INGA ĀBELE was born in Ri[illegible] studied biology at the University of Latvia, and worked for three years as a trainer on a horse-breeding farm. In 2001 she graduated from the Latvian Academy of Culture, and has been a full-time writer ever since. She has produced several collections of short stories, numerous plays and poetry collections. Some of her plays have been produced abroad, and her prose has been translated into several European languages. One other work of fiction has appeared in English: *High Tide* (2013). This present novel appeared in Latvia in 2017.

Her work shows evidence of her rigorous scientific training, balanced with her deep understanding of human motives. Her characters tend to be people whose values are put to the test, and who face great moral decisions. Ābele's prose works are the product of thorough research; she is fascinated by the little-known by-ways of Latvian history and its more unsung heroes. The novel which preceded this one, *Klūgu mūks* (The Wicker Monk, 2014) tells the extraordinary story of the disgraced Catholic priest and political activist Francis Trasuns, who championed the separate identity of Latvia's eastern province of Latgale – an area which also figures prominently in this novel. Inga Ābele is currently (2020) working on another novel based on Latvian history and further short stories.

CHRISTOPHER MOSELEY (b. 1950 in Australia) currently lives in the UK. He is a freelance translator into English from Estonian, Finnish, Latvian, and the Scandinavian languages. Previously a journalist and translator at the BBC Monitoring Service, he now teaches Estonian and Latvian at the School of Slavonic and East European Studies, UCL. He translated most of the short stories which appeared in the volume *From Baltic Shores* which he also edited (Norvik Press, 1994), and prepared a new translation of the novel *The Misadventures of the New Satan* by Anton Hansen Tammsaare (Norvik Press, 2006). He has also translated Andrus Kivirähk's novel *The Man Who Spoke Snakish* (2015) and Indrek Hargla's *Apothecary Melchior and the Ghost of Rataskaevu Street*, in 2016. For Norvik Press he translated Ilmar Taska's novel *Pobeda 1946: A Car Called Victory* (2018). *The Year the River Froze Twice* is his first full-length novel from Latvian.

Some other books from Norvik Press

Johan Borgen: *Little Lord* (Translated by Janet Garton)

Karin Boye: *Crisis* (Translated by Amanda Doxtater)

Jens Bjørneboe: *Moment of Freedom* (Translated by Esther Greenleaf Mürer)
Jens Bjørneboe: *Powderhouse* (Translated by Esther Greenleaf Mürer)
Jens Bjørneboe: *The Silence* (Translated by Esther Greenleaf Mürer)

Erik Fosnes Hansen: *Lobster Life* (Translated by Janet Garton)

Vigdis Hjorth: *A House in Norway* (Translated by Charlotte Barslund)

Jan Kjærstad: *Berge* (Translated by Janet Garton)

Hagar Olsson: *Chitambo* (Translated by Sarah Death)

Anton Tammsaare: *The Misadventures of the New Satan* (Translated by Olga Shartze and Christopher Moseley)

Ilmar Taska: *Pobeda 1946: A Car Called Victory* (Translated by Christopher Moseley)

Kirsten Thorup: *The God of Chance* (Translated by Janet Garton)

Selma Lagerlöf: *Mårbacka* (Translated by Sarah Death)

Viivi Luik: *The Beauty of History* (Translated by Hildi Hawkins)

Dorrit Willumsen: *Bang: A Novel about the Danish Writer* (Translated by Marina Allemano)

For our complete back catalogue, please visit
www.norvikpress.com

The Year the River Froze Twice

by

Inga Ābele

Translated from the Latvian
by Christopher Moseley

Norvik Press
2020

Norvik Press Series B: English Translations of Scandinavian Literature, no. 83.

A catalogue record for this book is available from the British Library.

ISBN: 978-1-909408-61-6

Norvik Press
Department of Scandinavian Studies
University College London
Gower Street
London WC1E 6BT
United Kingdom
Website: www.norvikpress.com
E-mail address: norvik.press@ucl.ac.uk

Managing editors: Elettra Carbone, Sarah Death, Janet Garton, C. Claire Thomson, Essi Viitanen.

Layout and cover design: Essi Viitanen.
Photo by Marylou Fortier on Unsplash.

This book was published with the support of the Latvian Literature platform together with the Ministry of Culture of the Republic of Latvia.

Contents

Author's Introduction

'Myth is much more important and true than history.
History is just journalism and you know how reliable that is."
Joseph Campbell

Language is the flesh of a novel. Language is a discrete reality; language depicts the world which probably could have existed, but we should not forget that it has never occurred. In the worst case, language illustrates. In the best, it demonstrates.

I have not lived in Latvia as a territory the entire time since World War II. From where can I draw my facts about it? For me the root of the Latvian word *vēsture*, "history", is found in the verb *vēstīt,* "to tell, narrate". Anything and anyone is capable of narrating: barbed wire found in a forest, or trenches, as well as museums and oaks, and people – the witnesses of events. As long as he who can tell exists, history survives. I often fall in love with the spoken word – not with its correctness, but just the opposite: with its originality, its unique style of expression. This is precisely how numerous pages of this novel evolved – I listened to eye-witness accounts and carried over to paper what I was told with minimal corrections. Time is an entity as thick as a tapestry, and, sewing its layers of style one on another, it is possible to achieve a dimension of depth.

In official history, a time is often appropriated by particular strong personalities. Typically one says "the Tsar's era", "the times of (Latvian president) Ulmanis", "the times of Hitler". The post-war period in Latvia was Stalin's time. Tragic, contradictory, one of the most complicated periods in Latvia's record, continuing till Stalin's death in 1953. Having occurred under the cover of the Second World War, the occupation of Latvia remained in force; the Europe that was divided as a result of the Molotov-Ribbentrop Pact continued to exist within its new borders despite the hopes of so many that the old ones would be restored. The winner is never judged. The world was jubilant about the end of the war, while in the Baltic region, part of the population left their houses for the forests, waiting for the arrival of Allied support. Instead they saw brutal repressions, deportation of whole groups of people to Siberia, shootings without trial. The impressive number of those choosing exile should be mentioned as well, people reaching Germany by sea in boats or Sweden by refugee craft. The forced collectivisation imposed by Moscow destroyed a great deal of the established farm-holdings, while their owners, branded as *kulaks* or "fatbags", were burdened with impossible duties to be paid to the state and, finally, deported to Siberia as part of Operation Coastal Surf *(Priboi)* on 25 March 1949. Of course there were those who threw themselves enthusiastically into the construction of the happy new Soviet life. The rest did not have much choice. If the most essential basis of human existence, freedom and homeland, have been taken away, the struggle becomes meaningless and the only remaining option is to try to adapt to power.

Stalin's era is marked by iron discipline, deafening propaganda, and elimination of the disgruntled; by Cheka (KGB) supervision of affairs and by impunity. However, as I have tried to demonstrate in this novel, everything depends on individual character. It was well said by the dissident political prisoner Lidia Lasmane-Doroņina, who had to spend 14 years of her life in Soviet prisons: "You could find considerate people even among KGB personnel who knew how to help you within the boundaries of the law. The most horrifying were those especially eager to please their bosses. They didn't act in the name of the law, you see, they acted to demonstrate their subservience to power. And those were the beastliest."

The currents of two times moving in parallel, rising from the lower River Daugava and from the town of Riga and flowing upwards, form the basic grid of the novel. At a certain moment in time, both of these time streams collide and get entangled into a knot, as the main character stands on the opposite banks, in the process of self-reflection through the curtain of time. However, a novel is not a painting, where two events can be presented *at the same moment*; a novel evolves linearly in time, which is why a simultaneous encounter on the opposite banks of the Daugava fails to occur. And it cannot be helped. In the words of the protagonist Andrievs Radvilis: "I was frustrated with art. It's all so imperfect. You always have to think up something more."

But it is precisely in this "additional inventing" that the perfection of all art resides. And the reader finds himself a participant in an event; turning from an observer into a creator. Thus a shared vertical is formed, the meaning of a work of art.

In turn, in the gently ascending flow of the novel, the vertical is the chapter entitled "Company Commander". Both occupying powers violated The Hague Convention (IV) of 1907 respecting the Laws and Customs of War on Land, which forbids them to mobilise the inhabitants of a country into the army of an occupying state or to involve them in paramilitary operations (article 52 of the Convention). Both occupying powers conscripted citizens of occupied Latvia into their armed forces and engaged them in various paramilitary formations. For evasion they were subjected to imprisonment in concentration camps or the death penalty. As a result, during the Second World War Latvian citizens had to fight against each other.

It is really difficult to explain the essence of the Latvian Legion to the world – the phenomenon of that generation that grew up in the period of the first independence or the so-called "free state" – the lost, or shredded generation, taking arms provided by the Nazis in their hands to defend the native land under their feet against the Bolshevik forces that far outnumbered them, creating the Kurzeme stronghold at the end of the war, which resisted the takeover by the Red Army right until the surrender of arms. In the words of the legionaries themselves:

"We knew it was the right adversary we fought; it was just a matter of the wrong ally". After the bitter humiliation of the Soviet invasion at the beginning of the war, having received refugees from all over the country toward the end of the war, Kurzeme came to symbolise the fight for the lost homeland.

As I prepared to write this novel, in my reflections on the territory of Latvia during World War Two and after, torn and shredded to pieces by varying countercurrents, my search was for the eye of the storm. And, as precisely as a clock, Riga racecourse seemed right for such a focal point – the powers came to replace one another, but on its tarmac the trotters raced every week, coaches and riders performed their functions and the stands were filled by the public. The racecourse leaflets for every race-day mirror their era. The languages change along with the riders and horses, but the legends are passed from one generation to the next. The horse has always been a trustworthy companion to man, the provider of food in times of hunger and comrade-in-arms for the serviceman. Riga racecourse was shut down in 1965. From then on a disruption in time has continued, regardless of the fact that we have outstanding jockeys and horses who win their contests in Tallinn or on the numerous racetracks in Lithuania, at a time of complete absence of racecourses in Latvia. So, Riga racecourse remains an Atlantis mentioned in their reminiscences by few, and signified now only by rows of trees lining the sides of its former cinder-paths, and one can still trace the name of their illustrious ancestor Poplar Hill in the pedigree of some of the horses. This horse has served as the prototype for Run Hill in my novel. In Raimonds Baltakmens' monograph *The Latvian Man and his Horse*, we read that "at Riga racecourse, the utmost value was assigned to the ex-world-record-holder of three-year-old horses (2.01,8) over the half-mile, Poplar Hill. (…) The Soviet men begrudged us our Poplar Hill by taking the horse to Gomel and slaughtering it there, sending this 22-year-old stallion to race unprepared. They had renamed him 'correctly' beforehand as Poplavok or Bobber. The old racecourse fighter won the race, but fell down behind the finish line, his heart succumbing to over-strain." Following in the footsteps of the legend, my novel was created.

The Stalin era described in this novel was also characterised by paranoid secrecy – it is difficult to find photographs, the relevant maps of Riga, and only very few cartographic town plans have survived, but it is an enormous delight to encounter people still preserving this time in their memory, to find documents and to have a dialogue with the streets and the buildings conserving and relating the history. And that is what happened with the prototype for Andrievs' father's house in my novel – the building found at 111 Krišjāņa Valdemāra Street. In the process of studying the documents regarding the deportation of the owners of this structure, I discovered that they had been taken away to be deported from the house at 17 Charlotte Street. As I tried to clarify the inconsistency, I came across the tiny Dārzniecības (or Gardening) Street connecting the Valdemāra and Šarlotes (Charlotte) Streets after the war. You can imagine my feelings as I saw the familiar palm of my town opening up completely unexpected lines to me on a hot July day – quite like in a dream where what was previously well known has suddenly changed its topography.

I have long since been fascinated by the Dreamtime of Australian Aborigines, and I find I can trust what was said by one of their Aboriginal artists: *Every water got a song. People got to tell you story to make you happy and safe. Every place got a story.* Close ties to our ancestors, our land, our nature, our animals, our sacred places and stories, and fables and legends, as well as parallels between the present day and history – I shall continue to observe that in everyday Latvia, although our era persists so strongly in severing this world from modern man.

Inga Ābele

ESTONIA
BALTIC SEA
Gulf of
Riga
RUSSIA
Vidzeme
RIGA
SALASPILS
OGRE
LIELVĀRDE
Daugava
AIZKRAUKLE
Aiviekste
RĒZEKNE
JĒKABPILS
Kurzeme
LATVIA
Zemgale
Latgale
DAUGAVPILS
BELARUS
LITHUANIA

Cīņa *newspaper, 10 March 1949*

Ice conditions on Latvia's rivers and at sea

Because of the cold weather, the ice cover on all of Latvia's rivers is strengthening. During the previous thaw, the ice shifted on some rivers and was released from the ice cover. Now the ice is forming again in the exposed areas. […] On the Daugava, in the rapids from Jēkabpils to Koknese, and downstream from Ķegums as far as Dole, there is intensive sludge formation. Ice thickness: 43 cm. at Daugavpils, 33 cm. at Jēkabpils, 30 cm. by the power station on Ķegums lake, about 10 cm. in Riga harbour. […] A shift of the ice on the Daugava is expected in the first days of April, and at the end of March on other rivers. The ice cover has grown considerably in the Gulf of Riga. Reconnaissance flights show that the whole northern section of the Gulf is covered with new, thin ice. […]

A. Pastors,
Head of the Sea and River Forecasting Section, Hydrometeorological Service

Summer Street

Curled up like a cat, the Pārdaugava district is snoozing under a hot July sun.

The lanes of Āgenskalns are the stripes on the cat's fur, winding and tangling under the trees and throwing broad, rustling shadows over the dusty gardens – 'Bees', 'Flowers', 'Honey'... then 'Lavīze's', 'Ernestīne's', 'Olga's'... When I finally find Summer Street after a long search, it turns out to be narrow and warm, as if split by a wooden knife in yellow plasticine. At the end of the street, around a grey rented house, the wind whistles and, shouting loudly, children are playing.

I leave the car in a line of others by the street door and go through the gateway into the yard, in the dazzling sunshine. In the staircase the windows are open, it's hot. The doors of the apartments – each with their own world of stories, smells and sounds. The house is silent, blown by the winds, warmed up by the summer, and yet it seems to be resounding; beyond this silence I sense the vibration of a beehive – as always in an apartment building, where dozens of lives are bound together in a single knot.

I have to climb to the fourth floor. Alongside the window you can see the darkening edge of a storm over the blue bend in the Daugava river.

The doorbell is powerful and purposeful, like lightning. The door is opened for me.

On the threshold stands a man of respectable age in bright linen trousers and a shirt. His grey hair, it seems, has just been ravaged by a nightmare or all ten fingers. His eyebrows, too, which lash whitely over his calm eyes. His prominent nose was burnished copper-brown in the long-ago summers of his childhood and since that time it has not given up its sunburn.

He invites me in.

"Hello! Please – sit down."

The apartment is tiny. From the entrance I can see through to the kitchen and a room which is piled up like a magpie's nest with books, bits of paper, paintings, ribbons, mementoes. Imants Ziedonis, the writer, is looking at me quizzically and a little ironically from a magazine cutting on the wall.*

I settle down in the only chair. He sits down on the bed behind the magazine table, folds his hands on his knees and begins a rapid, loud lecture about his book *Principles of Marshland Management*, speaking quickly, as if driven by someone, looking at the ceiling above his head, and when he occasionally stammers, it's hard to understand him.

I can't follow him, I fall into some sort of reverie at the point when he won't stop staring. I'm not thinking of anything specific, I'm cogitating on old age and how it is to be old and control your flesh, I'm thinking about eyeballs in their sockets and bones, about the burden of meat that the skeleton carries around for years, a co-ordinated, living and fluid, complex mechanism, created to serve the six senses and the heart. The excess kilograms of the soul. And what is the history of all that?

The ecosystem, structure and functions of a marsh, the circulation of matter and energy in the biosphere, is what I'm hearing as I emerge from his scrutiny.

He notices my wandering, inquisitive eyes, and is irritated.

"Why are you looking like that? Look, it's all described in my book. I don't understand why you rang me. You do have my book?"

"I will tomorrow."

I can't say that I don't have the book. And that it doesn't interest me at all. I didn't buy it when it came out, because it was hellishly expensive, and even now, when I looked up the book on an internet trading site, there was one copy of it and it was no cheaper. It had the author's signature, the seller explained to me when I tried to beat the price down.

But he looks at me stiffly, just like a moment ago. I'm a stranger to him.

He has a hearing-aid in one ear. I realize I have to speak louder.

"I will tomorrow. Tomorrow. I'm negotiating on the internet."

"Oh, are you?"

"Really I wanted to ask you about something quite different."

"About what? I'm deaf in one ear – please speak more clearly."

Bending forward, I say right into his face: "About Run Hill Dune."

A rapid mental process goes on before my eyes. Sudden memories, like a gust of wind, discompose his brows, and his eyes are clouded by a shadow – he's no longer living by clock time as the change comes – he's in some other world.

Then he settles down like earth after rain, pulls himself together, and at once he is terribly vigilant.

"But my dear, what do you know about old Hill?"

Now it seems he finally really notices me.

I pull from my bag a little programme from the Riga trotting track from 1943 and show him the name. Jockey: Radvilis; horse: Run Hill Dune; the race number.

"Andrievs Radvilis. So, is that you?"

For a moment he's prepared to deny it. Startled, he wipes his nose with a big checked handkerchief.

"I thought you were interested in my book… I'm sorry, I didn't catch your name on the telephone…"

"Alise."

His gaze is penetrating; the gaunt, rough fingers of both hands move spasmodically like roots around the trunk of a pine tree, clenching and unclenching. I would like to follow where his thoughts are involuntarily taking him.

"I didn't catch your name, but why do you want to know about that horse?"

"I'm looking for material about the Riga Racecourse. So little of it has been preserved… practically nothing. But when people talk about the track, they can't get away from that name, Run Hill Dune."

"I can't hear you. Old age, my dear, is a great misfortune that you can only avoid by dying young, and that's a great misfortune too. I remember little about that time."

"Tell me..."

"That horse has been dead for nearly a century now; you'll have to be satisfied with that."

I put an album of sketches in front of me and turn it towards Radvilis. The old man looks at the covers for a moment, incredulous.

"You were drawing him. For ten years," I say.

He looks searchingly at me with narrowed, thoughtful eyes, before summoning the courage to immerse his fingers in the album as if into a fire. At first he takes fright, pulls them away. Then he carefully strokes the pages, touches the cardboard, sniffs the paper. The album contains bigger and smaller sketches, drawings, paintings, most of them dated and signed.

"This was supposed to be lost!" he asserts with a stiff smile, turning his head incredulously. "It's not possible!"

I spread out one picture which is sketched in white chalk and charcoal pencil on a big sheet of brown wrapping paper, for which reason it has been folded into four for many years. The drawing rustles windily like an oak-leaf in autumn. A long table with people seated at it. In the background, behind the stove, a picture of Stalin. On the right side, in the light of a bare light-bulb, stands a horse, its head bent over some woman's shoulder. The woman is pregnant; next to her on the table lies an automatic rifle.

"Funny companions – a pregnant woman and a rifle...," I say.

"Why not? Padegs had a Madonna with a machine gun.* It's a composition."

"Strange – why a horse, indoors?"

"The horse is the wings of the human being, and she always has wings. There's plenty there, my dear – some made up, some real. But that's not the main thing."

"How come?"

"Thundering. That was a time of thundering. You understand?"

I nod.

"Although – how could you understand?" He sighs. "You can only imagine it."

Radvilis perfunctorily shoves the drawings into a heap and closes the covers.

"I was frustrated with art. It's all so imperfect. You always have to think up something more."

"What about with life? There are thirteen at the table."

"What?"

"Who was the betrayer?"

"That's not important any more."

"Why did you stop painting? Because of her?"

Radvilis tries to take back the album, but I'm quicker.

"Please, give it back! It mustn't get into strangers' hands. That wasn't the intention."

"All right, but first you have to tell me…"

"What?"

"About these drawings. What can be seen in them."

"But in art, everyone always sees themselves. Give it here!"

"Is that the Postwoman?"

He turns pale.

"Now go away! Right now!"

Suddenly as sprightly as a boy, the old man makes for the door, driving me out.

I place myself in the door-frame with my back to the flooding sunshine. The sketchbook is pressed to my chest. This is my last chance.

"We said on the telephone that we'd have a coffee in town!"

On his face, loathing contests with the afterglow of worry about his difficult nature, the imminent farewell and his loneliness.

"Shall we have a coffee?" I say, so that it thunders through the stairwell.

After a moment's reflection, he nods. Resistance has worn him out.

"Everything in life is decided by women," Radvilis mutters with dissatisfaction, pulling on his jacket. "They always get the last word. At least it's always been that way in my life."

Hot. Windows, doors open. The steps glitter under my feet. I run through the present, I run through the summer, I outrun myself anywhere and everywhere. What is the span of time after which the landscape stands before your eyes as memories? Is it long or short? Why is there no refuge anywhere?

"Nowhere, never," the stairs thunder under my heels. My eyes squint in the sharp light and the icy shadows, a sudden fear of the future grips the back of my neck. "Bang!" goes the street door. After a moment he comes out, gaunt and silent. A little knapsack on his shoulders, a jockey's cap on his head, but that's his style.

Along Vasaras iela, Summer Street, we go, shoulder to shoulder. All the time he's trying to keep next to his sketchbook, which I have like a faithful dog under my arm. A slow wind on the fences ruffles the furry Virginia creepers, and beyond them one can glimpse the ancient, half-collapsed walls and the private houses full of age and experience.

"Without anyone knowing, Lieutenant-Colonel Friedrich Sommer lived out his life here," says Radvilis, waving at some house beyond the fence. "You will have heard of his son, the lily-grower Jānis Vasarietis?"

I nod my head vaguely.

The only café, on the corner of Camp St. and Woodcock St., is sunk in half-twilight, with a milk chocolate colour. The gaunt figure of Radvilis, waiting for me, melts into it. The aroma of chocolate wafts around the freshly baked cookies, the agile, stout elbows of the women and the stooped heads of the men.

He stands looking at me, so serious, a little solemn. Perhaps he thinks I'm cruel. The sketchbook is still under my arm.

At one with the whole world, there we stand. And yet each of us separate, with our own – distant, incomprehensible – feelings.

"Two black coffees, please! And two white cream-cakes," I say.

On the terrace outside on the corner between the floral wall and the brick masonry is a heating flue for the winter season, on which is written *inferno*, so helplessly pale in the August heat. We sit down under it.

Meanwhile a thunderstorm is lumbering along Woodcock St. towards us, overtaken by a rapid tram, bringing clouds of dust with it. High in the sky, something like the composition before us on the table is moving against the wind – black, seething and light-headed, whipped cream. Here on the ground it is barely noticeable, only occasional gusts of wind like stray hands stroking the terrace with a feather, and the canvas roof shudders.

"You know, I wouldn't say no to the chance to look at another world in the near future," says Radvilis, looking heavenward. "Life is beautiful, but I've lived mine."

Confused, I ask him about his book. Momentarily enlivened, he declares that he could buy his time and extend his time, and as he simply loves his field to the depths of his heart, he starts telling me the principles of the science of marshes.

The different ecological structures and biotic interrelations… The qualities of the micro-relief of a bog… The influence of mechanical stress…

"Lately I've been most interested in the false seasonal changes in marsh pine trees," he states, pinching at his cake with his teaspoon. "In the published studies one comes across contradictory information about the possibility of false, unnatural seasonal changes in conifers that grow in Europe. It's been found that in conifers growing in the cool and mild climate of Europe, and in those that grow in unfavourable conditions, false seasonal changes don't usually happen. Other studies have been published, though, that indicate false seasons in pine trees that grow in bogs…"

"Where were you at the end of the war?"

He doesn't catch my words, and leans forward.

"I didn't hear you. The volume is good, but I didn't catch it. You don't have good articulation. I'm surprised! You're a journalist, your articulation must be correct, clear. But it isn't!"

Where did he find out I'm a journalist?

"Where did the war end for you? For *you*?"

The German tourists at the next table stop chewing and glance at us.

"In the the fortress of Kurzeme," he murmurs, suddenly grown quiet. "Where else?"

"And the filtration? Where did you go through filtration?"

"There wasn't any filtration. Not everything in the world is black and white. There's also the marsh."

He pushes the chair back and gets up. He bows, I don't know what for – for the coffee he has drunk, for me, or for his own disappointment – raises his cap and goes away.

And what had he been expecting? That we would only talk about high and low marshes while we drank our coffee?

At this moment the wind stretches out on the canvas of cloud and blows out its cheeks. It's a wild current that carries that old man away from me along the dusty vortex of the streets. This ship is half-wrecked. Undeniably well-built and full to the gunwales with experience, still proud and fiery in spirit. Where can one travel in it? The name of the current is Time, and that leads in only one direction – no return tickets are available.

I run up beside him and unfurl my umbrella.

"I'll walk with you – it's going to rain!" He no longer believes me, glances at me as if at a stranger, and continues on his way. I grasp his hand.

"I'll wait for your call, you hear? Please ring me! I'll be waiting, I'll keep waiting."

He nods unconsciously and, overtaking me, carries on his way. His neck retracted into his shoulders like a tortoise's. With the time he has lost, he's also lost the necessity to serve another's needs.

We are two independent dwellers in the marsh, who unfortunately owe each other nothing.

It starts to rain. He takes shelter and waits under the big elm at the Vasarietis house. So we stand awhile looking at each other. A car whips up a shower of gravel that clatters against the metal, while the rain pours down. Here is a man who, just like Lieutenant-Colonel Sommer, has lived out the end of his days on Summer Street, unobserved by anyone, but, unlike the lieutenant-colonel, doing it without honours or shiny medals, and wanting to leave this world – without a plaque on the wall of his house. Without a page in the history books.

But does that mean without memories either?

He was good to me and obliging about everything that didn't concern the past. It's commendable that the old man is resolved to live in the present, but am I guilty if I'm interested in his past?

I ring him a few more times. But when he realizes who is speaking he always falls silent and hangs up.

I mustn't wait too long. I remember the misfortune with the garages at the racetrack. I knew they contained boxes of valuable material. For too long I hung around, observing the garages changing hands, like high-class floozies choosing ever more exotic lovers. I should have broken in, even broken the law – I'm convinced of that now.

When I went away, it was a rainy April, and even from afar the scent of damp smoke assailed my nose – it made me sick at heart.

"You've come too late, Missus," declared a man with a Russian accent, standing by a pile of ashes with a rake in his hand. "It's all burned up."

"But don't worry yourself," he continued, noticing me reaching out to steady myself. "There was nothing valuable – just some old photographs on thick cardboard."

Seeing that this is no help and I'm becoming even paler, the man consoles me: "There was nothing valuable in the pictures either, just some horses and the race-track, just the Hippodrome."

I mustn't wait too long.

Yet I wait all autumn. And I've given up hope.

It's a black and damp snowless December when I spot the old man's name again lighting up the display on my mobile phone. For some reason I've picked up the phone, held it in my hand and waited for something. Perhaps at that moment, just as intently, he was looking at his own, and called my number, with firm intentions.

But perhaps we have both planned this call carefully and at length.

"Good evening. It's me – Andrievs Radvilis. How are you?"

My heart pounding, I reply that I'm well.

"Are you still interested in Run Hill? Might we meet tomorrow?"

"Of course. What time, and where?"

"I'd be pleased if we went out before dawn."

I agree without asking where we're going.

We fix a time to meet, before five in the morning.

"See you then," I say.

"See you then," he replies.

And he puts down the phone without ending the call. I continue listening. He sighs – his breathing is heavy, as if from the depths of a mountain. A bed squeaks, the receiver echoes a hollow rumble, the reverberations are slow and seem deliberately delayed, as if playing with the intervals. I realize that I'm hearing the beat of the old man's heart. Apparently he has lain down, his veined hands clasping the phone resting on his chest. I hang up.

After a moment I'm rewarded again. Sunset beyond the panes – as silent as a pink paper kite, caught in the hard, black branches of the oaks by the Daugava. The explosion of colour lasts only some ten minutes; after that everything pales and vanishes.

I fetch Radvilis' sketch album and leaf slowly through it. His drawings manage to capture activity. The lines are fine, nervous; a shadow seems to linger around the silhouettes. His jockeys on the track heave from side to side, but for the war horses the wet pen turns in rings, like constellations or a sprouting rye field. Of Radvilis' works, two ink drawings stand out: one a portrait of an old gentleman with a gaunt face and delicate features facing the viewer, and Radvilis' portrait of what is evidently the same person in profile – the head bent, the jaw muscles clenched in a bulldog bite. Both ink drawings are signed with the initials *B. f. E.* Then there are some pastels on black cardboard, in which you sense that Radvilis was trying out the style of the artist Voldemārs Irbe. There are sketches of the Daugava – flood-lands and a road, tussocks of grass, clusters of bushes and airy clouds above them – the lines stretch from infinity to infinity. In several of the ink drawings the war can be seen: garrisons, soldiers and the injured. Cripples too – people without legs and arms, solitary bedridden amputees with medals pinned to their chests and huge, other-worldly eyes. Their expressions are a curse that will pursue what they have seen to the end of their days.

For a long time I study the face of a much-sketched woman. Radvilis was a talented portraitist. Nothing about this woman is known to me, but what I see is contradictory, it doesn't add up. A delicate girl in a folk costume and white shawl, like the Russian painter Vrubel's swan princess, only the wings are missing… But in a sledge on a frozen river by the light of a full moon, with her hands upturned, she flies like a Valkyrie. A depraved boozing bitch with a heated expression, pictured with bare elbows and loose-hanging plaits, with vodka-drinkers in the background. Most of all I am fascinated by a drawing in which she is washing her hair in a forest, in the waters of a black marsh. Her hair is long and bristling, like a thicket of May roses, her face is as pale as moonlight, and her hands scratched, her expression gentle, questioning. On the other hand the face of a Soviet woman at a meeting at a long table is already burned like a Moor's in the summer sun, her white teeth flashing fiercely. Her expression has changed too – it is tired and malevolent.

In the morning I wake up well before the alarm clock rings. I stand silently in the room and I can't understand whether this is a dream or reality around me.

The night wind receives me in its cool hands as I leave by the familiar stairwell. He promised to wait for me, but there's no-one outside.

In the stairwell the lonely radiators wail. Bright rays of light pour from the old man's room as from a spaceship. Slowly I approach Radvilis' open door, stair by stair, until I catch sight of him down on his knees in the depths of the flat, writing something on a white page.

"Good morning!" he calls as he notices me, booming deep into the sleeping building. "I have to arrange some papers that might interest somebody. You understand, I'm an old man, I might die at any moment."

"Do you live alone?"

"I have relatives, but it's easier for them without me, thank God."

Having again dived into some drawer, he continues to pile up documents.

Then he gets up and announces, "We can go."

Radvilis puts a rucksack on his back, and jams a jockey's cap onto his head.

"My Papa always wore hats," he explains, as if feeling guilty, looking into the smoky hall mirror. "I only bought my first jockey cap when I couldn't find a proper hat."

Thereupon he proudly raises the collar of his jacket.

"This suit is from 1938, made in England. No-one else in Riga has one like it. Dad's suit."

The garment is dark blue with delicate pin-stripes. The elbows of the sleeves are worn to a preposterous sheen, but he doesn't notice that.

"Can you smell something?" Radvilis looks around the kitchen. "Is the gas turned off?"

He takes up his smoking equipment and takes a long farewell look over his dwelling.

In the car, Radvilis is unable to settle down, clutches at the safety belt and sighs guiltily. I help him and ask: "May I know where we're going?"

It's difficult to settle the old man in, as he twitches in his seat like a wolf-cub.

"First let's drive to the race-track," he says conspiratorially, observing me.

I nod happily, and off we go. Under cover of night the city seems different, a mysterious, empty place. Bulbs illuminate the shop windows, the damp asphalt swishes under my tyres, we are alone in the whole wide world. The Daugava is sleeping under the bridge like a lazy black ooze, not woken by the light before dawn. At night the car seems to run faster and all distances are shrunk by half. In the colonnade of high buildings along Valdemāra Street, darkness reigns, only an occasional light burns in a window.

"This is where Valdemāra Street used to end," Radvilis says, becoming restless. "And Vāgnera Street began – hard to believe, isn't it? Charlottenthal, or Charlotte's Valley, was once a wide plot of land that went up to the town's pasture-land. Until the twenties of the last century, the property belonged to the heirs of Wagner, the landscape gardener and nurseryman. There was a botanical garden, with tropical plants growing in the orangeries. After the republic was established, the land on the estate was parcelled into building plots and the network of roads called Nītaure, Aloja, Zaubes, Mālpils and Tomsona sprang up. Around these streets in my youth was the biggest new-built high-rise housing estate in Riga. My Dad built here too."

As we pass the corner of Mālpils Street, the old man points to the left.

"Here," he says.

We get out by a sporting complex illuminated by little globes, like an interplanetary craft. Radvilis steps into the middle of the road.

"Now we're standing on the track."

It's difficult to imagine a dust-covered track in a place completely covered with asphalt, glass and concrete.

"There, opposite, by Grostona Street, were the stands. They had burned down by the time the race-track closed."

"In what year?"

"Hard to say. I arrived here in May of seventy-eight, the stands were still there then. After that, when I returned in eighty, they weren't there any more. Sometime between those dates they burned down. It's built-up land everywhere; it used to be very low-lying. Veseta Street in those days ran along the avenue; one side of the avenue is still preserved, you see? Where the kindergarten is were the old stables, built with sturdy wooden beams. At the end of the field was a tree – it's been standing since ancient times."

We come up to a stout, wind-blown willow. Dewdrops twinkle on its dark branches. At the end of the new multi-storey block, a children's play area has been installed.

"This used to be the outflow of the Sarkandaugava River – to get to the race-track you had to cross little bridges. Over there, up-river by the Institute of Traumatology, there were always boats drawn up on the bank."

I try to imagine the stream, the horses running along the track, and the boats on the bank. Once again in the former stables stand former jockeys, now racing in the Hippodrome of Eternity. The shadows of the jockeys, the trainers, the grooms, the administrators and the audience are stirring; the apparently reserved, cool silence is overwhelmed by a thunder from the passionate stands, the wind-rustled, dusty prize rosettes on the riders' bridles, the normally unimpassioned people pay their money and cheer, watching their favourites on the track. The racecourse is not only entertainment but hard everyday work. A unique place with its history, its special events and its own language.

"The race-track is a purifying place," says Radvilis.

He is seated on the illuminated solitary children's swing and, clutching the chain, considering something.

"Did you know that the ancient Greeks and Romans purified the horses from evil after the military processions? They believed that speed can purify, just like fire."

After swinging a couple more times, he continues: "You know, that's the truth."

Snowing

Early on a Saturday morning in February 1949 the racetrack is still empty and seems abandoned. Through the motionless swathes of fog after the thaw, Riga rises up like an alien and oddly forbidding city. Having ridden on the straight, Andrievs dangles his legs over the edge of the cart and feels for a Belomorkanal cigarette in his pocket, letting the horse fall into an easy trot. Horseshoes rhythmically splash along the ice-and-water-covered track, cold swathes of light here and there fall through the mist like heavily brocaded curtains. The driver cleaves through them with his chest, and he feels a thrill. At such moments a subtle warmth flows around him, followed once more by a dive into the cold mist.

Where the fog has parted, the tangle of bare trees darkens, but on the right-hand side the empty stands are like a sinking ship.

The matches are damp. Trying to light up, Andrievs notices two men at the end of the straight with their hands in their trouser pockets. The horse stamps rapidly on the spot as she responds to Andrievs' agitation through the reins. But her rider has already collected himself. He puts the horse into a walk and slowly approaches the standing men, his lips fixed in an indifferent smirk.

Andrievs halts beside the two men.

They have oddly similar faces, like a pair of twins – just like Tweedledum and Tweedledee from *Through the Looking-Glass,* Andrievs thinks involuntarily. They are neither old nor young, neither ugly nor attractive – something in these faces is dangerous, precisely because of the lack of characteristic details. Low, flat foreheads and crests of blond hair. Both have lined eyelids, pinkish like ladies' handkerchiefs, no doubt caused by their night work. Their eyes carry the conviction of awareness of authority, acquired through self-torture, and now only death can erase it.

The self-confident faces of the powerful men are stiffer than the hump on a hunchback.

"Andrejs Jakovļevičs Radvilis?"

Andrievs nods silently.

"Great stuff!" The stouter one suddenly shifts and, quickly pulling his hand from his pocket, goes to pat the horse on the neck.

The rider, taken aback, starts to climb back up.

The taller one pulls out a lighter and offers it to Andrievs, having noticed the packet of *papirosy,* Russian cigarettes, in his hand.

"The horse is a bit tipsy – can't stand up," Andrievs ventures feebly.

"Yes, he can!" the tall one states calmly. His face is as symmetrical as a brick, the smile on it ploughs up a broad furrow of teeth.

"He'll wait! He'll wait!" The stout one pulls another hand from his pocket – quickly too, as if taking a shot – that is probably his way. He manages to catch the horse by the bridle. The stranger lets the rider know that he is no novice with horses and can even hold a racing stallion still.

The tall one introduces himself: "Major Mark Akimovich Krop, Ministry of State Security. And this is my colleague from Moscow, Vladimir Ivanovich Lyalyakin, an officer from the Department of Agriculture, getting acquainted with the situation in Latvia."

The stout one nods at the word "Moscow", and says nothing more. All three light up.

"Soon there'll be a biggish consignment of horses from Smolensk at the racecourse," says Krop, getting down to business. "Two jockeys as well, who are going to be working in Riga. We'd like you to get to know these comrades personally and get involved in the campaign. They'll give you further instructions. Is that clear?"

"What's he called?" the stout one enquires after the horse's name, not expecting Andrievs to answer. Yet his query was meant as a command, not a question.

"Grand Hill."

Lyalyakin grins.

"Grand Hill, San Hill, Admiral Hill. Bourgeois names. Pedigree?"

"Run Hill Dune and Diara."

"From Pet'ka Burzhuy! I thought so," the stout one says, turning knowingly to the tall one, tossing his fag in the sand and carefully stamping it under the sole of his boot.

Only then does he let go of the horse, which becomes restive, dribbling white foam on the ground.

"I saw his father recently in Gomel – they've renamed him Pet'ka! A dark reddish one… Racing trotter! The son is good too, good…Only here you've got some sort of uniformity about you, or rather, lack of sensitivity – in the blood, in the pedigree. The blood has got to be quickly changed to Soviet blood! You haven't seen any good racers here, I'll tell you that frankly. It's like you're sitting in a barrel. You've been carrying on your own thing, it's bad, bad, comrades…"

The horse won't keep still for a moment, and Andrievs pulls the reins tighter. For a racer that's a sign to start running fast.

Receding rapidly into the mist, Andrievs is surprised at how easily it can happen. All these years since the war he's been imagining a morning like this. Life in its craziness is like this racecourse – the straight leads you away, but the bend leads you back again, and there's no escaping the finish.

And yet – Smolensk? Why Smolensk – what has come out of Smolensk? What's this "campaign", and what will Andrievs have to do?

His hands tremble barely perceptibly, betraying him, hands that never tremble even after the tensest races. Andrievs releases the horse, lets him run at a pace that the racer himself chooses.

When the circuit is done, there's no sign of the two men. Only footprints remain in the wet sand in front of the stand – dark patches where the fag ends have been tossed.

After the training run, Andrievs' horse is taken over by the assistant jockey, Vanda, a tiny, slender lass, a pupil at Draudziņa secondary school. She's loyal, always turning up first on her days off, at the crack of dawn. Motley throngs of pupils and students turn up here at the racecourse in autumn to earn a bit extra. As the spring approaches, they're all hungry, and there are twice as many of them in spring as in autumn. Rumbling stomachs make them take on all sorts of casual jobs. A large proportion of these hungry ones are taken on by the port. Those who are stronger leave their lessons on hearing the long, low ship's whistle as it enters the harbour. The teachers don't object, because they know the harsh conditions since the war. Some of them load wagons in the goods yard or work on buildings to be demolished. Loading sugar is counted as a good wheeze, because you can pierce holes in the sack and pour sugar into your stomach, your pocket and whatever you have with you, a bag tied around your neck, and claim that the sack was already torn. But loading sugar is a job for the few who have the strength, certainly not for Vanda. A sack weighs 80 kilos; you have to drag it out of the wagon and carry it along a springy foot-bridge to the heap. For a joke, Andrievs sometimes weighs Vanda on the horse-scales – she never reaches even 50 kilos.

On ordinary days Vanda spends a rouble on her provisions. That goes on three slices of the moist, insipid briquettes called *buhanka*, little pies with plum jam called *povidlo*, and *kvass* to drink, but at home she and her cousin cook up a soup of carrots and potatoes.

Once every couple of months her mother sends the schoolgirl in Riga a large, bright red suitcase with a few loaves of rye bread, a few kilograms of smoked streaky bacon and a tin of twice skimmed, warmed cream, thick and yellow as butter, which will not go off – you can cut it with a knife. On the days when it arrives there is a party at the racecourse – the firm meat from pigs fed on rye is sliced and cooked on a Primus stove. Vanda treats her friends and schoolmates with it. If they buy in some good, cheap Caucasian or Moldavian wine too, they can have a real fling.

On the days when they get their grants or their racecourse wages, they treat each other to a slice of berry-bread or at least a spoonful of cream in their soup. Whatever it is, they know how to share.

Andrievs hands the racer over to Vanda and heads for the office of the course director, Pyotr Denisov, a former officer of the State Security Service.

"Good morning!"

The director, disturbed too early, is sullenly shuffling papers. Behind his massive bulk it seems that even the heavy oil painting, showing a Russian *troika* galloping along in a gilded frame, is lop-sided with dissatisfaction. It is no secret to anyone at the racecourse that lately the director has been going in for some heavy drinking.

"How am I supposed to train my horses and ride in races, Pyotr Gavrilovich, if I'm being run from your ministry? Since when have I been taking orders from them? Am I being threatened?"

For a moment the director hisses heavily like a samovar, through nostrils overgrown with thick wool.

"I give you my word of honour as an old Bolshevik – if I find out that you're being threatened, I'll tell you!"

"But why are they talking about Smolensk, about some *campaigns*? Why do they involve me?"

"No need to start exaggerating, comrade Radvilis!" Denisov wags his finger fiercely. "We all have our duties toward the Soviet homeland."

Andrievs swallows his spittle, bitter as poison, and goes away.

The transparency of dawn has died away, the fog has thickened into a grey glimmer, and over the city snow-clouds appear in the bluish gloom. On the racetrack several jockeys have appeared with their horses, the damp air vaporizing their hot breath, and the ground thunders with the pounding of powerful feet.

Andrievs stops next to Boriss Englards, his trainer, as he calls the old family friend, scion of a baron's clan, who for this reason sometimes gets chaffed at the racecourse as a baron or a colonel – in contrast to his bearing. A sufferer from tuberculosis for many years, delicate and desiccated, with his paltry little wages Englards supports a half-blind wife and helps a frail daughter. Dressed in a worn-out half-length sheepskin coat, buttoned up to the chin in a black camisole like a priest, on race days he withstands the winter blast in an unheated judges' stand. During training Englards always stands at the edge of the track with a chronometer and a notebook in his hand. Having returned to the Riga racecourse after discharge, Englards was formally taken on as a horse-breeder, but in fact he is the technical editor of the race programme, the training supervisor, the secretary to the college of judges, and the commentator – the soul of the course. After the war the baron rented Andrievs a narrow corner of his little flat, located in an old building next to St. Peter's church.

The old man meets the arrival with his peaceful gaze. His discoloured eyes seem to have been everywhere and seen everything. At first something sticks in Andrievs' throat. Sometimes it's easier just to stand beside him.

Quite a while passes as Boriss presses the chronometer, writing something in his little notebook.

"You're giving Reksis to Vanda?" asks Andrievs, as Vanda rides past.

The bay stallion Reksis II, born in Latgale in 1943 from Laurel Bingen and Vivat Valker, carries within him the blood of Riga's "golden division".

"On the sixth of March there'll be the International Women's Day prize. Let the girl have a go."

Englards sticks the stub of his pencil behind his ear and closes the notebook.

"The biggest pity is that blokes like that don't have the faintest idea about racers, let alone any knowledge," declares Andrievs, thinking aloud.

Boriss glances at him, raising his eyebrow quizzically.

"Denisov is hatching something against me," says Andrievs. "And I can't understand what."

"Have a chat with Eizens!"

Andrievs merely waves him away.

"Eizens himself has a noose around his neck. Oh, what will be, will be…"

In the afternoon, as a damp, gloomy darkness creeps over the city, Andrievs enters the stable dressing-room. Perched like swallows on a long wooden bench, the assistants are studying the race programmes and going over something quietly in the faint light of a lamp. Their young faces glow in the half-light like white apple-blossoms.

"I saw old Hill last summer in Gomel," Andrievs makes out Vanda's voice. "He looked in very bad shape."

She falls silent, catching sight of the arrival.

"Power cuts in Riga?" enquires Andrievs jauntily.

"*V Sovyetskom Soyuze ne byvaet, tovarishch Radvili!* We don't have those in the Soviet Union, Comrade Radvilis!"

Vanda laughs back. The room is vibrating with good humour.

"How do you like Reksis?" Andrievs asks Vanda.

"A lot!" Vanda exclaims. "Only… I don't like racing."

"Nor do I," adds Verinya Sokolova, a student of agronomy, gravely.

"So what do you like?"

"I like to saddle up Liepiņš' black Brinda and ride around Riga," says Vera. "We carry funeral parties, wedding parties, anything that's needed. She's really calm, and she lets us ride through Mežaparks* and everywhere."

"But I like it when I have to take Laže on horseback to the Ministry of Agriculture!" declares Helēna, a chubby dark-haired girl from the Printing and Publishing Trade School. "It's quite a performance when he goes to the ministry, you've got to see it! Laže doesn't go to the ministry by car on principle, although he does have one. Almuss is such a big, stately stallion! When Laže goes to the ministry, there's a cab with a leather cover, a driver with white gloves, a shiny harness, sparkling. A whole gang of correspondents is waiting there at the ministry. An impressive sight – a stallion with white feet, a driver with white gloves. Laže himself sitting there, and the driver – that's classy! It's quite a procession. Almuss gets put into harness at the stables on Ēveles Street; sometimes I take part in harnessing and getting him ready, but at other times I wait for them on Komunāru Boulevard, by the entrance to the ministry off Strēlnieku Street. The stallion too – tame, standing as if he's been put there, while Laže gets out. Then the driver hands the reins to me, for me to ride off while he goes for a feed."

"It's nice in the spring, when those stallions are got into some sort of condition," says Andis, a trainee veterinarian about thirty years old, from Odziena; the war and the post-war period have shuffled the cards – all on the same course you get youngsters straight out of school as well as "oldies" like Andis. "The state's own stallions that have gone off to be mated at country farms come back well-fed. Sausiņš, the son of San Valkers – he's a great big stallion, and pretty fast, but boy, what was he like when he came back!"

"Puffing and panting, he couldn't run!" agrees Ēriks, Andis' friend.

"I'd seen him before that, but afterwards I looked and I couldn't believe it – he was a bull! Was he the same stallion?" interjected Vanda. "Zeļčans gives me a horse and a box of twenty matches – here, this is for you now, a box of matches, off you go! It does a circuit – he takes out a match and puts it in another box. Ten laps in one box, ten in the other. It's boring going around alone, but with two, you can chat. We took it at a slow trot. Not everyone has girls that are happy to go round, the old chaps themselves have to do it."

The youngsters giggle and glance cautiously at Andrievs – after all, he hasn't got girls. Andrievs is known to everyone as a solitary, self-sufficient, reserved type, whose only friend is the old baron he lives with.

Vanda, though, continues enthusiastically: "The air is rainy beyond the horizon, and the birds are singing, but we just kept on riding, talking and talking... We'd forgotten all about the matches... You can forget the whole world like that. Didn't we just talk, the whole time! But ships' horns are blasting in the harbour..."

The girls' faces become transluscent, illuminated by the sap of life as if by oranges cast in bronze. A wistful, distant expression in their eyes.

"Oh, girls!" Andis slaps his knees. "What kind of a life is that? A cat's life?"

"From a slow trot you have to go to the finish," agrees Andrievs. "If you're committed to A, then you're ready for B too."

"I didn't say I don't like Reksis," Vanda corrects him. "I'm just afraid of racing. We don't have such strong arms as boys have."

"Is that what you think – that any person, either a man or a woman, can do anything with a horse, which weighs ten times as much as him or her and runs at a speed of sixty kilometres an hour? Motion equals mass times speed, after all – so have Newton's laws been suspended on the track?"

"On the track, the laws are always upset by chance," interjects Dzidra Baginska. "Otherwise the totalizator couldn't exist!"

As the gust of laughter dies away, Andrievs points out: "Thinking is power. You won't be able to ride if you get too sensitive. You have to be able to calculate distance. How did Saltupa ride in her day?... You probably don't remember, that was another time, but now… Take a look at how Mrs. Cīrulis rides! How Mrs. Mednis rides! You, Dzidra, are already a professional jockey… Ask their advice."

At that moment the door opens slightly and a middle-aged woman stumbles in, not old, not young, but elegant and dressed in a well-tailored coat. Her shoulders are covered by an old-fashioned but well-preserved calfskin pelerine in black. The newcomer is dragging a heavy suitcase with both hands, and puts it down at her feet with relief.

"Mum!" cries Dzidra, throwing herself on the woman's neck.

It is clear at once that she has come from the countryside. From some odd corner not touched by the wind of power. With light hand movements Dzidra brushes handfuls of wet snow off the wings of her mother's pelerine.

"Where did you get so much snow?"

"I was sitting in the freight car, because the carriages were full of men…. Good evening, trainers! There was a car going from the district centre to Riga, so I came to see my daughter and my Birztaliņa. How's she doing, how's she running?"

The Baginskis' home, Kalnaveseri, is located in Ogre district, not far from Skrīveri. In order to preserve even minimal security in insecure times, they have managed to re-establish Kalnaveseri as an auxiliary farm for the racecourse. Birztaliņa is the daughter of Run Hill Dune and Liara, born after the war, when Dzidra harrowed a field with the pregnant mare. Dzidra realized that wasn't a good idea, so she returned home, and right there in the little birch grove, or *birztaliņa*, the mare gave birth to the foal. So she was called Birztaliņa. For the sake of the little mare, Dzidra took up the reins at the racecourse.

"Birztaliņa's all right!" replies Andrievs. "How about you?"

Mrs. Baginskis suddenly collapses onto a bench and hides her face in her hands.

"I can't go on, Andrievs, my nerves can't take it. Every week there's some interrogation, they question me… The general atmosphere at our place in the country, too, it's - incomprehensible… We sense that something's going to happen, we just don't know what exactly. Will they let us live, or won't they?"

The youngsters act as if they haven't noticed Mrs. Baginskis' moment of weakness. In these times the normal thing is just to whisper about the inadmissible.

"You need to talk to Eizens," says Andrievs, and immediately realizes that this is the same advice he received from the baron.

Mrs. Baginskis pulls herself together and quickly wipes her eyes, reaching for her heavy suitcase.

"Yesterday I went down to the cellar and I realized this would be a good present for both you and Birztaliņa!"

The shiny locks snap open, the veneered lid bursts out, and a volley of summer smells is fired into the air. The suitcase is full of apples. The apples in the cellar have lasted well, in the greenery of pea-leaves. Some seem to be painted with a broad red brush. Some apples here have the lacquered rind of a black cherry – they have yellow flesh, and taste and smell like Muscatel grapes. Their hands are spattered, and their teeth crunch, as they bite into the juicy skins of the apples. Andrievs can't resist, either, and grabs one. Apples are now a great rarity in Riga – the city where, on the streets before the war, with every step you would encounter the powerful aroma from the cellarfuls of apples.

"They taste so good! What a unique taste! What varieties are they?" the youngsters exclaim to each other.

"The ones we know about – rose-apples, *serinkas*, Lithuanian pippins, and little bulbs – died back in the hard winters at the start of the war. These are kinds of autumn apple, ready for eating, but I put them in the cellar, and they don't have that bitter brown inside them. They're miracles from olden times, what varieties, I don't know."

After a while they're sitting there, confused and quiet, having swallowed the apples, cores and all – from the stems onwards, until there's only a little stalk in their fingers, to be crumpled with a regretful smile.

"The militia drew up a report on Filips when he was trading in apples without a variety name," says Vanda, and the others giggle.

Wanting to know the reason for the laughter, a man with a sleepy owlish face and a lantern in his hand looks in to the dressing-room. The drooping eyelids are hooded over the round eyes. He looks like Winston Churchill, only it's not a cigar in the corner of his mouth but a cigarette stuffed in a holder. This is Jānis Eizens, head of the Production department at the racecourse, a man trained in the old St. Petersburg school who, as the years passed, turned from a lawyer into a horse-trainer, and then from a horse-trainer into a book-keeper – of the racecourse's inventory of carriages, horseshoe nails or reins. Having spotted Mrs. Baginskis, the grandee comes to life. Right there on the threshold he combs his hedgehog of greying hair with his fingers, composes his bushy chin, and embraces the newcomer. Eizens' suit, strewn with cigarette ash, radiates a dusty homeliness from every pin-stripe.

"How nice to have blackouts in Riga! Without a trace of bad conscience I can give you a hug! ... Which winds have blown you in here, Mrs. Baginskis? Westerlies or easterlies?"

"We need to talk some more, Mr. Eizens..."

"If we need to, then come to my place. We'll put the tea machine on!"

Mrs. Baginskis pulls out a bag from behind the apples; the brown wrapping paper gives off a smell of smoked meat, and the fat stains clearly mark the places where the string is.

"I've got a little shoulder of pork tucked away here," the newcomer says apologetically. "Dzidra, let's meet this evening at Mrs. Cīrulis' place!"

"The girls will be right here." As he leaves, Eizens raises his lantern. "You know the old joke about the women's prison, don't you? After sitting together for years, when they're released they stick around inside for two more hours to have a natter."

The youngsters notice how the odour of smoked meat disperses into the dark corridor of the stables. The whole moisture of their bodies seems to come together in mouths full of saliva.

"There he goes, like, to Kirhenšteins'," Andulis tries to joke, but the joke falls flat.* He sighs, stretches an arm out and takes one more apple. The others follow his example; only Vanda gets up and starts to get dressed. Her boyish figure is elongated by the jacket, put together from off-cuts of broadcloth.

Clothing is a subject, like the past, that those tongues and teeth never bring up in conversation there. Before dances they exchange clothes, so as not to have to go in something boring, and that's all. How and out of what material somebody came by a blouse, from a relative, a colleague or some cheap tailor, you just accept it. Vanda's cambric blouses look home-made, and the thick *sarafan* jackets sewn by hand too, while the buttons are made of yarn. Many of them have the same kind of jackets – of thick grey broadcloth with colourful insets at the waist, the collars and the pockets, with a zipper in front, but pulled over the head. Vanda has a classic like that. High boots with laces too, with flat toe-caps as if cut across.

"You coming to Mrs. Cīrulis'?" asks Veriņa. "We'll listen to some music."

"It's snowing," Vanda sighs sadly.

It's no secret to anyone that the little lass is helping her landlady do her caretaker's duties. Especially when it's snowing, and every moment heavy lorries are driving up to her home and piles of snow swept off the pavement and the roadway are shovelled into the rear and taken out of town.

"But I'm expecting a load of firewood," Andrievs says in farewell. "See you in the morning!"

Silently they make their way in the darkness along the corridor of the stables.

The passage covered with chaff and sawdust is soft underfoot, like the skin of an animal lying on the ground. Every corner is familiar, and the horses standing in the stalls can be called by name. Light from the snow falls through the smoky panes. Some horses are rooting for hay on the ground with their velvety noses, but most are quietly breathing, easing themselves by shuffling their back legs, resting after a working day. Sometimes there is no electric light in the stables, but outside there is never any. The electric lighting system, begun in the days of the old republic and finished in the first Soviet year, was destroyed during the war and has still not been replaced. As the winter evenings darken, there can be no training and no racing.

Eizens' bunker is covered by a curtain; the candlelight stealing through the chinks throws long, flickering strands on the floor, and Eizens' and Mrs. Baginskis' muffled voices resound. Every now and then there's a whiff of an odour: of iodine and carbolic on Chief Veterinarian Serafim, of various salves and ointments in the jockeys' cubicle, of linseed oil and bitter leather in the saddling-room, of cold iron and heated polished nails in the farriers' apparatus. There are also the odours of sweet horse-sweat, of sawdust and hay, the warm odours of blankets and leg-guards. Finally Andrievs shoves the heavy outer door shut with his shoulder, and their faces are anointed by the shivering blast of snow.

"I'll come with you, Vanda!"

A slight surprise, along with gratitude, can be made out in Vanda's eyes, for the black city frightens her at night.

Over Riga the clouds are darkening, coloured by a muffled light – the reflection of the snow in the sky, or, who knows, the reflection of the heavens on earth. From this pillow of light hangs the thick, moving curtain of wet snow, which turns into a blue-tinged sticky wadding.

"Shall we go into the *bufete*?" asks Vanda. "You can get hot soup there up to eleven in the evening. Otherwise I won't be able to lift a shovel."

They set off along Mālpils Street up to the corner, where it merges with the bigger Šarlotes Street. Then they turn towards the centre along the little Dārzniecības Street, which until the Germans came bore the name Vāgnera Street, in honour of Wagner's horticultural work, and thus now called "Garden" Street, linking Šarlotes and Valdemāra Streets.

Along almost the whole length of Dārzniecības Street stretches Mrs. Cīrulis' wooden house, reminiscent of a small manor-house with a fenced-in yard. The ground floor of the house is like one large apartment; the upper floor is an uninhabited loft. The two walkers peer into the darkness beyond the shuttered windows.

"Empty and silent," declares Andrievs.

"Mrs. Cīrulis is with the student girls at the opera."

"You live with her too?"

"Mrs. Cīrulis would be happy to take me in, because she needs the money to keep her horses, but I don't have anything to pay her with. I live in a cheaper place. She has enough girls anyway. When the Russians came, so as not to have them put in just any old tenants, she picked some students and assigned them to her place. Then they issued that law about how many people there needed to be per square metre."

From Barbisa Street the wind pushes back a smell of cow-sheds through the snowy evening.

"It smells like the Liepiņš stables," exclaims Vanda. "Liepiņš recently showed us photographs of his Angora, the one he got after the First World War – a very pretty mare… At first I thought she had English blood; in the end they put her among the trotters.

She left a big impression – just one mare – on our stock of trotters."

"Through Draufgangers," Andrievs explains. "There was this stallion, Draufgangers, that she mated with. Draufgangers was small in size, but from Angora, Ango Draufgangers was born. After that, Ango Draufgangers sired a son, Angis, a black one."

"I know Angis, and Angis' offspring too – huge-sized horses, big and fast. And very good-natured. They're highly respected. Now when there's a need for big, fast horses like that, those are the ones. But the main thing is – they're good-natured."

"Who knows how much good stock Liepiņš has saved in that way," Andrievs observes. "He's from Krimulda, a large-scale farmer, but he had to hand his farm over to the Agricultural Academy; they only let him bring a couple of horses with him to Riga."

"Brinda and that other bay mare," Vanda adds. "And yet now he's keeping cows in his Riga stables. He even has a pedigree bull. It's not too bad – he brings hay, milks the cows, fills up litre bottles, and there are customers that come back – I've even brought some to Mrs. Cīrulis. The gentle treatment of Liepiņš, I think, was because of Professor Kirhenšteins. One part of Liepiņš' farm was counted as Kirhenšteins' rural farm. Were you at the agricultural show last summer at Grīzinkalns, when they demonstrated artificial insemination for the first time on two cows, apparently Kirhenšteins'? They were actually Liepiņš' cows."

Among the wooden shacks on the other side of the street, where the black holes of hovels appear, the two walkers notice dark figures behind a broken fence. Vanda slips in behind Andrievs' back. Their quiet breathing pervades the falling snow. After a moment they find that the two men behind the collapsed fence have been attending to their natural needs; now, looking back towards the banging wooden doors, they return to the buffet. There is a bigger building which appears through the curtain of snow, closer to Valdemāra Street. There, since time immemorial, stands a little pub, or "buffet", as drinking dens are called these days, a favourite with the jockeys. Sometimes it happens that someone arrives at the pub with a saddled horse, straight from the track – cutting a dark dash and making life brighter. Ordinary city drinkers come there too, but they are a minority.

"Now that's frightening," says Vanda. "I don't go to buffets on principle, because of those men, but when I really want to eat, I do come here; Nikolayevna always gives friendly service. And they have hot soup here."

The air in the buffet swallows the two visitors up like an unnameable, unclassifiable animal – hot, smelly, full of drunks, smoke and shouting. In the chimney-like furnace at the back of the place, tiny red tongues of flame squeak from a damp pine stump with an outstretched resinous foot. Over the fire, on a chain, a large soot-blackened soup cauldron is warming. There are not many customers on a Saturday at dusk. By the window, frothy glasses are being stared at by the two thick-set men who had been seen outside, evidently country people who have come into Riga with a load of hay or wood-chips, because the quilted jackets are pretty dusty. Some young, drunk and very ugly girl, wearing some sort of soiled rags, is insistently trying to engage their attention.

Nona Nikolayevna, the buffet keeper, is polishing the front of the counter with a cheesecloth rag, and cursing.

"Spitting here! What pigs!" Nona bellows, stooping down. Her legs, clad in brown, half-length socks, reveal the white knobbly flesh under her blue work apron.

"Hi there! What would you like, Andryusha?" Nona straightens herself, tossing her hair from her sweaty face.

"The usual, Nikolayevna! And a bowl of soup," he adds, as Vanda starts to fumble for kopecks in her pocket.

The girl grasps the minestrone soup bowl, filled to the brim, and moves out of sight of the drinkers on the other side of the room. Like a barge, Nikolayevna floats back out of the yellow smoke with a bottle of Crimean wine. And as a special sign of favour, she puts two warmed *ponchik* doughnuts cooked in oil in front of Vanda.

"One with *povidlo*!" Nona points out, graciously pointing a little finger. Vanda smiles humbly at her.

Andrievs finishes his cigarette and tilts the wine bottle.

"Good?"

Vanda grins.

"The usual."

"You don't know much about me yet, Vanda. I have a favour to ask."

Vanda nods understandingly – he wouldn't have suddenly come with her for no reason.

"I happened to hear that you'd seen old Hill in Gomel. Tell me about that."

Her green eyes darken like meadows overshadowed by a storm.

"Tell you everything?"

"Everything, everything," says Andrievs, topping up her glass. "I'm well prepared."

"It's a big stud for army horses, a structure that was ready in place in Byelorussia. After the war, trophy horses were arriving there from all over Germany, as well as trotters – although there aren't any good trotters there… But there are some from Austria and Hungary too – they picked everything they could. Well, and of course also American mares and stallions were brought in… The worst thing – when we were there – is the terrible disorder! Even the staff are hand-picked. There used to be families working at Russian stud farms from Count Orlov's time, who cared for the horses and understood a thing or two, but now – one or two of them do want to work, but don't understand a thing… The mess there was dreadful, muddy manure all around. The horses aren't cleaned. There isn't a good track – a galloping track. Heavy, sandy in the middle, so the trotters can only run on the inner and outer edges, where there's green grass. The main point is that they don't feed them… The American ones are quick growers, they need to be given monumental amounts when the foal is weaned from its mother. Even earlier – while the foal is still with the mare – you start to feed them up, because they grow quickly and they're already racing at two years. But there are really poor conditions for them there. The Ryazan Horse-breeding Institute wants to take over some of them, which would be a way out, because there in Gomel… I think nothing useful will come out of there…"

"Tell me about Hill."

"He was completely emaciated, he couldn't eat oats any more, but it hadn't occurred to anyone to feed him porridge. He looked terrible. Honestly, I've never seen such a wreck. There are plenty more like him there, without any names or documents, but you can see that they're really good horses."

Vanda glances drunkenly at Andrievs, having had more wine. She is simple, and at the same time as fragile as a mountain stream threading its way among the anemones.

"Conditions there are terrible. Those people might like horses, but they have no idea themselves, and there's no management there either. At the end I had to drink a full glass of vodka to Stalin's health. Ugh! I was thinking: even God would at least feed them, even if the management doesn't!"

On the day when the two dark silhouettes have driven Andrievs out from his imagined refuge, roughly stamping out their cigarette-ends with their boots on the banks built in the sand, he starts to admire Vanda's passionate attitude, instinctively trusting her and appreciating that he can talk seriously to this girl. There is something about Vanda of the ancient aristocrats, who do not feel a slavish dependence on a bowl of soup, but whose wealth of soul, whose layers of culture built up over generations, allow her to make free and independent judgments.

And above all, she is a really wonderful conversation partner.

"How did you get involved with horses?"

"At the funeral ceremonies," Vanda smiles. "That's where you could look most at horses, at those funerals. That's when they'd come together! Then there was something to see! You can't leave a stallion alone, someone always has to be standing by. Once at Skrīveri I took my friend with me, that Dzidra Baginska. We rode with the stallion Front, who was born at the Pskov stud; he'd been taken off the racetrack to the Baginskis' for mating. Really beautiful. Mrs. Baginskis said, 'Would you stand by that stallion while we're at the graves?' 'Sure, sure,' I said. 'But why is he pawing all the time?' They all came up to me and asked what he was – I said: 'This is a trotting stallion!' Beautiful."

"And how did you come to the racetrack?"

"You know Riekstiņš, the vet? A short chap? He was at the track a few times."

"I've heard of him. You know, Vanda, I'm so fed up with Natis Rindiņš, the vet at the track, that I don't feel I'll be interested in any of them ever again."

"Everyone respects Riekstiņš the vet," says Vanda, with slight reproach in her voice. "He was Professor Lejiņš' assistant in the Ulmanis days, and even in the German time. After the war he was given the job of entering horses in the pedigree register. I wanted to earn a bit extra in the summer, and Auntie arranged for me to be his technical secretary. I had a sort of board in front of me – he'd just call out, and I'd write. He took measurements, called out the colour of the hair, the features, the genealogy – we entered them in the pedigree book. Horses had to be inspected at the racecourse – I liked it there from the very beginning. And since Mrs. Baginskis' horses were also there at the track, we could ride the horses that belonged to her. Some other trainers offered to let me ride; that was interesting. You must know yourself that if a girl like me trots with them, it's a great relief for the trainers..."

"And you can earn money, too," says Andrievs, surveying Vanda's thin, stitched-together clothes.

"Most of the money I earned was in those two summers with Riekstiņš. I got to know the horse-breeders. The horses were taken to a particular place in the district. There are no hotels there, so you'd sleep in the parish council house – that was worse because there was nothing to eat. It was better with the breeders – they'd feed you, give you a bed. Because there were 'forest quotas' to be followed, but if the mare is in the pedigree book and is being mated, you're exempted from the quota. So there were whole groups in Vidzeme province, including Jēkabpils, that welcomed us with open arms. In some places *artel* co-operatives,* but mostly private. After all, they're all under an obligation to keep the army horses in good condition, in case there's a need for them. With Riekstiņš we covered all of Vidzeme province, including Jēkabpils, plus the whole of Jelgava district up to Jūrmala and the Tukums district, and finally I did the excursion to Gomel."

"Everything you're telling me is interesting," Andrievs marvelled. "Even if it isn't really like that in real life."

"What was most interesting for me was that through Riekstiņš I got to know Professor Lejiņš and learnt a lot. It's just a shame that I understood so little about it… There at Rāmava the professor has a summer cottage, where he lives, and when I was there once, I listened in, open-mouthed. Nowadays everywhere they teach the doctrines of Michurin and Lysenko – just them. Since Riekstiņš has worked together with Professor Lejiņš for many years – five or six – he's learned a few other things besides, hasn't he? They were very fruitful conversations there. Various people came together and talked about science, and I just listened, but I couldn't grasp much of it… It's a pity that I still don't appreciate the importance of what I heard."

"So what did they talk about?"

An impolite question at a time when people don't usually interrogate each other, when biographies are colourful, but what happens is often hushed up. For a moment Vanda feverishly rubs her temples with her delicate fingers, and then suddenly leans forward, and with flashing eyes, whispers softly, as if revealing a huge secret: "For example, the basics of genetics, as they teach it in Western Europe – we don't know about it yet. You know what determines fertility?"

"For what? For cows?"

"For all species. Fertility is determined by the ability to bind oxygen. For how short a time haemoglobin binds oxygen, and how. Breeding a cow is hugely expensive, but with this method you get to know immediately whether it will succeed or not. You know the prospects for reproduction. In English thoroughbred horses and Arab gallopers, the blood is best at binding oxygen. And for trotters this quality is important too. It determines sustained speed, because in a short time there has to be huge metabolism, the exchange of oxygen in the blood. That's an extremely important factor. And it's bred into them. The Americans have studied this a lot, they can immediately tell how a foal will run."

"And how does it seem to you – do you have any prospect yourself of spreading this knowledge?"

"The knowledge exists in itself." Vanda is peeved. "These are the basic laws of life – sooner or later the time will come when they'll be confirmed. The young generation is always better than the old. That's true of horses too – if you work it out right, every generation is much better and faster. Lejiņš and Riekstiņš said it too – there's no rubbish about those old guys! If it's useful to you and it's any good, take the young one and then you'll see how it turns out for you."

Andrievs grins.

"So you, like everyone else, say that the old must perish?"

"The old simply die out, that's the consequence of time," Vanda asserts. "For us it might be the other way around – the greatest pleasure is always to trace the old ones, who haven't perished in spite of time. I know that Nordpols, the stallion bred by the state, was found, the one who was bred in Brandenburg province in Germany. He was brought to the documentation commission by an old man. When they asked him the horse's name and where he had got him, the greybeard answered that this stallion was called Ješka and he'd got him from some internal army unit in the Kurzeme Pocket. The soldiers had confiscated the young horse that he'd raised himself, and replaced it with this weak, worn-out Ješka – Nordpols, one of the very best stallions out of Hanover. He was traced by the vet at the horse-breeding centre, who had himself once been on the commission that had bought Nordpols in Germany for Latvia."

"Wasn't he blind in one eye?" asks Andrievs, when he hears the name Ješka.

Lost in thought, the girl shrugs her shoulders vaguely.

"But it's a shame about Hill, because he's…" she says. "Hill's old, but he's lived the kind of life… he's…"

"Because he's Hill."

Vanda summons up her courage and asks: "In the stables you mentioned Saltupa. Was that Antonija Saltupa?"

Andrievs has to light up another cigarette hurriedly.

"What do you know about Saltupa, Vanda?"

"She drove with Hill at the age of fifteen and won the Grand Prize."

"That's right." Andrievs decides to be frank, so as to repay Vanda for her story. "That was in July 1939, she was almost fifteen. I had a finger in her getting onto the track, and then we won a prize and after that we got trounced. That's a legend, yeah – like Hill himself. Legends are ageless, but unfortunately I'm not a legend."

"You are a legend!" cries Vanda, adding in a conspiratorial tone: "I know that you led Hill off the battlefield!"

Andrievs is suddenly struck by the girl's forthright words. And her look, mixed with admiration. He doesn't know much about Vanda, but to Vanda Andrievs is definitely not a blank page.

"But then, I'm old already. As you just said: there's no rubbish about those old guys."

"That isn't old age, whatever you call it."

"Sometimes it seems quite the other way round – that I was born old, but with time I'm becoming younger," grinned Andrievs. "You saw Hill here at the track, you drove with him?"

"I didn't drive with him much – he went off for mating, and when I came here, they only took him out to exercise him… But I did see him. I was amazed at him – such a small size! Since he'd grown up in the south, in the great spaces, the boxes in the stalls for stallions in Ēveles Street would be too small for him. After that they moved him into the old stables at the racetracks – there were larger boxes there, and that was when I saw him the first time. And when it was possible they let him out on the circuit to have a run, but in the winter he was covered all the time with a blanket, because he was really freezing… He was a dark, dark, dark red – is there a better word?"

"When I had time on my hands, I thought up a description of him. He was chestnut. Dun chestnut – can you say that?"

"Like in the folk-songs…"

"And his offspring are like – you can't describe it. Mrs. Dubinskis' *Birztaliņa,* Birch-grove, for example – black chestnut. And my Grand Hill – if you look at him, he isn't a bay, as it says in the papers."

"You needed to know how to handle Hill. That nervousness was a bit worrying. If you were calm with him, it was all right. He was always walking – going round in circles in his box like a bear in a cage. There are horses that stamp around – luckily it wasn't that way with him. But walk, that he did. I don't remember clearly – I think it was only in one direction. He needed space… Did he walk like that even before the war?"

"Before and after the war, like a bear in a cage," Andrievs confirmed. "But during the war, strangely enough, he didn't. What else have you heard about Antonija Saltupa?"

Looking Andrievs helplessly in the eye, Vanda blushes to her ears. She's as red as a raspberry.

"That she was very beautiful and…"

"And?"

"…and carried on with the Germans."

"Put that kind of talk right out of your head, Miss Vītola! She was, and is, beautiful. But about the Germans – complete nonsense! She was simply a woman in love. Every moment of this damned life she's been up-front about everything. You're still too young to understand, but there's no need to pass on that kind of talk."

Andrievs feels he must have drunk too much. He feels sorry for the poor schoolgirl. Vanda's thin frame stoops and becomes almost transparent, dissolving in the smoky atmosphere. Her gaze is firmly fixed on a crack in the boards of the table; she has never in her life felt so humble and puny.

"Vanda, eat your soup! Calm yourself now," Andrievs commands soothingly, downing the last of the wine. "Nikolayevna, another bottle!"

"A glass, not a bottle, Nona!" Vanda abruptly and defiantly corrects him, adding more quietly: "You oughtn't to drink so much."

Andrievs grins. It's a long time since anyone cared about him that much.

A moment later Nikolayevna comes over decorously with a glass of wine, one ear cocked like a submarine periscope to the murmur coming from the other corner of the buffet. It's very pleasant to have Nona's attention diverted by something else. Otherwise she would sit down at their table and tell them about how she once saw Stalin, when he came visiting them at the Partisan collective farm near Yelizarovka, and Stalin was wearing his greatcoat and they were both photographed – Stalin put his hand on her shoulder and stood beside her. It was an unforgettable moment, worth revisiting in her memory for the rest of her life.

Nona Nikolayevna Vilna had arrived in Riga in spring 1945 together with the field kitchen of the Latvian Riflemen's Corps and its colonel, Pyotr Vilna. They had decided to stay here in their ancestral homeland. Apartments were freely given out to the newcomers, one of them near Padomju Boulevard, named after the Soviets, with undamaged Karelian birchwood bedroom fittings and Bukhara carpets – only the colonel soon died and occupied a place of honour in the Pokrov cemetery.

Nona Nikolayevna was ardent in her efforts to meet the targets of Stalin's Sovietization, learning to think "correctly" and "in the new way", taking part in the building of Communism, and yet every time lightning rolled over the city or a heap of ice fell from the roof, her hand made the sign of the cross purely out of instinct, her lips murmured a prayer by themselves and she felt like a backslider. That was Nona's misfortune, cleaving the depths of her being, something she didn't understand herself and didn't even try to understand, but just shoved somewhere into the attic of her personality, hoping that the cleft would be overgrown or covered in dust over the years, but it only grew deeper. She knew that she shouldn't hide behind the mask of a Soviet believer, and keep her feelings to herself. But these other feelings were stronger than her mind, and Nona didn't know where to begin. Therefore she turned her indignation with herself all the more vehemently on others, the ones who might not have such subversive feelings, but who still didn't know how to live in the marvellous new reality – on the drinkers, the speculators, the slovens, the backsliders.

"You don't smoke, child?" Having put the glass down in front of Andrievs, Nona leans over Vanda in amazement.

"There's a lot of smoking." Vanda revives like a river after the ice has melted and agilely picks up her spoon.

"Then just get that down you!" The buffet-keeper maternally strokes the girl's frail shoulder and goes.

"One of them is with jam," observes Andrievs. "Interesting – which one? And what does the other one have? I'll try my luck."

He grabs one of the *ponchik* pastries and rapidly bites into it. It reveals a filling of grey flakes. It is filled with the remains of fish.

Vanda has meanwhile recovered and slurped her soup. She collects herself and gives Andrievs a bright, broad smile, as she takes the other *ponchik*.

"I'm always lucky."

The few fine, pretty wrinkles around her mouth, as she bites into the *ponchik* and the brown jam smears the corners of her mouth, are really quite disarming. You can't get angry with Vanda.

"Where did you study?"

"This year I'm graduating from Draudziņa secondary school – my parents told me to do what I want."

"And what do you want to do?"

"Veterinary medicine."

"Really? You already know more than any academic professor!"

"See – even you make fun of me! You do!" Vanda snaps.

"It's the truth," Andrievs grins. "I always tell the truth, because it's the biggest joke. Veterinary medicine is a difficult job."

"All sorts of professionals are involved in veterinary medicine. Microbiologists and so forth – they don't have to be involved just with animals."

At this moment Nona's cries can be heard. It turns out that the main cause of her upset has been dozing all this time propped up against the wall – a young Russian boy, a war invalid without legs. His torso is attached to a little board, with ball-bearings screwed into it below. Evidently a little company has decided to ride out the blizzard in the buffet. The half-man, having woken up, is starting again to settle scores with the rest, spitting at them across the room, because that is his only weapon.

"We were fighting together, but who am I now?" the invalid screams at the other two, who are cowering guiltily in the candlelight. "I was a pianist, I became a communist. But you – millers! Scoundrels! And millers you always will be!"

"Drunk out of your skull like an animal!" screams Nona, standing over the invalid and threatening him with a broom. "Out of here!"

"No point! He's got concussion!" interjects the young girl with the pock-marked face.

But now the invalid is offended. Rowing himself with his hands, he moves toward the door. The ball-bearings squeak unpleasantly, the door opens; outside can be heard the loud victory song of the snow-shovels. The sweepers have started to clean the streets, and as soon as the snow is cleared, invalids have the opportunity to get moving. The girl snatches at her clothes and draws back for the invalid to pass, but the country proletariat, silent and guilty, remain by their glasses.

The incident has taken away their desire to talk. Andrievs and Vanda look at each other, and both get up at the same time. At the entrance, Andrievs hesitates: "I live by St. Peter's Church. And you?"

"On Lenču Street."

"Then let's go together down Valdemāra."

The heavy snowfall has eased off, light flakes are fluttering in the air and freezing. They walk quickly, to clear their heads from the smoke-filled bar and so that the cold can't bite through their thin clothes. As she goes, Vanda looks at the windows of the rental houses and says: "Doesn't it seem to you that houses, like people, each have their own face? Sometimes I look into windows and imagine all the faces, all the eyes, that have looked through those windows."

She stretches out her hand toward a window where a candle is shining warmly on the sill.

"You can imagine how someone has grown up and spent their life behind that window, for instance? Looked through it day and night, summer, autumn and winter, in childhood and right through their life…"

"No need to ponder over that," Andrievs pragmatically interrupts her daydream. "Look at me if you want to see that person – it was me! This is my father's house."

Vanda's eyes are wide with astonishment.

"Even when I was a schoolboy I used to look at the races on the track from my bedroom window. The garage wall in the yard almost touched the racetrack manager's building. I was one of the ones who used to walk around on moonlit nights and didn't remember anything in the morning. My mum was unhappy and used to cry often. Maybe because I was sleep-walking, but maybe because of my dad. They didn't live together. Dad and my elder brother Augusts were completely different sorts of people to Mum and me. They were energetic bosses with blond hair and blue eyes, we were dark-haired dreamers with green eyes. You know, as a child I hated the racetrack, because my mum was involved with one of the money-lenders from our building and started playing the totalizator."

Vanda tries to imagine old Radvilis, his beautiful Gypsy wife, Augusts and little Andrievs in the house opposite, on the stairs in the heat of some bygone summer. The house clearly reveals the essence of them all, their attitude to life, their sense of beauty and their struggles; it is finely designed and solidly built. Symmetrical, with a prominent bay window in the middle, where a portico built on the ground floor embraces a graceful heavy front door and a small coloured mosaic. The house is two-storeyed, built of light-coloured stone and looking like a conch-shell washed onto a Mediterranean shore.

"In the living-room I remember a piano that I was made to play, and I didn't like it. There was beautiful colourful furniture in the living-room – made by the craftsman Ansis Cīrulis, one of Mrs. Cīrulis' relatives. Dad said that Cīrulis had a special talent for understanding wood… What I liked most of all was drawing, I was always sketching something with a pencil on every bit of paper that came my way. I knew that hobo Irbīte* well, I would follow him on the streets; I also liked Romans Suta*, he even had horses on the track at one time."

Andrievs sighs heavily, letting out a white cloudlet of vapour.

"So, when you talk about windows, you have a good imagination, Miss, but I'm thinking more about the people who live there at the moment… The ones who were given the apartments of people murdered or sent to Siberia, with valuable furniture, earned by ceaseless hard toil. Are they moved to find out who owned the beds they sleep in, who owned the tables they eat and drink at? Hardly. I worked at the goods station for a while, loading trains that were used to transport stolen goods. Day and night there we were wrapping up the best furniture – whole suites, hundreds of paintings and pianos, and even palm-trees – with addresses out East attached to them."

Vanda is shivering with cold. Andrievs quickly pulls her along, forcing her into a snowdrift.

"Laugh! You see those two militiamen on duty there? They'll shoot at us for standing too long in one place."

Vanda gathers up a snowball and throws it at Andrievs.

"Were your parents deported?"

"Yes, in 'forty-one." Andrievs throws one back.

"And where did you end up?"

"At the racecourse. The course is like a father, it gives everyone shelter. Let's go!"

"But I thought – if you have a cow, then you're okay," Vanda breathlessly tries to keep up with Andrievs' rapid strides. "A cow is like a mother, it feeds the whole family."

At the junction of Red Army Street they are stopped by a cavalcade of dingy Russian trucks. Heavily loaded with wet snow, they brake with a squeal on the hill, and then turn along Valdemāra Street and vanish into the dark. By six o'clock in the morning all the snow must be cleared away.

"How strange, at a time when there's practically nothing, there are enough lorries to take the snow out of the city," declares Andrievs.

"That's discipline," replies Vanda, hastening her step. This evening, snow is also her concern.

"Why did you choose veterinary medicine?"

"My aunt – my mother's sister – is a veterinary surgeon, one of the first women in Latvia to graduate in veterinary science from the University, in 1926. My aunt, Mrs. Dzelde and Milda Skudiņa – three or four of them there were, they delivered a special appeal to President Čakste to let them study. And Kirhenšteins went along with them, he defended them."

"That old fool Kirhenšteins must be close to your heart."

"He's always been close to our family. He could have been an excellent microbiologist, world-class, but he preferred to be popular. The serum station that he set up used to make insulin for export, and the tuberculosis vaccine from Riga was rated the second best in the world. And yet, at academic graduations, he can still climb on a desk and conduct *"Pūt, vējiņi"**. I guess he's the kind of character that likes to get up on the table and conduct. There's a legend that in 1940, when the Soviet tanks rolled into Riga, he was sitting in Otto Schwarz' café and someone came up and summoned him to the Russian embassy. He got a fright, thinking he'd be sent to Siberia. But there they asked him if he'd like to be prime minister. He replied that he would. Ambitious, but with a soft heart. He likes being called Professor, although his lectures are more like interesting chats."

"The 'silver throat' of the Kremlin." Andrievs starts reciting a children's teasing rhyme: "'Big talk in the Kremlin from someone silly; why, it's that fisherman, Big Bear Willy; holding a placard is someone *klein,* Little Professor Kirchenstein…'"

"'Andrejs Upīts*, nose boozy and round, joins in the choir like a baying hound,'" Vanda finishes it off. "He's interesting, and hugely tragic. The great leader – but such a buffoon, coming in and getting up on the table! He doesn't realize that so many party members just don't get it. They call his institute 'a nest of Ulmanites'*, not a collective but a *sbrod*, a rabble. He supports the students and he always pays for them; he likes talking to students. Veriņa told me that sometimes he invites the students round to have a feed, to be honest. When they go to his place, they get chatting, they have a pie or two, but after that they have proper meat dishes and even sweets to follow."

"He could have just left it at pies! Can't make head or tail of his politics, from his actions, from what he does."

"And if it weren't him, instead it would be someone like Krūmiņš, Kalniņš, Čiekuriņš. Does choosing him make any big difference?"

"Maybe with Krūmiņš it would, but would it with Vanda Vītola? I don't think so."

Vanda doesn't reply, and Andrievs continues ironically: "Auntie, the first female veterinary doctor in Latvia – it's a beautiful legend, just like the stories about Kirhenšteins and his microbiology. Just read the papers, I'll bet they're full of news about aubergines, raccoon-dogs and Sosnowsky's hogweed. Do you really think you'd be allowed to work as a specialist? You'll get in all right, but after graduation the whole cohort of you will get sent off to some backwater where you'll starve and freeze, where you'll have to pull weakened cattle onto their feet by the tail, where what you earn you'll be giving away in taxes – if you don't give it away, you'll be given away yourselves, they'll brand you as a *kulak* and put you in prison… The five-year plan will be done in four years – you know that well. Your children will grow up on their own, your parents will die on their own, but your spouse will probably be bumped off by some KGB man, because your husband will turn out to be just as naively honest as you… In the end you'll have to join the Party and start talking about making 'life material' out of unstructured protein – if you're lucky, you'll get the Stalin prize…"

"I'll never ever join the Party!" interjects Vanda. "So what do you think I'm supposed to do? Go to Nikolayevna and be a dishwasher? Is that the way out?"

"You're right," – lowering his voice, Andrievs offers her his elbow. "You don't need to listen to a dinosaur like me. I'm a wolf who's left the pack, and I chose that myself. That's my way out."

Andrievs pulls the girl forward, but she, her feet dug into the pavement like a jockey on the track, doesn't budge.

"A month ago, we saw off our school headmistress, Miss Natālija Draudziņa, from the school to the Torņakalns Cemetery – this year she would have turned 85. She'd lived her whole life at the school; we'd curtsey out of respect when we met her in the corridors. When the Latvian army didn't have enough clothes during the liberation struggle, our headmistress organised the Women's Aid Corps, which sewed shirts for the soldiers out of used flour-bags. She was the first female Officer of the Order of the Three Stars before the war, but after the war she even got a personal pension from the Communists. What do you say to that?" Vanda asks.

Andrievs shrugs.

"Miss Draudziņa is the Communists' dream," he says, "her biography can't be separated from her work in the education field. She sacrificed everything, and willingly too. I'll salute you if you follow in her footsteps. But woe betide you if you want to preserve some little bit of yourself. Just think what they'll take away from you by force."

Vanda, caricaturing him, shrugs her shoulders too.

"And so what have you preserved of yourself, taking up a position like Hesse's *Steppenwolf*? Miss Draudziņa was always reminding us of two things: 'The greater the difficulty, the greater the desire to overcome it', and the other was: 'Remember you're all my daughters!' I'm going to remember that, but the forest doesn't listen to curses from a wolf. Goodbye! Sometimes it's not nice talking to you."

It's evident from her feverish breathing in the twilight just how much Andrievs, without wanting to, has annoyed Vanda.

"Miss Vītola!" He stretches out his hand beseechingly, but she has already vanished into the dusk of Ķieģeļu Street. It's a long way to Lenču Street, but she didn't want to spend a moment longer in Andrievs' presence. A frank conversation is a rare effort – she hasn't had one for a long time and she never will again. In future Andrievs will be talking only to history – to the buildings, the streets and bridges, the stones and the horses – ultimately to his baron – just as before. History is as secure a refuge as a hay-rack in a storm, and yet, it is a refuge.

He turns off past Olavs' business school, now the Academy of Art, where some of his classmates from the former Riga Number 2 Secondary School are studying. Andrievs himself has no opportunity to study, because his biography is a 'dirty page', as Denisov puts it, but perhaps he abandoned his hopes of being an artist when he understood that it was his mission in life to draw only one face.

Andrievs always tries to walk from the new town to Inner Riga by passing the Freedom Monument twice a day. The mighty stone images hypnotise him; he doesn't understand how they can wait so calmly. There flashes into his mind the anthem of the 19th Division:

We believe in the three stars of Latvia,
May the brilliance of their light become
Eternal beyond life.
And we walk and walk,
We keep sweeping forward,
For we must not arrive late.

At the ceremony here last October there was a gun "salute". The Freedom Monument was encircled by army searchlights, their beams of light directed at the three stars in the hands of the figure of Freedom. Soldiers who had climbed up onto the roofs of surrounding houses shot army signal flares into the air. It made Andrievs feel sick to the stomach. Freedom was being turned into a target for enemy cannon, exposing its fragility. After that, rumours spread again in the city that the Freedom Monument was due for demolition. Who knows who'd had the idea for this strange "salute"? Better for eternal night to reign, to let it stand in darkness, in a fog, spattered with mud, than in the depths of a lake, awaiting resurrection. After all, there are no such monuments on the Soviet tourist maps and sets of postcards.

At the ruins of Otto Schwarz' restaurant at the beginning of Kaļķu Street, where there is a cement monument to the "Mother seeing off her son to the partisans", mended and repainted several times, with its columns bisected, the war invalids are gathering as always. The monument is an offensive piece of primitivism, a crude, senseless misunderstanding, not a sculpture, but the invalids seem to belong to it – they are like that too, having lost all human scale. The loud shouting there is already an indication that the poor wretches are drunk as lords and have something they won't share. One of them, with hooks instead of hands, is threatening the ones who have their torsos fixed to boards, trying to hit them while wildly braying "*Rebyata, rebyata!* Boys, boys!"

Several invalids set off for the Kaļķu Square intersection, pushing their way crudely with their bare hands through the slushy snow. The ball bearings catch on the cracks in the stones, the swearing reverberates. Limping along, calling behind them, are the one-armed and one-legged ones in thin clothes, whose stench curdles the blood in your veins even from afar, a mixture of cheap tobacco, charcoal from remote hovels, piss and death. Among them is the girl he spotted in the buffet, who was thrown out of doors by Nikolayevna and the half-man. Some wretch is pushing his wheelbarrow with his torso, which is wrapped in a bag, leaving only his head and the ability to stare all around him with his black eyes. Following the curses, holding each other by the hand and bringing up the rear, are the blind ones – a man and two women. The invalids must be heading for the buffet on Marijas Street, where the beggars usually have their *zastolye* – equal distribution of the spoils of robberies, and drinking.

You can understand them: once they were soldiers, the eagles of their regiment, doing heroic deeds. Girls would swoon over them. A wound changed their lives in a moment. On the battlefield there were no drugs – at best a glass of vodka. Waking up without his arms, such an eagle would conclude that, in order to smoke a cigarette, for the rest of his life he'd have to beg for one. But he wouldn't beg at all – he'd open doors with his teeth, and swear and curse, just to avoid the humiliation.

Even the Party and the Executive Committee were afraid of them.

Trying to avoid the gaggle of cripples, Andrievs bumps against the pock-marked girl.

"Give a bit of bread to one of the raiders of Königsberg!" The girl recognizes him.

Andrievs steps away, but the girl, with outstretched hand, follows him as if attached to him, mechanically repeating like a wind-up doll: "A little cigarette for a shell-shocked man… He fought for his country, a hero! In a burning tank, he manned a battering-ram."

When Andrievs doesn't answer, she screams in exhaustion: "Gimme a fag, you bastard, I saw you smoking!"

Andrievs turns away in silence, and the girl goes back in the dark to the invalids.

In the gloom, he strides past empty-windowed houses, where at every step he can still make out the traces of war, past piles of rubble which are only gradually being cleared away. The torpor of darkness and cold seems to have completely taken over the city; only on the street corners are the militiamen morosely circulating. The wind from the river has ceased; the cold is pinching ever harder. Turning past the Schönfeld house on the corner by St. Peter's church, he notices by the courtyard door a pile of firewood that he had been chopping until midnight last night. On the chopping-block the baron is squatting motionless – on guard. Not a word does Englards say to suggest that Andrievs is back late. The new arrival immediately grabs some wood and lodges it in the crook of his arm.

On the narrow spiral staircase, scraping the walls like a sailing-ship, Andrievs manoeuvres through the ruined levels, up and down. The white, dense billets of aspen strike the nose just as sweetly as a trotter at evening pasture in summer sunshine. The wine he has drunk brings out the perspiration on his forehead, leaving a lingering emptiness and sullenness.

After a few hours the struggle with the firewood is over. Andrievs climbs up to his flat; in the kitchen he scoops water from a bucket and greedily fills his stomach, to mask his wild hunger. Standing by the window he notices in the twilight courtyard that the side door of the church, usually boarded up, is now half-open. Shadows are furtively merging into the black chink. The first one is the half-man. Then two others pull in their crutches. The last one to enter the church takes a secretive look around.

Marija, Englards' wife, squeaks her way along under the roof, sweeping up sawdust and wood-chips. Stricken with radiculitis since early youth, when she worked in a draught in a grain silo, her once supple body is now bent forward like an eel-hook.

"What's in the pot for us this evening?" Andrievs lights the floating candle and stirs the pot with a ladle. "Chicken soup with dumplings?"

Greyish pieces of chicken are floating in the soup – the neck, wings and legs, as well as the gizzard and liver. The former are sold tied up with twine, and the rest are the giblets. They are all boiled – they're cheap.

"Chicken soup from the giblets you brought the other day from the market," says Marija, looking at the worn toecaps of her slippers. "Just that washing, son…"

Day after day, sitting in a closet with a basin between her knees, Marija conjures away with various kinds of lye. She takes in white washing brought in by the madames of Red Army officers billeted in the surrounding apartments.

Andrievs needs no further explanation; carrying the linen up to the attic is his duty.

Having hung a string of pegs around his neck and put the heavy tub of washing on his shoulder, Andrievs climbs to the half-way level of the attic. He hangs up the linen, then pushes open the side window and looks at the snow on the fog-enveloped houses of Old Riga, taking in the overgrown ruins of the town hall and the ripped embankment of the Daugava. St. Peter's Church has no spire, it collapsed when it burned, so instead of the spire there is still an inadequate temporary roof covering, as meagre as chipboard thrown by the wind onto the mighty walls. The houses by the Daugava have burned down, because the wind at the time was "to the Daugava", as Marija says. A feeble light flashes through the high window openings of the church.

Seized by a sudden thought, Andrievs heads downstairs and goes across the yard to the door of St. Peter's Church. The nailed boards are holding only on one side; on the other side the long nails serve only as decoration. He applies his shoulder and opens it. The heavy door gives way; through the crack Andrievs enters the church. Under the high ribs of the starry vault, hidden behind a pillar, a little fire is burning. People are sitting around it.

The vast space, like a huge black and sooty, other-worldly threshing-barn with pits and piles of rubble in place of the threshing-floor, is enveloped in smoke and loud talk. Lying down on shards of marble, the half-man – the young invalid soldier seen earlier – is singing to the others.

"*Ya mogilu miloi iskal, serdce mnye tomila toska, serdcu bez lyubvi nelyegko, gde ti? Otzovis, Sulyiko!* I sought the grave of my beloved, it forced sadness in my heart, the heart is not easy without love, where are you? Answer, Suliko!"

Andrievs wanders among the mounds of crumbling rubble sinking into the darkness, and examines the peeling epitaphs. His feet catch on burned and crumpled ironwork, melted bronze, fused and smashed bells, crumbling profile portraits.

"*Uvidal ja rozu v lyesu, chto lila, kak slyozi, rosu. Ti-l tak rastsvela daleko, milaya moya Sulyiko!* I saw a rose in the forest, shedding dew like tears. Have you blossomed so far away, my beloved Suliko?"

Strewn among the ruins is the ancient store of Riga's graves – here and there are still some gravestones, worn to a dark lustre by time, the lids of vaults, chapel reliefs with epitaphs and the arms of the Aken, Barclay de Tolly, Renner, Vegesack, Grote, Widau, Schulzen, Fischer, Zuckerbäcker, Brewern, Hollander, Hepen, Kaspar, Mallen, Krieger, Pahlen, Reutersdorf families and other ancient Riga merchants, householders and landed gentry, who found their last resting-place here. Wisps of smoke in the greying light of the high windows are juxtaposed in places in white wraiths and it seems that, with pursed lips and grimly furrowed brows, even the ghosts of the dead are partaking of the strange evening. "*Nad lyubimoy rozoy svoyey pryatalsya v vetvyakh solovey. Ya sprosil, vzdokhnuv gluboko: Ti li zdesi, moya Sulyiko?* Above your rose, my beloved, a nightingale lingered on a branch. Then with a deep sigh I asked: Is that you, my Suliko?"

By the wrecked entrance of the chapel of Langenhausen mortuary there lies scattered the crumbling symbol of death – a skeleton with a scythe in its hand. With his fingertips Andrievs cleans the dust off the face of death which the pink ray of the fire has picked out of the darkness. Here, in this charnel-house of the world, where all the honours of the world are uniformly grey and crumbling, light celebrates its triumph.

"*Klyuvom k lyepestkam on prilnul, i, lyesov budya tishinu, zazvenyela trel solovya, budto on skazal: Eto ya.* It pressed its beak to the leaves, and, splitting the silence, the nightingale's voice rang out, replying: It is I."

As silence falls, Andrievs claps a few times. The four of them by the fire stiffen.

"Who's there? Come out!" commands the singer.

Andrievs emerges from the shadow of the pillar.

"What are you – crazy?"

"A neighbour of yours, don't be afraid. You've got a beautiful voice."

"Bloody bastard!" cries the pock-marked girl, who is here too. "Couldn't even spare you a single cigarette!"

"Maybe you'd like to find out where I fought?" the half-man asks jeeringly. "Where I lost my legs? You wouldn't? No-body wants to, see! I was beautiful myself, not just my voice. I performed with the Philharmonic, and my wife was a beauty. I didn't go back to her… What would she do with a bastard like me? I stayed with these useless *blackheads.** My wife must have my photograph up on her wall by now – there, look, my husband, died a hero's death!"

"Take them all – maybe we won't meet tomorrow," says Andrievs and, coming closer, hands a packet of cigarettes across the fire.

"Give me a drag!" screams the girl greedily; she starts sobbing and then falls silent.

The half-man accepts the packet with dignity and carelessly hides it under his armpit. His eyes, fixed on Andrievs, become suspicious. He is the only one of these "blackheads" who has retained a human face; the other faces look blunted and dirty, only registering a flicker of sense in their eyes when they catch sight of cigarettes or vodka.

"You feel sorry for me, right? Or are you afraid? Don't be afraid, I'm a free man, I say what I like. Better to be sorry for yourself, you slave. You must be thinking you've still got it all ahead of you!"

Andrievs shakes his head in denial.

"Don't fool yourself – I know, you believe it in your soul. With your brain you understand that it's all gone to shit, but the shit believes anyway. In some event, in a miracle… I know for sure that I've got nothing left ahead of me – no event, no miracle. Emptiness. I'm waiting for death."

"He might die too."

"Who?"

"Stalin."

The flames hiss around the wet wood, the smoke wafts over the smashed grandeur. Then the invalid suddenly bursts out laughing, even throws back his head. His eyes fill with tears. You can see that he's not laughing all that sincerely. The "blackheads" guffaw with him.

"Look, he made me laugh! Look, a miracle! And why not? He might… Stalin!... Come, sit down!" The invalid holds out a bottle of muddy liquid. "Let's drink to Stalin's death!"

And they would have done, if that muddy stuff hadn't been so disgusting. Andrievs, his hands jammed in his pockets, sets off. The one-legged man with crutches suddenly howls in a piercing voice like a circular saw, and the others join in: "*Iz dalyeka dolgo techot reka Volga*… From far and long the Volga River flows…"

On the narrow path Andrievs stumbles on Englards' pile of billets – the aspen-wood shines white in the darkness. Quick to get the scent of it, he nimbly kicks it aside. It's clear that the half-man doesn't have time to wait, he must survive.

He grows numb in the winter chill, as he pushes the door shut behind him with his shoulder.

The half-man must survive! What for, why, if emptiness and death await him? Maybe that is exactly why? Maybe in spite of it? But don't I have to survive? The invalid is free and says what he thinks. But do I have to live a lie? Is that how I will be picked up – lifted up like a chicken from my perch and have my neck wrung? He has to survive, but I – do I have to survive?

Having climbed back up to his apartment, Andrievs goes out through the narrow entrance-hall and sees that again they have been patiently waiting for him. Marija ladles out the soup and gives it first to Andrievs, then to Boriss. Both of them look furtively at Andrievs – does he like it? He does, but he has to eat carefully, because at times it has happened that something has fallen into the pot from tubs lifted over the stove – the odd dishcloth or sock.

After dinner Andrievs goes to his room, which used to be Englards' daughter's room. Sofija has fallen ill with a lung disease, like her father, and nowadays is living with some country friends where there is fresh pine-scented air. The only change that Andrievs has made is to paint the room in brighter, gayer colours. Just behind the door is a narrow couch, where Andrievs sleeps. All his books and clothes fit comfortably into two piles under the ceiling window on the metre-wide windowsill. At an angle to the opposite wall stands an old piece of furniture – a sort of sofa with curved, delicate legs, covered with a now faded cloth, where only some silver ornaments stand out from the general blackening. Almost every evening the baron settles on the sofa like a dove, puts a lamp on the radio table, and their conversations can begin. You have to stand in long queues for sugar, but conversation is free to enjoy, always available. They don't talk about trotters, maybe because that is everyday work, but most likely because "holy words should not be wasted."

This evening Boriss has with him several sheets of paper with tiny writing.

"I've started writing a new work, I'd like to read it to you and hear your reactions," he announces, clearing his throat. "This evening it's the electricity, dammit – I can't write."

"You said once you'd written a book already."

"That was *Potomivshy mir,* The Drowned World. But after the First World War I sold that one to the "Red Archive" for a derisory sum, a measly five thousand roubles, because I was hungry. I have to admit it – a mistake. No-one has ever seen that manuscript again. Perhaps it was for the best, like everything in this world, because the manuscript was a bit green. It was more of a description of society in my younger days, travels around the world and sporting events, horse-races, racecourses. In my youth I was keen on riding for sport, I took part in aristocratic, non-professional so-called gentlemen's gallops. One year I was even Russia's best rider in the steeplechase, I got a silver cup and golden roubles from the Tsarina. And in that same sporting discipline that Vronsky, the hero of Lev Tolstoy's novel *Anna Karenina,* takes part in, I won the Imperial Prize. I've probably already told you that the prototype for Karenin was the chairman of the Russian Horse-Breeding Board, and Vronksy's was Prince Golitsin in 1872… That book was also about Paris. In Denikin's government I was a sort of minister of propaganda, but at the end of the Civil War I emigrated and in Paris I worked as a taxi-driver. Then I started going to the races regularly …Yes, those were the days. That was the book. Nowadays I tend to write theses, not too much description… More like unusual ideas. Old age is like that. This one will be called *Revolyutsiya i kontrrevolyutsiya,* Revolution and Counter-Revolution, if you're interested. As you already know, in 1940, when the Red terrorists arrived here, the very next day they banged me up and, without any questions, sent me off to Tashkent. They thought I was some other Englards, a confectionery maker from Krimulda. I was saved from the Gulag by the skin of my teeth, and they sent me to the Tashkent racecourse. There I got to know and became friends with an amazing man – Shchokin, Professor of Equine Studies. He gave me a helping hand with just about everything. With this good man's assistance after the war my appeal for release reached Stalin. Perhaps I'll manage to publish the book…"

"Because in the end he might die," Andrievs said, recalling his unusual idea.

"Who?"

"Stalin."

Just as before, inside St. Peter's Church, silence reigned for a moment.

Then Englards bestirred himself: "Soviet power is repugnant to me, but I've never thought of that aspect. It's possible that he… But I'm not… I'm not banking on that. He might… But as a person I don't depend on that at all. I mustn't."

"If you're writing a book, you must surely have some hope of publishing it? Even if for quite a small…"

"I have to be free."

"But you can't."

"I can. I don't think about the end result – that might not even happen. I have to be free, regardless of the circumstances. Free in thought – in the actual process. That's what I wanted to write about, about the countless situations where I've felt independent in the face of death, not obsessed with some idea, but quite the opposite – freed from all ideas, fears, even from myself. I remember – at the end of January 1917… A big room. Everyone was there. Firstly, the members of the Progressive Bloc bureau and other notables from the State Council… others too that I didn't know… You could feel something unusual, mysterious and important in the air. We started talking about the topic, how the situation was getting worse every day and it couldn't continue that way… something had to be done… it had to be done right away… One needed the courage to take big decisions… take serious steps. But the mountain gave birth to a mouse. We talked – and we broke up. I had a vague feeling that something terrible was coming. But our efforts to avoid that terrible thing – pitiful! For the first time I looked into the eyes of the man next to me and I saw my own helplessness. I remember that after February 1917, when I was commandant in Petrograd, I went through such chaos that this time seems like mere child's play. Not only had the Party organizations crumbled to dust, the country's economic life had completely collapsed… It got to the point where one of the ministries, when sending coal for its agents in a distant governorate, put armed guards on the train, so that that coal wouldn't be confiscated by another authority on the way… The whole of the old state structure had broken down."

Andrievs gradually switches off from what the baron is relating; he can't take it in any more. He's thinking about the morning and the misty track, about the Cheka men* and Vanda's open, lively expression in the smoky bar, about the figure of

Freedom wrapped in fog, about the enigmatic face of the Sphinx high above the figures carved into the stone by Kārlis Zāle.* He thinks about the wisps of smoke wafting over the burned-out humans on the bare floor of St. Peter's Church.

His fingertips are itching with the desire to draw Vanda's face – if he weren't so very tired, he would draw it while listening to Englards or afterwards; he really would listen to the nice old man, as old as the world; Andrievs is already straining all his efforts to listen, but a dark heat is creeping over his brow, sleep is grabbing him by the scruff and forcefully robbing him of will-power. His fingers twitch and relax; on the border of sleep, Vanda's face is shuffled with Antonija's before his eyes, as if in a game of cards; if Vanda is tenderness, a gentle morning sun through the leaves of trees, then Antonija is a hot, eerie full moon and the rustling of foliage on a May night. For a moment it seems to him that both these women were the prototype for the silent, concentrated, downward-facing smiles of the symbol of Freedom. Definitely ambiguous: both a smile of joy and a sneer of pain, a grimace of passion along with a priestly silence; this world is a duality and it cannot be otherwise. Andrievs dreams that he has found out a secret and now he is completely free… at last… in the void between two mirrors… but at the moment of greatest harmony the beautiful face turns into a third – suddenly it is the dark pock-marked visage of the vagrant girl, and he sinks into slumber…

Englards stops reading and casts a glance at his sleeping sub-tenant. The slender young man is lying like a soldier fallen in battle, his palms open to the heavens. A wave of dark hair has tumbled onto the pillow. Only children and saints can sleep on their backs. Or very tired riders. Englards smiles. Then, quietly murmuring to himself, he releases one more sentence, finds it to his liking and gets off the sofa. He goes away, bearing the lamp with him and, at the threshold, turning back Marija and her silver salver, on which the tea-things are arrayed. Beyond the window the sky is clearing. It is a starry night with a full moon, when people are at their most fragile, and lunatics are unprotected.

Dreamtime Maps

"Where next?"

"Find the river Daugava."

We're travelling over the bridges as if over the bare rib-cage of a fallen dinosaur, we're rising over the suburbs as the multi-storey buildings and courtyards rise up out of the darkness, full of cars whose owners are enjoying an early Saturday morning in the warmth of their beds in black snowless December. The mind of man, which created these labyrinths, must have had its own intentions, but it is decidedly entangled in the creation of the world.

"You're doing well," the old man murmurs with satisfaction. "And now, turn up along the Daugava! To Sēla. *Selonia* – that name must have been borrowed into Latin from the Livonians. The Livonians called the Selonians *salli*. You know what *salli* means?"

"How would I know?"

"The higher people. The people upstream on the Daugava. And opposite – the Latgalians of Jersika."

I'm driving out along the quiet and empty Riga-Daugavpils highway. The car is smoothly gathering speed, the temperature is above zero, the road safe – the asphalt twinkles like anthracite in the arc of the headlights.

"To the Upland people. In German, *Oberkurland,* Upper Courland. Our Lithuanian neighbours – *aukštaičiai.*"

"Why are we going there?" I ask.

"Sorry?"

"You're from the Selonians? The Uplanders?"

"Yes indeed. It's my native place, I don't feel at home anywhere else in the world. Although there's nothing left for me there, just stones and graves."

Suddenly he chuckles like a cunning Mephisto and leans in closer.

"I decided to exploit you, my dear. To get there! That's the reason. Am I a scoundrel?"

"Who's exploiting whom here? I'll be leading you, as long as you're explaining to me!"

"You're mad," he says. "Your obsession is a riddle to me."

Like conspirators, we glance briefly at each other in the darkness.

"I'd like to find an explanation for it."

"I want to look at the snow falling," I reply. "I don't believe in explanations any more."

Thus this black world is exhausted. Even in dreams at night there is snow – white, delicate, beautiful.

Maybe he doesn't hear what I'm saying, but he doesn't ask again either.

"For some time I've been interested in Australian aboriginal art. Their stories about the creation of the world seem congenial to me, as well as their links to their ancestors and nature, the close bonds with the land."

"Maps from the Dreamtime, yes!" he exclaims.

I don't believe he can hear me, because I'm talking so quietly. But perhaps he can when he wants to.

"The meaning of life is to be a part of everything that exists, and the fact that you're alive connects you to everything that lives – I like that idea," says Radvilis. "Their desire to return to the sacred places of their ancestors. Sand dunes, deep waterholes, large boulders – everything has its symbols, its place in their life from generation to generation. A friend of mine ended up in Australia after the war. His son looked me up, we wrote to each other for quite a while. He was an artist, he was interested in *jukurrpa**. That is difficult, because non-initiates from another clan aren't admitted to it. Do you like those maps too?"

"Yes, that's why I don't want to explain anything any more. It only spoils everything. Instead it's enough to tell a story."

We stare fixedly at the winding road ahead.

This road is too dense a map for me, doubled over, too multi-layered. Now an old man is sitting beside me. I have no idea where we're going.

I turn on the radio. The wireless automatically seeks a station that is broadcasting at this early hour. Some little girl with a brisk voice from the Psychology Guard is announcing: "You're not old – you only have a little too much of a past… You can get ahead by leaving the past behind you…"

I turn off the radio – thanks for your trouble! The aborigines of Australia have about two hundred local language varieties, and not one of them has a word denoting time.

The yellow warning light on the car's dashboard comes on. At the next petrol station I stop to fill the tank. Radvilis gets out of the car too, bobbing like a float at first, stiff from sitting. We are embraced by the moist, fresh night air.

I go inside to pay. Perhaps where we're going there are no shops – I collect in my bag some apples and triangular sandwiches, some juice and bottles of mineral water. And the big take-away paper mugs of coffee are the religion of all night-time travellers. I watch as the spouting, hissing spurts of milk mix with the nocturnally black coffee. The salesgirl is a bit sleepy, another lazy observer of a Saturday morning.

Radvilis is standing away from the petrol pumps like a solitary mile-post. The light of his pipe flares up and dies away in the darkness, beyond which the village is slumbering, beyond which the road stretches out, beyond which the lights and signals of the railway line twinkle, beyond which, monotonously crackling in the damp, the veined high-tension wires are strung out and the colossal iron stanchions rear up out of the darkness, far over the Daugava, across the villages…

"I wake up at three," he says. "I smoke my first pipe around four, after breakfast. The second one before ten with coffee. I can't manage any more during the day, unless some smoker comes visiting. I must say there are less and less of those. And visitors in general."

I offer him a coffee. He looks at it suspiciously and declines.

We stand side by side, looking out into the dark. We are so light, as if we didn't exist at all. Absolutely senseless, but there is the illusion that it's possible to penetrate into the unknown.

The smoke is carried off by the wind.

Radvilis turns to go and glances at the bag of food by my feet. I lift it guiltily.

"We'll survive!" I say.

He smiles a quick, appealing grin, irony mixed with slight disdain.

"That's the least of what we need to survive, my girl!"

Surging across the horizon past us rumbles an empty early train. The lighted panes of the carriages rush into the darkness like warm amber beads. The windows of the village look blindly back at this intruder into their order. Silent are the yards, the gates, the sturdy frames of the houses. Various minds created these unfamiliar gardens, the people sleeping in the houses dream their various dreams.

The salesgirl peers out at us through the glass as we set off.

Comrade Riders

After the races on Sunday, when Andrievs raced with five horses, Monday at the track is a rest day.

The guests promised for late Tuesday afternoon from Smolensk have arrived.

Everything is as usual in the morning. At a slow trot Andrievs exercises the horses on the outer track, lazily rocking his legs splayed out from the cart in woollen socks and military boots. The light, brisk frost has again turned into a fine, slanting snow-storm, the horses lower their heads, while the riders are wrapped in quilted jackets.

The usually leisurely, decent director of the totalizator, Kārlis Grīnfelds, runs up breathlessly, waving from some distance away: "Andrievs, to the manager! Meeting!"

Andrievs doesn't hurry. Everything that has to be done will be done. He walks Kazarka back, unhitches her and leads her into the stable. After a light work-out, the mare is sweaty only under the straps of the harness. Andrievs rubs her body down with a hay-whisk, and wipes her eyes, nostrils and flanks with a damp cloth. He massages the trotter's shoulders with a fragrant mixture of camphor-oil, carnation and mustard-oil. Water is already boiling in the kettle on the thrifty stove; Andrievs pours it into a bucket, mixing it with a handful of coarse salt. Then he soaks towels in the bucket, squeezes out the excess water and lays a hot compress on the trotter's shoulders, back and sacrum. He covers it over with a tightly-woven gabardine cloth, with two woollen blankets on top, tying it all in place. Such a "salt blanket" freshens up the trotter's musculature. Kazarka stands, eyes alert, enjoying the warmth slowly soaking into her bones. Andrievs washes the mare's legs with warm water, then rubs them dry. He wraps them in bindings that have been soaked in a cold tincture of arnica. After that he smears her hooves with ointment and lanolin.

Into the stable comes Filip Boyev, the head of the training section.

"Well, what's keeping you? They're waiting for you."

"Right away – I can't just leave the horse! So what's happened?"

"Denisov from Smolensk has come back with a couple of Russians on his bridle... Right now they've got Sergey in front of them."

Sergey Orlovsky, the old trainer from the Ulmanis era, is the head of the training section in Latgale province and has been promoted to honorary unofficial scapegoat for the racecourse. As conditions in Latgale since the war have been miserable, so that trotters, a quick-growing breed, can't show their real paces, Orlovsky's charges only achieve their greatest speed after five years. But the five-year plan that the racecourse has undertaken to achieve in four, needs enacting right now, immediately!

Denisov rolls the whites of his eyes when the two riders come in and sit down in the empty chairs at the back. He coughs meaningfully and continues talking in Russian: "What we have here is a Soviet Latvian Hippodrome, not some national racetrack. It looks as if you've been abstracting yourselves from our socialist order, comrade riders. But you can't abstract yourselves. The day before yesterday there were over a thousand people at the track! Every job we do is the work of a Soviet trainer. Nobody likes criticism and self-criticism, but you have to put up with it like men – and that means you too, Orlovsky."

Sergey objects: "What does 'abstracting yourselves' mean? We can't expect great speeds out of our panicky foals for years yet! Many of them were literally rescued from starvation, Comrade Denisov!"

The director addresses him: "That's just excuses. No need to start discussing it, but get down to it! If you make a mistake, then you have to own up to your mistake and then you can work!"

"And the track we have isn't really a 'fast' one..." objects Eizens from his chair, puffing quietly on a cigarette. "Now if it were 1600 metres… But it's only 1043… That means – three sharp turns with low banking… Country tracks are much slower still… That's what Comrade Orlovsky is talking about. On an ideal track and in optimum breeding conditions our records would be at least a few seconds better."

Denisov wags his finger at Eizens.

"That's how a man might talk who has arrived from the Soviet Union and who can't think of any sort of nuances or shading. Your situation – your past – doesn't allow you to talk like that, Eizens! So far we don't have any respectable records at all, please don't forget that!"

"Absurd!" Andrievs whispers in Filip's ear. "He talks rubbish all the time…"

"And therefore we're going to introduce horses from the state's breeding stud! Our aim is, in the next few years, to obtain the rating 'Good' from the USSR Ministry of Agriculture. Let everyone get that into their heads! In the near future we will be bringing in most of them from number 18 stud-farm in Pskov, number 16 in Smolensk and number 59 in Gomel. We'll be converting the training departments into brigades and starting up socialist racing. With us today we have comrade riders from Smolensk, who've been putting it all into practice. Also a colleague from Moscow, Cavalry Instructor Colonel Vladimir Ivanovich Lyalyakin from the Department of Agriculture, who will be taking charge of the situation at the hippodrome."

Lyalyakin gets to his feet, bows and, wallowing in the applause, runs his gaze over the seated audience. His little black eyes dwell especially long on Andrievs. Lyalyakin is the same one who, together with the other Cheka man, caught him on the track before the races.

"Now we'll listen to them…"

"But –" interjects Sergey.

"No 'buts'! Your job is to listen and make use of the accumulation of great Soviet knowledge, and, most of all, to take on the rate of work of a Soviet trainer – something you're lacking! A style of working that's completely different to the racetracks in capitalist countries. Go ahead, Comrade Loginov!"

A lad sitting in the front row gets to his feet. Stumpy, with long arms hanging down to his knees. His head almost shaven, like a hooligan's.

"The basis of my work lies in the progressive discoveries of Michurin, Lysenko and Pavlov* in agrobiology and physiology, achieving progress under their guidance day by day, and I am convinced that here too, in the Riga collective, we will together achieve excellent new results, consciously following the words of Marshal Budyonny of the USSR:* 'Thanks to the support of the party and government, we have every possibility of creating a correct and fast trotter, on the outside.'"

Loginov smiles broadly and falls silent. His comrade, a tall, forward-stooping boy, turns his head and applauds.

"Hurrah!"

The others applaud too. Unexpectedly Serafim Stolbun, chief veterinary officer of the racecourse, raises his hand.

"Last week I was at one of our state farms, a large stud-farm raising foals, where they are constantly letting foals die. Finally the ministry sent me to inspect it. You could tell, even beforehand. I drew up a report. Most of Russia's veterinary surgeons were there. You don't know anything. My report was deliberately distorted, not acknowledging the unhygienic conditions and unhealthy maintenance. Other medical people have come from Russia, for example Kalniņš, who is very good. There are more still, very fine ones, but in many places there is no choice..."

Denisov and the secretary of the party organization at the course, Lopatin, smirk at each other. Serafim Stolbun, scion of an Old Believer family from Latgale, always says what he thinks, but the authorities do not really accept this bushy-whiskered figure, with his complacent, rounded, juicy jokes. A horse undergoing treatment once hit him on the head with the bit of its bridle, and since that time Denisov has called him "the battered one" behind his back. Stolbun is irreplaceable for examining and treating imported horses, so he can't be driven out of the racecourse.

After the meeting Andrievs returns to the stable alone. He presses his face against the horse's neck and takes a couple of deep breaths of its simple warm scent, starting to loosen the little braids which the girls had tied up before the races. Kazarka's mane is not submissive; on her forehead it is cut short, as on every trotter, but on the neck the stable-hands tie it in plaits. If life were as simple and logical as untying these little braids…

He takes off the "salt blanket" and rubs the mare's body with a straw whisk, then wipes her down with a towel and covers her with a dry blanket. When the coat is completely dried out, you can take it off. A horse's skin even in winter reminds you of ice with veins frozen into it – the bay coat is short and as smooth as silk, almost transparent. The stable on Ēveles Street is good; even in winter it keeps warm, unlike many others where draughts get in. Here you don't have to be afraid of freezing the trotter. Andrievs ties up the cold compress and rubs the runner's legs, especially under the fetlocks. He examines the hooves and concludes that the nails on the right front hoof have come loose. A farrier will have to be called.

Squatting on his haunches, Andrievs begins rubbing the trotter's legs with iodine liniment, to be bound up with warm bindings, when someone clears his throat in the corridor. He raises his head – there stand the two arrivals from Smolensk.

"Greetings!" says the one called Loginov, with a smile, extending his hand through the bars of the stall. "Let's get acquainted. Aleksandr Ivanovich Loginov – and this is my friend Aleksandr Ivanovich Stalnov – he's a nice chap."

Andrievs has no choice but to shake hands and quickly finish binding Kazarka's legs.

"How can I help?"

"We were sent to acquaint you with the situation. You show us around. We have to get to work, so to speak!"

Andrievs leads the comrades through the stables: "Tropa, Lyedokhod, Front, Talyanka, Magistral, Kupava, Zhemchug, Nyebosklon… And the Smolensk ones: Pravda, Perepyolka, Priskazka… The Riga racecourse has seven training sections, each of them taking about twenty horses for examination…"

Eizens comes running down the corridor and stuffs some sweaty roubles into Andrievs' palm.

"All the girls have disappeared, dammit! Send some lass to the special shop on Kirov Street for coffee," murmurs Eizens. "Banquet this evening, but there's no roasted coffee. Maybe you'll manage to jump the queue…"

Andrievs continues walking through the stables, relieved that no name was mentioned, because the Sashas are insistently grinding at him like a disc under a gramophone needle.

"We've heard a lot about you, a lot… Good things, of course, good things! Your course is popular with Riga people, they say, we hear you have a very active totalizator. And nowhere else do they look after horses like this. We call Riga the 'health spa', because horses don't come away from you 'broken down'."

"They say that Riga is famous for its processions, with all sorts of music, rousing commentaries and a festive atmosphere on race days," tall Sasha ventures to butt in. "You've got a flag too, they say, an emblem, and artistically designed posters. They say you haven't gone over to our long shorts and flat caps yet, you're still racing in sweaters and jockey-caps like the bourgeoisie! It's just as if you were copying the Latvian Riflemen's processions* led by Andrey Yakovlevich."

"We're trying," Andrievs says grudgingly, reasoning that it wasn't he who introduced himself to these comrades.

"They just need to run faster!" chuckles little Sasha. "We'll teach 'em! Efficiency has to be raised. Put an end to the 'health spa' era. What do you say about the Smolensk horses?"

"The Smolensk horses are very fast, but difficult to get to the start. Too nervous."

"Maybe hit them on the head," tall Sasha blurts out. "It all depends on the horse-breeder. The collective we have is of people from the front, you understand – sometimes some war invalid lashes out… But what blood they have! The blood of Petushok! Fairy tales, not horses!"

Andrievs recalls the coffee and looks into the dressing room. It's empty and silent, no-one even in the little booth, and even the veterinarians' bunker is like a graveyard. He turns the roubles over in his fingers.

"He said to go and get coffee, and yet, nobody…"

"Let the old women drink coffee!" enthuse the Russian boys. "This calls for a Cristal, that's what we should have. Let's go somewhere and sit down!"

"There'll be a banquet…"

"It's a long time to the banquet! Haven't you got some tavern near here, some snug little place? How do you manage?"

"There is…"

"Then let's go! We need to get to know it!"

Andrievs swaps his heavy boots for shoes and his padded jacket for a coat. The last thing in the world he wants to do is chat with the two Sashas at Nikolayevna's buffet. But they're sticking to him like thistles.

In the blizzard the trio turn down Dārzniecības Street. Andrievs drags himself on ahead of the two comrades as if to the firing-squad. The city is quiet and dark. Although the electricity supply is restored, it's a Tuesday evening, and because of the bad weather there are few people on the streets. A yellow, inviting light is shining brightly behind the shutters of Mrs. Cīrulis' place.

As if seeking a refuge, Andrievs suddenly shoves with his shoulders at Mrs. Cīrulis' garden gate. It opens.

Malvīne won't mind. Malvīne will understand. Malvīne can cope with anything, even with Russians.

The young comrades stop in surprise and look into the yard.

"One of our best riders lives here. And students – the jockeys' assistants."

"So it's like a *vecherinka,* an evening party?"

"Yes, yes! Just come inside!"

Mrs. Cīrulis' house has an asymmetrical mansard roof, onto the lower part of which on one side is built a whole two-storey extension, but only the bottom floor is lived in. At the front facing the street is a handsome outer door with steps and wooden columns, but it is always closed. Andrievs opens the garden door. Immediately to the left and right inside, in the half-darkness, are the kitchen and her daughter's room. On the wall of the corridor is a telephone. The corridor is separated from the visitors' room by a double frosted glass door, hinged to turn whichever way is needed. Light is shining through the door and girls' chatter can be heard.

When Andrievs and his companions clump in through the glass door, silence falls.

In the middle of the living-room a trotter is standing, wearing slippers and looking at the visitors with intelligent dark eyes. Then she twitches her nose and comes closer across the parquet floor.

"Don't be upset, she'll only sniff you!" says a middle-aged woman, with close-cropped wavy hair and red-painted lips. She is wearing a dark blue trouser-suit and a velvet jacket that has seen better days.

"The only horse I know that judges everything by smell," Andrievs explains in Russian to the two visitors. "She'll smell out from a distance what sort of person you are. If she accepts you, she'll let you pat her; if she doesn't, she won't let you near…"

"Like a dog," a guest ventures uncertainly.

The dark bay racing mare sniffs at both Sashas' faces, snorts at the stink of *makhorka* tobacco and angrily flattens her ears. It's clear to everyone that they won't be special friends here. The guests pull the snowy fur hats off their heads, and taking a couple of shy steps backwards, stumble and fall over the thick matting of sacks piled by the windows.

"Careful!" cries Mrs. Cīrulis. "Those are potatoes from the country, covered up so they won't turn green."

She casts a quick questioning glance at Andrievs, while the guests take off their coats and gather in the corner.

"You're sitting here listening to music, but I have to manage with the Great Wide Homeland on my own," says Andrievs quietly in Latvian to Malvīne.

Malvīne puts a comforting hand on Andrievs' shoulder, and then turns to the two newcomers: "Her name is Rasbine. American, but a pretty big one..."

"You ride her?"

"She's my horse," sighs Malvīne. "Before the war I had a whole stable, but now I've given it all back to the racecourse. I can't pay for the upkeep."

The guests nod, but it's evident there's a lot here they don't understand.

On the big table there is *kvass* to drink and berry-bread, a bottle of bitter orange liqueur and red Moldavian wine, and various snacks from the country. The students are squatting on the edges of the sofa – Ērika, Helēna, Veriņa Sokolova and a couple of unknown ones. There are also Mrs. Baginskis with Dzidra and Vanda, but Andrievs immediately senses pure ice in Vanda's gaze. The students clear a place for the guests at the end of the table.

"What are we celebrating, girls?" tall Sasha exclaims cheerfully across their knees, having got over the initial surprise.

"You see, Comrade Baginska has arrived from the country, a horse-breeder, getting ready for the International Women's Day prize! That's what we're celebrating."

"Any old day, until the suitcase is empty," confirms Mrs. Baginskis.

"You have your own horse too?"

"Yes, of course, several of them."

"Wow, will you listen to that!" Sasha turns to Sasha. "No collective farms, everyone has their own horse. Trotters walking around the room with slippers on. Will you have a liqueur?"

The addressee winces.

"And you probably only have girls at the reins?"

"Just wait for the banquet – then it will be blokes only!" quips Andrievs.

"Please, help yourselves," Malvīne invites them. "I'm passing round the bread myself, as you see. We won't leave it on the table, because Rasbine likes a bit too. Usually she lives in the stable, but sometimes she comes in – to listen to music."

"She likes music?"

"Classical especially."

"You go out to *vecherinkas,* girls?" Sasha, confused, changes the subject, pouring plenty more of the liqueur for himself and his comrade. "In Smolensk, we all get together for a *sklyachina* – just like what you do, one person brings the vodka, another one something to eat – we get together, have dances – *plyaskas* – with *garmoshkas,* accordions. Then we let rip!"

"Can you separate students and dancing?" asks Helēna. "The dance-halls are as full as sausages. You can't get a turn at the English waltz or the tango – my favourite dances, and they need a lot of space."

"But my favourite dances are the marathon waltzes," Veriņa chimes in. "You don't need much room for that – you can just turn on the spot, if you're not too dizzy."

"What are marathon waltzes?"

"You don't know? Waltzing in a circle, non-stop. Which couple lasts longest! After that you can squeeze out your clothes, they've got so wet!"

The girls giggle; the comrades, quivering, knock back the sweetish liqueur. What is happening seems like a play put on for their benefit.

Meanwhile Mrs. Cīrulis has gone over to the grand piano in the corner of the living-room and plugged it in to the electricity. She hunts for a wicker box on the shelf and takes off the lid. In the box are lots of discs.

"What shall we listen to this evening?" she asks, looking thoughtfully at the guests. "Let's have this one, in honour of the visitors!"

Malvīne puts a roll inside the pianola and sits down at the table. The instrument pipes up, the music starts. The keys move by themselves, no-one is playing it.

The two Sashas look on in surprise as Rasbine approaches the piano at the first notes and stays beside it, listening attentively.

The music is brisk, and at the same time gentle. The keys, moving by themselves, and the horse by the piano create a strangely ghostly atmosphere, as if the crepuscular room were interwoven with invisible pendants of crystal. As the last notes are heard, the guests wake up as if from slumber.

"What was that?" Tall Sasha wants to know.

"Tchaikovsky. A fragment of the ballet 'Swan Lake'."

"Shame on you, idiot!" Little Sasha digs his friend in the ribs. "I knew that one straight away."

"What, because you didn't have a single *swan lake* on your school certificate?" he says, stung at being called an idiot.

"Because there isn't a whiff of socialist realism in it

Seeing that Malvīne is looking for the next disc, *Romeo and Juliet,* the Soviet guests get to their feet. orange liqueur is all gone. They collect their coats and bow.

"Time for our banquet! Coming with us, girls? Well, okay then… It's your loss. Bye, mare!"

Rasbine swishes her tail brusquely.

Andrievs also takes his leave.

"I've still got a couple of horses under blankets," he explains. "And I have to think of how to escape from the banquet alive."

Before closing the frosted glass door, he tries to catch Vanda's eye.

But she doesn't look.

Late the next afternoon Andrievs is occupied in re-shoeing his horses. The racecourse's driver, Knaksis from Jelgava, has brought master farrier Jānis Ziemelis – with his big leather apron across his belly he looks like the Father of Devils himself, the Thunderer, the Roarer, the Smith of the Heavens. From his meal Ziemelis has saved a sandwich, and he offers a bit of it, wrapped in parchment, to Andrievs.

"Eat, son, you're looking a bit weak to me," he says in Latgalian.

It's heartwarming that he's offering a sandwich with his unwashed filth-covered hands.

Observing Ziemelis bending over in the middle of the stable with his box of instruments, the jockeys are swarming around like bees near honey, promising the farrier power over the heavens, if only he has the time to examine their trotters.

Malvīne insists on Ziemelis re-shoeing Rasbine and Rasma, her other mare, Rasbine's mother. Dzidra calls him over to Birztaliņa and Poplar Lī, which Eizens has talked her into riding for the Women's Day Cup. Valdemārs is fretting that Valka is completely lame, and has lost a shoe; Filip reminds them that Ziemelis has promised to shoe Karsoņa, while Helēna already has Pollija by the bridle and is saying she was first in the queue. Vanda says she is prepared to wait for the master farrier until the middle of the night…

The smith lets his discoloured eyes roam over the supplicants and cracks juicy jokes about "first-night conjugal rights".

There are two farriers working at the racecourse, but Ziemelis is a high-class master. Having grown up in Selonia, his language rolls low and round like lumps of clay. His hands are as knotty as oak roots – they say that in his youth he was a wrestler who laid everyone on the mat. Yet these hands are able to hold a two-year-old foal's hoof as gently as a baby lark, and shoe it with a prophylactic horseshoe, driving the self-forged nails straight in along the white line, screwing the spikes into the shoe for safety on the icy track. The master himself claims that he's able to forge twenty-six different types of shoe.

"I'm the son of a farrier myself," Ziemelis tells them in Latgalian, holding a horse's leg in his lap and trimming its hoof with a file – "as a teenager I was working in a smithy to earn the money to go to commercial school. I can even shoe a bull, but you need eight shoes for that!"

Ziemelis gives speed to a trotter, protects the joints of a jumper, working his stubby fingers like tubers, operating nimbly not only with a hammer and hoof-knife, but also with a scalpel. Listening to his flat speech, even the most skittish trotters are calmed, when their nerves have been stretched like strings to breaking point. Even the hopeless ones improve their gait and are saved from the knacker's yard.

The Soviet visitors can't talk with Ziemelis, because the smith doesn't understand Russian.

The two guests walk around, morose from their fierce hangovers, as betrayed by their heavy breathing. The day passes in acquainting them with the training plan and technical matters. The best Russian trotting horses will go to them. The administration scurries around like the inmates of an anthill stepped on by a bear's foot.

Andrievs is now giving instructions to the stable-hand and making ready to go home, when the two Sashas suddenly stop him and want to talk. Let them come with him to Nikolayevna's – otherwise there will be too much "dry talking".

Yesterday they were properly introduced to the town, thinks Andrievs.

Nikolayevna, catching sight of the trio, breaks into a smile and leads them to a separate space deep down beyond the chimney-breast.

"There's a thing we wanted to talk about," explains little Sasha, even before ripping the silver cap off a Cristal champagne bottle. All three of them light up.

"It's about our *campaign*."

"What campaign?" – Andrievs looks foolish.

The comrades look at each other.

"Time's passing quickly – in two weeks it's the Great Prize," the little one says patiently, embroidering his words stitch by stitch as if for a feeble mind. "It wouldn't be good for the prestige of the Soviet homeland if our arrival went unnoticed."

"Oh, it wouldn't be liked!" agrees the tall one.

"Who wouldn't like it?"

"The party and the government… Did they really not warn you?"

"What do you want?"

"To win."

"Where's the problem? You've been given some fast horses."

"Grand Hill is the fastest."

They trample their fag-ends on the stones by the chimney-breast as the Cheka men did that time, although they could have thrown them into the fire, and the party's over. With concentration and care they render the fags harmless with the soles of their boots; perhaps that is the Soviet way. Tall Sasha spits on top of it.

"Trotting races are a sport and a battle; it's not realistic to predict a certain outcome. Then it wouldn't be interesting to watch – see, this is what we're talking about! We need to surprise the public… so they'll know how strong our Soviet homeland is, and its horses – unbeatable!"

"Come to the point – what's this about?"

"It's about a specific way of riding. Five horses have been entered for the Baltic Military District Prize. Grand Hill might win, but he might also lose…"

"…because a good rider knows not only how to win brilliantly, but also to lose by a nose, if need be…"

"Let us win! Would it be right for a bourgeois to beat Soviet horses for the Baltic Military District Prize? We'll share the money equally."

This last sentence enrages Andrievs.

"Prestige of the Soviet homeland? So is this about money or about prestige?"

"What's the difference for you? You do the riding, we'll do the rest."

"I won't go along with it!"

Andrievs turns around and walks out of the pub.

"Aborigine! Damn you!" spits the tall one.

"He won't get anywhere," the little one soothes him. "He's still green. We've got Lyalyakin behind us… Nikolayevna – the bill!"

Andrievs sets off for the racecourse, right down the middle of the street. All this dashing around, this twaddle about the racetrack's ratings and records – was it all just for money? What was that Sasha waffling about at the meeting? Budyonny, Michurin, Lysenko… the party, and the fast horses from the state studs… Fiddlesticks! So vulgar.

Andrievs recalls that in November 1939 Run Hill Dune's win brought in 4014 lats for his Dad, which was the value of three horses. Although the individual record pay-out wasn't expected for a win, this pay-out did cover a lot – the average prize-money at the time was such that one win would keep a horse in oats for a year. That interested the leading trainers, horse-owners and the totalizator customers enough for them to combine forces and discover the most talented horses.

On the other hand, in these Soviet times the totalizator works so strangely: it builds stands to accommodate the public at any cost, yet the miserable income from a win – a trifecta or a quinella – makes the riders work in their own selfish interests. There's no place for the big traditional prizes, where the amounts are quite different.

Of course he has heard of such things, but he's never come into direct contact with such dirty dealings.

If you consider it with a cool head, what Andrievs stands to gain by taking part in the "campaign" would be huge…

What's he thinking now! Has he gone quite mad?

Get thee behind me!

Ready to hit himself in the face from shame, the betrayer throws open the door of Grand Hill's box.

It wasn't by chance that they had sought out Andrievs! Not just incidentally. The Cheka have some strings to pull. And he jumps to their tune – like a puppet! Hundreds, thousands, are doing that already…

He can't look Grand Hill – the son of Run Hill Dune – in the face. The offspring of the horse that Dad bought, the continuer of the line. As the grass-roots and the blood sink through the humus, that same look sinks through time, through the veins, through the genes, through the brains in the skull – such is this look with white shoots of light in the dark eyeballs, that nameless trust, and the question: *et tu, Brute?*

Someone is standing in the corridor; Andrievs swings around – it's Eizens.

"I'm going away, I'm leaving," Andrievs murmurs incoherently. "Give me the paper, I'll resign!"

"Come!" The old accountant immediately perceives the seriousness of the situation. "Let's go and have tea and a chat."

Andrievs crosses the threshold into Eizens' peeling cubby-hole. The Head of Production has a different office in the administration building, still with the lustre of the old times. Yet you can't be sure there that the Cheka aren't listening in. This is quite different – you can feel free here. That is why Eizens sits in a stable until late at night and sometimes even spends the night here.

On the cooling cast-iron of the little economy stove a tea-machine is hissing cosily. Eizens pours a large draught of China tea into a big glass and then adds something stronger from a little bottle in the desk drawer.

"Drink your grog, relax. Where are you going to run to, where will you bolt off to in the middle of the night… Tell me everything, who and how…"

Andrievs' teeth chatter against the edge of the glass.

"All of them… the actual controllers, the Party people, the major-generals in the Air Force, the colonels, the rear-admirals – the Yeryomins, the Lopatins, the Kiselevs, the Vasilevs, the Lyalyakins, the Denisovs, the Rindiņas, their relatives and hangers-on, they all play the totalizator – but the blame falls on the administration and the riders. You think I don't know? The deputy director, Colonel Mikhailov, Vice-Captain Svidovoy, Major Pimenov of the Veterinary Service, Senior Lieutenant Kleshchevsky… A real Red Army horse-racing club! The so-called primary Party organization! And these constant complaints about 'not loving' the Russians! If any one of those third-rate 'jockeys' violates the racing rules, or the code of behaviour in the stables, or work discipline or, God forbid, trespasses on the track, then there's a great stink and they grab us by the short-and-curlies! They're reforming the management – now, you see, they're going to merge the training sections into brigades, and make our riders answer to the senior brigadiers, their own people… Of course, they'll do the right thing; I don't know any one of the older riders who's caught the Red fever. They have their own favourites out of the trotters from the State stud-farms, and they're thinking as well of blaming Sergey for the starved nags from Latgale not running as fast as their own! The minority of the double, even triple, race-winners among our riders, who've won several prizes – well, because of their 'smudged copy-books' Denisov gives them the title of second-category jockeys… This is derogation… derogation of our horses and ourselves! I can't breathe here, I'm going! Riff-raff they are, *svolochi,* scum! I don't understand how you can sit at the same table with them!"

From a whisper Andrievs has progressed to a scream. Then he controls himself and takes a good swig of grog from his glass.

"Have you calmed down?" asks Eizens. "Now perhaps you can tell me what this is all about."

Andrievs looks on, shocked, as Eizens, no friend of Soviet power, nervously pulls at the drawers of the desk, where he keeps the *konchiki*, the tips put by for a rainy day.

"What's the point in being honest and keeping clean, not accepting anything underhand in your business, if their whole system is falsified and corrupt?"

Eizens leans his chin, covered in long stubble, on his palm and looks at Andrievs.

"The Cheka major let me keep Grand," Andrievs admits with downcast eyes. "If I don't do it and they catch me, I'll be dropping you in it too…"

Eizens picks out a thick yearbook, alphabetized by himself, in which, at the end of every race-day, he has entered the result for every horse that started, so that each horse's career can be followed.

"You see this?"

"I know that for every horse you can write down the pedigree over four generations."

"On forms that date back to German times!" Eizens laughs, pouring into his glass from the bottle left in the drawer.

Andrievs doesn't understand what his patron, who put him up all through the war years and has saved his life more than once, is now trying to say.

"Believe me – there was a time when I was shouting like you are now: I'm leaving, that's enough, I can't breathe!"

"I'm really astonished that you can put up with it."

"There are two rulers in this world – money and power," explains the old man. "I've experienced both. And you know – they're both good!"

"There's a third one as well," Andrievs objects. "Beauty."

"Leave beauty to the artists and those who are in love. Perhaps you don't know that the first racecourse in Riga is one of the oldest in Europe. It was created in 1891 and it was the fourth largest in the empire in terms of numbers of horses – after Moscow, St. Petersburg and Kiev. After the First World War, with the independent state, they created the Rīgas Hipodroms limited company, which unfortunately had quite a short life. The shareholders invested a lot of capital in that. At the end of Antonijas Street they built a covered stand for the spectators, winter and summer stables, the wooden ones where the private horses still stand, a kilometre-long racetrack with electric lighting – nowadays the stable grounds beyond the gates. In those days I was one of them, but I came in almost without any funds, only with Lamsters' protection. Young and green I was..."

Someone is fidgeting and coughing behind the curtain.

"Ziemelis," Eizens reassures Andrievs and continues his story.

"Most of the shareholders were distillers, they were only interested in the income that they lost when Latvia closed the lottery clubs that had been popular before the war. These gentlemen didn't understand a thing about horse-breeding, and so they didn't fulfil the main task, the one that every racecourse in the world has – to test the abilities of their horses, improve the thoroughbred qualities of the trotters. In half a year they bought only one stallion – Ansis, who turned out to be no good at racing, bit off a jockey's finger, and was given away for street-sweeping duties. Secondly, in all the important well-paid administrative jobs at the racecourse they appointed their relatives. As a result, the public lost faith in them, and the quality of the game declined."

Eizens is silent for a moment and, wrapping his cigarette in a strip of newspaper, checks that Andrievs is listening. The latter, with head bowed, is sucking long draughts of grog through clenched teeth.

"Before the First World War the best professional jockeys were earning up to 60,000 gold roubles a year, so the totalizator wasn't interested in them. After the war, as the prizes collapsed, the jockeys themselves started doing deals and keeping horses. Their relatives, the stewards, not being professionals, couldn't spot the illegalities. The owner would fix it with the jockey that the public would stop betting on his horse, but afterwards, in the deciding heat, he would buy up several tickets and easily win big sums. But the public is no fool; the affair came to light. You can't fail to notice that a complete novice is winning, while at the same time the other horses are going 6 to 10 seconds slower than usual… a scandal! If the public anger became too great, the management of the course would ban the offending jockey from the game for two race-days – whereas in other countries you'd be banned for several years for doing the same, or even… And another scandal: thirty horse-owners refused to take part in races, demanding equal rights for foreign and local horses. It turned out that two horses in Riga and Berlin were registering the same time, but in Latvia, for some reason, the foreign horse was given a handicap. This advantage of seconds allowed it to get all the main prizes. The Latgalian owners were forced to withdraw their horses, because they couldn't compete with the unknown imported foreigners. So that they wouldn't have to cancel races because of a lack of horses, they started breaking the rules. In one race Hermanis Liepiņš' own horse took part, as well as his daughter's horse, his son-in-law's horse, and an unknown owner's horse, which turned out to belong to Liepiņš anyway, because on the programme a couple of days later it was entered as the building contractor Liepiņš' horse. When the press got wind of this… a scandal! 'Why is Mr. Liepiņš allowed to organize a stitch-up against the rules of the racecourse? How can the public play the totalizator if all the horses are from the same stable, all controlled by one and the same well-known Mr. Otardi? Are horse-races being turned into "family deals"?' As a young lawyer, I got involved in unpicking those deals. But I didn't call them machinations, as the press did, and I didn't blame Pētersons, Lamsters, or Liepiņš – they were horse-breeders in the true sense of the word, they understood that a racecourse is like a clock that must not be stopped, the races can't be called off… They supported the horse-breeders of Latvia, buying up not only many good foals but also excellent sires from abroad and giving them to local farmers to mate."

Eizens wipes his eyes, into which the draught is constantly blowing dust.

"What seemed much worse to me were those speculators, whom I won't name, but I know for a fact that they buy up first-class racehorses abroad, and bring them in without passports or track records. Over here these horses get into lower classes without any trouble and win big money. Everywhere else in the world, foreign horses could take part in races only if they outrun the local first-class horses. Here they hide their names, they start under pseudonyms, the public isn't allowed to see them being trained. Several times a jockey would hold a horse back, but the fourth time, when the public no longer believed in this trotter, he simply took the whole bank."

"And how did it end?" Andrievs lights up a cigarette.

"As it had to. The upper stand was half-empty, the music no longer played, every second totalizator cash office was boarded up... 'With the autumn, the Riga Hipprodome is dying', the papers wrote. In the spring of 1924 the Cabinet allocated a concession to the totalizator, but by the end of 1925 the members of parliament voted to close it. Fēlikss Cielēns was able to give a fervent address to a session of parliament: a small handful of businessmen were winning millions upon millions at the cost of the people's tears, while the mothers of all the officials and citizens and the little folk were crying and wailing about the money they'd lost on the totalizator. The Social Democrats, from the very beginning, were shocked at how the racecourse was ruining the citizens of Riga."

Andrievs imagines his own mother. Yes, but for her the racecourse came with passion for a certain person – the totalizator couldn't be blamed for that.

"Of course the Rīgas Hipodroms company went bankrupt. The horse-owners established a Latvian association for promoting thoroughbreds, headed by Hermanis Liepiņš, and tried to play it with the bookmakers, but that wasn't allowed, and the police quickly drove them out. Meanwhile people kept coming to the racecourse – the flower of Riga society, the intelligentsia of town and country. According to the number of admission tickets sold, about a thousand spectators came on weekdays, on Sundays about six thousand, although there were hardly more than seven hundred seats in the stands; the rest were standing. Even for equestrian events the place was packed. That meant that this kind of sport attracted and interested the Riga public."

The curtain at the back of Eizens' office trembles and for a moment billows in all directions, as if an enchanted castle were rising into the air; then a calloused hand appears, fumbling its way along the cloth and sweeping it apart. Bare feet step onto the stone floor. The farrier stretches and blinks his sleepy eyes in the lamp-light like an eagle-owl.

"And then the Saltups came!" he says. "Ontonija might have been wetting her pants, I don't know, but Staņislavs, Francis, Jezups, Donats, Ludvigs – Latgalians, in other words... They got a majority in Parliament for the totalizator. All the Latgalian groups in Parliament were for the totalizator – they've been holding races in Latgale for ages and they're hoping to send horses to Riga... You woke me up with your chattering, damn you, I want to eat right away... Here, Jon, a pretzel!"

"No thanks, I've already eaten," Eizens replies.

"Then you, sonny!" Ziemelis offers it to Andrievs, and he doesn't refuse; suddenly he feels as famished as a wolf. "There's never a time when a man can do without a bit of food, you won't tell me that... Yesterday there was sausage too, my son-in-law brought it from the country, but my grandson caught sight of it and – gobbled it, I didn't even get a whiff..."

"Latgalians have to eat too, of course," says Eizens, pouring some grog for the farrier.

"Boy, how they put it away there!"....

"Some Latgalian groups even put the issue forward as a categorical demand. But only in 1932 did the deputies decide to reform the racecourse and the totalizator and put the matter in the hands of the Army Equestrian Sport Club. Men for whom horses were more important than themselves. At first there was still no confidence in them, but after the first year attitudes changed. And so the matter went away."

"And boy, what men they were!" Ziemelis nods vigorously, devouring the stale water-pretzel. "Our own racing specialist, Boriss Englards! The veterinary doctor, Lieutenant-Colonel Rusaus, General Eduards Kalniņš and General Hermanis Buks. Colonel Dannenbergs, Colonel Dūms and Lieutenant-Colonel

Kuplais. Rappa, from the General Staff. Captain Marnics, and Zutis from the Equestrian club."

"Rūdolfs Lamsters and his nephew Reinholds Beķeris," Eizens chimes in.

"Beķeris sure was a jockey! Unique! First win in his very first race riding the record-breaker, Kvarnozors! But he was trained up by those foreign jockeys – the Estonian Juulius Lond and the Canadian Joe Reimer, at least that's what Beķeris himself told me. I hear tell that Beķeris is in Germany now, on the Hamburg track, and Vērītis in Sweden – or the other way round. Vērītis was a great jockey too, marvellous! Won the derby four times! Looked after his horses. They were good friends. I remember how Beķeris, in the German days, helped Vērītis to get his record back – Beķeris' Meteors was the main rival to Vērītis' Adlons. Beķeris was alongside Vērītis, on Meteors, like an assistant jockey – and Adlons just couldn't get past Meteors, and then it happened – Vērītis beat Beķeris' record with Beķeris' help!"

"But the track has never been a place just for jockeys and gallopers," says Eizens. "There were cyclists performing there too, they started air-balloon flights, there were Flying Days – that's where the Wright brothers' first aeroplane went up, marathons were run, there were even athletics, and football matches. They built a hill of ice for toboggan riders, the distance walker Jānis Daliņš set his first world record; even fashion shows! Every year they used to hold the National Equestrian Cup here. You remember the Latvian team rider, Captain Teodors Broks? Ludvigs Ozols, our leader, and his national team got wins at the games in Insterburg, Königsberg, Tilsit, Gumbinnen, Nice, Warsaw, Sopot."

"I was told about Ozols by his father; we were both together at Ezere, where I was treating the horses' hooves, and he was levelling the ground at the communists' airfield," coughs Ziemelis. "For the first Soviet honours the unit's political leader from Jelgava wanted Ludis' horse. He'd been bought in Finland – a beautiful thoroughbred English horse. The political leader was supposed to have defaced Stalin's portrait in the office, and Ludis turned out to be the culprit. The First Lieutenant was seen for the last time at Jelgava railway station yard, lining up among the men condemned to hard labour… But as for Broks, while he was working in the Taišeta camp on construction, the guards are supposed to have beaten him up, because he'd been in some bad fights with them… The light of eternity bless them all! All of their horses I remember by their feet – Broks' Oreba and Oriente, Ozols' Nargusa and Greja, Klaipa, the English one, Vakarvējš – that one had such hard hooves! And your father's old Hill, I remember him too… And your father too, Andrievs. May he rest in peace!"

The three men drain their fire-water dry, with a gasp.

Andrievs bends his head.

"I'll go now."

"Off you go," replies Eizens. "And remember – the racetrack didn't start with us, and it won't end with us."

"But what shall I do?"

"Do what you have to do. Don't worry about me."

Andrievs stops short at the threshold.

"For them it was the Patriotic War, after all. I have disappeared, because my homeland has been taken away. Look – a war invalid on the street, half a man, in the mud and snow! A hero! Think clearly – for or against! There's no middle way. What am I to do, with nothing to die for?"

"You still have a horse. For a man, a horse is the hour of truth."

About a Horse

"Riding calls for huge amounts of imagination, especially with young horses you've just started trying out on the track," says Radvilis. "Each one of them has its brilliant individuality, coming from far away, far back in its pedigree and its experience. Usually this experience is only two years' worth, but it can be sad, even tragic… The first year is usually 'in the dark'. You can feel its talent, but it isn't clear it will have enough sense to bring the talent out. You know what it is that marks out the high-grade horses?"

"Speed?"

"Not at all, it's the brains," laughs the old man. "It's not worth investing in mediocrity, but genius demands a congenial jockey in return, with the patience of genius, with empathy, endurance and a whole complex of other things. Instead, sometimes you have just sheer nerves, drawn taut like strings…"

"You're talking about horses, but you might just as well be talking about life."

"It's all about a horse," says Radvilis. "I don't know anything at all that's not about a horse. Look at it how you like, but a horse is a sort of symbol of life. You feel life, you know life, you tame life – as you do to a horse. To ride a horse subtly. To hold the horse's reins surely. Not to abandon a horse. A horse carries you."

Agony

At the beginning of March, life goes on at its customary pace. As usual, in the two weeks between the Cup races, Andrievs is working out with Grand Hill for two days at a fast pace, and on the others, alternating a trot with a rest. Apart from Grand he has another six, at various stages of ripeness for racing, with training sessions twice a day, morning and evening, so there's no time to be bored. He avoids the comrade visitors as much as he can, although they always impose themselves on meeting, with warm handshakes and cigarettes.

In the middle of the week he gets an invitation from his colleague Valdemārs Jurgensons. Old Mrs. Jurgensons, a former friend of Andrievs' mother, has penned these lines in a calligraphic hand on writing-paper: *"The honour of your presence is cordially requested by Marta Jurgensons to celebrate my birthday at Old St. Gertrude's Church on Saturday at two p.m., after service, and thereafter to share in the celebrations at the house on Tomsona Street."*

Thank you! I'll definitely be there.

On Friday evening the gusty winds buffet the attic room with an icy blast. Under three blankets and two coats, he's hot. Andrievs just can't get to sleep. The clock strikes one, two, three, four. Before his eyes, a trotter, the finish line, and the command to "stop" the horse. He reasons out dozens of ways of finishing, carrying out planned tactics, but in the end he wins anyway.

Before five o'clock, in the dark, Marija and Boriss get up. Feet start shuffling, they clean out the night-bucket, the door of the stove opens and closes with a squeak, the first smoke wafts through the cold room, salty and warm like the splashing of little waves in July. Making the fire goes slowly for Boriss, because while he is lighting it he sits on a small log by the stove, reading through every page of the newspaper that meets his eyes. Marija, in her corner, is murmuring her morning prayers. Andrievs listens in to the morning symphony, and his run-down brain finally weakens. He falls asleep.

Morning!

Morning cuts like a dagger – a bright blue, broad sunny morning over all of Riga. Andrievs jumps up and over to the window, shuffling from one foot to the other on the icy cold floor. Yes, this is worth something! Repayment for the mares of the night. For the weeks of cement covering the city. The sunny Saturday morning is invigorating like a rolled-out crisp white linen tablecloth. It booms with countless possibilities. Does Andrievs believe in God? Marija once asked him that, and he answered: So am I living in the Middle Ages? He saw that she was grieving, sorrowful. Today he must go to church. How that excites him, and he doesn't know why. The wish to live, to feel young? He could avoid it, but he must go, this morning. Afraid even to admit to himself how deeply rooted life is within him.

First of all Andrievs hurries to the racetrack, where his colleagues are cracking jokes like firebrands as they harness their horses. The track is frozen, but after a couple of hours the sun begins to thaw it. Fine tendrils of water twist through the sand; the hooves, cleaving into the ice, grind it into the sand. The jockeys can't avoid a mudbath. Only their white teeth glow in their faces. They can't use glasses, because behind the mud-spattered lenses they would simply be blind. Their hands hold the reins, the whip and the chronometer to check their times, and conserve the horses' strength over a distance.

After working out, Andrievs feeds the horses and washes himself down in the shower, but once home he assiduously washes and combs his hair. His shirt has been cleaned to a shine by Marija's skilful hands and smoothed with the coal-iron, but it is no longer new. On a sudden decision he takes from his suitcase a white scarf, a shiny white handkerchief, and gaiters. The pre-war dandy's outfit, inherited from his brother. For a moment he presses them to his face – these things still bear the scent of his mother's flat, along with a slight yellowing, of decay. His father's staghorn cigarette-holder falls out of some written sheets of paper – Antonija's letters. He quickly reads one and stuffs it in his pocket for safe-keeping. Then he sets off from inner Riga and, so as not to be late, jumps onto a number 1 tram to the corner of Brīvības and Kirova Streets.

His brother's coat is warm, the shoulders as wide as a tent. He's wearing Boriss' Panama hat. Padegs, Padegs, mutters some woman, looking back at Andrievs as she steps off.

As he runs he is assailed by the memory of a scene from the artist Kārlis Padegs' funeral – everyone is walking along Barona Street, full of sadness and bitter bravado, thinned out in a chain along the walls of the houses, so that approaching people are forced to step off the pavement. The funeral feast was at Padegs' favourite, the White Mare on Dzirnavu Street, full to overflowing; Andrievs, then a boy, could hardly get in because there was no room; women were sitting on their husbands' laps, there weren't enough plates, but Padegs' plate and his overturned glass stood untouched. It was a third-rate pub, which closed at ten in the evening, and the rest of them then went on to Māmuļa, but Andrievs stayed behind and thought about the weak and consumptive Padegs, and wondered if they, the rest of them, would have it any easier at the hour of their death. It was April 1940. Nothing had started yet, but Padegs was already dead. On that night of death Riga was struck by the first thunder; there were rumblings from Europe too, and distant lightning, but they didn't yet sense that this would be not a storm but a war. Irbīte, the barefoot painter, had invited Andrievs along to the funeral, as he knew the teenager who often knocked about with him in the market and the outskirts. Andrievs didn't know Padegs personally, only that he used to turn up at the racetrack when he had money, or from scandalous rumours. Padegs needed publicity – to be written about, where he drank and where he'd fallen, sitting alone at Schwartz's or the "Luna" for hours on end, sunk into himself, suffering his *Weltschmerz*. It was a pose, but in the pose there was a truth about life, a sense that many others would live and walk along these streets longer than he would. Fate had shoved Padegs onto the stage, and he died on the stage. At the cemetery during the funeral Irbīte painted a pastel of the scene.

As he daydreams, Andrievs travels too far, and arrives late at Vecā Ģertrūde, the most magnificent sacral building by the Riga architect Johan Daniel Felsko. This edifice, swept clean, smells of whitewash, and only last year it was given back its congregation, composed of three parishes, now called the Parish of Old St. Gertrude, officially registered with the Commissioner of the Council for Religious Cults' Affairs at the Council of Ministers of the Latvian Soviet Socialist Republic, Pēteris Pizāns, and now forced to pay disproportionately high property insurance premiums for this confiscated neo-Gothic pearl.

Mrs. Jurgensons is one of the pillars of the congregation. God is her fortress, helping her to endure the war and her husband's passing, helping her to bring up a clever son, endowed with ambition. He is also going to help her deal with her son's tuberculosis and to pay off the taxes. In the front row she benevolently nods her wavy grey head, with a broad-brimmed hat jammed on top. Her voice dominates the others, melodic and sonorous. Andrievs observes the ritual from behind. Some young couple has chosen today to christen their child, and before that, get married. The young bride in her thin dress with her infant wrapped in sheepskin on her arm is standing at the altar. The Reverend Pāvils Pečaks spends too long commanding them not to be like draughty houses in life, so harshly that the bride's shoulders start to shake.

As promised, after the services have ended, Mrs. Jurgensons' guests set off for the house on Tomsona Street, the Jurgensons' flat. There are about thirty guests, relatives of the Jurgensons. Most of them from academic circles, chemists, because Mr. Jurgensons was a professor of chemistry, and Valdemārs is also studying chemistry.

Stopping on the sunny steps, Andrievs chats with Valdemārs. Mrs. Jurgensons comes with her retinue, and one of them is – Vanda. Andrievs suddenly sees what good physique and clothing do to a woman. Without her stitched jacket and laced boots Vanda is just as slender and upright as the church on whose steps they are standing.

"You've been cut from the same image," observes Valdemārs jealously.

She has spruced herself up; under her grey coat she is wearing a new dark green dress with pleats. On her feet are black half-length boots, with galoshes over them. She's wearing a silk scarf with tassels. The trump card is the newly bought white handbag she's carrying. Valdemārs is meanwhile waving at the Moskvich; the older people and the priest are climbing into it. The rest of the happy group is hurrying to Tomsona Street.

From the racetrack, only Vanda and Andrievs are invited to the party. Yet Vanda is keeping her distance. On the staircase Andrievs manages to press a little piece of writing-paper that he had previously found in his suitcase into the hurrying girl's hand.

Outer clothing and footwear are left in the corridor, where a bright-coloured, plush-upholstered sofa and three matching chairs are luxuriating. Andrievs sees Vanda taking off her galoshes and surreptitiously inspecting herself from all angles in the big cheval-glass.

An elegant luncheon is laid out in the reception room, eloquent proof that the Jurgensons family was once very prominent. Mrs. Jurgensons herself is sitting in a chair, served by two waiters proffering wine. The guests are talking quietly, Valdemārs helping them to their places.

"Dear God!" Vanda whispers, shocked, into Andrievs' ear, looking in awe at the dark oak furniture and the tableware set out before her – porcelain, silver, crystal and starched napkins. "Proper high-class."

A waiter arrives with Gewürztraminer on a salver, tapping Vanda on the shoulder and saying familiarly: "Here you go!"

The table is arranged so that Vanda is sitting next to Valdemārs. Andrievs observes them from the other side.

There is no soup.

Vanda is served a veal cutlet, but sits thinking of something.

Three knives, three forks on silver holders, a little painted porcelain plate beside the main plates, onto which you put your bread after biting a morsel. A crystal dish of piquant marmalade, like pink dewy amber.

The gentleman sitting beside her, some professor, offers her something, but Vanda manages to avoid making it obvious that she doesn't understand a thing.

The company is strangely quiet, the guests talking almost in whispers. There is a discussion of Professor Lejiņš, whom the apologists for progressive biology and functionaries of Soviet science want to drive out of the chair of the President of the Academy of Sciences. They say the old pillar of science is too much in favour of clover and cultivated pasture, defending the possibility of competition between private farms and collectivisation.

"A new genre of science is flourishing" – a political denunciation.

It would be hard, they say, to "dig him out", but he was going to be excluded from working with students at the Academy, so as not to spoil young minds with his nationalism.

"Professor Lejiņš is still in intellectual thrall to the Western authorities, they say – he even tries to indoctrinate students with the kind of distortions they have in bourgeois science."

"Even Kirhenšteins is accused of liberalism! At the Institute of Microbiology there's said to be a nest of 'bourgeois nationalists and enemies of the people', but communists and the Russian comrades aren't given jobs. It's not any sort of serious scientific research institute, just a gravy train for bourgeois nationalists."

"Then let's drink to that! Let's wish happiness to Latvia, and to our dear Mrs. Jurgensons!"

They all get to their feet and sing the old song of praise by Andrejs Jurjāns,* but there is something odd in their sad faces and eyes, a fearful questioning, and they sing not loudly, from joy, more despite themselves, murmuring a string of words under their breath which have no significance under these circumstances.

The men fall silent and reach for their vodka bottles. The drinking is perfunctory, from fluted shot glasses, raised quickly.

Andrievs takes some fish. At this dinner he feels secure, because every Saturday his mother used to host a salon – invited friends and laid the table. Table manners, once acquired, are not forgotten. It's amusing to savour the wine and witness poor Vanda's torture. He has to admit that the girl is acquitting herself well.

The dessert is fruit.

"Some sort of little balls," Vanda observes, choosing one for good luck. "I can't understand what's inside."

"That's a grapefruit glaze," says Valdemārs.

"Tasty!"

Vanda picks out another ball, but observes that this one isn't to her liking.

The waiter brings coffee, a little droplet in the bottom of the cup.

"Very strong," Vanda declares.

"Please put some cream in the young lady's coffee," Andrievs commands the waiter across the table. Vanda looks at him with grateful eyes.

After a while the gentlemen go into the professor's study to smoke. Mrs. Jurgensons chats to the ladies, but her smile is mournful. Vanda gets purposefully to her feet and goes to the window to cool off. Andrievs sees her taking the scrap of paper from her white handbag and skimming quickly over it. Thereupon she presses herself against the sill, her eyes scrutinising the cumulus clouds over the distant racetrack.

Valdemārs comes up to her; they start chatting. Dark silhouettes against the background of the dim yellowing sky.

The light in the guest-room gradually becomes mellow, like smoky glass. With the dusk, Andrievs' resolve is fading; suddenly he feels broken. He ruminates to himself about the past night spent awake. The table- and ceiling-lamps are not yet lit, people's faces take on a greenish patina and their eyes twinkle as if set in black mountain rocks.

"The grey hour," says Mrs. Jurgensons. "Son, play me my favourite song!"

Valdemārs sits down at the piano, and starts to play Čaks' "Recognition". Mrs. Jurgensons sings.

"Do you read the papers?" asks Valdemārs in the moment of silence that falls after the song. "They've started a campaign against Čaks* too. They say he's trying in vain to climb up the 'sunny Soviet mountain'. He's being called a 'cosmopolitan', the theatre reviews accuse him of *nizkopoklonstvo pered Zapadom,* kowtowing to the West."

"How is a campaign possible against a sick man?" declares Mrs. Jurgensons. "His heart's as fragile as newly mown hay."

"But you know: the highest idea doesn't acknowledge human compassion," Vanda suddenly interjects ironically, quoting Rainis'* words. "He who sets them on fire doesn't ask whether he will perish. He pays no heed to himself or others, only sacrifices what is dearest to him."

In the interval between songs, Andrievs exchanges a few words with the hostess and takes his leave. It's time to head back to the stables. Seeing this, Vanda also says goodbye. Valdemārs holds her coat.

"How did you like it?"

"Oh, it's nice that the old lady invited me!"

When Andrievs and Vanda are going out onto the street, she jokes: "I say – at elegant dinners like that, God help you! When I went up to that table, I thought – I'll probably go hungry. There were all sorts of things there, you only had to know how to eat them. The first little ball was good, the second had a hard fruit in it that I couldn't bite; after that I didn't take anything more. So much to eat, but you have to go home practically starving!"

"Why did that waiter tap you on the shoulder at the beginning?"

"Oh, him!" Vanda laughs. "We met at some do at Kirhenšteins' place. It was simpler there, but the waiters were the same. As I was going I joked to him, 'Well, we probably won't see each other again…'"

Since there is no sun, the cold seeps into their bones. Andrievs pulls up his coat collar. They stand face to face and really seem to be cut from the same mould.

"That thing you handed to me was sad and very beautiful," says Vanda suddenly, looking him in the eyes. "The beauty gave me back my sense of proportion. I recovered, and I didn't mind not being able to tell the three knives apart."

From the freshness of her pink mouth, warm puffs of breath are rising. Andrievs thinks: just like his young racing mare after a fast run, airing her flanks.

"That's what beauty is." He sinks into thought. "Forgive me for that time."

"No, you forgive me!" Vanda rapidly interjects, turning her handbag over in her fingers. "It was my frustration, not yours. I don't know how to eat elegantly, or hold a conversation – once a boor, always a boor! That time, I didn't have any kind of apology in mind, I simply wanted to say – first of all, the war is over and we're alive, Andrievs! May I call you *tu*?"

Andrievs hadn't expected this move.

"Why ever not?" he says, confused.

"We're young, no-one will ever be allowed to shoot us down in the street for no reason, because of the war. The papers tell us the terrible numbers of war dead, but we are alive!"

The little white bag in a young girl's hand. A handbag – bright white. The key to everything.

"The five-year plan – in four years!" Against his better intentions, Andrievs is unable to hide the sting of irony. "For the ideas of Marx, Lenin and Stalin – proletarians of all lands, unite!"

Vanda is silent.

"Humiliation," he says. "The dead can manage it. What are the living supposed to do?"

The dark streets and the yellow lamps, her breath and marble skin, full of light.

"Shall we go?" he says, turning his shoulder to the wind and the racecourse.

"I'm done with everything there." She turns the other way. "We'll meet tomorrow."

The first steps are halting, as if something important had been forgotten. As if tomorrow might not come.

"Vanda," says Andrievs, observing her. "Can you read English? Maybe you'll come and visit tomorrow? I have a book that might interest you."

"Tomorrow evening my classmates and I are going to the Daile Theatre."

"What's on?"

"*The Character of Muscovites.*"

"Interesting. So then" – in English – "*good afternoon!*"

"Thanks for the poem!" Vanda calls out. "Why does it seem to me like a woman's handwriting?"

"It's Čaks' handwriting," he laughs.

The bright scarf and slender figure gradually merge with the black city. The very last shaft of light is her white handbag, in which rests the scrap of paper written in Antonija's hand.

No, he doesn't feel like a traitor at all. Damn it, she's right, that girl! The old man is digging his own grave, even though he doesn't want to. But what is written on the scrap will live on – he knows it by heart.

Agony

On the roadway opposite the finest bar the cabman's mare had fallen.
She lay in the dirty snow between the dropped shafts
As if on a bed with yellow foam on her lips, as if she'd been drinking beer.
She was beaten meanly with the juniper whip-handle by the cabman,
To get her up quickly to carry the gentleman to his club.
The gentleman collared him angrily and threatened to pay him only half.
But the mare – she lay heavy, like a woman weak from pleasure,
Merely breathing she raised her flanks with her feeble powers
And as sharply as a fish's gills out of water.
Then the cabman caught her by the tail and lifted it as if by the hand.
A crowd of women were swearing around them, and the teenagers guffawed

With pleasure, while the men gave advice.
The mare just gave up the ghost, frozen in a little puddle
On the pavement with her cooling nostrils.
And the policeman who arrived said: better hurry
To get matting and a cart to dispose of the corpse.
Then, yelling at the citizens to disperse, he returned solemnly to the corner.
On the roadway opposite the finest bar the cabman's mare had fallen.

Dawn

The little towns and villages glow yellow in the dark as they come within the ring of the horizon. Then they vanish behind us. I don't know whether it's a natural phenomenon or the military airfield on the left side of the road that is sending a reddish pillar of fire into the sky which, reflected against a cloud, collapses downward like a billowing rosy curtain.

"Where the northern lights are, there are the battles of soldiers' souls," says Radvilis, guessing my thoughts.

The old man turns his head timidly, as if wanting to avoid anything frightening. Soon I understand – something unavoidable is just over the hilltop, and that is the dawn.

At this time of year and in these weather conditions it has nothing to do with sunrise.

In the east, in the bosom of the dark, gleams a dark blue point, and then, as powerful as high tide, the blue colour fills the whole area. The bluish tinge lasts perhaps twenty minutes. As soon as the eye perceives it and the mind grows accustomed to it, the blue is already fading, bleaching like a water-colour, awash with a mist-like, fine texture, until it fades to pale grey like a wet linen towel from edge to edge, soiled in places with a yellowish clay. In the hollows, the fog stands in battalions.

With the greyness, the old man's energy ebbs away. The night seems to have given him wings; now it has vanished and his flight threatens to end. In a funny way, I start to get the same feeling. The day is calling us back into our roles. Calculating roughly, he must be aged about a hundred, I'm about half as old. He's striving to live in the present, holding stubbornly onto the rope that stretches from the past to the future. I have brought him something from the abyss of that haze, and he has grasped it. And now his vitality is his own undoing, because a complete denial would have allowed him to hold out indifferently against the temptations of time. Something within him has not quite taken leave of this world of illusions.

The Grand Prize

The morning of the races arrives as clear and cold as the previous one. Andrievs, in spite of his anxiety and excitement, has slept like a log, so it is no problem to get up a little while before Boriss. On race-days he doesn't rely on the stable-hands, but looks over his mounts himself, from early morning until late evening.

He hurries to the racetrack, with little energetic jumps, and is observed with astonishment by the dishevelled rooks in the willows on Ķieģeļu Street. At the fence of the stables, Andrievs stops for a smoke. This is a high place where, at sunset, you have a good view of the quiet racetrack and the stands, which a couple of hours later you wouldn't even recognize. Bright hooves speed along the track, the colourful shafts flash, the horses that have become legendary in the public eye will fly along with the leading jockeys – the little determined dun horse Karsoņa, the old but phenomenally vigorous cup-winner Irmans, the delicate stallion Auris from the wartime, Lielvārdis, the famous son of old Hill, the bay winner Front from Pskov, who is heavy at the start but flies like a cannonball once he gets going. In the intervals between races there will be music, and the announcer will pronounce exotic-sounding names – Čum Čum, Dāvids Hells, Dyerzky Ukor, Dufiņš, Hasti Langina, Heinrihs Juniors, Marsiks, Pobedonosnaya, Poplar Li, Reksis II, Skrīveriete, Vakarzvaigzne, Uhar Kupets, Nebosklon, and so on, and so on.

Meanwhile the public will be thronging into the stands, studying the race programmes, examining each individual horse's form and the jockeys' rankings, making pencil marks, calculating odds and going to the totalizator tills, for pairs, doubles and express. Actually there isn't a single person who would win particularly large sums on the "tote", nor are there any who would fritter away all their assets. In playing other games of chance – cards, for example – the situation can change in a matter of minutes, one person being ruined by blind accident and passionate playing, while another can make himself rich in the course of an hour. At the races that isn't possible at all – the individual races take place at twenty-minute intervals, or even longer. It has been shown – the longer the interval, the greater the stakes played on the "tote". Excitement is reduced, but the public has more time to consider the horse's form and prospects. That means that the races are not a game of chance at all, as must appear at first glance. The players are not counting on their luck but taking a decision based on facts. It's an intellectual kind of game.

How much will Andrievs Radvilis earn today?

Of the prize-money, almost half goes to the breeding stud, but of the rest, a third goes to the jockey. Until February last year the prize-money was reckoned in roubles, but now the prizes are counted only in points. The monetary value of the points on racecourses in the Soviet Union varies. At the Riga Hippodrome one point is worth one rouble. The greatest amount of winnings since the end of the war went to the legendary Irmans – one hundred and ten and a half thousand roubles. Auris, the stallion saved from the knacker in the fortress of Kurzeme by Zemištēvs, with whom the old chap used to wake up and go to sleep, was registered among the Russian trotters and after the war assigned to Soviet farm number 16 in Kaliningrad, earning almost 59 thousand.

Andrievs has no hope of getting any better than third place with Vaida, out of his fifth group of three-year-olds. For third place - 22 points, that works out as – half goes to the owner Petrovs in Ludza; out of the rest, one third would be about four roubles. Not bad. Enough for some *kvass* to drink.

He could hope for a win with the little bay Imaks, the fine-legged, talented son of old Signal Hall, reared by Mrs. Baginskis. A win would bring him 108 points, about half of which would go to Mrs. Baginskis, leaving about twenty roubles out of the remaining third, enough for "cigars" one fine day. But it will be running against Jānis Ārs from Number 5 Training Section on the grey, Klarnets, and the Soviet comrade Loginov on Kolonija, the fast-paced one from Smolensk. He'll have a fight on his hands, and the outcome isn't certain. For the race-track is the sign of infinity.

He can't hope for anything much from three-year-old Pilots, for the Ministry of Agriculture Stud Farm Cup. Spodris, sired by old Hill, will be running, and the talented Bajans from Ludza. Again those four roubles, if he's lucky.

The same goes for Kazaka in the Minor Cup for three-year-olds. Kazaka isn't ready yet.

But for Grand Hill in the Baltic Military District Grand Cup, victory is as good as in his hands. Over several years Andrievs has trained up a real cracker from a non-starter– a true fighter on the race-track. The winner would get 5,000 roubles; half would have to be given back, and out of the rest he would get one third himself. But if he held out, he could get the whole 5,000 from the two comrade jockeys; that's what they promised.

In the cup race for Women's Day, for horses of the older generation, there will be Dzidra Baginska on Eizens' Poplar Li, Mrs. Cīrulis on Mrs. Baginskis' Birztaliņš, Veriņa Sokolova on Valcis, Helēna Vētra on Mrs. Cīrulis' Rasbine, Renāte Pleša on Signal Boy from Latgale, from the stables of Staņislavs Trasuns, abolished by the Bolsheviks, and – finally – Vanda Vītola on Reksis II.

At the memory of Vanda his heart is pierced by a shard. Unhurriedly Andrievs lights up the next cigarette. She is a marvellous girl, yet so poor. With his betrayal money he could buy Vanda a white handbag! Ah, not a handbag, she already has one, but he could go to the Central Market for some silk material, to Kvīns or Rozenblūms, who sell industrial goods, or to Fišmans the milliner, where the salesgirls in winter walk around the shop in long, real felt boots. If, as once happened, someone offered antique silver earrings for 200 roubles, he wouldn't say no, he wouldn't be such a fool. If he did hold back the horse, in time he could save up and even buy a two-storey summer-house at

Ķemeri. What's he dreaming about? He could simply support Vanda in her studies!

The shard that has penetrated his heart gradually freezes his limbs and paralyses his mind. To the very last moment he can't decide what to do. Obey and go off into the unknown or take a risk and remain free, which might also mean destruction?

As in his dreams, Andrievs dresses in his colours – a black peaked jockey cap and a blue shirt. He sits in the booth and in his hands turns the racing whip of walrus whiskers, left to him by the best pre-war jockey on leaving his homeland, the legendary Reinholds Beķeris. Walrus whiskers used to be highly regarded. They were the most famous whips. Walrus whips were hard to get, and they went to the greatest masters. The shaft is short and light, it is very supple at the end. The old jockeys – Morozov, Beķeris, Vērītis – they had them. But Andrievs' good friends – such as Valdemārs and Antons, for example – don't. The first to use them were the Canadians, who rode American mounts, but they wouldn't ever sell them. Price didn't come into it – simply none of them were sold.

Valdemārs enters, dressed in his own colours – a red shirt with a red cap, the bright yellow ribbon of the training section across his chest.

"Has something happened?"

"Everything's all right."

Vanda runs in, dressed in a black shirt with a black cap, bridle in hand, looking even more lanky and flushed with over-excitement. "They're complaining at the weighing-post. Serafim is looking for you."

Andrievs looks back at her with a vacant expression. Vanda slams the door.

The minutes pass as if under a frozen lake. Andrievs mechanically gets to his feet and goes out of the stable, where he is received and swallowed up like a fading note by the thunder of the racecourse. Towards him along the track come the runners, their jockeys warming them up for the first race. Viktors is chatting with Antons, shouting at Andrejs; Donats and Jānis are laughing loudly about something. They are casual and unhurried, that is their job, their job is their passion, their passion is excitement for other people. The first races are usually not especially important, the strongest horses don't take part in them, so the stands are still half-empty.

The loudspeakers screech out the Russian song *Stepy' da step' krugom,* All Around The Steppes, sung by the People's Singer Lidiya Ruslanova, born Praskovya Leykina in the Volga village of Danilovka, who began her life begging for alms in the courtyards of the old people of Saratov, but who after the capture of Berlin on 2nd May gave a concert in the ruins of the collapsed Reichstag. According to the latest reports, she is under arrest for looting during the war. As always under Stalin, nothing is really known and it might only be a rumour. Riga Hippodrome, however, plays it as safe as safe can be, Ruslanova is cut short, and replaced by the chorale of the Leningrad State Academic Choir.

The gong rings out, Englards' voice announces the parade, and the colourfully dressed riders, lined up according to their numbers, drive their horses past the stands, the thills yoked to the buggies.

Andrievs goes up to the scales in the stable yard, where the weight check before the race is being done. The course's veterinarians, led by Serafim, carefully check over the horses, led out by the stable-hands. Serafim examines each runner thoroughly and exhaustively, including taking its pulse. At a mere glance, he feels the horse's "form" and determines its measurements and weight to the nearest fraction. The invited Professor Pēteris Apse, a lecturer at the Agricultural Academy, who was treating the horses even before the war, is also to be thanked for the fact that under the favourable circumstances of the Riga Hippodrome the horses are so well cared for, not driven to destruction as at many other unregulated tracks.

Brencītis, a stablehand, a little round man who looks like the long-nosed dwarf in Wilhelm Hauff's tales, comes up to Vaida, who is called Voodoo, to affix the *oberčeks* – the strap attached to the head. Andrievs turns away to the track, warming up the horse.

More spectators are arriving in the stands. People are coming to the totalizator, coming to play. At the track they are very interested, children too, in how the horses start. The spectators assess the horses' chances, both from the information in the programme and from observing the horses as they warm up – how they run, how firmly they handle the "false starts" or trial runs.

While the next ones are warming up, the runners in the previous race get their awards. Applause, ovations, coloured rosettes on the bridles. Assistants run up, take over the tired runners from the jockeys, throw blankets over their backs and set off, at a walk. In summer they walk longer, but in winter they have to mind that the runners don't get cold, they have to take the horses back faster to the stables, every few moments giving them a few draughts of warm water. The weather is sunny, a couple of degrees above zero, yet the ice and snow are still clinging firmly to the ground.

Now that the next jockeys are warmed up, Andrievs takes his turn.

The parade ride is announced, the participants gather on the track by the gates to the stable yard, where the controller checks that everyone has arrived. At a signal from the controller the jockeys start riding in the parade past the stands, one behind the other, in numerical order.

Andrievs is the first to ride, going up to the last of the stands, making a turn to the right, back again along the same track past the stands, followed by the others in strict order.

The announcer's voice rings out: "The cashiers close in three minutes." The "tote" players hurry to buy tickets for their chosen option, observing each other, especially the more hardened ones – what will they buy? The cashiers cease accepting payments as the starter's signal is heard. If a cashier has received money up until the start signal but has not had time to issue all the tickets requested, ticket sales are curtailed, and the money for the unissued tickets is immediately paid back.

On hearing "Runners to the start!" the starter raises a flag; all the runners go over to starter's orders. After the starter's flag is raised, a jockey may get out of his buggy only with the starter's permission.

A bell rings, and Englards' shrill voice calls: "Runners, to your places!" They go up to their starting positions, fully prepared to start the race. At the starter's order "Back!" the jockeys immediately retreat to ten metres behind the starting position, adjusting their speed, and all at once in a specified order make a turn toward the race-track.

The trotters rush past – the starter lets down the red flag. With the bell, the call goes out: "Go!"

Voodoo is usually obedient and thoughtful, but today, with the ends of the reins trailing behind her, she hangs about, an insensible lump of ice. There are no tactics, there's no technical finesse. Andrievs doesn't help the trotter: he makes no contact with her during the race, and the mare is bewildered and tries to manage on her own. But nothing changes, and at the finish, quite some way behind, offended, she starts jumping, overtakes the others and ends up finishing on the outer edge.

"He jumped into the post." Bewildered, those who placed their hopes and money on number one – Andrievs and Vaida – are digging each other in the ribs. Of course that is not a literal description; the finishing post is on the edge of the track, but if the horse goes out at a trot through the finish, then that's what they say: "jumped into the post".

The stands tremble with indignation, whistling and braying are heard as Andrievs heads back at a slow trot to the gates of the stable yard. Evidently quite a few people who believed in the jockey's talent are disappointed. It says in black and white in the programme that during a race, and especially as the horses approach the winning post, patrons need to observe silence, because screams, applause and other kinds of noise frighten the horses and may affect the result. However, the spectators, carried away with excitement, quickly forget that, and the stands, filled with many thousands, sometimes thunder like a storm.

Andrievs doesn't care. He's looking down into the mud, and he doesn't see his own shame.

The assistant jockey takes over the exhausted Voodoo. Andrievs takes off his cap and heads for the booth to wash his face. Someone passes him a towel – he's taken aback, it's Vanda.

"What's happened to you?"

"Nothing."

"That is something, that 'nothing'. You have to do your job, but what are you doing?"

He wipes his face in silence and gives the towel back to Vanda. As he tries to say something his lips move, but his head lolls and he doesn't utter a word. Vanda extends her slender, cool hand to the jockey's flushed brow.

"Your face is on fire. Let's go to Apse!"

Andrievs doesn't listen, but climbs into Imaks' buggy, brought to him by an assistant, and rapidly turns to the track.

On the shiny back of the trotter, like dark ice, the sun has burnished such a glow that it hurts the eyes to look at it. The stallion, raised by Mrs. Baginskis, is good-natured, accustomed to hands and to human love. The powerful, playful energy feels good at the end of the reins, seeming to be driven forward like a gust of wind, communicating every moment with his rider through mouth and reins. What would you like? May I run now? I can go even faster!

Andrievs can still feel Vanda's cool hand on his brow. He gradually comes to his senses. "You have to do your job, you have to do your job…" He counts out Vanda's words like a prayer, seizes them as his life-line.

In the next race he is held up for a long time by his fellow rider Loginov. Kolonija, the mare from Smolensk, called Lyalya, is fast, but with a tight mouth, like all Russian trotters. For a long time Sasha can't get her to line up with the others at the start. First there is a false start, the starter waves the flag like mad, Englards screams out: "Start cancelled, start cancelled, on your marks!" and then the same in Russian. Sasha hears, but turns around in a half-circle, unable to control Kolonija. The other horses also gradually get skittish; white foam covers their breech-bands like towels. Jānis with blue-grey Klarnets makes another false start. The grey mane and silky tail rush past; the riders return to the start once more.

The third time they all manage to start at once. Little Imaks is especially lively today, but perhaps it only seems so to Andrievs, because he himself feels he has just woken up to daylight.

In the heat of the struggle, as Loginov's buggy approaches, Andrievs notices Sasha's face turned toward him. It is red and knotted with anger. His fellow jockey cries out to Lyalya and loudly smites her with the shaft of his whip across the bridle. That is forbidden, because it might upset the other jockeys. Imaks, who at that moment is next to Loginov's buggy, takes fright, but continues running to the finish.

Since the previous tactic didn't work, Sasha starts waving his whip in all directions, even backwards and to the sides, to get at Imaks next to him. The blow misses, and strikes Andrievs in the face.

Andrievs' whip is always lying in the buggy, below his hip. He takes it with him only as a talisman, because, working with horses as he does, he gets to know them intimately over a long period, calculating tactics before every race, working out the pace far in advance like a chess-player, taking the horse's talent and competitive qualities into account. Everything necessary and possible for a win he works out to the finish, so he feels no need to crack the whip; for him the racecourse is the glory of the most intelligent jockey.

Frightened by Sasha, Imaks rushes forward, and Andrievs only manages by a hair's breadth to keep the horse in check. Yet he does. To everyone's joy and surprise, Imaks takes first place in the hard competition. Second is Kolonija, third Klarnets. The stands are roaring; they whistle and stamp their feet. The commentator loses his voice like copper in bright sunlight – Englards will no doubt be wiping his nose, because at beautiful finishes the old man always gets tearful. Of course the first three were the leaders in this race, but the surprise was the order.

At the award-giving, Andrievs climbs out of his buggy and kisses Imaks' dark silky nostrils, which are fluttering rapidly, like two bat-wings, after the race.

He hands the horse back to an assistant and goes to the stable yard. Colleagues are running around him, greeting him and looking with concern at the red welt on his face.

Sasha extends his hands exaggeratedly. "Did I hurt you there? Forgive me, for God's sake!"

Andrievs turns away from him. "I know your God."

Serafim runs up to him and applies a stinging ointment to his cheek.

"We'll have to report Loginov to the judges," Vanda says, also shocked.

"No need," says Andrievs. "Only if the use of the whip causes a hindrance. But I won after all."

It's a surprise to everyone how happy Andrievs is. He doesn't even sense that he has just removed the burden of a heavy shameful choice from himself and has dashed to freedom.

It was achieved by a friend's hand on his brow and an enemy's scorching blow on his face.

"There is a need," mutters Serafim. "Too much has been allowed, there's disorder in the ranks. There are still no ruddy noses with our lot, but they're always drunk! Vodka's too expensive for them, they drink Gypsy vodka – ether… From that you get belching and biliousness, girls won't look at you. Now they're after me and Pēteris to prescribe bitter gentian in 25 gramme doses on various prescriptions – *dlya kobili grazhdanina S*, for Citizen S.' mare."

Meanwhile the female jockeys are preparing for the Women's Day Cup. Right next to her, Vanda receives Reksis from Filip's hands. Filip is a masterful jockey, a sincere Latgalian, a man who carries out his duties, who was even director of the racecourse for a time after the war, before the old Bolshevik Denisov was imported from the Union. Filip hands over the reins.

"Now girl, you let fly!"

Vanda grins, but you can see that she's no longer here – her whole being is already flying along the track.

"Light as a feather," chuckles the old experienced jockey, looking over the beautiful pair. "Reksis can't even feel he has someone on his back. I paired him with my prize buggy! That girl is smart – she'll get going!"

Andrievs doesn't have a race; he sets off in a hurry to the stables on Ēveles Street to saddle up Grand Hill for the Grand Cup.

Polished to a shine like a bronze statue, with his ears pricked up, his old battle companion is waiting for him in his box. On hearing Andrievs' steps on the dark, cool passageway, the horse briefly whinnies. Andrievs is no longer ashamed to look at him.

"Hi! Let's go!"

At the entrance to the corridor Grand is nimbly dressed by the stable-hands, fussing like bees around their queen – one of them puts a chest-belt picked out with silver threads across his chest, inherited from Beķeris, another places over his head a bridle with a sheepskin muff on the snout, so that the horse won't see more than a few metres' distance, and, if he is frightened by puddles or shadows, doesn't jump over them. Precious seconds would be lost setting the horse back on course; it is March, in the sun the racetrack has thawed in patches like the bark of a plane-tree. Another one clips thick leg-shields to his legs – prophylactic footwear, because since the winter they still have studs attached to their hooves. The shields protect the horse's legs from grazing by its hooves.

Andrievs finds the other jockeys ready to go, and all together in a long stream they set off along the road to the track. It looks like a carnival – the jockeys in their bright shirts, the slender-legged trotters decked out for sport. Passers-by smile and wave, open their house windows, children shout from the window-sills. At the end of Zirņu Street there is a solid bridge over a brook – a tributary of the Sarkandaugava River that traverses the ditch and separates the racecourse from the upper town.

The planks echo hollowly under the hooves, the stream of jockeys floods onto the track, and then they set off along the inner track to the stable yard, so as not to disturb those warming up for the next race.

Vanda comes up to Andrievs, her flushed face smiling from ear to ear, a woollen scarf loose around her neck.

"How did it go?"

Vanda pulls a white envelope out of her pocket.

"Andrievs – first place! No silly vases or watches, no – cash in an envelope, my first money!"

"I thought so," says Andrievs. "You're walking a metre above the ground!"

"Reksis was so strong! He was running at the back, we got to the tape, I turned at the tape, let go of the reins. Reksis was very good at the finish. He was off and away! At the finish he wouldn't let anyone past him."

"Filip even gave you his *amerikanka*!"

"They only give *amerikanka* buggies to the best, and only for the Grand Cup!" exclaims Vanda joyfully. "It's all thanks to him; the Russian buggies are so long and heavy, I wouldn't manage them. Although – at first it's so strange, such a funny ride – you're sitting right under the horse's tail… I used to wonder what they saw in that Reksis. American, sturdy, small, but so affectionate! Now I understand – such a fighter Reksis was at the finish – I've never seen a horse like him! His mouth is soft, a soft little mouth – men probably couldn't ride him. Somehow we fit together well. He feels me, and I feel him."

"You still in the races? Or would you rather go to Mežaparks, to give the funeral-goers a ride?" asks Andrievs teasingly.

"I'm not afraid any more! Now I understand better what you once said about thinking. I solved the problem: there are horses that lead the running, there are horses that go to the finish, and there are horses that break down at the finish. The hardest part for me is still the turn towards the start, to straighten up, all in the same line. Reksis is very stubborn – and then I thought: maybe it's safer for the first line to go and I go behind the first horse. I thought that up myself!"

"Great," Andrievs tells the girl. "That's called tactics. And which one was behind you?"

"Second was Dzidra on Poplar Li, third Mrs. Cīrulis on Birztaliņa."

Vanda goes away with a smile. On the way, Eizens calls to her: "Congratulations, featherweight! Now you'll have to collect the first prize!"

He comes up to Andrievs and attaches the *oberčeks* to Grand Hill.

"Apse thinks that Pilots is limping, though I don't see any great problem there. Come to the judges after the finish!"

Andrievs nods. But Eizens is in no hurry to go. "What have you decided?"

"I'm going to go for it."

Eizens shakes his head, and momentarily rubbing his reddened pug-dog eyes, follows Andrievs with his gaze for a long time.

Everyone comes from a different direction as Sasha is warming up.

"To the friendship of peoples, Andryusha! To us!"

It seems to his fellow jockeys that everything has been agreed. The stocky one sits at the reins of Front, the tall one is driving the very large, fast, emaciated mare Prost', nicknamed Proshka. Also taking part in the races are Valdemārs on Bārītie and Sergey Orlovsky with a state-bred stallion from Latgale, Dyerzky Ukor.

The stands are fit to burst. Englards' frail little voice almost fails with excitement as he calls out shrilly like a country cockerel: "The most intense racing competition of the winter season! The stake in prizes: ten thousand points. The winner of the first prize will get five thousand, second place three thousand, third place fifteen hundred and fourth five hundred. We're about to see with our own eyes how it will turn out. Prizes for the jockey and stable-hand of the winning horse. In starting-place number one, in Category Two, jockey Aleksandr Loginov with the experienced bay stallion Front, from the Pskov stud, out of Tunok by Feja – individual record, 2.24. Number two, Category Two, jockey Aleksandr Stalnov, on the mare Prost' from the Bronyevik collective farm in Gorky District, best speed 2.26, as you can read in your papers. Number three – our own talented, well-known Andrievs Radvilis, with the race champion Grand Hill, out of the legendary American former record-holder Run Hill Dune by Diara, owned by the Ministry of Agriculture of the Latvian SSR, individual record – remember this, esteemed spectators – 2.17!"

The stands crash like the ocean against rocks in a storm. Andrievs waves as he rides past his fans.

"Number four, our most experienced jockey, Valdemārs Jurgensons."

Another ovation. Valdemārs waves to the stands.

"He will be riding Bārīte, the mare from the Riga State Hippodrome, out of Dāvids Dufi and Bārenīte, whose sire is the famous Adlon from the wartime, with a record of two minutes fourteen seconds. Bārīte's best time is 2.20 – bear that in mind! And last, number five, our good old – the most straightforward and yet the most experienced jockey – Sergey Orlovsky, who is leading on points at the Riga Hippodrome, and who rides horses from Latgale – this time too, on the beautiful, grey, very promising stallion Dyerzky Ukor, from the Orlov stud in Latgale, out of Ulov by Draga, whose best time over this distance has been 2.22. Place your bets, citizens, and remember, the judges' decision is final. We remind you that admission tickets are to be kept until the end of the races and shown to the inspector on request."

Warming-up time is coming to an end. Just like yesterday at about this time, a bank of clouds has appeared in the sky. At the moment when they obscure the sun, the race-track seems to have goose-pimples. Andrievs' self-confidence is ebbing away – always before the start he feels ill at ease – his stomach churns and his heart has to be held in his throat to keep from jumping out of his mouth.

"The Great Winter Cup of the Baltic Military District and the most important event of the season," Englards carries on. "Shoulder to shoulder with the jockeys of the Riga Hippodrome there will be comrade jockeys from Smolensk, who have come here with the fastest horses in the Soviet Union from our fraternal Soviet Russia, to help us forge new victories for communism. How they will succeed we shall soon see. We wish them all success. Riders, please, on parade!"

The track spins and sucks Andrievs in; everyone else seems distant. There remains only a thundering in the ears – his own heart and the horse's.

"Cashiers' desks close in three minutes! Riders, to the start!"

Grand Hill responds with a neigh, shakes his head and dances on the spot. He feels like the king of the races, but he's not alone in that. Front, with his dark eye staring through the straps of the bridle, tries to look sideways at his rivals. Dyerzky Ukor is also ready to crush any opponent to a pulp. These are mighty adult stallions, the cracks of the track, as they call the fast, strong, hardy fighters on the racecourse, who fight their own battles on the track, and humans have no inkling of what they themselves think of losing.

Grand Hill likes to lead the race – and that will be Andrievs' tactic. Quite straightforward, going for broke. The horse is on good form – let him do battle!

"Riders, on your marks!"

The red flag.

The bell.

"Go!"

With the bell, the feeling of unease passes like the shadow of a cloud. With the race, another time begins.

The first silence that envelops the racecourse after the start is hypnotic. Thousands of gazing eyes, thousands of held breaths, fingers clinging tightly to the programmes in their fists, only their hearts beating in their chests. It is such a short moment – about two minutes, until the huge moan, the tide of encouraging cries, or sighs of disappointment, the rustle of whispers – bah! But that is at the finish.

For one moment his whole life flashes before his eyes. It isn't possible to think, because the speed with its white-hot power tears time and space to shreds, recreating itself.

Is this eternity, this rhythmic, shamanic thundering of hooves?

Beyond the first curve, having got past the leaders, Andrievs lets his horse take up the position of "first buggy" and take the lead. At his shoulder he notices the muzzle of Front, just behind him, that rhythmic hot breath. Beside Front runs Prost'. Andrievs knows that Front can't be caught at the finish, so he has to hold the leading position for as long as possible. Stalnov, for his part, is driving Proshka quite wrongly, because the mare, if driven hard at the start, tends to flag at the finish.

Grand Hill is leading convincingly on the straight, leering backwards with a white eye. He always runs in the lead in a contained way, as if to keep his rivals at a particular distance, not letting them pass at any cost. Andrievs doesn't spur him on – he has to preserve his strength for the last surge. The loudspeakers announce the quarter-distance results. Despite the poor track, the speed is good.

Front draws ahead at the curve. Knowing that Loginov usually responds to his neighbours, Andrievs holds his horse back a little, as a precaution. Their fellow riders, convinced this is a manoeuvre agreed beforehand, start thrashing their horses with their whips and the two move into the lead. All the others are behind them. For a while all one can hear is the horses' panting and the thunder of hooves. The stands are approaching like an alien, dark shape with its own sharp shadow. Proshka is gradually losing strength and, despite the jockey's efforts, falls behind. Andrievs turns Grand into his place and picks up the reins. Do what you can, my steed!

Recovering on the lee side, on the final straight Grand Hill goes to pass Front like a flash of light over the icy track. His legs no longer seem to touch the ground; it is one continuous moment of flight.

This is a magical moment: for Andrievs the most beautiful one in the race. To let the horse run on his own at his own pace. It feels almost secretive, like reviewing your whole life. To be released into freedom at the price of life, as the blood surges in the lungs and emerges as breath, the muscle fibres vibrate tensely under the skin like an iron wicker-basket.

With a strange light feeling Andrievs merges with his buggy, sinks into it, so as not to interfere, not to be present, as the trotter fights out his duel with the track. At the same time he maintains the sensitivity of his fingertips, communicating with Grand through the reins – you are not alone! If you need me, I will come to your aid.

When Front falls behind, Comrade Loginov is transfixed, with a gaping mouth, letting go of the whip. His stupefaction affects everything – Loginov doesn't realize that Valdemārs is approaching swiftly and stealthily on Bārīte.

And so they finish – Grand Hill, then Bārīte, beating Front by a nose, thereafter Dyerzky Ukor and Proshka.

The stand is ready to collapse like a listing ship, because thousands have jumped to their feet, whistling, screaming, applauding.

The competitors ride around the track at a slow trot, calming their mounts and wiping their mud-spattered eyes. Sergey praises his Dyerzky Ukor, stroking him with the reins across his back. Valdemārs shakes his palms alternately – because of his weak joints, he is in pain after the strain.

The comrade jockeys sit in their buggies with transformed faces. Stalnov is spitting like mad in all directions and angrily pulling at Proshka. The mare pricks up her ears in response – her mouth is already stuffed with complex irons, because she appears hard to control. Loginov swipes the whip-handle across his own throat expressively. It looks so ridiculous, as if they were boys in a sand-pit playing Indians. In his childhood, too, Andrievs had to squat on strangers' staircases, because boys from his yard were waiting outside, threatening him with a gesture just like this. So he was afraid to open the door onto the sunny courtyard. But the door had to be opened sooner or later.

Childhood is over. He understands that, and is no longer afraid.

At the prize-giving Eizens embraces Andrievs. That is worth more than gold cups, red rosettes and money.

The public is cheering lustily for the horses to start dancing – then, as sudden as the snow that falls in a heap from the roof, they set off for the cash-booths to collect their honestly gotten money. Half of them didn't bet on Grand Hill, as one can easily observe – the bosses of the comrade jockeys, their deputies, officers, political instructors, allies and fellow travellers. Dark figures with drooping walrus moustaches loll dejectedly in the trampled stands, studying their programmes in disappointment.

The loudspeakers wheeze into life, and start blaring out "Latvians cheer for Stalin".

Vanda comes toward him with her bright icicle of hair dishevelled about her neck. Right there by the stands, Andrievs, black as a Moor, jumps out of his buggy and greets her.

"Congratulations!" exclaims Vanda. "That was such a beautiful win!"

"Of course." His white eyes flash in his mud-drenched face and he puts the envelope of money in her hands. "Will you take Grand? I have to go to the judges. Keep my prize in a safe place too!"

Grand Hill sighs like a steam engine, giving off the aura of a lake at dawn. Vapour rolls off his back in swathes against the sky. Vanda quickly takes the *oberčeks* and throws a heavy blanket over the horse's back. Then she sits in the buggy and waves.

"By the guard hut, let him drink a couple of gulps of warm water, ask for it from Shevchenko's water-tank," Andrievs calls after her, "and again after every circuit."

Running up the steps with one bound, Andrievs gets an icy shower in the face in the judges' stand.

As if carved from ebony, Cheka Major Mark Krop stands against the crepuscular Riga skyline, and, cigarette in hand, appraises the winner with cool eyes. Next to him, Lyalyakin stares at the track, bored.

At the table with a half-emptied bottle of Redhead and glasses sit Eizens, the judges Mārtiņš Kalpiņš and Aleksandrs Vēbers, next to them two men in grey hats. Right at the end of the table is the director of the totalizator, Grīnfelds. In the middle are Denisov the director, the book-keeper Captain of 2nd Class Svidovoy, Major Pimenov of the veterinary service, the Party organiser Senior Lieutenant Kleshchevsky and the chief veterinary officer, the Communist Natālija Rindiņa. At their own end of the table, their relatives, friends and retired Soviet Army officers appointed to the Party organisation.

On the table, a dish of little sausages. Probably just brought in from the buffet.

By the open window at the end of the room, Englards is calmly talking into a microphone. He is sitting on a little stool, holding the microphone in one hand, in the other a chronometer. In this way, with some intermissions, he has spent fifteen winters of a baron's life in the cold judges' stand. After each trotting race he has to write a report, and it must not be written with a pencil.

Being the technical secretary, Englards holds a little bottle of ink next to his bare skin, so it won't freeze. He is so very used to doing this that he can't wear the ink-bottle on his chest any other way. It suddenly occurs to Andrievs that no-one has ever seen Englards eating at the racecourse. In winter on the judges' stand, so as not to go numb with cold, the judges often bring in sausages to munch on, but Englards doesn't take part. They are also reluctant to offer him any, so as not to offend him, because he wouldn't accept.

Seeing Andrievs come in, the two men in grey hats jump to their feet and shake him warmly by the hand.

"Congratulations! You showed us that you can do your work better than we can!"

"May I introduce – Dolmatov, director of the Moscow Hippodrome, and former adjutant to Marshal Semyon Budyonny," says Eizens. "He has come to inspect our hippodrome."

"Hello," says the other man, pressing into Andrievs' hand a block of dark, bitter, rationed Gvardeysky chocolate, made for pilots by the Krasny Oktyabr factory. "I'm your colleague from the Moscow Hippodrome, Viktor Ratomsky."

"From the old Ratomsky dynasty," declares Eizens in Latvian, then continuing in Russian: "I highly recommend him – an enthusiast! A decent and collegial man. Come, Andrievs, sit down!"

"Thank you, I still have races..." Astonished by this appreciation from his Moscow colleagues, Andrievs only says: "What about Pilot?"

"Pilot is taken. You'll be riding Kazarka."

In the vestibule of the stand, on the first floor, the directors of the racecourse have put out leaflets and posters as well as announcements and photographs showing the "qualities of the best thoroughbred horses in the republic", as the humorous Professor Apse would put it when he was in a good mood and without a headache. Visitors are looking over the exhibition "informing you of the development of pedigree horse-breeding in the republic and the Hippodrome's achievements in improving the horses' performance". Hanging on hooks next to these are inventories of the horses' training and testing programme. Andrievs sees that a girl of primary-school age, with two dark plaits emerging from under a white kerchief, with hanging bunches of ribbons, is shyly touching the bit on the bridle.

"Don't touch it!" cries her mother.

The little girl catches sight of Andrievs. He is climbing the stairs like a mystical figure from another world, with a mud-spattered blue shirt, a sunburned face, white riding breeches, black boots, and a walrus-whiskered whip in his hand.

Usually the public don't meet their heroes face to face. A jockey is allowed to mix with the public only after his last ride on race day, when visiting the upper stands is otherwise forbidden to them.

"Mummy, mummy, look!" the little one whispers, tugging her mother's sleeve.

Andrievs bends over the little girl and looks searchingly into her eyes. "You like racehorses?"

"Yes," she nods timidly.

"Come here some day after school. I'll take you for a ride, eh?" says Andrievs, pressing some chocolate into her hand. "Agreed?"

The little girl has Vanda's eyes; they have the light of snowdrops in them.

The Moscow colleagues' handshakes were so hearty and firm that Andrievs' palm is smarting. Going to the stable yard, his eyes catch Lyalyakin's and Krop's frosty looks, and Ratomsky's flashing smile. Suddenly he understands Eizens, the eternal mediator, the conciliator. Eizens has always done his work and never asked: what's in it for me? He loves horses, respects and honours them, and tries to love people. If he doesn't succeed, he appears not to notice it, but his main consideration is: will it be good for the racecourse? If anyone at all in this whole gang in which he has been forced to involve himself over the years knows horses and understands trotters, then, with a noose around his neck, he might even drink vodka with a hangman.

In the sentry-box of Shevchenko's, another company is gathered around the well-heated economy stove. A snack at the table too, but instead of sausages, stewed cabbages. Ziemelis is drinking with the racecourse farriers Augusts and Silvestrs, and there also are the old harness-maker Aldmanis from the St. Petersburg Hippodrome of Tsarist times, and Professor Apse. The veterinarians, with flushed faces, sit next to Mesdames Cīrulis and Baginskis, who are equally flushed.

"Boy!" cries Ziemelis, having caught sight of Andrievs. "I was expecting – I couldn't wait to see you beating those Russians. At the last turn you were gobbling them up like berries! Grand Hill – what a pace he set! Just like old Hill!"

"What about Pilot?"

"He's lame in the right front leg. Ziemelis must have banged the nail too far into the hoof when shoeing him," says Apse.

Ziemelis dismisses this with his hand.

"According to the professor's findings, it's rare for any horse to be completely healthy."

"Just like ourselves. My head aches enough to give it to the dog to gnaw on," Apse grumbles.

"A good headache lasts three days!" laughs Mrs. Cīrulis.

"Are you celebrating?" inquires Andrievs.

"We'll have to get started on – Women's Day! You know, son, when God judges a man, he takes away his sense and gives him a woman. Come, sit down!"

"I still have one more race."

"Well then, keep on your toes, boy!"

The March afternoon gradually takes on that slow, clear, pure tone that is characteristic of spring evenings. The town is no longer flat, as if drawn on a sheet of cardboard; it has taken on depth. The snow, enveloped in a crust of ice, crunches underfoot, but the black silhouettes of the trees seem to be melted into the azure of dusk.

Mazā, or Little One, as Kazarka is known at the racecourse, is brought up to Andrievs. Sitting in the buggy, he can feel every bone painfully. His tiredness is considerable after the long day and the nervous strain; he thanks Fate that the ride with Pilot fell through. After the main races the stands are half-empty; most citizens have gone back to town to spend their Sunday evening.

Until now Little One has been running on Wednesdays, when they hold the races for young novices which are just starting to run at the course. In summer, on the harbour side, in a place well protected from the wind in the Hippodrome garden, Eizens is growing fabulous tomatoes. When the skittish, uncontrollable two-year-olds arrived in town from the countryside, it occasionally happened that one of them didn't take the curve and ran over Eizens' tomatoes. Even for Andrievs and Little One it had happened, "running over Eizens' tomatoes".

Kazarka's pedigree is from the Trasuns horses. Staņislavs Trasuns was a diligent model farmer at Rubulnieks in Rēzekne district, one of the most influential breeders of Latgale trotters. Trasuns was deported to Siberia in June 1941. The horses were nationalised, most of them killed in the war. But even today, the pedigree stories relate, there are often references to "Trasuns blood", although Trasuns' branch of the family was wiped off the face of the earth, an empty place among many other thousands of places.

Over the winter the small but fast black mare has got used to the conditions at the racecourse, but it still happens that in a fierce competition with a rival she "jumps out". Galloping in a trotting race is a big transgression, called "jumping out". For three-year-old and older horses, fifteen jumps count as galloping. The horse has to be stopped, because the thirteenth jump is counted as a "skip", for which it is eliminated and sent home. If a pair wants to claim prize money, then there must be no more than three jumps over a distance of 1600 metres.

It's good that the little mare is easily led and can be quickly put back "on pace". What complicates matters is that she likes to lead a race. If she gets behind someone somewhere, her drive disappears and the results are not so good. So all the time she is balanced on a knife-edge – one has to give her head and make sure she doesn't "jump out".

In the Minor Cup, Kazarka starts off a fairly fast race, shoulder to shoulder with Sergey Orlov's Lira, from Ludza. Behind them, moving up, is Comrade Jockey Stalnov with Sud'ba, a rapid steed from Stud Number 5, who, however, before even reaching the stand, makes two jumps out and is overtaken by Valdemārs with Sun Hill. Both of them race some way away from the leaders. Far behind them lingers Veriņa Sokolova with Zhemchug. At the next turn Lira starts to "jump" and falls back, and Kazarka does a "jump" too, but she keeps second place behind Sun Hill. At the end of the opposite straight Stalnov and Sud'ba enter the space between the two leading horses, who diverge to the left and right, so as not to block the middle path of the interloper. At the turn, Stalnov levels with Andrievs, but then, suddenly running on, crosses Kazarka's path. This "crossing", as it is always called, is a strictly forbidden manoeuvre. It means forfeiting the right to a prize, and a heavy penalty for the jockey.

The loudspeakers are silent, because the horses are close together, and from the stands one can't see what is happening on the curve. Andrievs realizes that this is a planned tactic of Stalnov's in which his fellow jockey takes revenge for Grand Hill's victory. He tries to prevent Sud'ba from deflecting Kazarka on the bend, but this is very dangerous. The hooves of the two contenders are audibly scraping. Little One stumbles, but miraculously, after being intercepted, she carries on trotting. The roar of the horses behind them can be heard – Lira and Sun Hill are both there. At the end of the turn, Stalnov tries a couple of times to strike Kazarka across the head with his whip – even more, to drive her off the track. There's nothing else Andrievs can do but try to get ahead and pray to God that the enraged Kazarka won't carry him off the track.

And then it happens – the wheels interlock.

Stalnov falls out of the buggy. Sud'ba, left without a driver, gallops off to one side with the empty cart. Andrievs carries on as before, and finishes first; second is Sun Hill; third, Lira. Zhemchug comes last.

Having given Little One to an assistant, Andrievs goes immediately to Stalnov, prostrate in the mud. A doctor runs over too, with his bag, along with the quarter-track judges, the starter, and a throng of people. Lira and Sun Hill have gone right past the stricken jockey in their duel without touching him. Eizens rushes up, along with others from the judges' stand.

"What happened?"

Stalnov pulls two front teeth out of his mouth. At a quite inappropriate time it occurs to Andrievs that now it will be easier for his comrade to spit.

In the spectators' eyes, Andrievs is the guilty one; whistles and curses are heard, demanding that Kazarka does not get the prize.

The colleagues from Moscow are calling for witnesses. No-one helps Andrievs – the quarter judge, retired Air Force Major Yeryomin, is so drunk that he can hardly stand up, let alone testify.

"A jockey who hinders his competitor's ride is either clumsy or dishonest," says Andrievs indignantly. "Either way, he has no place among the jockeys on the course!"

Rindiņa, the Communist, wipes Stalnov's flabby, bloody mouth with a handkerchief and shouts at Andrievs: "There used to be 'competitors' in your bourgeois days. Now there is no place on the course for those who call their comrades 'competitors'!"

Stalnov makes a special effort to limp, to engage the spectators' sympathy, dragging himself toward the stands like a shot swan. Eizens and the judges go back to confer.

The spectators are murmuring with dissatisfaction, awaiting the verdict of the college of judges. There are not many who put their money on Kazarka. The potential favourite in the race was Sud'ba. Of course it's in the interest of the majority to disqualify Andrievs and declare the race null and void.

"Attention, race-goers!" cries Englards into the loudspeakers. "All totalizator tickets should be kept until the final verdict of the college of judges about the proper order of the horses at the winning post in the relevant race, which will be put up on the board in front of the stands. The announcement of the result on the radio is to be regarded as preliminary information."

One freezing, noticeably intoxicated proletarian, who is longing to get to the hot buffet along with his friends, makes an open threat: "A brick across the snout for Radvilis and our money back! How much longer do we have to sit around here?"

Eizens comes in and puts the confirmatory decision up on the board. The race counts as valid.

The spectators let out a dissatisfied groan.

The proletarian shouts: "Let's go to the cashiers! Get our money back and string up the judges!"

Some totalizator players start breaking boards, but the angriest are already going up the steps to the judges' stand. Confusion is breaking out. The administrators, forced to retreat, have barricaded themselves inside the judges' lodge, and Englards declares the last race invalid over the loudspeakers. The spectators get their money back at the cash-desks against their tickets and head into town in little groups.

Andrievs sits in the stands, his head hanging. No-one will acknowledge him any more. Lyalyakin, Denisov and Krop walk silently past. Stalnov is talking to the men from Moscow. Stalnov doesn't seem to be suffering any more, though previously he couldn't take a step properly.

Eizens and Englards arrive and send Andrievs to the stables.

"It was a crossing, pure and simple!" declares Andrievs despairingly. "Any change of direction on the final straight is seen as a racing infringement."

The red weal glows fiery on his cheek.

"The fact is, it happened on the curve," replies Eizens. "And no-one really knows what happened there."

"That's just the way things are," adds Englards. "You are overheated, and now you're rapidly cooling. Go and get warm."

Walking to look after his horses, Andrievs thinks of how a whole life can be changed in a moment.

"One moment a winner, the next moment in the mud," he tells Vanda, who is fussing around Reksis, binding his legs.

Without saying a word, Vanda gives him back his prize – the envelope of money.

"You don't believe me either, like them?" Andrievs asks her.

"The Hippodrome is a game of chance," replies Vanda coldly.

"I don't agree with you!" cries Andrievs, going up to Little One.

"If you could tell us," he says to the mare, changing her blanket. Her breathing has now calmed; Kazarka looks with serious eyes at her trainer.

By the railings they take off the muddy protective footwear. Before starting to care for her legs, Andrievs casts an eye over them. On the right side, holes have been knocked in the protective leather of the leggings. He examines the horse, then carefully looks over Kazarka's front leg. Small tear-wounds are clearly visible, from which a liquid is leaking into the fur. The leggings have no doubt protected the horse from any worse injuries.

Andrievs shows Vanda the leg-protectors.

"Look! This is the right front leg. What do you think – can a horse knock such holes in herself – and on the outside edge too? This happened when he ran across my legs. I clearly remember the noise when the hooves hit each other! These are the traces of Sud'ba's studs!"

Vanda examines the leather on the leggings.

"I can't understand it. I've never seen anything like it!"

Andrievs peels off the protective coverings, dries them off and puts them in a container on the bench.

Late that evening, Apse is walking through the stables. Andrievs calls the veterinarian over to Kazarka's box.

"No doubt about it, you'll have to show this to Denisov tomorrow! I ought to fill in a report, but my head hurts like hell. Tomorrow!"

On the way home, the dark city absorbs everything, even their breathing, so that you can't tell whether these are winners or losers walking.

The next day is a day off, but at lunchtime Englards comes up behind Andrievs with an announcement that he must appear in the administration building before a hastily convened court of comrades – the renamed Hippodrome Jockeys' Court of Honour.

Before the court session, Andrievs goes to the stable to pick up the material evidence – Kazark's leg protectors. Great is his surprise when he can't find them anywhere. He searches on the bench and under it, among the saddlery items and farriers' boxes, checks through the blanket stores and the fodder troughs – they are nowhere to be found. They were big and heavy; where can they have got to?

Everyone has the day off, even Vanda. There is no-one to ask.

The stable-hands shrug their shoulders, saying they know nothing.

Baffled, Andrievs drags himself over to the administration building. In the director's office is assembled the flower of the Hippodrome management, including his colleague from Moscow, Lyalyakin; the instructor from the Department of Agriculture, Major Krop from the security service; Secretary Lopatin from the Party organisation; and the veterinary specialist Natālija Rindiņa. Also present are Comrade Jockey Loginov and the injured Stalnov, with his bandaged elbow; Donāts, Jānis and Valdemārs, representing the jockeys, and the witnesses Orlovsky and Sokolova.

As chairman of the consistory court, Eizens begins: "I asked Comrade Radvilis to appear so that we can examine this case. Yesterday in the last race there was an incident where, when the wheels interlocked, Comrade Jockey Stalnov was thrown out and sustained light injuries."

"Serious injuries," cries Denisov. "He has a doctor's report."

"Comrade Jockey Stalnov sustained serious injuries. Today we must examine jockey Radvilis' action in this situation and assess the nature of the damage," says Eizens, turning to Stalnov. "I wish to remind you – no jockey must forget that a horse-race is a matter of a jockey's honour, that inadmissible action by a jockey upsets the spectators, arouses angry allegations, causes distrust in jockeys and objections to the rulings of the college of judges – all of this happened yesterday, unfortunately, when the cashiers were forced to yield to growing discontent from the spectators and pay back money, thus causing losses for the Hippodrome. I give the floor to Director Denisov."

Denisov has already scrambled onto a chair at the mention of his name.

"The Hippodrome must in the first place work in the interests of Soviet citizens, and only secondarily in its own self-interest. Yet the Hippodrome is also a centre of propaganda! How can anything like this be allowed? The biggest mistake, comrades, is that we are not fulfilling the directions of our leader, Comrade

Stalin, and our Party, and are not mastering the theory of Marxism-Leninism!"

Andrievs stares fixedly at the short, thin tie of the Soviet official, with its huge knot. How does he tie it? Does his wife, guided by instinct, tackle this gigantic example of Soviet applied art every morning?

Valdemārs is asked to describe Comrade Jockey Radvilis. He rises stiffly to his feet and reads from some sentences hastily written on a piece of paper.

"Comrade Jockey Andrievs Radvilis is a very experienced trotting jockey. Deeply erudite, very familiar with a horse's anatomy. A highly qualified jockey. He rides at a high level, is technically masterful, understands tactical matters. He is an authority among other jockeys and the administrators. He strives to raise his political-ideological level –"

Rindiņa, the veterinarian, cannot restrain herself and gets to her feet, flourishing her huge bosom before her colleagues.

"Outright lies! To talk like that is to say nothing, Comrade Jurgensons. We must speak the plain truth – Radvilis does not take part in public work. In his activities he commits errors of an ideological nature. He receives criticism incorrectly and does not try to correct his errors. He has not yet liberated himself from nationalist attitudes. He avoids new cadres and does not train them. He associates with compromised persons, who stand apart from the campaign to re-educate the bourgeois intelligentsia."

"At their place the horse lives indoors next to the piano!" cries Stalnov indignantly. "But the piano plays itself. I saw it with my own eyes."

"See! So much for their authority! Allow me to differ!" continues Rindiņa. "In my eyes, Andrievs Jakovļevičs Radvilis is a bad element. Surely we're capable of finding proper Soviet people!"

Andrievs' gaze is fixed on the deep cleavage that is ominously darkening between Rindiņa's breasts, where a button has burst. She suits Denisov well, he thinks – his short jacket won't close over his watermelon belly.

"How can the plaintiff explain what happened on the track?" asks Eizens.

"If a space is created between two horses running side by side, and a cart runs into it from behind, then the latter has the right to ride through the space; those are the rules," declares Stalnov, with a frown. "Andrievs Jakovļevičs didn't want to allow that; as a result I was injured, and so was our common cause."

"Comrades Orlovsky and Jurgensons were riding alongside," interjects Grīnfelds. "Perhaps they can testify as to how the incident happened?"

Both merely shrug.

"To be honest, I didn't see anything," says Orlovsky. "You know yourselves what the track was like yesterday. My face was completely covered in mud, and I rode turning toward the stands. I only noticed that Comrade Stalnov's horse jumped past me with an empty buggy."

Veriņa Sokolova, too, who was riding far behind on Zhemchug, claims to know nothing. Finally the floor is given to Andrievs.

"In the third race Loginov tried to upset me and my horse when I overtook him, and here," Andrievs continues, indicating his bandaged cheek, where a cherry-coloured shadow of a bruise is now darkening around the pink wound, "is the actual evidence."

"Lies!" screams Stalnov. "It was an accident! I already apologised!"

Loginov silences him and pulls him back into his chair.

"And then you decided to take revenge on Comrade Stalnov?" demands Comrade Rindiņa sternly.

Andrievs is confused.

"No, not at all. Quite the contrary – he took revenge on me. In the final stretch, knowing that it is forbidden for one horse to shove another off the track, like in the highway code, even in a straight line, Stalnov risked doing it anyway, almost running me off the track. Unfortunately he himself fell out of his buggy."

"And where is the evidence?" smirks Loginov.

"There was evidence yesterday; with my own eyes I saw stud holes in the right-hand side leg-protectors on Kazarka's leg, scraped by Sud'ba, when Stalnov made the crossing on the last curve. He likes curves, because there it's hard for spectators to follow his illegal actions…"

"You can lie like a dog, but where's the evidence?" Loginov is becoming indignant.

"Unfortunately today the leg-protectors have disappeared."

"What does this mean – the leg-protectors have disappeared?" Comrade Rindiņa is shocked. "Such things never disappear, and now suddenly – gone. It's not a little needle. So did they grow wings? Do you, Comrade Radvilis, want to claim that there are thieves in our collective?"

"I don't want to claim anything, but Kazarka's right front leg is injured. Professor Apse can confirm that. Yesterday he was going to compile a report, but he had a headache."

"Professor Apse, can you confirm that Sud'ba cut through the leg-protectors with her studs and injured Comrade Radvilis' horse?" asks Denisov.

"How could I, if I haven't seen the leg-protectors?" replies Apse, bewildered. "The injuries that Kazarka had yesterday might in theory have been caused on the track, or in the stable, by hitting a sharp object, for example prongs. Of course, if we could see the holes in the leg-protectors, we could conclude that they were caused by incorrect riding. A horse cannot injure the outside of its own leg. I am very sorry. Please take no account of me; I really did have a headache yesterday, and I still have one today."

The members of the court whisper among themselves, dissatisfied; Lyalyakin quietly confers with Krop.

"And why did you say at first that Comrade Stalnov wanted to take revenge on you?" Denisov asks suddenly.

"Everyone knows – in every race a jockey has to ride to win." Andrievs tries to swallow saliva, but his throat is completely dry, as if scraped with a wire brush. "If he didn't make every effort to win, he'd be deprived of a jockey's rights for a period, or even forever. Comrade jockeys Loginov and Stalnov, since they arrived from Smolensk, have wanted to involve me in a campaign to hold back Grand Hill in the contest for the Grand Cup of the Baltic Military District, for a certain payment, and I didn't do that."

The comrade jockeys look at each other.

"He's lost his mind," says Loginov. "What nonsense!"

"I have witnesses," says Andrievs, looking at Krop and Lyalyakin, "and they are here."

The silence of the grave sets in. It seems that even on the street you can hear Andrievs' heart pounding, the sweat is heavy on Rindiņa's brow, Denisov's mouth gaping like a fish on a hook as his fingers try to button up his unbuttonable jacket.

"He's drunk, or he's lost his mind; comrades, you won't allow these lies, will you?" roars Denisov, jumping to his feet.

"To tell the truth, it's hard for me to follow what's being said here," begins Krop ominously, enjoining silence with a wave of his hand, still in his place, as if he'd expected such a turn of events. "Right at the start I wanted to say – there will be some bitter words, but it's better to say those words than to keep your bitterness in your heart. This incident does not have a very good political resonance. What is important is the tendentiousness of what has been expressed here. Its whole essence is mistaken, misleading and incorrect. We understand very well that under the Soviet system we are moving forward rapidly. Here we have an incorrect, slightly nationalistic tone, if I may put it that way, which should be recognized and condemned. Our Soviet Hippodrome in Riga has succeeded in acquiring comrade jockeys from Smolensk, and now, in the first great race meeting, we have reached the pass we now find ourselves in. We cannot pass over it indifferently, because otherwise we would seem to be siding with that position. Perhaps this is bitter, perhaps it is unpleasant, to talk among ourselves about these issues, but ultimately I am forced to note that in our Soviet system it is a common phenomenon, that criticism and self-criticism are an important weapon without which we cannot manage. With the help of this criticism and self-criticism, which maybe no-one likes, but which has to be manfully endured – with its help, we must be able to eliminate the mistakes and shortcomings, the incorrect political tendencies, which are evident to us in this situation. It seems to me that Comrade Radvilis aspires to be a true Soviet trotting jockey, and it seems to me that in essence he is one, so that he too needs to take a position against his own line, and the court of comrades also needs to condemn that position as such a position needs to be condemned."

As Krop speaks, everyone gradually calms down and takes a breath; even the clock on the wall seems to resume ticking.

"It seems to me that it was simply an unfortunate way of expressing himself on the part pf Comrade Radvilis," says Eizens, trying to save the situation. "Politically, it was an absolutely incorrect performance."

"And it seems to me," Denisov interrupts emphatically, "that many people are using Radvilis as a banner! Your friends are your worst enemies, Eizens. You ought to stand up to them yourself. Now as to the essence of the case: I'm aware of the question of cadres, and with every worker there are very many problems. At the Hippodrome there remained only 66 trotters; of the cadres, Eizens, Grīnfelds and a couple of jockeys. Especially when the war ended, there were many difficulties. We needed to turn to Moscow to select the sort of cadres which would help Latvia to keep more or less in line. Now we have received them, and we will continue to receive ever greater numbers of both horses and jockeys; it's a very great, fraternal, friendly, humane assistance that we're receiving. It seems to me that the comrades' court ought to recognize – if it can be called such – the unwelcome and harmful nature of this conflict."

"Yes, I demand an apology!" sputters Stalnov.

"So do I!" Loginov chimes in. "Apologise to your comrades, *ti blya!* you bastard!"

"Please, Comrade Radvilis, apologise to the comrade jockeys for the slanders, the fabrications, and for the incident in the race," Denisov intercedes.

Andrievs involuntarily places his fingers on the scratch left by the whiplash; he feels as if he's been struck with the whip again.

"I apologise."

"Why does it seem to me now," Loginov continues to mock Andrievs, "that what you just said doesn't agree with what you're thinking? Why are you trying to explain away an incorrect idea as a correct one? If you said: 'Esteemed colleagues, forgive me,

I messed it up this time' – no-one would criticise you. And yet your words and your thoughts are different! You don't have to humiliate your Soviet colleagues."

"I don't like Comrade Radvilis' words either!" Stalnov whistles. "He came here with a different intention. He said something quite different at first, and now he's apologising. You could hear from his own words that there was no misunderstanding; from his side it was a condemnation of his Soviet comrade jockeys. Why are you trying to apologise? Say what you said at the beginning. Why do you want to say you're sorry now?"

"I said one set of words, then another."

"I'm simply shocked that you can take that attitude to this question. I am reacting to these totally incorrect slanders. Only in this way can we really establish anything. If we take that attitude to the case, then we will simply have to investigate the matter. Only in that way can we agree to go on working here. But the case is clear, it seems to me. There is no evidence, only slander."

Everyone sits still as if under water. Not even Englards' blue carpenter's pencil can be heard scraping, the one he uses to draw sketches while sitting in meetings. Stalnov still wants to say something, but Lyalyakin silences him with an angry glare.

"Comrades, may we ratify the words I spoke earlier?" Krop summarises, surveying the assembly cold-bloodedly. "We're gathered here to acknowledge your actions during the races, as well as your statements, Comrade Radvilis, about your politically incorrect and contemptible action. Let us take a vote!"

Andrievs bows his head so as not to see the raised hands which surround him with their throttling shadows like a forest of club-moss.

"Have you nothing to add, Comrade Radvilis?" asks Denisov, still not leaving him in peace.

"Thank you for the admonitions, and I will take account of them," Andrievs forces out of himself, as he hears the scraping of chair-legs and the tramp of departing feet.

*

Englards arrives home late and sits down next to Andrievs' camp-bed.

"This is for you," he says.

Andrievs, who is staring wide-eyed out of the window at the twinkling stars, like wisps of saffron, of a March night, examines in the circle of lamplight the sketch drawn during the meeting. It's a portrait of Andrievs in profile. The averted eyes. A knot of muscle is bunched over clenched swollen jaws. He already has one gift – a self-portrait by Englards. The old man's portraits are well executed – the anatomy of a bare, truthful face. "Look at that when I'm no longer around, and you'll draw strength from it," says the old man. "You have your whole life ahead of you. Plenty more things will pass through your head."

Going to his own corner, he adds: "Eizens has been suspended from his post."

"Why?"

"Quite without reason, he was given the blame for the mess with the totalizator players."

Beauty

"Straight along the detour! Why are you turning right?"

"I want to see what that white dune is on the bank of the Daugava," I say.

"That isn't a dune, and that isn't the Daugava, it's the silo of the Pļaviņas dolomite factory, and there hasn't been anything to see there for ages!"

Radvilis retracts his head into his collar and looks offended.

"Hey, what now?"

"If your eyes are looking for what mine are looking for, you wouldn't take a step here. That's not a river, it's a tub, a vat, a pigs' trough – look at it as much as you like, you won't see anything!"

"That is my Daugava. I wouldn't have any other."

I get out of the car in the middle of a lonely road. Shamefully, as if browbeaten, the old man struggles out and hobbles backwards.

"This was the most unique natural formation in the whole Baltic region – the so-called 'primeval Daugava' with its precipitous canyons, with castle mounds one on top of another! Not on any river embankment can you find as many castle mounds as on the Daugava. You just have to believe that what you find here is the ancient Gardariki, the land of castles. Imagine a gorge of outcrops of dolomites, wavy, bending, overgrown with blackberries, with countless rivulets, which freeze over the banks in winter like white curtains. Here were the Lorelei Rock and the huge Grūbe rapids, with its strong constant rushing in summer, when the water was low. You could wander for a whole day along the bed of the Daugava jumping from rock to rock along the Aldiņu sandbanks. One of my schoolmates lived in Pļaviņas. On summer nights with an open window that rushing noise would put you to sleep."

Sceptically, without moving, I look at the line of wagons running along the foot of the hill of shards, the cranes enveloped in shrubbery, and the concrete bunkers beyond the meadow, frayed and ragged like a moth-eaten bit of wool.

I can see how she parts the curtains on the first floor. From the piano onto the windowsill jumps a tom-cat, the darling of the house, asking to be let out. She half-opens the window. It smells of hoarfrost, which has touched the fields of bent-grass behind the factory workers' houses. There is no snow, the bank down to the edge of the Daugava is billowing rosily like the cat's fur. Beyond the window a dusty road, beyond the road an oily railway, beyond the railway a dirty, mud-spattered side-track. But suddenly she is seized by a yearning for the Daugava, so strong that it causes a pang in the pit of her stomach. She tears herself away from the window and calls to the girls to get dressed. They are as tiny and light as butterflies, with wavy hair and greenish-grey eyes like hers. For several years now she has dyed her hair black and cut it short to have less trouble with it. She is tall of build, in mourning her mother she has lost weight this autumn, but that makes her step lighter. The top-boots embrace her calves comfortingly. They're suitable for both city pavements and wading in the dolomite mud. Only this morning – the bent-grass smells strongly of frozen, freshly washed clothes and she is as much in need of the Daugava as a mother, the closeness, so strong that it stings the pit of her stomach... The sharp grass comes up to her armpits and over the girls' heads – there are paths trampled in it all the way to the river. Walkers are standing on the bank, where the grey blocks of dolomite reach down to the depths. The ginger tom-cat runs up too. So do they come here often? The Daugava is not welcoming. In summer, sometimes boys dive in and go for fast swims. Now a damp wind blows into her face from afar and thundering can be heard. She can't understand it – those are separate thunderclaps or a cannonade. "Mummy, they're shooting!" says the youngest daughter, covering her face with her fingers, striving with her gaze to hold back the huge body of water that is hazily steaming. There, above the compact bank of clouds, there must definitely be the sun. She pats her pocket and pulls out a cigarette. It's good to smoke and look into the distance, as if passing over yourself and being able to see your life before you, and even beyond that. Beside her is not her mother, but the Daugava. It may be unclean, unlovely and dangerous, but it's always beside you and always in spate. "Let yourself pass through, wash away, don't hold back, don't stop," the river quietly gurgles to the rock. Beyond it are the dark forests of Sēlija. "It's Saturday, darling," she says. "They're shooting elks in Sēlpils."

"Now there's nothing – the banks are as full of water as bathtubs," Radvilis' strong voice rings in my ears. "Around there were the Lorelei, the Devil's magnificent whirlpool, and many rapids, Pērse's waterfall and the pretty, weeping Staburadze with the Linden Fountain, Jumiezis – the rock, sloping like a roof, farmsteads and graves, and Bebruleja – a whole village. Lokstene castle mound, too, which the locals wrongly call Jersika. Maybe the headman Loker is mentioned in Saxo Grammaticus' *Gesta Danorum** – he took the Danish Viking Hading prisoner, he was the lord of *Locesten*. What do you think?"

I wasn't thinking about that at the moment, and yet I said: "I don't know, the names sound similar, but Loker was a Curonian*, anyway. Lettgallians and Selians settled around the Daugava."

"But why, when he had put the guards to sleep with his tales, did Hading immediately set off up the Daugava – Duna, Dyna, Wina, Weina – and attack the Latgalian king Handuvans, who had fortified himself in the Daugava castle yard – *apud Dunam urbem*? So then Loker's home was also by the Daugava?"

"We can't know that; *Duna urbs* might just as well be the town of Dona, and Handuvans not our home-grown Andiņš, but some Hans. So which one would be called the Castle of the Daugava? Olinkalns? Sēlpils?"

"No-one knows – the main thing is that *Duna, Dyna, Dūne, Dyn, Djuna, Duin, Dunē, Dune, Dzjuna, Dunlear, Dina, Duno, Dyyni, Dwyni* – in German and Swedish, French and Frisian, Albanian, Azeri, Belarusian, Basque and Bosnian, Bulgarian, Czech and

Esperanto, Galician, Croatian, Italian, Latin, as well as Kazakh, Slovak, Spanish, Ukrainian, Welsh and Hungarian…"

"…in a word, in many languages *Duna* means 'dune'," * I said, impatient for the end of the sentence.

"What?"

"Dune!"

"Exactly!" For a moment Radvilis catches his breath as if after a fast climb. "A sandy hill. And even if we don't know where the Daugava castle was, we can picture it well, because we know how the Latvian folk songs, *dainas*, describe it, what the pillagers saw as they entered the Daugava estuary – 'sandy hills all around, Riga itself in water'."

"Why should I have to see what I don't see?"

"Sorry?"

"Why is it important to think about what no longer exists?"

"Time is a fatal yet light veil. All the most magnificent fruits of human activity – oral folklore, writing, painting, photography – are created with one aim – to see through time, transmit history, and once you have climbed out of the monotonous banks of your own life, you don't want to return to them. You see, it's simple – you're either a bank or a river! This flesh, no doubt, is a splendid thing, but it stops right here. It is my bank at the moment, though it's uncertain and decayed. But thinking is fine and deeply serious, like the Daugava, if I may paraphrase Jaunsudrabiņš*. Yes, I choose to be a river, if I'm allowed to choose. How much there is you will know well yourself if you've studied *jukurrpa.*"

"From a bird's eye view, everything looks simple and uniform. Those who lived down here had to work hard."

"Did I claim the opposite? They lived and worked, but did it in beauty, which didn't cost them a cent! They only had to lift their eyes. Beauty, of course, is not popular these days. It is an eternally unattainable ideal, which keeps creating unrest in the world, reminding you at every step of the dead God. Look, there in the depths, eight metres below the water is the drowned Bebruleja, the village of raftsmen. Originally it was the Polish and Lithuanian rebels, persecuted by the Tsar, who fled there; later they mixed with local people, and it changed. The Stukmanites used to laugh at the Bebruleja folk – "they sit on the bank and wait for bread to come into their mouths". The Daugava was the main provider of both work and bread for them. Their little houses were in small clusters right on the bank, but their meagre strips of fields stretched inland. On the river opposite the village were treacherous places with many rocks and whirlpools – the Pačiņa dam, the Časkiņa whirlpool, the Rubka stream, the Aldiņš whirlpool, the Kapu sandbank. To ruin a raft or barge was an expensive pleasure for the owner. If the raftsman was bad or inexperienced and did not hit the *uļica*, the road, by which the raft was to be brought ashore, then the beams got tangled and the barges were overturned in the Bebruleja rapids, the bags of grain and buckets of hemp were poured into the water. The assistants from Bebruleja, who came in work-gangs to put everything back together again, earned their keep. There were those among them who earned their living in trade or by breaking the dolomite with their hands in the Bebruleja quarries. It was very heavy work for both people and horses, and yet, if they wanted, they could stop for a moment on a rock in the middle of the river. The ceaseless bubbling of the rapids, amplified in the depths, the high white cliffs on the banks, richly overgrown with jungles of lilacs, barberries and brambles, the resinous scent from the thick forest of spruce and mast-pines, by the Riga-Daugavpils road – the echoes in late spring, amplified tenfold by the banks – you can imagine it! Now the work is just as hard, but the beauty is taken out of it. Beauty is traded for big money on the stock exchange. Doesn't it seem unfair to you? As the sun shines for everyone, so the beauty of the Daugava was meant for everyone in this flooded village – from a child who is just learning to sense beauty like the warmth of the sun on his skin, to the grey-haired old man, accompanied only by his memories."

The landscape seems deserted, but mist is moving in the air – dark, doomed, as if dragged along in the mud. Like the current of the Daugava with its muddy banks. For some reason I recall the migrating dunes on the east coast of America – quiet, bright light radiated by the ocean and the sand. There's some connection between these two apparently irreconcilable landscapes. Maybe –

that one greyish, genuine snapshot among many enhanced copies in the computer.

"Once in America I saw a similar landscape," I say to Radvilis, when we have stood silently for a while on a little stretch of patched road. "The dunes on the outer sandbanks of the coast."

"Pardon?" Radvilis turns his good ear toward me.

"There's a dune in America like this place."

"Yeah?" He is interested. "I've been in America – with a choir. And what's the name of the dune in America?"

Radvilis listens so intently that his mouth is twisted and his eyes stand out in an effort to read the words on my lips.

"Run Hill Dune."

Now I am the one who doesn't avert my eyes from his face. I want to observe the slightest nuance of emotion.

But the old man quickly turns his head away.

"Run Hill! He was from Carolina, of course. I thought so – why are you telling me this? Let's go!"

I want to go too.

Beyond the rails of the Pļaviņas dolomite works I notice the workers' houses, built of white bricks. Over the fields of bent-grass on the Daugava side moves a tall figure, followed by three little girls. It's her, I think. The one I saw first! Just like a partridge moving with its chicks across the field. Is that why it's important to see that it's possible to observe a complete landscape, while time shows us the same thing in sequence? A pity that she and her daughters are deprived of the beautiful Daugava. They have deserved it, but now they have to create it for themselves through the dense shroud of time and water. I know that she will be wise and teach her daughters to observe. She has the raftsmen's blood in her – the soul of a poet.

Through the Glass

In the following days, time runs backwards, as if the world has been overturned and is ruled by shadows, on prancing feet. All the trotting jockeys must fill in reports on the compulsory course "Lenin and Stalin and the training of Young Communists". A lecture timetable is appended to it. Rindiņa the veterinarian will present the only lecture, "Applying Lysenko's genetic teachings to horse-breeding, and the latest achievements in it"; a guest lecturer from the Ministry of Agriculture will read a necessary work, "Stalin's Great Plan for the Transformation of Nature"; Colonel Vasiliev on "Stalin on the Struggle with Contradictions in Nature".

Eizens is temporarily suspended from the Hippodrome. The booth in the stables stands empty. For a couple of evenings Andrievs walks past his former habitation in the German time – the Petersons house on Tomsona Street. There Eizens had a flat dating back to the era of President Ulmanis. Now it is a communal flat, but the window of Eizens' room is dark. There are some rumours that he has gone to his sister's.

In the wall newspaper on the Hippodrome's noticeboard – that all-seeing eye of the nation – a large, anonymous revelatory article has been published about the jockey-mauler, Andrievs Radvilis, son of Jēkabs. He is claimed to be the son of an element hostile to Soviet power, whose activities have been noted for a long time. He does no public work, he compromises Young Communists – he is said to have dissuaded the young jockeys from joining the Young Communists. He justifies himself by the different material conditions in the hunt for money. He is said to be reading bourgeois poets, books in English, and is alleged to have said that the Hippodrome was created long before the establishment of Soviet power in Latvia. It is apparently impossible to ban Radvilis from anywhere, but he must understand that the question must be examined by the highest organs. "People like Radvilis must be swept onto the dungheap of history!"

Stumbling and falling, Andrievs slides along the black ice to the stable, bent double against the strong north-east wind which shakes the town, and at the same time wishes to run to the opposite side – to be somewhere else, a hundred thousand versts away from this cursed place.

As gloomy as the edge of a storm, he enters the stables' dressing-room, where Helēna, Veriņa Sokolova, Valdemārs and Ēriks are gathered. Mrs. Cīrulis is carefully sprucing up the trotters' bridles by her box, treating them with saddle-soap.

"Where is Vanda? Congratulations, you've succeeded! And those drawings – they must be by Veriņa?"

"What are you talking about?" Mrs. Cīrulis asks cautiously.

"About the wall newspaper, what else? I'm supposed to have declared that all the records belong to horses from capitalist countries! What a sin! Am I supposed to have doctored the record books?"

Blushing, Helēna looks at the toe-caps of her boots.

"You, Helēna! How could you?"

"Denisov made me…"

"Leave her in peace!" Veriņa Sokolova bursts out in defence of her friend. "First of all you learn to drive yourself, and then you judge others! You blame the whole world, but nobody, not even the judge in the court, can find in your favour."

"Major-General Yeryomin of the Air Force? As if you didn't know that his chronometer is always fixed? I really don't understand what such a stupid creature was doing in the Air Force."

"You're the stupid one!" shrieks Vera, hugging the weeping Helēna's shoulders. "You're a… backsliding reptile. A haughty fellow! For years, no-one has seen you smiling, you won't come down off your throne to talk to nobodies like us. And now you come asking to be defended! For what? It's the truth – people like you belong on the dungheap of history!"

"In a liar's mouth, even the truth turns to lies!" Andrievs hits back, and goes away.

Unexpectedly, he catches sight of Vanda. She is standing by Grand Hill's box. In the half-light her face is pale, her eyes turned toward the horse.

"I gave you a present of the 'bourgeois' Čaks' poem, I wanted to show you a book in English! You told them all that, did you?"

"I only told Helēna. I had no idea that she could do something like that! My friend… Forgive me, please!"

"Where did Kazarka's leg-protectors get to? You were the only one who saw."

"I wasn't the only one. Loginov led Kazarka off the track to the stables."

"Loginov, not Brencītis?"

"Yes, Loginov! I had just arrived with Sud'ba. Maybe I disturbed him and he didn't have time to hide them straight away…"

"That explains a lot… Although – what are we left with? I don't want to make you choose. Be happy!"

He sets off, following his nose.

Of course he ends up at Nona's, and spends the evening drinking with the crippled half-man and his girlfriend.

He tells them eagerly about his favourite book – Lewis Carroll's *Through the Looking-Glass, and What Alice Found There.* Andrievs likes the English language, English concepts and the English character, which is such a strange contrast to *nonsense* – with its various strange creatures, clodhoppers and the author's flights of fancy. Before the war, everyone who wanted to keep up their own style was mad about *nonsense.* It was a characteristic of Padegs, of the turbulent artist Romans Suta, of the vagabond Irbīte.

"See, reality even comes into our simple fairy tale!" Andrievs explains in bad Russian to the invalid, standing on tiptoe, conducting with his hands. "In a poisonous lethal form like a cobra, which strikes quickly! Or like fly-agaric, whose spawn slowly spreads under the moss… Da da da dum – strike up the band! We're all behind the glass – the Red King and the White Knight are leading the parade, Tweedledum and Tweedledee have joined the party in countless numbers and are holding mad duels, the little shops are bare, and the shopkeepers are talking sheep… Just like in Renaissance times, it's popular here to play chess on huge chessboards, living people take the place of the chess-pieces, only the game is even more absurd. The pawns are moving like knights, but the knights only imagine that they're knights – they've long been consigned to the abattoir or to Siberia. The pieces make moves that they think they're doing themselves, but no – there's an invisible hand… Da da da dum! The stakes are lower than low – survival. Only one character is just as in the story – the girl! A clear-headed, pure girl, who wants to know everything and take part in it. And most importantly, a *thinking* girl…"

The ugly strumpet laughs as if tickled: "A girl," she brays , "a *thinking* girl!"

"Here behind the glass, words have long been replaced by word-play, that's why it's hard to pronounce them… But the eternal mystery is the Red Queen. Who is the Red Queen?"

Drink is having its effect and it seems to Andrievs that there's no more important question in the world. He blubbers vacantly at Nona's breasts: "The Red Queen has drowned in the Daugava…"

"And so what about Stalin? Will he die too?" asks the half-man, jeering.

"He'll die too!" Andrievs bangs his fist on the table.

"And Beria?"

"Beria will die after him!"

The two of them clink glasses, and with one gulp, empty their tea-glasses of vodka. For Nikolayevna this is too much; she says she'll call the militia.

Andrievs' envelope of prize-money is often pulled out of his breast-pocket. The half-man's friends gather round, a few unknown passers-by sit down too, with swarthy faces like trolls, and jingling medals, leaning in ever closer to Andrievs in the yellow light of the lamp. He is generous, treating them all, right and left – Satan's prize has to be drunk away! The toothless mouths are all screaming something at once, they sing, they smoke, they want to drink to brotherhood and kiss, until finally Andrievs feels he's stinking…

He forces his way out of the drinkers' embrace, he wants to go home. He takes a couple of steps and falls on his face, tries to get to his feet – and falls back. All he understands is that, if he holds onto the wall, he can reach the crossroads, where the militia are on duty.

In this state he is received by Marija at the front door and she carefully leads him to his bed.

He falls into a black dreamless sleep, drunk as a lord.

The next morning Andrievs forces open his sticky eyelids and lingers for a moment in another world. The juices of life slowly return to his heart, the light stings his eyes mildly, his breathing wheezes in his chest – dirty, hot and shallow. Everything that happened dawns on his memory.

He drags himself to the kitchen and drinks half a bucket of water. Then he plunges his head into the remainder and snorts like a horse.

Gulping some roasted beet coffee from a big jug, Andrievs goes over to the window. Outside the rusty window-ledge the wind is whistling, and the sun looks on, pale and severe, as if red with weeping.

What is Andrievs? Is he still a trotting jockey?

He sits down on the floor beside his suitcase and opens it. Palmer's book of poetry. Between its pages, crumpled letters.

Even when his father had just brought that book back from America, it lay at night under Andrievs' pillow, and every word seemed full of strange sensations. Similar feelings steal over him as he wanders in a graveyard, reading the inscriptions on the headstones.

Walter Butler Palmer was a breeder of racehorses, a jockey and a poet. He died in 1932 at the age of 71 in an accident on the track.

His father had met Palmer several years before Palmer's death and was enchanted by this man's spiritual power. He always recalled Palmer's face – like a root, he said, a pine-root, bright and at the same time tightly twisted like a rope. His father was surprised at how similar those two places were, on opposite sides of the globe – the dunes on the east coast of America were just like Kolka in Latvia! Just like Kolka, so it was at Run Hill Dune – huge white rising dunes of sand, whose name was later carried to Latvia by a horse bought there, at the confluence of two powerful streams. Jātnieka kore, or Rider's Ridge, is the largest of the four remaining great dunes on the outer banks of the coast, remembered in many stories and sayings about the coastal sandbanks. The name *Kolka* arose from an exclamation of the Livonian grave-robbers, the so-called "foot-turners" – *kuol ka!* – "die now!" There is also the story of Blackbeard the pirate, saying that the ancient inhabitants of the little town of Klepergalva, or Nag's Head, used to suspend a lantern from the neck of a mare and do a circuit at night along the Rider's Ridge. Sailors on a passing ship, thinking that the lantern-light came from a port, approached the coast and ran aground. The next morning the local people would go to the beach to collect goods washed up on the shore from the shipwreck. That is how the town names of Rider's Ridge and Nag's Head came about.

Andrievs turns over a page. On yellowed squared paper – his own clumsy attempts to translate. The addendum to the translation releases old feelings, memories of a crepuscular room, the atmosphere that prevailed there. He sniffs the paper. The text is magical as an attestation of dedication, only the writer knows the reason for every crossing-out, and the ravines of doubts that are often hidden by a deleted word.

The horse*

The horse is the thing;
You may have the thrills
That come with the gasoline,
You may have the spills
And the pace that kills,
In your auto or flying machine,
For the flier that flies

In the vaulted skies
Must come to earth if his engine dies,
But the fire that lies
In a horse's eyes
Is the spark that lives and intensifies,
So here's to the horse – THE KING.

In his childhood, riding his bicycle along the sandy Zirņu Street, he readily recognized the tracks of the rubber tyres of the heavy haulier or carrier as Gustavs. The carters speeding along Andrejosta to Katrīndambis loved to flick the boys with their whips deliberately, but Gustavs was a great friend to the boys. Gustavs was the only one who owned a dray with all four rubber tyres. The other rubber-tyred ones were only on the back wheels, and the rest had all wheels on metal hoops, which rattled nastily on the pavement, and on a sandy road with a heavy load sank in the ruts and annoyed the horse. Gustavs always greeted the boys in the Riga fashion: "I is a Riga man!" And he even called his leather carter's apron, in the Riga way, a *širce*. But the main thing that distinguished Gustavs from the others was his horse. Ordinary draymen had *zirģeļi* nags, mostly bought in the countryside for the price of the leather and just skin and bone, having worked their whole lives, while the *ardeņi* steeds of the heavy hauliers, even badly fed ones, looked grand. Such a one was Gustavs' huge, sun-warmed Princis, with his white mane. The drying-rooms on Šarlotes Street froze, and the warehouses had a hitch-bar, where the draymen waited for deliveries from customers, having a quick drink. There for the first time in his life Andrievs glimpsed the vagabond artist Irbīte – he was drawing Princis, who was gnawing the hitch-bar from boredom. Looking over his shoulder, Andrievs stiffened – he seemed to see before his eyes an image on cardboard from long ago, a pastel drawing by the artist's hand.

As he sketched, Irbīte liked to chat to the boys, telling them that he liked pastel drawings on a black background, because then you had to get light out of the dark. In all other forms of painting, the light has to be submerged into the black.

Andrievs still didn't really understand why, but he knew that he also liked this process. Princis was the first subject of his sketches. Inspired by Irbīte, the boy tried to emulate in pencil the horse's magnificent muscles, like loaves. When Princis put his tired foot forward, the pattern of shadow changed, and he had to start again.

The times were such that Andrievs didn't become a painter.

But he did become a trotting jockey. Even though he had never especially wanted to. The horse had in a way become his father, the racecourse his refuge.

He browses through the well-thumbed, crumpled little book *Heart Throbs and Hoof Beats: poems of track, stable and fireside.*

In his high-school years, when Andrievs had already discovered the racecourse and met Antonija, Palmer's book became the first impulse for them to write to each other. They exchanged their letters in the hollow of an old ash-tree in the lane off Veseta Street.

They were romantic letters. Taking care not even to look at each other on the track or in the stables, in their letters they confided in each other and revealed themselves completely. Andrievs left his first translations and sketches in the hollow, Antonija her experiences and dreams. Antonija always signed her letters with another name: it was Crown Princess of Sweden for a while, and Countess Diana, even Antonie van Leeuwenhoek when the mood took her for joking and there was a lesson at the Sisters' school about the development of the microscope.

The letters were like a diary for a duet.

Andrievs has kept a score of Antonija's letters – the ones that had been hidden behind the torn lining. Only a few of his own – unsent, erased, rewritten.

There are also a few sketches of Run Hill Dune on squared paper.

Is the cup of sorrow being spared for Andrievs' horse at this moment?

Then why would anything be spared for his master?

At the racecourse, from the back door of the stables, Englards, having waited a long time, slips out, making signs in the air with his arms and whispering quietly: "Denisov's looking for you – get away somewhere!"

"Where is there for me to go?" laughs Andrievs. "Sign on at the Ministry of Forestry, become a thief?"

He goes to the office and looks in at the director's room. Denisov, in a pale shirt, like a cloud of mist, is spread out under the oil painting of a Russian *troika,* with its exuberant colours.

"Why didn't you come straight to me, instead of the stable?"

"But I always do that!" replies Andrievs. "I didn't know you were looking for me."

"Take a seat at the desk."

Andrievs sits down in the empty chair by Eizens' desk. He takes up Palmer's little book which, as he was leaving the house, he'd slipped into his inside pocket, as if expecting to have to wait.

Denisov's telephone rings.

"Yes, he's arrived."

The director says: "Go outside! They're waiting for you in the stairwell."

Andrievs enquires: "Do you remember, Pyotr Gavrilovich, that you gave your word of honour as an old Bolshevik that if I was in danger…"

"Out!" screams Denisov, spitting out his dentures. "Still expecting honour, are you? You've brought shame on our Hippodrome!"

Andrievs goes away quickly, so that the red-faced man won't have an apoplexy.

Standing by the stairwell are two unknown men. One of them asks Andrievs' surname, indicates a badge on his lapel, and says: "You are under arrest. Follow me."

The man walks ahead, the prisoner behind him, and behind the prisoner is another Cheka man. A black limousine is waiting in the street.

Andrievs perceives every tiniest crack in the cement steps, and after that every tiniest frozen spring streamlet on the pavement. The world has crumbled into fragments as in a kaleidoscope, it is no longer a single big whole. It occurs to him that maybe it's like this when you're dying. This fragmentation, the slowed-down course of time, and against that, the brain working at breakneck speed.

They walk past Englards, who, with his veined arms, clutches an invisible bottle of ink to his chest. The old baron's eyes are an indescribable reflection of his feelings – weariness and despair – as if observing a conflagration.

Andrievs reassures him with a look. Hundreds and thousands of different nationalities have walked this same path of disintegration, martyrs known and unknown, who have disappeared without trace or memory.

They walked, and Andrievs will walk.

The walkers climb into the black car, vanishing into the soft bed of leather, and after a short while the car stops in front of the notorious Corner House.

Andrievs is led up to the second floor, and left alone in some empty office. Looking around him, once again he takes out Palmer's little book of poetry.*

> Did you ever, dear reader, really love a horse? Have you been one of those fortunate mortals who have lived a portion of their lives out in the gorgeous freedom of God's open country? Have you ever as a child confided your joys and sorrows to a pony or poured out to some equine friend, tried and true, the anguish of your soul? Have you ever looked into those great, limpid, hazel eyes when all the world seemed against you and read therein the promise to share your successes and reverses through the sunshine and shadow of life? If so, then there has come to you that supreme satisfaction that comes from an intimate association with man's best friend, a satisfaction which can not emanate elsewhere and which all the mechanical things in Christendom can not produce.
>
> I have come to look with compassion upon those unfortunate individuals into whose lives there has never come the lasting influence of AN OLD ROAN MARE; possibly she was as white as the drifting snows that hid the hedge rows in winter; mayhap she was as black as

> the cawing crows that voiced a vigorous protest at your untimely intrusion; perchance she was the color of your own chubby hands in butter-nut time. Be that as it may, a memory of her faithfulness and constancy has abided with you on down through the years and prompted you to purer motives and higher ideals. Undaunted by heat or cold, she served you on festive occasions, and brought succor and relief in the hour of your affliction. Through the inky blackness of the night and against the fury of the tempest, the old mare brought you home, where warmth and comfort and loved ones awaited your coming, and where her deeds and the deeds of her progeny were an oft-told tale. The ingenuity of man may devise other methods of tilling the soil; uncertain devices will emancipate our animals from the drudgery of menial labor, but time can not efface the record or dim the achievements of those sturdy, faithful steeds whose service so largely aided and abetted the pioneers in the development of this great country, and so to their memory and to the friends of horses everywhere, this book is respectfully dedicated.
>
> *Walter Butler Palmer*

Occupied in this way, Andrievs sits for an hour or so in the office.

The arresters return and lead Andrievs to a cellar, handing him over to a quite fearsome-looking guard. She is a two-metre tall woman dressed in a grey quilted jacket, riding-breeches and box-calf boots. An oval face with stiff features and hair tied in a rat-tail. The woman is still young, but her hair is already old. She comes up so close that the acrid odour of her body can be sensed, she makes him stand astraddle and explores the crevices of Andrievs' body, searching for a weapon. She shoves him to the cattle-pen side of the cloakroom.

"Get undressed! Trousers too!"

Andrievs stands completely naked in the pen, and watches while the woman cuts the buttons and elastic bands off his clothes with a long knife at a metal table.

Then she gropes him once more. For a moment he enjoys the clipped tail of her hair on his fingertips like a precious cloth. Andrievs turns away.

"Just write – write out your chit, my beauty!" booms the guard bleakly, tearing the rubber band out of her hair. "Give it all back, is that clear?"

Her large cold hands slide down his naked thighs, exploring. Andrievs pushes the guard away.

"*Popitka nye pitka, a spros nye beda!* Nothing ventured, nothing gained!" She sniggers shamelessly in his face, and it is even worse than a scream, so diabolical.

The guard tosses him his clothes and makes him dress.

"Get moving!" she commands brusquely.

His braces are confiscated, his trousers won't stay up with just a hook; Andrievs holds them up by hand. He walks along a corridor covered in red carpets. The air is full of dampness and fumes, it stinks just like the guard – of long-term communal premises and unwashed linen. On both sides he can see black padded doors of cells. The two of them stop by one of the cells. The guard unlocks the door and makes Andrievs go inside.

He is dumbfounded – the room is thronged with naked men.

"Hello!" a student calls out to Andrievs. "Come right inside and get undressed. They're taking us to the bath-house."

The guard closes the door. The key squeaks in the lock. There's just one mouthful of air here for each of them.

After washing right there in the cellar all the prisoners are called to a little room, where a Cheka doctor and a young nurse in a white robe carefully inspect and record each of them.

The officer lifts up their arms, looking in their armpits for tattoos of the Legionaries. He studies the left-hand side with its burn-mark. However, he asks no questions, only writing down his observations in his document. Finally, with rubber-covered fingers, the nurse goes into his anus, and Andrievs may leave.

He spends the night with his steam-bath-mates in the big cell. A guard unlocks it and lets down nine metal beds from the wall. There are twenty prisoners, the beds go to the older men, so the others are forced to sleep on the concrete floor. There are no sheets, or pillows or blankets, you have to make a pillow of your clothes. The cell is brightly lit.

"Don't cover your faces or the lamps!" commands the guard as he goes. *"A to kapzdyets!* Otherwise shut up!"

The heat and the light are gradually exhausting them. When the first attempts to get to sleep have failed, Andrievs sighs: *"Une Saison en Enfer"*…

"Quiet, poet!" calls another man. "There's a little eye in the door, and other ones you can't see in the wall next to the door, for questioning…"

"I didn't say anything that was worth questioning!"

"The main thing for them is confession, because confession shows the accused is guilty," whispers a slightly older man. "Don't confess to anything! They'll do everything possible to get you to confess, and after that the evidence or the lack of it won't change anything. From the start you're offered the chance to confess freely, and sign the indictment for attempting to 'undermine Soviet power.' If not, you'll face rotting with the polar bears…"

"How come you know all this so well?" another one calls out. "Maybe you're a 'cell agent'?"

"Don't talk rubbish!" says the first one, offended. "I was here in forty-one."

"Then you ought to know how kindly they treat you here. When they start kicking, beating, pulling out your nails, all your advice will be gone with the wind."

"That's for everyone to know – I know it from experience," the first one justifies himself. "They threatened me that my family would suffer, and that put the wind up me… Now, after the war and the camp by the Amur river, I have no family, I have no fear."

Andrievs would give anything for a glass of water. His hangover is burning his stomach, and the heat in the cell is unbearable. A toilet barrel is set up in a corner of the cell. The sour fumes of excrement are soon mixed with the heat.

In this state, stupefied with the heat and the stinking fumes, in the morning Andrievs is conveyed in a lift to one of the upper floors – to the investigator.

Holding up his trousers with his hands, he stands before Major Mark Krop.

"Citizen Radvilis, good morning!" he smiles broadly. "Hold your trousers with one hand! The other behind your back."

Then he indicates a chair at the end of the table.

On the table next to Krop are arranged Andrievs' personal possessions and his suitcase.

While I was sitting in the empty room yesterday they were ransacking Englards' flat, Andrievs realizes.

Antonija's letters have been translated and copied. The cigarette packets have been ripped up and the cigarettes tipped into a paper bag. There is also Palmer's little book, confiscated by the guard-woman. Nothing special there, little trifling things, soiled nothings – a child's first shirt, father's shaving set, mother's wedding ring carved out of a silver five-lats piece, but now dulled. Still shiny is Run Hill Dune's horseshoe – a worn little trotter's shoe, with broad nail-holes, slightly deformed.

In this nightmare from which it's impossible to wake, Andrievs can only clearly make out the decanter – four-square, of thick glass with a stopper. It stands on the table in front of Krop, full to the brim with water.

Examining the material, Krop raises his eyes to Andrievs for a moment.

Then he leans forward and asks: "Where is the Postwoman?"

Andrievs is enlightened – so that's what they want!

That is why everything has happened that has been poured over Andrievs' head lately! And any knowledge, even the gloomiest, is better than not knowing. Desperate, and at the same time relieved, the accused lets out a wheeze from his throat: "Drink!"

"You'll drink afterwards," Krop replies benevolently. "Where is the Postwoman?"

Fortunately the last of his common sense has not deserted Andrievs. He remembers *Through the Looking-Glass, and What Alice*

Found There. Of course that isn't the question! This is a word-game.

So, with his dry mouth, he doesn't whisper "I don't know," but asks: "Who is the Postwoman?"

Checkmate.

Dissatisfied, Krop rubs his face with his stumpy fingers and lights a smoke.

"So we won't get around to drinking."

But at this point Andrievs makes a move with his knight.

He jumps to his feet, runs, and grabbing the decanter, drinks eagerly, in great gulps, protecting himself with his elbows. Only supernatural powers could prise the precious vessel away from him. With every mouthful the water refreshes him – suddenly Andrievs understands the miraculous tales of the water of life and death. It's no metaphor! Krop takes fright, and straightens himself up. For a brief moment Andrievs has the urge to strike. Now what would it be – whack! – across his red forehead! The Cheka man would collapse. Then he'd rip open the door and bolt outside – down the steps to freedom, on the streets of Riga.

Has Krop called out, or pressed some emergency button, is there a guard listening at the door – who knows? The guard's black rubber truncheon bruises Andrievs' neck and ribs. Krop indicates that that's enough. The prisoner is shoved back into his chair. The guard remains in the office, by the door.

His flesh is singed by the blows. For the few years of peace Andrievs has not been used to physical threats. If the Cheka succeeds and they know how, they will take this even further – to hell, where even your inner life no longer belongs to you, where confessions of what you have done and haven't done are mixed with nightmares and imaginings.

Krop compiles his report and leaves.

At first Andrievs is pleased to be sitting in an office – at least it is light here, though the windows are barred. But when sleep finally overcomes him, as painful and deep as floodwater, the guard rushes up to him and hits him with the truncheon. When that doesn't help and, having dropped off to sleep, Andrievs rolls off the chair, the guard rushes at him, swearing, and with a few kicks forces him to his feet.

This accursed time draws out slowly. Clouds gather behind the barred windows and wet sleet starts to fall, steaming up Stalin's family portraits on the wall in bluish shadows.

Instead of lunch Andrievs is shown the kindness of a trip to the toilet.

Then, more standing, sitting, beating, standing, beating…

In the evening, as the yellow lamps on the town's streets are coming on, Krop arrives. He no longer asks about the Postwoman, but starts from another point – surname, name and patronymic, date and place of birth, composition and location of family, a brief account of his whole life.

Had he worn a uniform, borne arms, taken Hitler's oath, and so on. Grinding round and round the subject, indefinitely.

Gradually Andrievs realized that the Cheka man doesn't know much about him. He has to know how not to get his answers muddled.

"So, in the Legion, you were nothing more than a combatant and a soldier in a unit whose job was to treat sick and injured horses?"

"Yes."

"You're telling me fairy tales! You must have been mobilised into the German army."

"I was a trotting jockey, I had a UK Schein* from the racecourse, but since it was no longer valid, I hid at the home of the keeper of my father's horse this summer."

"Not your father's horse, but Run Hill Dune, a stallion belonging to the Ministry of Agrculture!" Krop corrects him. "That's the same horse that is now at Gomel?"

"You know better where he is now," grins Andrievs, recalling the morning on the track.

"You didn't go into the *Schutzmann* units?"*

"Murdering hostages on the spot, unarmed people? That's not for me."

"Good. Go on."

"We've talked through it all once already…"

"I'll decide here what we've talked through and what we haven't!"

Silence.

"I've got plenty of time," says Krop, lighting up.

"Well," concedes Andrievs. "It happened because of the horse…"

"Let's start at the beginning – your father Jēkabs Radvilis owned the trotter Run Hill Dune before the war," Krop declares.

"Yes."

"In the first Soviet year he was nationalised under the Ministry of Agriculture of the LSSR. During the war he was periodically at the Hippodrome and with farmers in the country. At the beginning of 1944 you found out that other horse-owners were preparing to leave Latvia and travel to Germany, taking their best trotters with them. They wanted to talk you into going with them and taking Hill too."

"Yes."

"These were Reinholds and Georgs Beķeris?"

"Yes."

"You didn't agree to it. Why?"

Andrievs hesitates. He mustn't say he would have been happy to escape, but he couldn't because he was held up near the front line.

"It was too dangerous…"

"Go on."

"At that time Hill was with a farmer on the Anna estate. I did go there."

"How?"

"By bicycle."

"Which farmer?"

Everyone he mentions by name is threatened with the same fate as his own.

"I don't remember – it was over beyond Nītaure."

"What's the name of the farm?"

"Maybe Papardes… As the front was approaching, one day I got sent to a smith to make a wheel for the carriages – the Germans made the farmer go with the refugees. When I got there I found out that there had been a ROA group* on the farm, requisitioning horses for service on the front, and Hill had been taken. I got on my bike and set off to trace him. I found him to the north of Nītaure, where the military carriages that weren't needed for supplies had been transferred. About that time they had realized that Hill was no good for haulage. He was assigned to the abbatoir group. Luckily, there I spotted a two-horse wagon. I decided to yoke the two of them to it, him and Maška, because Hill had been there at Papardes with her. She was a carter's mare, very sensible, they'd been together through the summer. Hill was calmer with her. She also pulled in a pair, she was powerful. I showed my racecourse documents at the command point of Number 44 Grenadier Regiment."

"And they accepted you?"

"At first they laughed – any good for shooting? They said: if you're from the racecourse, then you can tell a horse's head from its tail, you've been told not to hit it on the arse. I was to write my application to the commander of Number 1 Company. Luckily the previous jockey had just taken to his heels."

"That is – voluntarily left his position?"

"At that time there were a lot of absconders, going into hiding."

"But you weren't intending to stand in the ranks of the fascist forces, sowing death and destruction, for the sake of a horse?"

"I was a battlefield jockey, a carrier of the wounded. Mobilization in the territories of occupied countries isn't lawful on either the brown or the red side – so what's the difference which side you're on?"

Krop is carefully writing down Andrievs' statements. For a moment he drums his fingers on the table, as if wanting to say something, then reconsiders, waves to the guard and lights up again. Andrievs is led away.

This time the guard leads him to a small but just as brightly lit and hot little cell, where on an open metal bed there sits an imposing grey-haired man in a dark woollen cassock. Sweat is streaming down his ruddy face. The two raise their eyes to each other.

"Jesus Christ be praised," says the old man.

"Forever and ever."

"Should we know each other?"

"You're Dean Viļums of the Madaliņa Catholic church in Jersika."

The old man nods.

"That I am. For three years under the Germans I was sitting in the Salaspils concentration camp for condemning the annihilation of the Jews from the church pulpit. And now I'm sitting here for speaking out from the same pulpit against excessive taxes on those who are counted as rich farmers." The dean wipes the sweat off his face with his hand and flings it onto the concrete. "But you – eat first, then we'll continue talking. Otherwise they'll take it away."

Placed on the bed are an iron mug and a bowl. In the mug, black tea; in the bowl, millet porridge. Andrievs falls on the miserly portion of prison food.

The Catholic church of Madaliņa at Jersika is located right on the bank of the Daugava, near Gospari. On the site of an old cemetery, the little church, built in the Romanesque style out of rubble, is extremely beautiful – like a mirage, floating airily in the sunshine over the secular world. Not far from the church flows the Svētavots, the Holy Fount, to whose waters miraculous powers have been ascribed for centuries.

"I was betrayed when I was praying in public for them during Mass."

"For whom?"

"For the women! Women plough and harrow with horses. Women go to the pine forest to fetch their quota of firewood. The war has taken away the men to God knows where – in directions known and unknown. The marshes of Volkhova, the so-called 'Courland Pocket', to camps in the west and the east. Others are hiding in the forest… The women are waiting; the work won't. But who is imposing the impossible taxes on them? In my congregation now you can count the women on your fingers. The prisons are overflowing with farm-women – young, strong ones, and old, incapable ones…"

The cell door bursts open, and a rubber truncheon is aimed at the shoulders of the seated men. *"Spat'!* Sleep!" roars the guard. "*Ne bazarit'!* Don't chatter!"

When the prisoners are placed slantwise, the guard unlocks the third and fourth beds. Another guard brings in a boy aged about fourteen or fifteen, and a thick-set man in a worn-out homespun suit.

Then the door shuts. The key squeaks in the lock.

The boy throws himself under his bed and falls asleep on the floor, with his coat under his head.

Andrievs, who has dozed during the day standing up, like a horse, is again burned out by the heat and the blinding light. Sleep can no longer be summoned. His mind, like an abacus, rattles away in memory through every word uttered by the investigator, considers his mistakes and counts up the ensuing replies.

The dean quietly mutters his evening prayers.

Andrievs is overcome by a strange lethargy; he doesn't know whether he's asleep or awake. Thoughts that start like a dream end like memories, and vice versa.

"Holy Mary, Mother of God, pray for us sinners, now and at the hour of our death. Amen," the priest's prayer rustles like a dry autumn leaf across the room.

Someone is standing in the corner of the cell, with a white, illuminated face.

"From my company?" guesses Andrievs, getting to his feet in a moment. At what time was a fifth man let into the cell? Had Andrievs really dozed off and not noticed?

"Where?" ask his cellmates, looking up from their sleeping-places.

The guards come in again; Andrievs' alarm is a good reason to exercise their muscles.

When the disturbance has quietened down, Andrievs slowly, millimetre by millimetre, turns his eyes toward the corner of the cell. Hope rises in his heart of once more catching sight, even in a nightmare, of his company commander.

But the features of the seated man are changing; in the dazzling light his face drips like candle-wax, and from his skull

Andrievs suddenly recognizes the sitting man – it's Pavārs! Paulis Pavārs: the first man to fall in the battle of More. A man whom life had allowed to live on for a little while, but death had long since swept from memory.

Why has he come? Is this Paulis' dream in which he dreams Andrievs, or is Andrievs dreaming Paulis?

It was Paulis. Known on the battlefield, lost on the battlefield. Andrievs draws his knees up under his nose, trying to recall him.

And that strong smell of marsh tea?

On the red pine tree, dripping with resin.

Company Commander

As dawn breaks, the division is hiding in its resting place.

Andrievs is sleeping on a horse-blanket with his head against the reddish trunk of a pine tree, with his knees hunched up to his forehead, curled up like an embryo in its mother's womb. He tries to snooze, but a hawk screeching somewhere high in the sky disturbs him.

As he closes his eyelids, his internal vision will not cease showing him a jerky black and white film of country roads in pale moonlight. He has travelled all night, with short breaks. Hard days have been spent where they disembarked, in combat with forward Russian units. Nītaure, More, and closer and closer to the Vidzeme highway, which is the aim of the massive Russian army push.

All around are the black outlines of the sleepers. They've been allowed to fall asleep on their feet, falling over their weapons. Company Number 1 of the 44th Grenadiers' regiment of the 19th Division. Smiling in their sleep, because they are the covering unit, still happy to have got out alive from the Kārzdaba dunes, that hell on earth, in the fearsome fire of the Russian artillery.

Andrievs tries to recall the position of the platoons in yesterday's battle, the nests of weapons, the postings. Useless – he has no memory. An empty slate, thoroughly erased by the bloody rag of war. The past and the future are knocked down and laid waste. In this situation the only permanent thing is the endless tension, battle by days and movement by night – map and compass, a pocket torch by the light of which appear dead-end roads, woodpile paths, marshy meadows, bogs, spruce forests, brushwood, pine-forests, woods, glades, stands of pine, sandy paths, footways, saplings, thickets… Houses abandoned by refugees with bereft chained dogs and wandering stray livestock. And his mouth tastes of dust and bloody salt.

Draught horses are at pasture on the hem of a marsh in the thick September fog. Andrievs catches sight of Run Hill. His fine russet head above the mist. Maška is there too. Rest is brief in this charnel-ground. They are always on the point of getting injured. Only the horses, unlike Andrievs, have no idea why they are drawn into this slaughter.

It's difficult to imagine a more contrasting pair than Hill and Maška. For a war-horse the work is pure punishment. The delicate and fiery trotter and the plodding, heavy draught mare. When Maška is shot at, in a dangerous situation, Hill, rushing forward, jerks the harness crosswise. Yet the front offers no choice.

He has never seen such a strange relationship between a mare and a stallion. There is nothing procreative or generative about it. The horses behave as if they were two tree-stumps on an island in a marsh, and when Hill leans his neck over Maška's, or Maška picks at Hill's mane over the shaft, there is nothing carnal, only a wish to calm herself, to be beside another sentient creature.

It's a little past six o'clock, and delicate curling beams spread out over the oily darkness. Under the mist the silhouettes of small pines in the marsh are fading. A couple of hours' snooze is needed before the German units draw in. But sleep is nowhere near, despite the exhaustion.

And that hawk too!

In the dawn light one can't make out whether the bird is sitting somewhere on a treetop or circling high over the marsh. Only the persistent ones – piu, piu! – like arrows with sharply honed tips, are wandering in the burnished light over the dozing forest.

The hawk screeches and screams – a coded message, a telegram – for whom, from whom, about what?

The marsh breathes coils of haze into the air. A light breeze rocks the frightened swathes, and slowly sweeps them along the bright horizon like stooping regiments of soldiers. Above the figures in the mist the hawks are wheeling in the clear azure; there are countless numbers of them, circling and screeching plangently, and the marsh subsides along with their suppressed wheezes, their dull sobs.

Andrievs wants to wake the sleepers, but he's afraid they'll think he's not in his right mind.

No-one around him is even raising his head.

Even the horses are standing serenely.

Maybe the battlefield will tell Andrievs alone what will happen today, through the hawks' mouths?

Is the message that Andrievs must fall? Today? Tomorrow? Maybe Pavārs? Afanasyev? Laizāns, Levi, Ikše? Or Spārniņš? Someone else? The battlefield knows. The ground is bloodthirsty. This apparently peaceful scene is already smacking its lips for blood. Just now a portion of young flesh has been stuffed into the maw of the marsh; time is inexorably, unavoidably thrusting it forward. Thousands of black sundews are excitedly trembling with the desire to swallow. This is an unusually warm autumn, but the blackness of the marsh is still spreading the sense of Hell, because down there under the moss is a quagmire of peat and water, dark, full of unknowing.

Andrievs touches his forehead and trembles from the coldness of his hands.

He mustn't go around examining the dying with cold hands, Antonija once told him.

They aren't dying yet. Only the sky above his head is as broad and white as a highway, and the horses stand immobile in the bright morning mist.

The company's runner and chief cartographer, Jānis Spārniņš, Andrievs' former schoolmate at Riga High School number 2, arrives unobtrusively. Noticing that Andrievs' eyes are open, he sits down on a mound and lights a cigarette for himself and Andrievs.

"We'll have to let Fritz' units through, you know, and we'll have to take up positions. And what's that unit up there looking down on us, a red one? The last units are about to go off. They got down in time… Vanished! They even took the artillery munitions with them. Not a single Fritz left on the whole front.

This will be a battle for the Latvians against the Russians, pure and simple, I tell you!"

They both sit quietly smoking. Over their heads, circling indecently low, roaring like bumble-bees, are the aircraft of the Russian reconnaissance force.

"Jančuk, another one, quick!"

"You're inhaling as if it's fresh air!" Spārniņš glances at the map, then stares at the marsh. "There, in front, across the marsh, is a trench-path left over from the First World War. They sent me to find out where it starts; they'll send a battalion over. In 'nineteen this is where the Fifth Zemgale Latvian Riflemen's Regiment under Jukums Vācietis fought it out. We learned about it in history lessons at school. What's that strange look for?"

"Can't you hear the hawks screaming too?"

"The hawks? Hawks scream in August; now it's September." Spārniņš walks away, but calls back from the mist: "Pavārs is looking for you by the draught-horses!"

Light as a bird, brittle as ice, Spārniņš crosses the waterfall. Walking over the mounds, he lifts his legs ridiculously like a heron, seeming to bend his knees in every direction. His blue-grey eyes behind the lenses of his thin glasses narrow as he laughs, into gleeful slits.

Good old Jančuk! How can he go on for months in battle conditions keeping such a clean uniform and shiny polished boots?

While others talk about girls, Spārniņš goes quiet and blushes.

Spārniņš' father, the businessman Hermanis Spārniņš, one of the founders of the Latvian Chamber of Trade, was arrested in Riga on 14 June 1941 and deported to Siberia. Only by a fluke were his wife and two children not at home; otherwise they would all have been consigned to oblivion.

The deportation deranged his mother's mind and made her go off after her husband. Jānis' sister had tracked down an elderly relative, who looked after Mrs. Rūta day and night. She collected her things for the journey to her husband and screamed that she couldn't die without seeing *it*...

What? An icy hell? A disappearance?

Hell, thought the mother, would be better than the empty space that the deportation had torn out of the family's living flesh. Jānis, unable to stand his mother's madness, lived elsewhere.

After a while, Andrievs goes off to the horses. A few long shafts of sunlight have thawed the mist around the cranberry-flecked hillocks of the marsh.

Hill stands with head bent down, indifferently, with every draught of breath quietly expanding his lean flanks. He doesn't seem to know that Andrievs is placing a blanket over him; only his pointed ears twitch and pin themselves back malevolently.

The war has healed Hill's nervousness, his ceaseless wish to go in a circle as he has always done at every stable where he has been. This decisiveness struck at Andrievs' heart.

He puts the nosebags around the draught-horses' necks. To Hill he gives some dark bread he has saved. He strokes Hill's neck, with its prominent veins.

"I'm taking you home," he whispers. "I promise."

Andrievs casts a quick glance over the sleeping men and the loaded carts – the draughts. Munitions supplies, transport for the wounded, provisions – those are draught jobs. The field-kitchen with the cooks, the slaughterhouse company, the weapon-maker with his workshop, the quartermaster with his store-cart, the clerk, the rations supervisor, the messenger, the communications officers, the machine gun staff – they're all Latvians. The Fritzes are saving their own skins. All along the front – twelve kilometres – not a single German unit. Abandoned for the Red dogs to tear apart.

As they left they took care to prepare everything – the positions are already erected. Trenches, bunkers, barbed-wire fences, minefields – everything prepared in time and by the rules. "We'll just deepen the machine gunners' positions," the company man explained yesterday, "the German regulations aren't good enough about that; the Russians always put their snipers in among the attacking lines, and the machine gunners get the bullets in the face..."

Andrievs seeks out his companion Paulis Pavārs, with whom, the previous evening, he'd talked about looking for Pavārs' father's house.

The senior sergeant in charge of supplies lets them go, and the two set off across the main road.

"I can't stand that pig, I can't, I can't!" roars Pavārs, barking with a congested throat, looking obliquely back at the senior sergeant. "When the Fritzes are next to us, he always screams at us in German, *Götterdämmerung!* He's sucking up to them, the damn dog. I can tell you something else – his friend Ēršķis, that first-class soldier, is the ultimate bastard, an accuser, an informer, a real arse-licker. He reports everyone who hasn't disembarked properly! After this they're sending him onto the attack, to certain death..."

"The company has been given new weapons. More fire-power for the German bone-saw – Ivan won't get anywhere near it."

"But more for the bone-saw to consume too. Supplies will be difficult, if the fighting goes on... It'll be hell here, it will be hell." Pavārs is panting at the back of Andrievs' head like Fate. "The Russians won't do any reconnaissance before the attack, they'll come straight over, thinking that they'll frighten people away."

The mist rolls along the ground like a heavy wet bath-towel. The distance smells intoxicatingly gently of smoke and milk. In the Pavārs' yard, under a great oak, whose bark is grey and streaked like a hunk of rye bread, branches have fallen. Other trees scatter leaves, but in autumn the oaks cast off twigs, red, hard, coppery plumes.

The path hasn't been swept. Full churns of milk on the steps. A cow is stretching its head by the wattle feed-lot.

Paulis presses the moulded clapper on the front door. An inviting warmth from the burned-out stove. The smell of bread. The lower part of the kneading-trough is still full of dough. All around in a circle there are beds with white pillows and striped blankets, the corners turned back. Entranced, Paulis wanders from item to item, touching them.

Peacetime life.

On the door-post, a notch cut by Paulis' knife, when he was still a herd-boy... He'd hang his cap on a peg. Over there, the corner is dark from Grandpa's spitting, where in old age he'd withdrawn, lost his mind and stopped washing… But around the stove is Mother's shadow, as she throws flour into the mouth of the oven, to check whether she can shove in some rye bread. The dough still preserves her fingerprints.

They must have left a few hours ago. On the wall a big clock ticks loudly in its cherrywood case.

Maybe half an hour ago.

Swept away… Empty.

The two of them go back outside. The tabby cat observes them with its green eyes.

"What will be left, what won't? What if it's a direct hit? Not one stone left on another." Paulis looks around, puts his weapon on his shoulder and shoots one of the sheep that are scattering in fright by the door of the byre.

Andrievs hears the hollow purring of the reconnaissance aircraft over the marsh. He remembers about the hawks, takes Pavārs' carbine and doesn't give it back.

"No need!"

Paulis doesn't listen, he's a ruthless destroyer of everything. With an axe he smashes the bottles in a cupboard. The beautiful big cheval-glass he shatters with the butt of his rifle. Milk spills out, the churns are sent flying. Breaking down the garden fence, he flings it with full force at the window!

"I won't leave a thing for those buggers! Whenever will the great day of revenge come upon them?"

"This isn't the French Legion, Paulis! This is your own land… Don't destroy things!"

Paulis recovers from his rage. He cuts off the sheep's head, expertly extracting the innards. He rolls up the carcass onto his shoulders and starts moving forward.

"At least we won't go hungry when we leave," says Andrievs, following behind.

"Now you're talking, Andžu! Good that the sergeant can't hear us, otherwise tomorrow morning we'd be going on the attack. We're straightening out the front, straightening it out, not retreating… Svilāns just brought in a bucket of honey. You heard how he takes the honey? With his head wrapped up, he pours water over the bees!"

In his mind's eye Andrievs suddenly sees Antonija, hiding a gun in a beehive. The pink dimples of Tone's cheeks in a snowfall and her ice-blue eyes. The red woollen scarf with long trails over her fair hair. She is looking at Andrievs with tenderness. This vision is so vivid, like a bright painting standing in front of Andrievs, framed in a misty morning.

"What are you thinking about? Why have you gone quiet?" Paulis calls out.

"I'm... about that trip to the church. That'll be a death trip again. Down by the Mergupe the bushes are full of friends of the Reds. It's hard for me with two horses."

"Let's hitch up my black one, to give yours a rest!"

"You're riding like Chapayev* – standing up under fire! You'll get the Iron Cross."

"The Iron Cross or a smashed face... No, not a smashed face, now I have a horse like that! It'll pull us out of hell – the one we caught at Skujene. You can do damage with one like that. When the machine guns are barking, he walks on two legs. I control him, this isn't his first time, I think. A proper war-horse. The main thing is, he's young. How old is your trotter?"

"He'll be fifteen."

"Oh, oh," moans Paulis, walking on with the sheep on his shoulders. "How do you look after him in this madness?"

"He looks after me."

"Well, look to yourself. If I were in your shoes I'd head for the forest. Yesterday the chaps were saying that the average life expectancy here, even for officers, is two weeks."

Paulis swings around and, before going onto the highway, takes one more long hard look back at his father's house, left behind in the distance.

"What if I stayed here?"

"Stay, Paulis. The war is over."

Bombed telephone poles, tangles of wires along the hazel-grove. Not a single human soul. A hawk is sitting on a haystack from last year, carefully observing the pair.

"*Legio patria nostra*," Paulis quotes the motto of the French Foreign Legion, and turns to go. "Don't pay it any mind – everyone goes all weak at the sight of their birthplace... You said yourself we're in Latvia after all, our own land, every inch of the land is ours. And how will you get along without me, going alone to the church?"

Meanwhile the positions are surrounded by barbed-wire fences and mined with anti-tank mines. There's febrile movement all around. Every company is allocated to bunkers according to taste and needs. The soldiers are in a good mood, because they've got to their places and can rest for a while. One Russian reconnaissance plane has been shot down, the pilot ejected, but they haven't managed to catch him. It's become clear why the Germans' movement along detours was done in the morning light this time. The enemy was deceived about the division's aims, but all roads except one are mined. Now the Reds are approaching along that road.

Paulis and Andrievs are sent to the church to fetch munitions. They hitch up Paulis' black horse.

The highways are full of refugees. Combatants are sitting in carts, going against the current. It's hard to struggle against the sniggering, against the people with demented eyes, not looking back, abandoning their homes. Their expressions are like drained mud, their children are as silent as stones, their horses are skittish, just as stupefied as the harnessed sheep.

Down in front of the church the road remains empty and broad. Faint crackling of machine guns is heard in the bushes, at first sparsely, but then gaining in force.

Paulis senses the imminent attack, jumps onto the cart standing up and lashes the black horse with the reins across his back.

"Hold on, Andžu!"

Andrievs doesn't hold on; at this moment his gaze is fixed on the clouds. The mist has risen into the air and been transformed into elephant-coloured accumulations over the crests of the maples, the tarnished green of the avenue of lindens. The white clouds are woven into the brocade of the dark-blue sky.

s moment might last an eternity.

y then does Andrievs understand what is going on. With its ears pinned back, the black horse is galloping as fast as it can. Does the horse sense that Death wants to take a seat in the cart?

The horse carries on up the hill, snorting among the whining bullets.

"Hurrah!" comes the roar of the Bolsheviks' attack from behind his back. The battle has begun, but it no longer affects the travellers.

"There is, there is a God in Heaven!" Paulis reins in the horse and sits back in the cart.

The ammunition is unloaded onto the ground.

In a ditch behind the church they can hear a horse.

Paulis happily slaps the black horse across his bony crupper.

"He's so ridiculous! You could say he has no fear. One time, going through the brushwood pell-mell, all the others have cleared off long ago, this one has his head in the air like a moose, he bends down into the bushes to check what's going on there… Or what about the time I'm going back early in the morning to the meadow – and he's sitting there! Sitting like a puppy, looking at me. I say 'Good morning! What are you sitting there for?' He looks at me, lowering his head – 'I'm sitting, yeah!' Ridiculous! What a joker."

The horse drinks water. His flanks are dilating rapidly. The black forehead. Veined skin and bloodshot eyes. A nameless horse. War changes everything.

They load the ammunition onto the cart. Now they have to get back.

On both sides of the bridge is a precipice, beyond which alluvial flood-land spreads out. On the north side, at the bend in the river, fighting is going on for every foot of mud. Pillars of artillery fire rise up high against the sky, together with sludge and trees, huge spruces flying through the air, roots and all. Machine guns are barking like dogs.

Every few moments the black horse rears up on his hind legs and then jibs, until the wheels with their load on the side of the cart slide down over the precipice.

In great somersaults the heavy cart, together with the horse, rolls downwards. Down by the river the black horse lies immobile in the tomb of its yoked load. Paulis, his arms outstretched, runs after it.

When Andrievs arrives on the scene, with a brief shot to the head the animal's sufferings are ended.

"*Coup de grace,*" says Paulis.

The black, shaggy legs point stiffly to the sky like a curse.

It's useless to try to cut through the straps or release the saddle-pad. The harness is soaked through with the incessant rain and the quagmire of war, made of good leather by a saddler in peacetime; it has constricted the horse.

The black horse's eyes fall into their sockets and his nostrils grow cold. The grimace of extreme agony on the horse's lips is more expressive than what one sees on the face of a dead soldier. Andrievs pulls his cap off his head.

"Who would have thought it?" says Paulis, as if in wonderment.

Then he nimbly inserts his arms up to the elbows in the half-open mouth between the yellowish bared teeth, cuts off the horse's still-hot tongue with all its root, and extracts it from his throat like a foamy fish.

"You think only about what you can eat!"

Paulis laughs, and cleans the sand and mucus off the horse's tongue with his knife.

"And what do you think about? Eternal love?"

"You're going to get it in the mouth soon! Earlier he saved your life, by the church."

"So what? I'd cut off his balls as well, but they've already been cut. I'd fry them on a piece of shrapnel – a delicacy! If I fall in the war, cut off my balls – you hear, soldier?"

"If yours haven't been cut off already too!"

"You should've been at Volkhova, matey, at Ostrov, Opochka or Zilupe. In my place you'd have been bored to death long ago! But how do you end it, how do you end it?"

The scattered ammunition has to be collected and brought up onto the road.

Climbing up over the crumbling gravel, Paulis measures against his shoulder a Panzerfaust flame-thrower fallen from the load.

"They say it's that new Panzerschreck grenade-thrower… Fuck, it's heavy. Andž?"

Andrievs doesn't respond. Temporary exhaustion. Paulis seems to him like a big silly child, amazed to have ended up in a war.

"Andžu, listen! Now it's stopped after all, just creep up and keep going, like a louse."

"What's up?"

"An animal really means more to you than a human?"

For losing the cargo and for swearing at the *Spiess* sergeant Pavārs will be sent to the *Stoss* attack – to the front line.

Andrievs harnesses Maška and Hill, and goes to collect the ammunition by the bridge.

Down by the river a black smudge is still visible. Who will bury him? Most likely the foxes and stray dogs, after that the rainfall.

He no longer encounters firing along the way. Returning, he discovers that in the afternoon there was a small skirmish of forward reconnaissance troops with a brief exchange of fire.

Since then everything has been quiet.

At the field kitchen they've lit a fire and boiled up the sheep that Paulis brought. In the trenches the men are eating and enjoying it. They're licking the fat from their fingers. The commanders have let them break out the vodka. Andrievs enjoys some from his dish at the edge of the garden and stares at the forest of graves, past which, blowing the yellowed leaves with his nostrils, Hill moves about among the crosses, as if searching for the past summer.

Meanwhile Paulis grandly holds aloft the bluish pike of the black horse's tongue with both hands. Might the animal's tongue have to be marinated with some herbs and roots, and smoked on some logs, to turn it into a tasty morsel? It makes the men's mouths water.

Through the occasional rumblings of artillery can be heard something like the noise of tanks. A messenger arrives from company command. About fifty Russian infantrymen and armoured carriers have been observed on the main road, transporting the infantry's heavy weapons.

The men are quickly ready for combat. Andrievs, having harnessed the horses, lingers on the ground shielded from bullets behind the school. The wounded will have to be transported to get first aid from the base hospital set up in the school at the back of the battalion's dressing station.

The forward group also returns with the news that Bolsheviks are approaching with a T-34 tank.

The tank is approaching about seventy metres from the forward combat positions. A few dozen metres more and it will run over anti-tank mines. The men with the flame-throwers are now waiting to be within firing distance.

But just then the tank stops.

Paulis is a grenadier. You can see him clearly from the school, sitting in a dug-out, turning his head with its bright helmet.

"Sit quietly!" Andrievs whispers, as if Paulis could hear. "Why are you always fidgeting?"

But now Paulis has got up, with the flame-thrower on his shoulder. He approaches within shooting distance of the tank. The primitive iron turret seeks its target and finds it.

A shot rings out, and Paulis is no more. With a direct hit the tank wipes out one life story.

All around there is deep silence.

On the first days there is still no artillery support, even the anti-tank cannon is silent, not being allowed to reveal the company's positions to the enemy's advance group.

After a little while a small Russian infantry group runs out and prepares for battle. The company's machine gun on the right flank lets them get closer, then mows the Bolshevik infantrymen into the dust of the road.

The tank retreats.

"The battlefield has taken its first life," cry hundreds of hawks, painfully striking across Andrievs' temples.

*

At that moment the door of the prison cell strikes against Andrievs' bed with a metallic slam. Two guards come in.

"*Podyom*! Up!" they shout. "*Vstat*! Get up!"

Andrievs stands dumbly in the row beside the others he still can't get out of his dream – his memories.

*

Soldiers carry the shattered Paulis in their arms and roll him up in the canvas from the cart. A dishevelled teddy-bear falls out of Paulis' breast pocket.

Andrievs carries the deceased out to the back of the Vibotnes field hospital and lays him out temporarily under a currant bush. Paulis will have a place in the Brothers' cemetery with his plush talisman. He will have a plaque with his dates of birth and death, and a memorial inscription. But if the Bolsheviks come back into power, he won't even have that.

Andrievs rummages among the empty, abandoned houses of the village. He is looking for pillows. His fellow combatants are either tired or bored, and they laugh at Andrievs: "Are you looking for Mummy's tit?"

"Ten days," murmurs Andrievs, confused, putting his hand on Hill's forehead. "Ten days."

He thinks about mothers every time a grown man cries like a baby, calling for his mother, in his cart. In his mind's eye he sees an ephemeral shadow bending over each wounded man. This is the consummation of a mother's task – to be drawn into this illogical, senseless world. Reunification, as at the moment of creation. Any mother would scold a driver who didn't find a pillow to put under her son's head in his hour of suffering… Andrievs can testify to such sights in his battle-carts. He's only afraid that he'll be seen as deluded. He's already regarded as obsessed by horses, the only thing on his mind.

So therefore he is quietly collecting pillows, collecting them like a German. Many, many pillows. Big and small, of down, wadding and wool. Some still bear the impression of the head of their sleeper. Or the breath from the mouth of a baby. Andrievs piles up the pillows in the cart, and from the cart he tosses them into an empty corner of the dressing-station set up at the school.

An impressive pile. The command is to keep hold of More for ten days – many pillows will be needed.

*

At this moment he gets a painful prod with a rubber truncheon over the ear.

"*Ne spat', ti blya!* Don't sleep, you bugger!"

It's good that he's out of it. If he'd remained in his memories, he'd get a smack on the nose.

The guards are only imitating alarm, falsely so as not to let them sleep. Maybe it's an order. Or maybe they're keeping themselves awake because they're bored.

The door closes again. But this time there aren't even any memories. Andrievs collapses onto his plank bed like melting snow. Bare walls, a bare bulb, heat from the crackling heating pipes.

"Where are you from?" he asks the boy in a whisper, looking down.

"From Nurmiži."

"What's your name?"

"Gatis."

"What are you doing here?"

"They say I've been supplying food in the forest," Gatis whispers. "But there aren't any Forest Brothers left there! After the war my father went into the forest, but later he volunteered at Cēsis, when they found their bunker and shot four others dead. He hasn't come home, he's probably been sent off to the polar bears… I'll hold out. Good that they've left Mum alone, she's desperately sick."

"Nurmiži – is that near Sigulda?"

"Yes."

"Why are you sleeping on the floor?"

"My uncle and I were jockeys. The Russian army ordered us to do ten days' corvée work, collecting and burying the dead. They all needed to be brought together, the ones that were shot on the front line. We had these low grain-carts, seven or eight inside, and then on to the graveyards. We weren't allowed to bury anything – not a horse, not a cow, not a German – until the Red Army men had been buried. So what do we do? We're not going to just go past them ten times. There was a whole week of fighting, and the ones that fell on the first days got mixed up. We had those Germans by the braces, but the Russians, though, by the straps, the belts… The ones that fell on the last days, you could grab them by the arms, by their clothes, but the ones from the first days – they already had worms in them… You boil up the ashes in lye, otherwise you can't get the terrible smell out of their clothes. At night you couldn't get to sleep, you had to scream. That's why I can't sleep in a bed – I'm afraid I'll fall out."

"Did you run away?"

"What else? The Germans were driving everyone out of their houses in a zone twenty kilometres from the front. It wasn't that they were much interested in the people, Dad said – the Germans only want to get hold of the animals, and if they don't drive out the farmers, they'll hide their animals and the Germans won't get hold of meat… We hid under the rocks by the Gauja river. There were three or four families of us there. There was a running spring there, you could give the animals water, cut down oats in the fields. The Germans burned down about fourteen houses up by Nurmiži, to have a bit of ground for fighting. My auntie was lying injured at home – she was burned to death. Afterwards I collected her bones in a coffin and kept it in the barn. The hillside was cut bare, the Russians came from Cēsis and from Nurmiži too. The Germans were sitting quietly with their bone-saw. A Russian fired a pistol from their side – hurrah, *za rodinyu!* For the Fatherland! So they throw their greatcoats onto the barbed wire and get over, again shouting, hurrah, *za Stalinu!* For Stalin! And they jump into the trenches, but the Germans are waiting for their moment and mow them down… It was mad there. After that, Dad sent me on home, to look and see if anyone was left alive or not. On the way a Russian officer wanted to shoot me, because I was wearing a knitted shirt exchanged with a German soldier. '*Ti nyemetsky fashist!* You're a German fascist!' I said: '*Nye fashist ya!* I not fascist!' Just a *fascist*, good that another officer winked at me – I cleared off..."

The cell door opens: "*Na bukvu 'K'!* With the letter 'K'!"

The boy waves his hand and goes off.

Over the next days the four of them start to understand the system at the Corner House. Interrogation takes place at night, but if a person has been questioned all night, then they won't let him sleep even in the daytime, they leave him to stand in the investigator's office and keep a guard standing by or send him to his cell. In each cell there's a bucket for a toilet. Once a day the prisoners are led to the toilet, and then they have to carry this bucket and empty it.

After several days like this, any sense of reality has vanished.

What happens is so absurd, and the interrogator's questions so senseless, round and round, that the only reality is memory.

*

The main battle line stretches along the slope of the hillside.

In the darkness beyond the distant field, like a rosy spot in the twilight, the Bolsheviks' heavy automatic weapons are ceaselessly firing. Over the field the wind thrusts the torn clouds. It isn't raining, yet the wind has the force of a storm.

At three o'clock in the morning a communications check at the local school, the company command post, is scheduled.

"Legionaries! The companies are not at full strength, because during the battles in Vidzeme province we have suffered losses, but morale is high. Everyone must be responsible for himself and those he holds dear. We are in Latvia, our own land; every foot of ground here is ours. Again the bloody hands of the Bolsheviks are reaching out for the lives and property of our own. We have only one course – to fight. That will decide whether we will survive as a nation or die in the Siberian tundra."

Andrievs is standing outside by an open window, listening to the commander's speech and smoking, along with many others who have been unable to squeeze into the school classroom.

"Our positions are suitable for defensive fighting – the enemy's main roads are clearly visible from our side. Before the main battle line lies Gulspurvs, a bog which will create great difficulties for the enemy if he tries to attack with tank forces. The divisions are crowded into a very narrow area, so they will send only two infantry regiments into battle; three will remain in reserve for the division."

The school is of two storeys, and the window-sills are a metre wide, the walls built of split stones, thick and compact. Infantry weapons are unable to shoot through it.

"There are telephone connections to every platoon commander; they're backed up by radio transmitters. On the front lines there are signallers with walkie-talkies from the artillerymen and grenadiers. The first time in all the battles of Vidzeme that we have such good communications with both platoons and headquarters. The messenger group functions as a reserve, which in case of need is used as an assault group and armed like the platoons, with bone-saws and other weapons."

Andrievs leans in beside Jančuks, who is listening, his elbows pressed against the windowsill.

"Do you know about Pavārs?"

"Yes. Poor devil. His nerves gave out."

The commander continues: "The first aid point is located on the southwest side of the school. During battle, aid will be given by medical staff from the 1st Orderly Company. We only have three combat riders left – Ērglis, Akmens and Radvilis. Radvilis, as you know, with his two horses is standing in for three."

At this rare joke, the men take the opportunity to snigger. Andrievs casts a glance backwards, where in the lean-to shed he glimpses Hill's head hanging low.

"The first three days will be the hardest, because the ammunition situation for intense combat is completely insufficient. We will defend ourselves with only light infantry weapons and in hand-to-hand combat. I don't want to make fine speeches; everyone knows his duty. Battle experience dictates its own rules. The main thing is: we must hold these positions until 5th October. Now you have rested, I hope the night will be peaceful. May God protect you!"

It is not sleep at all that overcomes Andrievs in the dirty room, littered with straw and human excrement, but a choking sack.

The Vibotnes house has been abandoned for quite a while now, the room long unheated and damp, like an empty well. For the first moment he is quite stunned, not understanding why he is in a well, or whether it is morning or evening streaming greyly through the window. Then he recalls the commander's speech, the hundred grammes of vodka offered afterwards, and understands that for a couple of hours he has been as if submerged in water, and yet he hasn't been able to get the rest he longs for. His heart is working even harder, as if after a huge burden, while he, eaten up by lice, scratching and wobbling, gets to his feet.

A new morning has jerked back into this world. The floor rattles with the men's boots and shoes. Brooms sweep clouds of dust into his face, brushing the rubbish toward the exit.

"Stand up on your hind legs now!" cries Vilis Ērglis, throwing bricks onto a pile so as to barricade the lower panes of the window. "The Russian's woken up too, you hear?"

Andrievs is already able to discern the intensity of a battle from the sound of it. He quickly perceives that at the moment it is only getting started. The Russian grenadiers rumble lazily, firing at the tracks.

On the threshold he lights up. Smoke curls into the fabric of the day; Andrievs starts to regain his orientation in space and time.

See the fresh morning in the half-light. It must still be September!

See Andrievs' horses in the apple orchard. Andrievs calls to them, they raise their heads and look back. With a soft thud, red apples tumble over the horses' backs, as in some other, peaceful life that exists right beside him.

With a rough jute bag Andrievs rubs Hill's temples and nose. He cleans Maška and Akmens' dun mount, as well as Ērglis' squat bay mare. He takes two buckets in each hand and goes to fetch water. In front of the school is a well with a pump. You have to go there to pump water for your own needs and to water the horses.

Andrievs walks past the parish hall, then along the path. The avenue of birches is sparse. The path is strewn with yellowing leaves. In peacetime, a few steps, nothing. But now, every few moments mortars are falling on the path.

With a hollow wail, the mist parts, and in a low flight over the birch avenue appear two enemy aircraft. Andrievs jumps into the ditch and lies prostrate. He digs his face into the mud, and for a moment his whole body is absorbed into the ground. It is a brief but intense moment of weakness – the temptation to let go and become part of that ground.

Burning bullets are fired from the aircraft. Right next to them the school's woodshed catches fire. The firewood is dry, it burns with a crackle like a midsummer bonfire. He quickly realizes that at the moment he is only getting ready. Cautiously Andrievs moves his buckets and walks along the ditch to the well.

The soldier who has been pumping water before him is bent over his bucket. Andrievs conceals himself out of reach of the firing, behind the well-frame, dragging the corpse over to him. That's Spārniņš! As tidy and well-groomed as ever. Maybe only injured? Andrievs searches for a pulse. There is none. Nor does he have a legionary's badge around his neck – he must have thrown it away because of the lice that love to nestle around it. Blond hair, the parting on the left. Eyes closed, seems to be asleep, because no wound is visible. Even the glasses intact. Andrievs turns his friend over, finally noticing a small wound between the brows. A drop of blood, the size of an awl-stab, and yet some stray splinter has brought the boy his death.

Together with a hot moisture in his eyes, for one moment of deep sorrow Andrievs' world is dissolved into a realm of distorting mirrors.

But there's no time for sorrow – the Reds' aircraft are howling in the clouds again.

A couple more times Andrievs covers the difficult distance to the well and back, until the horses are watered and the order comes to go and fetch the wounded. He drives the pair behind the school.

The orderlies are carrying a piece of burned raw flesh that was once a man.

"Corporal Akots, from operational command. Take him alone, check that no-one is looking, he's in great pain."

Orderly Vilciņš passes Andrievs the corporal's cap, full of singed personal belongings.

A belt buckle, a badge in a leather pouch, a rosy crystal bead, a cupronickel cigar-case engraved "Riga 1914".

The wind whips out of the cigar-case a yellowed, dirt-smeared piece of squared paper – Andrievs examines it. These are the 'bullet words' – a soldier's mother's writing in blue ink and a shaky hand:

"God's promise to him who believes the book that he will truly see no bodily harm and will not suffer. I commend all spears and wounds to the Lord. Bear witness that no fatal spear can do any harm. God the Father will stand by you in all your sorrows. M.T.D.I.L.T.P.D.N.K.L.D.F.T.H.I.W.M.D.ch.D.L.Z.L.U.ch.xAmen*. These are the words confirmed by God. These are holy words for men."

On the other side of the page is a hastily written, uncompleted poem.

Andrievs encounters the mute gaze of Akots. The eyeballs of his burned face seem strangely white, but the expression in that gaze says nothing, because there is no more face. Andrievs hurriedly covers the helmet in the cart. The orderlies lay the injured man on pillows, which gradually turn red, as if steeped in currant juice, while the victim grows ever paler. They have to travel uphill past the main battle line along a dangerous road, shot at by mortars. Every few moments the artillery fire comes closer. After every explosion the horse's skin twitches nervously as in a time of horseflies.

"Now we need to go, not just dance, brother!" Andrievs assures him.

Pulling on the reins, he makes the pair walk slowly, although the bullets are whining around them all the way to the battalion's field hospital. He feels the wounded corporal's pain and the gaze of his closed eyes in his back like precisely aimed bullet-holes.

At the crossing, where the road turns off to the battalion's dressing station, Andrievs notices that there is no longer cause to hurry. The wounded man is dead.

Coming toward him is a lieutenant with a brilliant white dressing around his arm. He must be going back from the hospital to the trenches.

High above his head, shrapnel is bursting in a cloud of coloured smoke. With a clatter and a dull thud, a fragment hits Andrievs' helmet. Right beside him, the lieutenant suddenly lets out a howl and grabs his leg below the knee.

"Mummy, save me! Save me!"

Rags of skin and sinews from the lieutenant's leg are hanging down, bleeding heavily. The man is writhing like a worm on the sandy road. Andrievs unties the binding from the stranger's mess-tin, and makes a tourniquet for his leg above the knee to stop the blood. He stands up and pulls him up, helping the wounded man to lie down in the cart, pushes him on top of the corpse and flicks the reins over the horses' backs.

"Go slowly, that's an order! Slower! I'm in terrible pain!" screams the lieutenant.

He can't. You'll bleed to death, thinks Andrievs, urging on the lazy Maška. The cart clatters and jolts over the ruts.

The air from the shooting is boiling like porridge. The orderlies lift the wounded man out of the cart and immediately apply a bottle of brandy to his lips, and the unfortunate man swigs it in great gulps like fire-water. While the nurses apply a splint to his leg, the lieutenant hands Andrievs his sub-machine gun and pants: "Lieutenant Jēkabsons, number 3 company, I have a personal request."

Meanwhile a doctor is registering the death of the corporal who expired in Andrievs' cart. Now the battle cargo is unloaded and the driver can go back. Handing over the corporal's belongings, Andrievs opens the cigar-case and transfers the carefully preserved cigarettes to his own. The day's yield is seven cigarettes, but it's something for him to smoke!

He also stuffs the scrap of written paper in his own pocket.

The convoy crosses the shot-up junction at as great a speed as the horses can muster. Behind the big shed, lined up in a row, are soldiers whose lives were extinguished by grenade shrapnel. The young boys seem to be dozing in the shade, fallen asleep. Jančuks Spārniņš is there too. Two of them are still moving; Andrievs feels their heartbeats and rolls them into the cart to take them to the hospital. At that moment, Russian tanks break out onto the road, attacking from behind. The artillerymen run into the stone stable and call Andrievs to come too. He doesn't listen, driving the horses to the long stable wall, remaining with the wounded. Childishly he covers Hill's ears with his hand. The horse trembles with every shot. The tanks are bombarding the stable; several grenades burst not far from the cart. The roof of planks is punctured like a cotton rag.

When the salvos from the tanks have retreated, Andrievs surveys the wounded and the horses. Amazingly, this time they have again escaped death.

Andrievs and the wounded men are halfway to the hospital. When, senselessly shaking along the edge of a potato field, the cart reaches a courtyard, a Bolshevik attack suddenly starts, and the apparent salvation is suddenly transformed into a sea of fire. Artillery fire is bursting ceaselessly on all sides. Andrievs presses himself under a tree and holds the horses by the bridles. Doctors and orderlies are hiding in the cellar or the bunkers; the wounded are helplessly yelling for aid in the middle of the shooting.

"Is this a joke, that we're still alive?" one wounded man calls out when the attack suddenly stops and the courtyard goes quiet. "You've still got your guts, old chap!"

"Say thanks to the horses," replies Andrievs, dusting down the animals' backs. The chestnut tree above his head is ripped out, torn to pieces, the cart is strewn with leaves and pulverised fragments of chestnut.

"Pleased with yourself, are you, sonny?" says the wounded man. "It's God you have to thank!"

"But I say: the horse."

"Well, anyway," sniggers another one. "If they shoot you, they shoot you, and if they don't, they don't, but if you fall, what can you do then?"

Having handed the wounded over to the doctors, Andrievs receives an order to appear at the command post by the school.

The first-aid room beside the command post is overflowing with the wounded. A crowd is thronging the corridors. Making his way through it to the commander's office, Andrievs runs into the head doctor of Number 1 Medical Company, Major Jānis Lauskis.

"How's it going?"

"If you start badly, it goes badly."

"Yeah, the enemy's no fool, he can tell that our artillery still doesn't have any ammunition."

Outside, the Bolshevik machine guns are ceaselessly braying, and every few moments the squeal of Stalin's Organ, or Katyusha, the BM-13 rocket-launcher, rings out.

"My God, where's the organ going?"

"To Kārtūžu Manor. They want to knock it down. Thank God they don't have enough sense to deploy their Maxims sensibly," declares Lauskis. "Behind the school there's a good dead ground for bullets."

At that moment an anti-tank cannon shell hits the upper floor of the school. The ancient walls tremble, but after a doubtful moment, when it seems they will collapse in fragments, they decide to stick together after all. Plaster crumbles from the ceiling, showering the heads of young soldiers with grey.

"Ivan's looking for Ūdris!"* laughs someone.

"We're not so stupid as to keep Ūdris on the roof. Ūdris is on the front line, in the forest!"

The upper floor, spotted by artillery fire, with its rhomboid windows, really would be an ideal observation point. That is why the commander has forbidden soldiers to be there, because the roof is under constant heavy fire.

> There once was Bunker Thirteen, where lived many a man.
> When a grenade was thrown in there, the shit hit the fan.
> A blast rings out that's fit to frighten the very devil,
> Where once there stood a bunker, now the ground is level.

Who knows where it started from, like a little flame the cheeky song bounces like wildfire off the peeling ceiling that constantly shudders under the enemy's artillery.

> Death shines before our helmets, and goes with us to battle,
> The enemy's heart trembles with fear, when we begin to cackle.
> You'd better clear off, Ivan, you'd best be much afeard,
> Because my nimble fingers are itching to grab your beard!

The song is well known, and it gains strength as it grows, like the transparent juice in a fruit.

> Hey, you old devils, just look at all your talents!
> Drink vodka, catch flies in your ears, walk on your toes for balance.
> But anyone who's not friends with us had surely better beat it.
> 'Cause we'll shoot without mercy, what we don't like – we'll defeat it.

Next to Andrievs a mud-smeared soldier collapses, with a shattered shoulder, shards of bones in an open wound mixed with mucus and earth. The soldier, supporting himself on a doorpost, waits for the end of the song and then screams something, spreadeagled on the ground. Immediately two orderlies and Dr. Lauskis bend over him.

"Legionaries!" shouts the commander across the overcrowded room, and silence falls. "Today the premises of Numbers 1 and 3 Company were attacked by four enemy battalions. After brief preparatory firing on our positions, in their attack the Bolsheviks captured the Mazratnieki house and some of the trenches of Number 1 Platoon of Number 1 Company. In both of these attacks our soldiers recaptured their trenches from the enemy in close combat. At present there is no support from heavy weaponry. The MG-42 requires a lot of ammunition, as you well know. Orderlies and soldiers who are constantly going your rounds with the wounded and ammunition! Military riders! You will supply the men with food. We were hoping for a rest tonight, but that might not happen. The Bolsheviks are constantly attacking… That means that soldiers are in a permanent state of combat. I have no fears for them – they are trained and very experienced, they have been in rearguard action, on reconnaissance patrols, to say nothing of attacks and close combat. But no matter how tough the opposition, rest is necessary; they need a breather, but they don't get one!... We must hold our positions. You know that the German soldiers' fighting spirit has disappeared. It's every man for himself. Their mood is one of panic: get home, to the fatherland, to hell with this war!... But we have nowhere to go. Our homeland is here, under our feet. Here at More we're defending Riga! And the fight is for the supreme goal – for freedom!"

The commander leaves the room. After a moment the former bustling and hubbub resumes at the first-aid station, the orderlies bring in a couple of men whose bodies are mincemeat, but unfortunately they are not dead, they wail with the voices of owls, and someone is already calling for the cart convoy. Andrievs raises his hand – his thoughts had been straying, to Tone, to his brother and his little girls, to Riga…

"I'll take them, bring them over!" he hears himself saying. Then he remembers Hill, who's out there alone, in the rapidly darkening night, and sets off along the corridor to the door, ahead of the soldiers, who reach out from stretchers for an orderly, a young girl whose jaw has been shot away, her eyes big, dark, questioning, but her arm, in the sleeve of her overalls, hanging down to the ground.

Soup, coffee, bread, as much as you like – the food is as good as it can be in Latvia. It's not the first time Andrievs has heard these assertions. In the short snatches in battle the men doze off right there in the trenches, always ready for combat. Ready to eat whenever someone touches them on the shoulder… Weakened, but always ready for combat and food.

See, there's one. A chap with no name.

His face is reflected in the light of separate gusts of fire deep in the bottom of a trench. His gaunt arms reach out of the dark and gratefully grasp a bowl of food.

"It's terribly cold in the mornings; I don't know how I'm going to stand this cold… Boils, I've got these boils on my left leg… Everyone here has boils, the boils fester because they're poisoned where the shrapnel hits; even the ones who aren't hit have boils, boils everywhere… Those who have boils are in awful pain… On the cold ground. I don't want to finish my life here. In the background I have to hear that terrible shooting and the roar of the tanks."

"Can't sleep?"

"Me? I sleep very badly. Can't close my eyes, sleep won't come, the food stays in my head, and if it's not that, it's my son and my wife again, I'm tortured by it from one day to the next… The soup for dinner is smoked herring, boiled, very tasty. God helps me, next to Bērtulis, he's got swollen boils, his legs, his face and thighs, he had to hand over a urine sample to the doctors and in the end they hauled him off for an examination…"

"Have a cigarette!"

"Thanks! At home I don't smoke at night, but now I can't get by without them, I wait for them like bread, usually, it's hunger. I can't get to sleep, the front stays in my head. It's freezing at night, there's no warm room, I can't remember the last time I was in one of those. I really want some of that warm macaroni soup. When they take you to the bath-house here, I only wash my head, hands, legs, face, there isn't enough water for anything more. They haven't changed my clothes, they say there aren't any. We keep putting the same dirty ones on again. Full of lice. You have to dig in the ground, when you leave the sleeve hanging out, then all the lice gather there at the end of the sleeve, and then you burn them off – that's the Russian fashion. What's that funny noise?"

"My horses are snorting."

"I don't know why I can't get to sleep at night, I've even asked for injections and powders to be able to sleep better – they won't give them out. Since my bladder's frozen, at night I often have to go walking, which disturbs my sleep. I had herbs to drink, I got one little jug of camomile tea, that's the medicine I have now. The days are beautiful, but I've got tears in my eyes, I just don't want to hear that terrible noise… Every day I have a cry by myself, because it eases my heart. Go wherever you want, everywhere they're waiting for us Latvians, sorrow and death, because there's not enough space for us anywhere like in the old war, but our place is at the front. Even when you ask them to hold on, they just laugh and say that we Latvians are only around the front lines."

"Take some more soup!" Andrievs shakes the thermos flask.

"My stomach's already like a barrel. Thank God. When the sun doesn't shine, it's a gloomy day. I'm depressed. In the morning I have a cry, to ease my heart. Am I fated to return to my dear home? I'm waiting for that precious moment, I pray to God to help me, and I don't know if my wife will be mine or not. When the sun disappears, it's so cold I have to put mittens on. How awful it will be to freeze again, for the umpteenth winter. I just get tears in my eyes, I don't want to fight any more. In the morning, I feel, it'll be cold, about five degrees below. Today I took a piece of shrapnel out of my left arm."

Andrievs is called by an orderly, and says goodbye to his companion.

"Off you go, goodbye, who knows whether we'll meet again sometime," says the fellow.

The night is relatively peaceful. The Bolsheviks are not preparing for a night attack. Grenade-throwers, cannon and anti-tank cannon shoot in occasional bursts of fire, as well as deterrent fire.

Having got permission to rest the horses, Andrievs sets up camp in Vibotnes stables, in Hill's manger. The stables aren't secure, because there may be a direct hit, but it's all the same to Andrievs. He feels too tired to look for any special comfort for himself. He strews the manger with straw from the big pile, puts his helmet over his face and falls asleep as if in his mother's lap.

He's slept so sweetly that he overslept. He wakes to a sound like a mad dog howling – the voice of the Katyusha rocket-launcher. Andrievs rushes to the entrance and calls to the orderly in the yard: "What's the time?"

"Good morning to you! Nine. You've had a sweet sleep – it's a wonder. Since eight o'clock this morning Ivan's been at the organ again."

There's been a frost in the night. Andrievs is intoxicated by the scent of fallen leaves emanating from the earth. The air is slightly bitter and fresh like water from a clay jug, asking nothing more than to be drunk. Hill and Maška too, give out lengthy snorts as they're led out of their stable, their nostrils sharpened by the crisp, frozen air.

Harnessing the horses, Andrievs looks for a moment at the scene playing out before him on Gulspurvs, unfolding like dappled skin, with its greenish belt of forest at the edge, and the tendrils of paths like dark veins.

See, about twenty tiny figurines spill out of the forest and, crying "hurrah!", try to reach the main line of battle at a run. A cannon placed to the left side of the houses mows down the first of the advance group, and they remain hanging on the wicker of barbed wire. The rest dig themselves into the side of the forest.

See, the confluence of the Bolshevik forces at the Russian advance post at Zavadas, distant houses in the marshy lowland. Back and forth run the light trucks, the yoked pairs are driven about, the horses are whinnying, people are moving, repairing the bridge over the stream; five tanks or so are standing beyond the bridge as if penned in. Along the edge of the road toward the Russian post toddles a fat pig, from who knows which house, which sty. Soon it is spotted by the soldiers, and only a squeal is left of it. See, the enemy forces, company after company of them, wriggling out of the forest like little snakes, writhing toward the horizon. An apparently peaceful scene. Nobody knows that the hawks are calling out that the great field is lusting after their flesh.

That is all that shapes their lives at this moment.

There is no let-up from the Russian air-force – over his head there is the hollow roar of bomb-carriers, and past the cart come bullets from weapons on board… Andrievs pulls on the reins and mentally begs the horses to forgive him for such a dreamscape.

*

One night Gatiņš is shoved back into the cell with a bloody battered face and his teeth knocked out. Trails of spittle and blood stream from his mouth as from a deep piercing wound. His upper lip is swollen dark blue, like a boil. The boy can't speak, sits down on his bed and looks around with the eyes of a hunted animal.

After a while the others realize this, trying clumsily as best they can to help. The priest wipes the boy's bloody face with a pocket handkerchief.

"Good God! How can you look on calmly while innocent people are tortured like this?" asks the fourth cellmate angrily, having suffered in silence all this time.

"Father, forgive them, for they know not what they do."

"Stupid talk – you can't forgive ignorance!" the man growls, clenching his fists. "What's needed here is Arājs!* He was a proper guy, no fooling around with these Russian Jewish bastards."

The fellow leans over toward the door and shouts out: "I've shot about twenty myself!"

Andrievs and the priest stop what they are doing with the battered boy, looking nervously at the door.

"Nothing to be proud of," says Andrievs, as if the oppressive silence required the last word from him.

"Simons Šustins* can be proud, and so why not Viktors Arājs?" The fellow's angry chest is puffed out like a rooster's. "So why did Arājs' live wires call their boss Šustins? At the start of the war Šustins, even when he was on the run, lined them all up against the wall – a hundred people or so, guilty or not – and buried them in the courtyard of the Central Prison! How did they behave in June and July of 'forty? They poured out of their underground rat-holes – communists, Young Communists, prisoners. They all got promoted to responsible posts in the party, the unions and where the hell else! Berkovics – propagandist for the Cheka, Jofe – commissioner for health, Blūmentāls, director of the National Bank, in the Riga Infantry School, the police, the army – up the greasy pole they all went. When they set up the Riflemen's Guard, the auxiliary police – that's where absolutely all the Jews went, people who'd been in the Bund* and the Poale

Cion*! In the Guards' Clubs and the centres, at all the events they almost all spoke Yiddish."

Andrievs flew into a rage: "It can't be that everyone is guilty just because they're Jews! There were plenty of Latvians too – honestly naïve ones and cynics, as well as careerists and lickspittles."

"That's what I've been saying! If Stalin hadn't shot Latvians even before the war, then the Latvian Bolsheviks would be robbing us blind now, faithful Communist Party members, led by Jēkabs Peterss* and Lācis-Sudrabs*," scoffed the man. "Now there's nothing! Dirty work has to be left to the Jews."

"One force took away my parents, my schoolmates, my neighbours, in 'forty-one; a month later another force shot all the Jews. So what's the difference?"

"The Jews are the guilty ones. I was a *Schutzmann* myself at Pļaviņas, I saw with my own eyes – in 'forty, when the Reds came in, then the Jews and the Russians went on demonstrations, columns of red flags marching from the station to Gostiņi and back. They had *garmoshkas* and *gulyankas*, accordeons and parties, in the station square. But after that, when the Germans came in then there were red-white-and-red Latvian flags at Gostiņi. Collaborators, my arse!"

"And what's bad about that?" Andrievs cuts in. "It's natural. Of course power changes hands, but the great majority of people think about their families. They simply want to survive!"

"Hold your tongue, boy! You're still wet behind the ears, you've got your mother's milk on your lips."

"Hold your tongue yourself! I was in the Legion. Heroes like you didn't come anywhere near the front, because the ones like you got shot."

Before they grab each other by the hair, they are finally overheard. The door opens, and the big fighter is shoved into the corridor. Andrievs gets it in the back as well. The priest is pushed into place.

"Ne sobachtes' vy tut! No barking here!" screams the guard. *"A to mozgi vybyu!* Otherwise I'll smash your brains out!"

The night seems to last an eternity; there's no inkling of what the time might be. Andrievs thinks about the company commander. This man is like bright back-lighting. As long as Andrievs is able to recall him, even the agonies of death can be kept in proportion.

*

On the evening of the fifth of October the division departs from More, leaving several combat groups behind as cover and decoy. The cloud is forced down to ground level, the fog drips onto one's face. The night is so dark that nothing can be seen. Andrievs walks ahead of the cart between Maška and Hill, leading them by hand, encouraging them. Andrievs' cart is full of wounded who can't walk, but in his mind he is taking leave of those who stayed in the trenches of More, gradually mouldering into the black earth and the ashes of their ancestors.

Night in the Irbīte school. Alarm! Everyone runs outside. In the distance can be heard the firing of machine guns and carbines, with the occasional grenade explosion, until an uneasy silence sets in. It's no longer possible to sleep.

The order is that they may resume the journey only at 10 in the morning. The withdrawal will be up to the Peļņu house by the Nītaure-Mālpils road. There they must take up defensive positions and the time for resuming the withdrawal will be indicated. In the afternoon the first Russian advance groups have already arrived, forming into a chain, starting to fire with mortars, but they are not allowed to retreat yet.

In the early evening, on time, they must leave the defensive positions they have taken up.

Having sought out Andrievs with his gaze, the commander waves, and sits down in Andrievs' cart. During the day the officer has been slightly wounded in the leg. Orderlies have bound it up, everything seems in order, and yet he can't walk far. The cart is now layered with the wounded and soldiers' belongings, so the officer and Andrievs sit pressed shoulder to shoulder.

Swaying in the cart, they survey the refugees who are wandering along the side of the road and in overloaded wagons across the fields. Like the soldiers, they have long since forgotten peace and rest. The weather has begun to clear, beyond the swathes of fog the moon comes out every few moments and looks down on the bent heads of the refugees. Farmers' wives trudge behind the wagons, shrivelled and shrunken as if behind a coffin. From the wealth of former farmhouses there remains whatever is on the cart, and a bleeding wound in the chest in place of a heart. Feet move forward, but the soul stays behind, not wanting to part from its farmyard birthplace. So they move now like mechanical wind-up dolls toward the darkening west. Over toward Sigulda, the northern sky is pink from flashes of fire. There the Germans are hurrying to burn down whatever they can.

"I'd like to get written permission to visit relatives in Riga," Andrievs tells the commander.

"I don't have the authority to give permission like that, and nor has the battalion commander," he replies. "You'll have to go absent without leave, preferably without the horses. Find a bicycle!"

"I really need the horses," says Andrievs, without explaining further.

"Then you must be careful, don't cross bridges on any account! In the past few days the Germans have shot nine convoy attendants who arrived in Riga without documents. The Germans like to shoot Latvians rather than Germans, to frighten the others."

"With More behind me, I've no longer got anything to be afraid of."

"Yes, More has been the biggest close combat arena in the Legion's history," the commander agrees.

"I just can't understand the Russian soldiers' actions – why so many rapid assaults and then just as rapid surrender?"

"What is there to understand? It's every man for himself. During an attack they have barrage units – *zagraditelnyy otryad* – which shoot at their own soldiers from behind, forcing them forwards. Half of them have no weapons at all, they're given the job of taking them from their fallen comrades. The Russians are bold and even defiant when they're in a big group, but as individual soldiers they're cowards."

There's a hint of exhaustion in the commander's voice; he wraps himself in a blanket and tries to doze.

Behind the birch grove, an enormous full moon.

And the birch grove is made of silver.

Life.

What can be more sacred than that?

They stride out. They walk and walk. In a rapid procession throughout the night the soldiers arrive at the Jugla paper-mill by the lakeside, and stumble into the newly built barracks.

Finally they can rest their bones on the plank-beds of the barracks.

Having left the horses hobbled in the meadow by the lake, Andrievs comes in to join his companions. The sleepless nights at More, the constant anxiety, the nervous tension, the need to always be alert, have had their consequences. Some of them are raving, some can't get to sleep from over-exhaustion. But when they do, they sleep the sleep of the dead, round the clock.

Every few moments Andrievs wakes up, turning from side to side. It's so strange to have a soft place to sleep, not pressing on his bones.

The next morning a messenger comes hurrying in from battalion headquarters. The company commander is being called upon to check for positions that the company will take up in the battle to defend Riga.

The fog has fallen from their eyes like a veil, and the autumnal scene is unveiled in all its glory – in gold and purple. Morning has dawned with sunshine and a light wind. The men from the trenches go out and look around, feasting themselves – they drink, eat and inhale, gorging on the beauty in great hunks, like bread. A blue sky and tender twigs of the birches, shaken by the wind. Aspen trees tremble their leaves like gold coins sewn into the skirts of Gypsy women. Never mind that the wind has a dark blue icy lining. The soldiers reach for their bowls and set about washing themselves and rubbing themselves down. They indulge the luxury of shaving their beards, so they won't get itchy necks. They boil up their lousy shirts in big pots. Washed garments are hung up on birch branches to dry.

One or two of them realize for the first time that they are alive.

They even strike up a song – not out of defiance as in the trenches, when singing will drag their tired frames by the hair out of the slough of unconsciousness, but out of a fire in the heart – for the joy of it.

There isn't a single *Oberfeltwebel, Unteroffizier* or *Hauptmann* to command *Ein Lied!* so the song is not one of those drilled in the barracks, such as "Erika", "Drei Lilien", "Alte Kameraden" or some such. Nor is it one of those beloved by the Legion, such as "Kad ar uzvaru", "Ak, latvju meiten" or "Div' dūjiņas" (When in Victory; Oh Latvian Girl; or Two Little Doves). Only one song is suitable for the defenders of Riga: "19. divīzijas dziesma" (Song of the 19th Division).

Under our feet the highway's white,
To Latvia it leads,
To Latvia, where the enemy
In our fields sows Death's seeds.
We're marching boldly and proudly,
And we've rifles on our shoulders,
And the words of ancient heroes
Bequeathed to us Latvian soldiers.
We're coming soon, wait, Latvia,
We're bringing freedom to you,
Precious to us!
And we stride and stride,
We rush and we hurry,
For we must not be late.

The text has been set to music, known also in Europe as "The Devil's Song". This melody was appropriated by the Third Reich when it began to form its own Kondor air-force legion. Later unknown authors wrote the song "SS marschiert in Feindesland"

(The SS Marches on Enemy Land) to the same music, popular with the SS and its allies during the war.

The song became the anthem of the 19th Division in the last year of the war, so the text of the Latvian version of the song has nothing of Satan or of devilish laughter about it. It has only heartache and the desire to regain the lost homeland.

> We believe in the three stars of Latvia,
> May the bright fires burn on
> For ever and ever!
> And we stride and stride,
> Forward ever we rush,
> For we must not be late.

In the early afternoon, when the clothes are dried, the company commander arrives, tired but happy. He gathers the legionaries together.

"The battalion commander announced that Riga will not be defended, but will be declared an open city. The leaders of the Legion have the Germans' agreement that there will be no fighting in Riga, so as not to lay it waste like Jelgava. So we have to prepare to continue on our way at nightfall to Kurzeme. We will move at night through Jaunjumprava, across the Daugava River over the temporary pontoon bridge, through the Riga marches and forests, coming out on the Kalnciems road heading for Džūkste."

Many who have heard this go off without leave to say goodbye to their loved ones. Armed with the commander's fixed gaze and several handbooks, Andrievs also harnesses the horses and sets off for Riga.

*

When daybreak is already sitting on the roof of the Corner House like a grey pigeon with pink breast feathers, the guards fling the old *Schutzmann* into the cell. His arms are scalded with boiling water up to the elbows.

The fellow's energy is exhausted, his eyes are tearful. He sits under the bare bulb, nursing the raw red pieces of meat in his lap, and humming incessantly to himself:

> Hitler's sitting on a rubber tree
> Watching his grave dug in the cemetery.
> Oh how funny it will be
> When it breaks, that rubber tree.

His mumbling was like the prayer of someone who has lost his mind, merged with the morning orisons of a Catholic priest.

Four men in an underground cell, curled up like worms, and none of them worth any sympathy. For a start, sympathy is banned from this cell. And there isn't a single victim in the past war who is greater or lesser: sufferings are not comparable. Consider it: the first breath of a baby against the death-throes of an old man! One woman killed against two men? Three Jews from the ghetto against two Latvians in Vyatlaga or a dozen Lithuanian Forest Brothers blown up in a bunker?

*

For the first time Andrievs clearly appreciates what light is.

He remembers that joke about the rubber tree breaking. At the time of Hitler's death-throes, Andrievs had arrived in Riga, and his heart was singing in his breast like a red clay pot in the kiln – new and resonant. Pleased about one old trotter being rescued.

Riga has been dug up like one great molehill. The Germans have tried every way of reinforcing it, mobilising people to dig anti-tank trenches. On every corner one is stopped by gendarmes and SS soldiers. They show unashamed disdain for the documents of a Latvian Legion soldier, probably recognising only a German SS *Soldbuch*. Yet, the documents are in order, and Andrievs hitches up to continue his journey.

Near Grīziņkalns he gets safely past the *Schutzmänner*, who are rounding up civilians for the last ships to Germany. In front of Andrievs a carter gets caught, and has to abandon his horse and cart right there on the street. So is a man who pulls away from them and shouts that he is a widower and out to buy bread for his children. The gendarmes don't respond at all, but a group of four people calm the screaming man – they say that they're just going to inspect his documents and let him go... But the captured ones, arranged in lines, are led away. The women who are following them at a distance with bags of food and packages of clothes call out that they will be driven to the harbour at the end of Ausekļa Street.

Andrievs pulls on the reins to go faster. The air raid warning sounds, he has to drive the pair under the Air Bridge, Gaisa tilts. The warning goes on for a long time, until finally it ends. Freedom Street, Brīvības iela, now called Adolf Hitler Strasse, is covered with animal dung to a depth of two fingers. Mooing and neighing are intermingled in the stretch between the Air Bridge and the Pontoon Bridge, Pontonu tilts.

Andrievs turns off along Debesbraukšanas Street past the Pokrov cemetery.

Someone clears his throat in the cart – Andrievs looks back. A man is sitting on the cart in grey tatters – his shaggy hair and straggly beard billow in the air, his legs dangle over the wagon-rack, as bare and grey as sole-leather. His mischievous eyes blink in the ripples of sunshine and shadow; from his shoulder hangs a little sack in pastel colours like a shepherd's bag.

"How's it going now, how's it going now?" the shepherd-like vagabond asks rapidly, sitting right there on the wagon in the way he is accustomed to, swaying, bending forward.

"I'm going to war."

"Oh really, boy?" The artist pulls a face. "You must go to civvy street, not to war. To shoot is a great sin! Shooters will burn in the fires of hell."

"They're already burning," sighs Andrievs. "I'm not shooting, I'm carrying the wounded. You could say I am going to civvy street, if you prefer. Say, which is better – sin or shame?"

"Look to yourself, if you want to be resurrected. If you're Orthodox or Lutheran – good. But if you're godless – that's also good. My tragedy is that I'm sort of half-way. I'd like to have real power. I have only one thought in my head – how to get more light into the picture. Or else paint on sandpaper? Sandpaper has a good light of its own."

The horses walk on calmly; over those sitting in the wagon the silky rays of sunlight are spread out like a spider-web fluttering in the wind. The artist raises his soiled fingers and looks at the sun through them.

"No, no, I can't do it. No-one can. God created light!"

He waves a little piece of black tar-paper, on which is a layer of bright autumnal pastel chalk.

"Want it for yourself? I've painted this scene a hundred and fifty times! I've got to raise a little bit of money."

"I've got nowhere to put it."

"You have no home? A shame that I'm so dirty – you could stay with me, but you'd get lice."

"I have my own."

"Do you know, I've got a new thing now: a shop in Pārdaugava, on Tilzites Avenue. Will you take me? No… That's a shame; it's just that I've just exchanged one work on a panel for a berry-bucket, I could treat you. I had visitors there from a gallery as far away as Dresden – as if they were coming to a great man! They haven't visited a single Latvian artist, only me! Hush hush, mustn't brag about it, the director will get to hear about it and throw my paintings out of the museum… They promised me a whole heap of Reichsmarks for one market scene – take note, not Ostmarks, but Reichsmarks – and food vouchers! I didn't sell it! Enamelled eyes for soldiers, I didn't sell. You ought to be painted yourself – there's a lot of light in your eyes."

"I have to go to war."

"You're not afraid! It's safest in a cabman's cart. When the air-raids start, I jump in a cart…"

"What's so safe about a cart?"

"The horse is a shield," explains Irbe. "The horse is praying when he runs. You pray too when you ride. You pray as long as you live. Life is praying. When nobody is praying any more, then God will be dead, I don't want to see such times… Cool shadows, see – autumn's arrived!"

Closer to the racecourse the commotion grows greater – pedestrians and small drays are mixed with carriers, who are overtaken by army units. With an effort Andrievs gets across the crossing to Miera Street, draws on the reins, looks back – the vagabond is no longer in the cart. As if an Art Nouveau sculpture, carved from shimmering dark granite, had taken a ride in Andrievs' wagon and then fallen back off in the shade. All that's left in the cart is a tiny pastel drawing like a messenger-pigeon's note from the great painter Voldemārs Irbe.*

Andrievs saves it in his sketch album.

This is the area of Andrievs' childhood and youth. How strange to see with his own eyes the familiar houses and streets! Many times he has taken leave of all this, with no hope of seeing it again. It seems that now with his battle-cart he has entered a time machine, where everything has stopped, where everything is as before.

Having got near the racecourse, Andrievs confirms to himself that the postcard-like bliss is only an illusion. Between Šarlotes and Tomsona Streets are long rows of German army barracks. SS soldiers patrol the gates of the site. The courtyards are full of heavy Belgian thoroughbred horses belonging to the artillery divisions, resting there, their heads lowered indifferently. Yoked together in groups of eight, they will have to pull cannon and a gun-carriage weighing four tonnes along trackless stretches to Kurzeme.

Andrievs leads his tired horse across to the old stables. He himself goes around the corner to Eizens.

The Pētersons' rented house, built in the functionalist style in the mid-thirties, retains at its entrance traces of the romantic period – supple curved forms invite one to explore a staircase like a mysterious sandstone grotto. In some fine details the architect has refrained from the forced geometrization of modernism and put the main emphasis on the sensuousness of the material. Andrievs enters the shade of the building, disturbing the quiet peacetime dust with his rough army riding boots. The air on the staircase does not stink of medicines, old blood, bullet-riddled intestines – it is untouched by the war and fusty from his boyhood summers.

He rings the doorbell, then bangs the bronze clapper – a dragon's head – and finally Andrievs beats persistently on the door with his fists.

Eventually it springs open like a sesame pod, and Eizens stands in the doorway, startled. He is sleepy and stubbly, clad in a striped dressing-gown.

"You're listening to the gramophone, old fellow, so you don't hear me?" asks Andrievs, as Eizens can't stop staring at him like a wonder.

"And we were just thinking that you were already eating a *Muschelsalat* and *Blutwurst* at the Wintergarten." Eizens beckons him inside. "So you haven't gone off with Gogis and Reinholds, then?"

When Andrievs wants to enter his room, Eizens pulls the door shut in front of his nose.

"Yesterday there was a bit of a session…"

"I see," says Andrievs, taking out the pastel drawing and handing it to Eizens. "Put it among my things later – I met Irbīte on my travels. Just don't give it to one of your Fräuleins…"

Eizens takes the board, looks at it closely, then puts it on the dining table and steps back.

"Brilliant…He's a genius… What brings you here, and in that uniform too?"

"I've brought Hill to you," says Andrievs. There's something in his statement that makes Eizens turn serious for a moment. His round, eagle-owl eyes become moist, and the curve of his lips bends like a wave on the sea. Eizens hugs the boy, squeezing him in a pincer.

How has Andrievs failed to notice that the old fellow's head is trembling so much?

"Come, sit down, tell me!" – the old man beckons him toward the ash-strewn sofa. "Where did you get him?"

"I'll tell you that along the way, I don't have much time. I have to get to Džūkste by morning. I'll leave Hill with you. It's just a miracle that he was saved at More, but in Kurzeme nothing will save anyone."

Eizens lights the cigarette that has gone out in its holder and breathes the smoke in deeply. His cheeks flatten against the bones like dark pools. His gaze lingers on the red-white-and-red shield on Andrievs' sleeve.

"You've got to get to Džūkste? I've got a Fräulein who can bring a passport from the bank, with a stamp and everything… Change your clothes and you'll get to Germany, you'll be guzzling Faschinger Bier with the Russian generals."

Andrievs conceals a smile – probably the same Fräulein whose silk stockings are hanging like a snakeskin over the back of the chair and whose patent leather shoes are discarded in the middle of the room.

"I'm expected there, they trust me. It'd be a betrayal to do that, even dishonest toward her."

Eizens grimaces knowingly.

"Right here at this table yesterday an officer was saying: *Militärisch haben wir den Krieg verspielt, aber politisch wird gewonnen.* Militarily we've lost the war, but won it politically. He also said he'd heard that in Berlin from a German doctor, a political commentator."

"Is anyone allowed to tell that to the soldiers in the Legion?"

"And why these unnecessary losses? Hundreds of thousands fallen for nothing! Any thinking person can see that there's no sense in it any more…"

"If the Latvians hadn't held onto More at the cost of their lives, then people in Vidzeme province would have had no chance of being evacuated, and Riga would be left in ruins! Kurzeme, full of refugees like a ship to the gunwales! I'm defending my homeland, nothing more."

"What's happened to you?" His old friend examines Andrievs carefully.

"I…I saw it all with my own eyes."

"You used to be the first one to laugh, all this didn't matter to you… But now you're just like Eizens. You see, I'm not planning to go anywhere – when the Russians throw 'Christmas trees'* at the window, I sit peacefully reading the *Tēvija*."*

"What good stuff do they write in that?"

Eizens dismisses it with a wave of his hand.

"The editor is a right bastard! The twaddle he comes up with! How the Germans will defend Latvia, there's nothing to fear!"

"We have no hope of holding out against the Russians."

Eizens hitches up his trousers, which won't stay up over his round belly without braces.

"What do you want from me, old chap?"

"A good, steady battle horse."

"Steady!" growls Eizens, scratching his neck. "I do have one – he'll be good for mincemeat at Džūkste. But we'll have to go to the Lapenes property."

"How long have you had horses at Lapenes?"

"So could I keep them here?" says Eizens, dressing quickly. "They're requisitioning everything. When the Russians made a run for it in 'forty-one, we were hiding the good trotters out at Lapenes even then – you don't remember it, you were in the countryside… Then we'd collected all of them from the stables at the racecourse – the ones that had owners were taken back to their homes, but those that weren't taken we kept in those huts… But those horses neigh, dammit! They can't keep their traps shut. What can you do – stuff them with oats from the nose-bag to keep them eating? Good that the Russians got out quick. Let's hope the Germans won't be long about it."

In the stable Eizens examines the racer.

"Run Hill – he's alive! For this I award you, mate, the Orders of the Three Stars, Viesturs and the Iron Cross!"

Andrievs has to relate in all its details how Hill came to be one of a pair on battle duties.

"Yoked together with a mare! You're a mad boy. What I marvel at most is that grasshoppers like you can be taken to war at all!"

"If you'd seen them in the *ROA*, you wouldn't marvel at all. *Vlasovites**, supporting the Germans. Sub-machine guns on their shoulders, pistols, and about ten hand-grenades hanging off the waists of each of them. Dogs on leads with them. A terrible sight. They took to it, they accepted it."

The two of them accompany Hill out of the stable. Maška neighs softly behind him, then sighs. She probably senses her fate now. Hill looks back too, as he takes in the autumn air with his broad nostrils. At the gate to Grostona Street Eizens waves to the guard, and he lets the head of the Hippodrome through, without questioning him.

The three of them plunge into the garden area, walking along paths overgrown with shaggy grass, among the apple-trees, pear-trees, huge blackcurrant bushes, untended onion beds and collapsed hothouses. This autumn has been virtually without rain, with few exceptions. The sun, bright and white, casts an unnatural light across the blue sky and the world, like an opera set. The air smells of rancid inundations and rotting, diseased flesh. The Lapenes property is a place that has managed to remain unscathed by all authorities, retaining an air of abandonment and isolation.

Starting with a gift of land from the town in the Ulmanis presidential era to the Mazpulcēni youth organisation – adolescents who were learning to drain, plant and water the low-lying land, the allotments are laid out in the place of the town pasture-lands from the racecourse right up to the Pasture Embankment. In the time of Tsar Peter the First, the Pasture Embankment was an avenue planted with four rows of willows with a cattle-track beside it, a popular promenade for the townspeople, along which the patricians of the town built their little summer retreats. The unhealthy air of the low, marshy place and the clouds of midges forced them to sell their properties, however. Later, sleepers were laid in the marsh, reinforced by rails laid out over them – along the Pasture Embankment was a goods station of the burgeoning Riga rail network. There's a depot here for receiving and dispatching trains, a place for uncoupling wagons, loading and unloading tracks, high loading platforms and vast storehouses. Here, race-horses are also dispatched and received.

"Unnaturally warm autumn," observes Eizens, puffing on a cigarette. "The refugees will have to get out in time, otherwise they'll freeze to death in their carts."

They come out onto the rutted Skansts Road, with the Lapenes property extending on both sides. Under a burned cherry-tree sit three carousers, emptying a vodka flask.

"The Russians are coming, and we can't do anything about it," one of them grumbles.

"You're short of brains, Ans!" parries another. "The Russians can't get into Latvia a second time! That's why the English are giving them arms and tinned meat. As soon as the Russians start coming into Latvia, the English won't give them any more arms, and they'll be done for!"

The fellows fall silent and cast long stares at the newcomers.

"Everyone in Riga is sitting around discussing what to do – to go or not to go," says Eizens. "People's mood is mostly undecided: to get away, or stay? They're weighing up the pros and cons. Fleeing is no walk in the park."

"Today I saw *Schutzmänner* rounding people up and forcing them onto ships to Germany."

"Up to now only the Bolsheviks have been rounding up slaves here. I see the Germans hunting people down as a betrayal."

The autumnal smell of the earth is intoxicating. They seem to be walking along the branched lungs of a giant injured organism which is still continuing to breathe of its own accord, until the final move stiffens and freezes it.

Far beyond the rails, the water-tower of the town's abattoir glistens. Finally Eizens turns left. In a little summer stable, rebuilt from a cowshed, Andrievs catches sight of a black horse. With its head poking far out over the half-door, it neighs loudly, having seen the newcomers. The wave of whinnying even makes the other sheds in the garden shudder.

"Now he's mooing like Hitler's cow!" declares Eizens.

"I don't need a mad one like that!" Andrievs is taken aback. "I have to yoke him to a mare, I have to carry the wounded… What will I do with a wild beast like him in war?"

"I don't have another one! This one has papers that will let him leave Riga with you, without a word."

At a time when documents are of more value than lives, the argument is effective. Andrievs takes the bridle and approaches the horse.

The black beast has only one eye. A long bright scar like a lightning bolt stretches across his brow, touching the empty socket of his right eye and passing down to his nose. It gives the horse a severe, contemptuous expression, but the look of the single eye is firm and wise.

"Just go up to him!" urges Eizens. "When he understands what sort of slaughterhouse you're leading him to, he'll tear your head off."

Andrievs hasn't said much of a farewell to Hill. He strokes him and presses his head against the horse's warm forehead. Warmth – that is what every living being in this world must know of another. There is no other wealth.

Time is rapidly flying toward evening, pulling the world forward and moving the angelically beautiful, frosty, colourful leaves, the bluish shadows of branches on the path, shaking the distended, shaggy fox-fur-like grass-stems. On the horizon the locomotives at the goods station are whistling, pushing military wagons along the track, loaded with ammunition and cannon; ships blow their horns in the harbour, carrying thousands to their fates across the sea.

"Sendergruppe Ostland! Hier spricht Riga, Goldingen und Libau! Auf die Reichsgebiete befindet sich kein feindliches Kampfverband. Eastern broadcasting group! This is Riga, Kuldīga and Liepāja! There are no enemy military units on the territory of the Reich," a radio loudspeaker announces at the goods station, constantly reporting on the situation in the skies above the Reich.

Time drives far away what was close, taking it back. Only one thing can save you – to love your own time.

"Never stand next to the black one, so he doesn't bite your ear off," warns Eizens in the stable. "I got him as an exchange from some artillerymen who couldn't cope with him. He's nice to women, but he goes on the attack with men. Someone probably mistreated him. There's no point in hitting him; once a horse-breeder tried thrashing him with a whip, and after that the horse noticed the whip lying against the wall and bit it in half. This is how I manage him – when he gets uppity, I give him a light slap on his muzzle, as if to say, I won't be a tyrant, but I don't like your pace!"

"What's his name?" sighs Andrievs. "At least you'll tell me that?"

"How would I know? Insbergs' artillerymen swore at him as Ješka."

As soon as he is being yoked up, there's a difference of opinion. Ješka doesn't like Maška, and he wastes no time in biting into her shoulder. Maška bites back.

"Do it the right way round!" instructs Eizens. "Yoke him with the blind eye facing inwards, so that Ješka doesn't see Maška."

As they are saying farewell, Eizens asks him: "So you said – the Russians will be here?"

"After a while maybe – at least a few days, while they bring in more forces... At More they lost a lot of blood. But then they'll be here."

"All sorts of things are being said here... Maybe the Legion will hold onto Riga? Maybe Latvia will declare the restoration of independence and fight against the Germans and Russians at the same time? Maybe Latvia will be divided into Soviet and Western zones?"

"Utopias! Be thankful that it won't be bombed to bits like Jelgava. Don't forget – keep Hill under a blanket! He's always freezing."

"Don't teach an old dog new tricks," retorts Eizens. "Look after yourself, boy!"

"Any news of Antonija?" asks Andrievs.

"Nothing much... That Kraut ran off to Riga a second time, they say, and crept away, leaving her to get on with it. Tone asked: so why didn't he take me with him the first time? He said: But I knew you didn't love Hitler!" Eizens laughs heartily. "Tone replied: whoever's gone away, let him go! That's what my Fräulein told me, she was actually there. It seems to me that Tonija is back in Latgale. She hasn't been spotted here."

"Goodbye then," says Andrievs, pulling on the reins. Eizens remains in the doorway.

Officers are conferring by the gate of the stable yard.

These are men who in peacetime were Andrievs' authorities, acquaintances and colleagues, but now between them are not only several dozen steps and three years of war, but also a huge difference in rank, the hell of battle, and Iron Crosses. Andrievs passes by them with his cart and its rack, with a one-eyed black horse yoked to a clumsy mare of a bluish granite colour.

There stand the commander of number 19 Artillery Regiment, Major Voldemārs Grāvelis, and the commanders of II and III Divisions, Majors Kristaps Insbergs and Jānis Ozols. They break off conversing and look back. Andrievs salutes – the only thing he has learned in the war, because he already knew how to ride horses long ago.

Through them Andrievs glimpses himself as a boy, cutting photographs out of magazines showing the riders in the national team – officers – at a time when the new state's cavalry, just formed, was not only holding its own, but even competing with nations with huge reserves of riders and horses and ancient traditions with famous training schools for riding. In Andrievs' collection is a cutting from the ninth issue in 1933 of the military review, *Militārais Apskats,* in which Lieutenant-Colonel Voldemārs Šēnfelds, also known as a publicist and poet under the pseudonym Skaistlauks, wrote: "In the Riga Cup race, Etimoloģija, ridden by 1st Lt. Ludvigs Ozols, was only 160 cm. behind the foreign celebrities whose value is estimated at up to 12 thousand lats." In the German period Voldemārs Skaistlauks was the director of the Hippodrome, but now he was an officer at the Battle of More. This man, who for his victories in the First World War and the War of Liberation over the Reds, the Landeswehr and the Bermontians,* was awarded the Military Order of Lāčplēsis, the Orders of the Three Stars and of Viesturs, and for the defensive battles on Latvian territory was also awarded the Iron Cross,

Classes I and II, is probably even now on his way to Kurzeme, as commander of Artillery Regiment number 15, a first lieutenant.

The distinguished racing jockey Kristaps Insbergs took part several times in the Warsaw races, where, in the park of Belvedere Castle, the cream of the world's jockeys and horses gather. Another place where the Latvian riding team were frequent guests was Insterburg, the heart of the East Prussian Cavalry horses. Andrievs' father never ceased to praise the way that Insbergs didn't rein back his horse in front of every hurdle, as the Poles did. That cost them seconds. Kristaps knew how to lead a horse to a hurdle by the shortest route, sharply cutting off the corners on the turns and saving time. That was said to be his advantage, honed in hard training over many years.

"Insterburg supports our aspirations," Jēkabs Radvilis was told by Kristaps Insbergs after his return from the races. "East Prussia reminds you of Latvia: separate, single farms, fields and coppices, buildings, but what is most surprising are the Latvian names of the houses: Vējlauki and Lazdupes, Lauksargi and Bajārgali. If all we can hope for is to get official kindness and sometimes admiration in the big racing centres like Warsaw, Romania, France, Aachen, then at Insterburg we're received with sincerity and even friendship."

Andrievs remembers well the names of the first horses to be honoured – legends for little boys: Greja, Burggrāfs, Etimoloģija, Altgolds, Erbitans, Klaips, Ērpe, Valkīre…

The officers recognize Andrievs and see the red-white-and-red shield on his arm. Kristaps Insbergs suddenly raises his arm and waves to Andrievs. He waves back.

And remembers the 16th June 1940 issue of the Latvian Soldier magazine, *Latvijas Kareivis* – right there it was, lying on Andrievs' desk, where his shocked mother had put it. During the independence period this newspaper was an organ of high culture with varied content, much smaller than *Jaunākās Ziņas,* the Latest News, which is highly regarded by the Radvilis family. A day before the Red Army's attack on Latvia, it had published the Soviet Union's announcement to Lithuania and described a shocking incident at Maslenkiai near the border, to which an investigation commission had been sent, led by General Bolšteins. Then, taking up the second page of the paper, a poem by Andrejs Eglītis.

> Put a sword under your head
> And do not sleep profoundly –
> Your honour and your fatherland
> Forbid you to rest soundly.
> Put a sword under your head,
> Have it for your pillow,
> The last statement you will make
> Must be to strike a blow.

If until now there have been doubts in his mind as to whether he is doing the right thing, then since Insbergs' comradely greeting they are blown away with the smoke of the town. Andrievs no longer feels ridiculous, the cart is not awkward and the horses are not clumsy. He is a battle rider who saves the wounded. There are no higher or lower things in the world, everything is determined by the constant source deep in the human heart – a sense of purpose. If this source is pure, it changes the world.

His beloved Riga lies behind him, hidden in the sandy hills, lashed by a storm under a lightning whip.

The road to Kalnciems is empty, without a living soul. Andrievs feels uneasy – who owns this territory now? He urges the pair onward. It doesn't help much – Ješka is an excellent puller, but Maška is tired. It's getting dark – Andrievs would be ready to attach the shafts to himself if it helped.

In the distance, between the steep walls of the forest, a little black spot appears on the rutted road. After a while Andrievs reaches the company commander, pushing a bicycle.

"The horse man!" cries the commander joyfully, on recognizing Andrievs. "What luck! The bike had a mishap. The front tyre won't hold air, but I don't have any repair kit."

The commander throws his things into the cart and takes a seat himself.

"I came away with a wet back. I was only a few hours at home, saying goodbye to my folks. And what about you?"

"I've changed my horse for a better one from the Gypsy," jokes Andrievs.

Having got through the big forest, the horses become uneasy. Refugees are gathered in an open field.

It's a clear, warm October evening. Far and wide, people are spread out beside their unyoked cart-horses to spend the night, their horses skittish, the smoke from fires wafting around. Most of them are cart-teams from Vidzeme province, but around some of the carts the Latgalian language can occasionally be heard. The eyes of domestic animals driven from their hopes stare mournfully among the dusty bent-grass – exhausted cows that have been taken along, with swollen legs bound in rags, sheep, and dogs.

The travellers finally catch sight of their company, which has settled down to rest in the open field. Andrievs unyokes the horses and lies down on the cart, feeling the dampness biting into his shoulders. Yet his exhaustion is too great to find the strength to get up and seek cover. The commander, hurrying past, covers him with a coat. That was what his father used to do early in the morning. Andrievs falls asleep in a moment.

The next morning the soldiers cheerfully greet Andrievs and throw their bags onto the cart, so moving them around has become easier. But for the horses the journey is harder and harder. The gravel, worn down by the refugees' cart-teams and the military wagons, is being repaired in places by sappers. Bundles of planks, laid crosswise, are buried in the fine-ground sand; elsewhere beams are laid transversely over bog-crossings; in places a pavement has been formed out of tree-stumps as the easiest substitute. Yet from time to time the horses have to almost kneel in order to haul out the wheels, sunk up to their hubs in the quagmires along the way.

By the Lielupe river, in place of the blown-up Kalnciems bridge, the sappers are building a pontoon bridge.

On the way to Džūkste the company commander is taken ill. He sits in the cart, his back leaning against Andrievs' back, breathing heavily. Every few moments he is shaken by a fever. With shallow, thin panting like a dog's, the first lieutenant slumps back moment by moment – either dozing or, who knows, losing consciousness.

On 12th October 1944, number 19 division replaces the German 81st infantry division. On 15th October the ruthless struggle for the Lestene battlefield begins. A battle for houses that are razed from the surface of the earth, but will remain in the soldiers' hearts until death. Pūces and Nabadziņi, Putnakrogs, Ķempji, Spriguļi, Eglītes and Miekuļi, Āmari and Jaunmestri, Bitšķēpi, Rumbas and Birznieki, Dirbas, Priežusargi, Rimeikas, Ērmes and Vamži, Vanagi, Jāņukrogs, Vidiņi and Ģibelas, Brūnumuiža, Lestene, Bērzupe station and many more – these are not merely house-names.

Their names recall the six great battles for the fortress of Kurzeme.

*

From time to time the prisoners are allowed a little walk to a small space in a courtyard. They circulate in single file, their hands behind their backs. Without stopping, conversing, or sitting down. The yard is covered by a wire roof, over which a little bridge has been built, on which an armed guard stands.

Here and there in the corners, dirty snow and ice are still lying. Over the expanse of the courtyard stretches the endless sky, a heavenly blue, and the brisk outdoors air caresses the body outside and inside. It is the only proof that the world still exists somewhere. Returning from these walks to the narrow, hot, brightly lit cell is a descent into hell.

At night the interrogation continues. Krop pesters him with questions about everything that occurs to him, returning senselessly often to the same subject. It is this senselessness that most irks Andrievs.

"Why did so many desert?" asks the investigator.

"In October they deserted, in November they no longer did, it appears."

"Why?"

"Well, because it wasn't clear what Hitler was going to do with Kurzeme. When they found out there was a command to defend it, then they came out. Kurzeme was flooded with refugees from every part and every district of Latvia; that led to a lift in their morale. The only line of defence left was the line of soldiers."

*

On the wooded hills along the battle-line, things are boiling like a witches' cauldron.

In the November night Andrievs wakes up and looks for the company commander – evidently he is desperately ill.

The company's command post is built into a wooded slope, at a position on the forward bridge over the Bērze river. When Andrievs asks after the commander, the men point to the pine trees.

"He's there. Not listening to anyone, talking to himself."

Andrievs approaches a figure in the darkness.

"I'm not going in yet. I want to understand what I'm really hearing," says the commander.

"You're hearing the pines. Right over the bunker there are big pine trees rustling. The autumn winds are resonating into the bunker."

For a moment the commander considers what he's heard, then asks gratefully: "Is that you? The horse-man?"

"Yes. I'm supposed to bring you to the regimental first aid station. You have a very high temperature. Come with me."

The commander follows Andrievs obediently and lies down on the cart. He is thoroughly exhausted, as he has not yet recuperated after the battles of Vidzeme.

"For the third night I've been waking the company command group and sending them to the front line. It seems to me that the Russians are coming on the attack, bellowing Hurrah! Autumn nights are dark, you can't see anything. When we got there, it turned out that Ivan wasn't on the attack. The men are starting to look apprehensive."

"You have a very high temperature."

"I have diphtheria."

"Getting diphtheria in trench conditions – that isn't serious?"

"I just don't know why they didn't send me to the field hospital. Such a strange feeling all the time. As if I was in an army camp somewhere in peacetime. One chap told me we're at Pūces. Some corporal reported that they'd gone on the counter-attack at night, and while they were clearing Russians out of the trenches they'd used little boards and hunters' rattles to make it sound like pistol-fire, and the Russians had fled – apparently also without ammunition. That's the only conversation with the corporal that I remember. It's dark in the bunker, I lie down in my allotted sleeping-place and I switch off again. Were they investigating me? The battalion commander sent me to search for the company. I did, they were standing in formation together with the whole battalion. The lieutenant colonel made a speech. They were led into battle by a band; the whole battalion sang with all their might "The Lord God is our strong fortress" and "God bless Latvia", then they played "As I go off to war" and after that "As now in peace all those blessed ones who went into battle in strong faith" – they didn't need that, that's a funeral song, everyone understands that – when they lie in their graves, then they won't have any more time, they'll be raking sand over them right there in the trench… let it all be done as was probably intended… But we just go on and on, rushing forward… Massed artillery fire. Exploding grenades flashing to the ground in the dark. The Maxim guns are howling, the bone-saws are rumbling.* The fire rages in the foreground with an indescribable fierceness. You hold your weapons covered with coats, to work when the attack begins! Everything around like gravel-pits. There isn't any more level ground, it's been ransacked. When dawn breaks, the trenches filled up with earth start moving, the soldiers leap out and rush to take up their positions. The earth is steaming from its warmth, morning breaks, exploded shells are smoking. A bloody sun rises, what does it promise? Finally they come out, count to eight, come over to us, the infantry close behind them. We crawl out of the sand and go towards them, looking into the white fires

– we respond with counter-fire. Three shot-up tanks are stopped in the space between, but five went back, damn it! When the battle ends, you can only guess how many are left alive. I can't shoot the wounded, however much you ask. Those who are capable of turning the barrel of a gun on themselves have done it already. The one who shot up the tank, whose face is covered in blood, with a hole in place of an eye, begs not to be left alive, to let him die and go and help others. Better to die an honourable death by your own hand than be tortured by the enemy. Machine-gunners, along with all the machine guns, have been squashed flat by a Russian tank. Many of our wounded from the front line, besides the wounded and fallen Red Latvians, are also begging to be shot dead. You have to save bullets; only twenty out of eighty of ours are left. When did you last eat? The clock has stopped, unwound. Silence in the trenches. Both sides bloodied. You have to help the seriously wounded to get to the back lines. Good that Laumanis' battalion heard our SOS and arrived to stand in our place. He and his men have gone through the fire of a lot of battles and made their reckoning with life, not afraid of death. A senior sergeant from number 7 company had gone over to the enemy side, and must have informed the Reds about our activities. The Russians forced this senior sergeant to come out in front with a megaphone to invite us to go over to the Russian side. Soldiers of the seventh company crept over to the front, found him and shot him dead, giving a traitor a traitor's fate. The houses at Āmari have been destroyed, where there had been fighting. Communications were cut off. We retreated. That was when Laumanis' men arrived here. After a short discussion we went over to counter-attack. The Russians retreated. It turned out they were Red Latvian units who called out as they went not to shoot, they were Latvians. We stopped shooting, but we went on the attack at a more intense rate and invited them to come over to us. There was no reply. Give up. I forced a crossing over the Bērze river; the water was up to our waists. Laumanis' men took the Dobele road, which we needed to capture. The regimental commander gave the order to return to the starting positions. Why? The battle went on all day long, the men hadn't eaten, they were tired. Many, me included, were wet.

There was nowhere to dry out. Everyone slept as best they could. The next day it all started again. Since my company suffered the most, it was replaced, and for a while Laumanis' men stayed in its place. We were sent into the reserves to recuperate. How many were captured, how many lost their lives, how many were injured and how many went over to the *kurelieši*, General Jānis Kurelis' military grouping?"

The Number 1 Company cart approaches Bitšķēpi, the regiment's first aid station headed by Dr. Lauskis.

"We're here," says Andrievs, halting the pair. "So now, Senior Lieutenant, with your permission…"

Carefully he lifts the feeble commander out and carries him a hundred metres alongside Bitšķēpi farmhouse, where there is a dug-out shelter in the ground built as a first aid post.

"How is he?" asks the doctor, feeling the lymph nodes in the patient's neck.

"He was raving the whole way," explains Andrievs.

"Because of the seriousness of the illness he can't be transported," declares the doctor. "He must stay here and be watched over by his own soldiers."

The doctor prepares a syringe for an injection. Andrievs goes away.

Bitšķēpi is a long adobe-walled building. Opposite the farmhouse is a shed with grain-bins and a byre with a cow. Špiss, the company's senior sergeant, and his helpful assistant First Class Private Ēršķis, are settled in at one end of the house. The riders are given some room. Andrievs' sleeping place is on a sweating-shelf on the first floor. Not far from the house is a field kitchen, half-submerged in the earth, to protect it from artillery shooting. Two cooks are fussing around it. A couple of kilometres to the south is the front. Sporadic shooting resounds from there, otherwise all is calm. When the automatic weapons start to clatter and a chorus of "Hurrah!" is heard, that will be the attack.

The cart is sent for the fallen. They are buried in a hillside near the forest. But while the fighting is going on round about, it isn't possible to carry the fallen anywhere. Quite often they are laid right there in a trench, a new trench is dug beside them and earth thrown over them.

Young girls from neighbouring houses are working as nurses – tending to the wounded, because those are extremely numerous. Helping to bury the fallen, Andrievs tells the youngest nurse, who is working at the regimental dressing station: "Hermінīte, take a piece of paper, pen and ink and write the surnames of the fallen men; make notes on those pieces – how many steps to the trench, how many full rows there are."

"And where would I put a paper like that?" The girl is confused.

"Roll it up in a bottle and bury it somewhere. After the war the field will be ploughed up, then it will be necessary to recall them."

The company's senior sergeant sends many of the military riders off to the front lines – here a horse isn't likely to be wiped down, nor well fed, and one word against those in charge – off to the trenches! The sergeant keeps his distance from Andrievs, because he's afraid of his one-eyed Ješka. One morning the sergeant's batman, a sturdy young lad, takes Andrievs to task in the courtyard: "Senior sergeant, sir, his belt isn't done up properly, the buttons on his coat haven't been polished!"

"He's got so stiff, he'll have to be sent to the trenches to get shot. What else…?"

"You hear, you'll need to send him off to the infantry, into position for attack!" cries the private, encouraged by the senior sergeant.

Ješka gets close to him and grabs him by the shoulder. Having extracted himself from the horse's teeth, the batman slinks away as fast as his legs can carry him.

After that incident Ēršķis keeps on thinking how to get Ješka to the cook, to turn her into rissoles, but he leaves Andrievs alone. The military rider doesn't doze either – for his black guardian angel he's awake day and night, his sheepskin half-coat folded up, spending the night in Ješka's trough.

"This is the hundredth soldier I've accompanied on his last walk," the sergeant sighs over one of the fallen, an old man whom he had himself sent to the battle-lines. After a couple of days the company commander sends the sergeant together with his first-class private to the trenches, and the senior sergeant himself becomes the hundred and first.

The sergeant's batman is shot by a sniper. The bullet has caught him just above the brow, a groove driven into his hair. He calls for help. An orderly immediately sets off to help, but as soon as the orderly gets over to the injured man, he himself is shot dead. Two more men creep up to help, but they are also shot down by a direct hit to the forehead. One student who has just been sent from Laumanis' battalion, gets hit near the ear. The last one to crawl up to help is the sergeant. Even he is shot dead.

This morning Andrievs has picked up eight fallen men near the barn. With her whinnying, Ješka is sniffing the scent of her most mortal enemy – death.

All of them have their boots pulled off.

When they are interred in Sveikuli cemetery – twenty-six together with those who fell yesterday – some girl is looking for her boyfriend or brother among the dead. Languidly she eddies about in a pale, thin coat, like a fallen leaf, driven by the wind from one to another; she bends down, gets up, pushes her scarf around her neck, bends down, gets up, tries to be quiet and respectful and smother her desperation, but the pain is stronger, seeming to rupture her body into pieces from within. The young legionaries have been shattered – which one is which? – unrecognizable.

They all lie in a single grave, covered over by a tarpaulin.

At Bitšķēpi a furlough of some weeks sets in, because the mean commanders are away from home. The new senior sergeant has a good voice; in the evenings they gather together and sing or talk. The girls also sing, having arrived from nearby houses to cheer up and soothe the soldiers before they go to their deaths. On the sweating-shelves on the first floor they pass from hand to hand in the darkness of the night. By day they tend the cow and wash the soldiers' clothes in front of the door.

The company commander sleeps behind curtains in a dark corner, quite unnoticed. Doctor Lauskis and the paramedic Senior Sergeant Brunovskis inject him with drugs three times a day.

One evening the commander asks Andrievs to yoke up the one-eye to a light buggy. Ješka has become a symbol of success in everyone's eyes, is trusted, and it's regarded as a good sign if anyone has to go somewhere with the black horse. He's going to a gathering of officers, with the table laid.

"I feel bloody lousy – the paramedic won't let me get up. I know what diphtheria is. Perhaps vodka will save me?"

Andrievs helps the senior sergeant to get up and dress in clean clothes. He is severely weakened, the bones of his hips are poking through the skin. Grey rain is falling. The two of them are awaited in the courtyard by a lieutenant, and Andrievs breathes a sigh of relief – the party is not a delusion of the commander.

Andrievs on the coach-box, the officers in the hooded cart. The roads near the front lead from ruin to ruin. Beyond the bend in the river, over a little bridge, finally an undamaged farm can be descried in the fog. The ancient houses, built of stone, slowly emerge from the mist like a symbol of peacetime.

The officers go inside. As the door is opened they can hear that the party is in full swing. Andrievs doesn't unharness. He only takes the bit out of the horse's mouth and puts an armful of hay down in front of her, to refresh her. Ješka, snorting peacefully, chews the hay. Her driver sits, withdraws into the hooded cart, and stares into the darkness of the night, bewitched.

For a moment the rain is replaced by wet snow. Large lumps, like descending butterflies, cut through the blackness with radiance, and vanish in the mud. The front, nearby, is wakeful.

Heavy weapons speak in various voices. The most beautiful voice is of the shells in their barrels. In flight they scream like swans heading south in the autumn. But that is the voice of death. An attack usually begins with artillery fire. The machine guns bark. One machine-gunner with an old Russian Maxim shoots with a beat, that of danger. The anti-tank and cannon shots come overhead almost without a sound. The explosion happens before you hear the shell flying. The most characteristic is the musical key of the mortar, if there are not many mortars and they aren't fired in a mad rush, as they are here. The firing reminds you of the noise of champagne corks being pulled with great force outdoors. Often you can escape from a mortar, of course, if there's somewhere to run to, because it flies considerably more slowly than its sound. In flight the sound is like quiet whispering: *kutch-kutch-kutch*. Having flown the intended distance, the mortar falls silent and comes down upright.

Unexpectedly the company commander climbs into the carriage.

"Let's go. I'm not staying. I feel pretty bad after all."

He hands his driver a small measure of fire-water. Andrievs sniffs it and spits indignantly.

"What the hell is that swill?"

"Made by Latgalians in a petrol barrel," replies the officer. "If I had to choose which soldiers to take into battle, I'd choose Latgalians. You can rely on them on the battlefield."

The black horse doesn't need to be coaxed; the ghost of the farmstead soon vanishes behind them. The riders are swallowed up by the dark, in which only the voice of the front can be heard in the sky, and the horse's hooves on the stones. Andrievs loosens the reins, leaving the homeward route to the horse. Though he is one-eyed, instinct drives him on more surely than eyesight.

"Commander, what helps you in battle? Your thoughts?"

"Thoughts help you between battles. In battle there's no place for them. You can't keep up with events. Only instinct drives you on."

"Instinct?"

"Instinct, presentiment. It's always saved both my life and many other people's. Sometimes I rely on instinct and go against what seems like common sense. Only then do I realize what it was trying to tell me…"

"But surely war is a circumstance that goes against all common sense?"

"What is meant by circumstance? Man is endlessly hoping for external circumstances which will force him take a particular attitude. If for example it was officially confirmed that God exists, the great majority would have no trouble in becoming believers in God. How different would that be from a sheep's obedience to a sheepdog, which bites it in the leg if it doesn't do as it's told?

Man is not a sheep, and God is not a sheepdog. Man must realize how colossal a strength lies within his psychic powers. Man has to create God in the circumstances where God is most lacking… Just as He created us – from nothing. External circumstances, though, are only an illusion – day, night, life, death – or does this crazy confusion appear real to you? The only thing that exists is what we ourselves create, what we believe in. Unfortunately this one thing that he needs to know, man does not know or understand. And God, seeing how pitiful is man's awareness, hides these great powers from himself – still deeply concealed, flashing only occasionally – in instinct, dreams or presentiments…"

For a moment the officer struggles to breathe; then he says: "And what is war? All of us who are here now in Kurzeme, have been born and raised in a free Latvia, and it's clear to all of us what we're fighting for and fighting against… This summer the Germans arrested my younger brother Helmuts in Riga – I hear they took him off to Germany, and assigned him to a unit that is meant to be fighting the British and the Americans. My brother refused to fight, because it wasn't his war. And he was shot dead – not without the collusion of Latvians. He was only seventeen years old. Now tell me, horse-man – what is war?"

"Whereabouts are you from?"

"I'm from Riga, from Āgenskalns. Before the revolution my mother worked for the Tsar's family as a governess. My father was the son of a farmer with a large farm from Kherson district; he served in the Tsar's Crimean Guard as a clerk – that's where they met. After the revolution my mother was allowed to travel back home, but my father was imprisoned, being from a rich farming family. He escaped being shot by the Feodosiya Cheka in 1922; he went incognito on foot right across the Crimea, Ukraine and Belarus; from Sebezha he crawled the last fifteen kilometres, because he didn't know where the Latvian border actually was. The Latgalians found him unconscious in a field and delivered him to Rēzekne hospital with typhus. I don't know much about all that. We didn't talk about it at home. Even when I mentioned it sometimes, talking about myself, there was always silence – sometimes tears. But when the Stalinists came into Latvia in 'forty, my father knew what to expect from them. He lived his life so that only mother knew where he was."

In the darkness they have to cross a draining-ditch. Andrievs recalls that the little bridge is rotten right in the middle. He tries to steer Ješka away, but the horse is pulling to the side. Of course the cart tumbles into the ditch, where the cold black water is flowing up to knee height.

"That'll be just great for your health!" Andrievs curses, trying to help the senior lieutenant to wade to the shore. "This Ješka is only good for carrying corpses!"

"You're a decent man, and you don't even whip your horse!" says the officer, as Andrievs is pouring the water out of his boots. "Thank you! I've never seen soldiers who aren't decent – with a few exceptions. If I had to sum it up, I'd say: you can tell if a man's a soldier. Working with people in extreme circumstances, I've never been wrong in my assessment at first glance. You are a soldier."

Andrievs bites his lip so as not to ask: is that bad or good? And what does that mean: soldier?

Having got out of the ditch, they travel on. The horse's back and knees are dripping; the wet snow has again turned to rain.

"And in spite of first glances, I still try to upset predictions. You remember that young boy from student days who turned up among twenty other men as an extra? He hadn't taken part in the war. I felt he had to be saved. What to do? I couldn't send him to the rear, that takes time – it has to be co-ordinated with the higher ranks. I ordered him to Number 1 Platoon under Lieutenant Jurisons, recommending he should be looked after and not go anywhere outside the bunker without needing to. When there was no-one in the bunker, the young soldier went out and joined up with the machine gun crew. He said he'd be glad to stay with the machine gun, to let the men have a rest for a while. The men did lie down right there in the trenches. Not long passed before a Red patrol from the bushes shot the student dead, point-blank. You can't second-guess fate."

At Bitšķēpi, Dr. Lauskis immediately has the company commander conveyed along with other patients to Lestene church, a collection point for the injured. Command of Company Number 1 is in future entrusted to Senior Lieutenant Ernests Brūns.

"You're suffering from alimentary dystrophy," explains the doctor, taking leave of the officer. "Rest and get nourishment! The nurses at the Aizupes field hospital will give you sandwiches."

It's late at night when Andrievs and his cart arrive at Lestene. The church is in darkness; only in the high windows is there a light like that of flitting bats. There the orderlies are doing the rounds of the wounded with candles and checking whether anyone is in need, or whether anyone has departed this life. The extensive quarters are overflowing with the wounded; they are lying not only on benches but even under them and in the main passage.

One of the dead is carried out of the church, and in his place the company commander is laid on a bench. Before they part, he still has something to say to Andrievs.

"The men were in a depressed mood when I left them… My men," whispers the officer, staring wide-eyed at the high ceiling.

"And how can you help them?"

The officer waves briefly, and Andrievs leaves, swallowed up by the fog.

*

"Are there any witnesses who can say anything more about what you did in the Džūkste operation?" Krop asks Andrievs. "Anyone from your company?"

"The company was completely wiped out in the Christmas battle near Bitšķēpi."*

"How so? A hardened company that had been fighting all over Vidzeme – even at More."

"They couldn't call on the artillery for support. In the course of an hour in the morning there was heavy Russian artillery fire, they lost communications, neither the telephone nor the wireless worked. The company was engaged in close combat with about two Russian battalions. It was terrible close fighting – right down to the last breath."

"But what about the prisoners, the wounded?" Krop persists.

"You could ask one of the political leaders. Fighting opposite us was the 125th Latvian Riflemen's regiment. No-one got out of Bitšķēpi, not even the wounded, who couldn't move by themselves, let alone those who were taken prisoner, when the ammunition ran out. When the battle had died down, they were still shooting. Not only in the trenches, but at the rear too. That's a war crime in wartime. In the First World War the Red riflemen committed the same crimes; the actions of Stučka's soldiers in the War of Liberation were also a crime. To shoot the wounded on the battlefield, or those taken prisoner, is not forgivable!"

"Don't tell me your made-up stories that you can't know about! Just tell me what you've experienced yourself," shouts the investigator, yet still writing something down hastily.

Andrievs dully inspects the illuminated map of Latvia which is pinned up on the wall behind the colonel's head. The colours of Kurzeme on this map are a raw blue, pale green and linoleum brown, like sawdust. And then, as if bit by bit a stone resting in the ground had been exposed in the tortuous heat and bright light of these days and nights, he glimpses the real landscape of Kurzeme.

Kurzeme is red and black. And astonishing in its size.

The fortress of Kurzeme, the cauldron of Kurzeme, the spoon-net of Courland – call it what you will. For the Germans: "*Scheisse mit dem Krieg!* To hell with the war!" and intimations of collapse; for the Russians: "*Za rodinu! Za Stalina!* For the Fatherland! For Stalin!" and anger about the unconquerable fortress, when victory is so close; for the Latvians – their homeland under their feet. The peace of the fallen, which none can ever again disturb from their deep dreaming, the senseless feast of the living, which lashes the bodies with an even more painful whip than the peace of the fallen, the cauldron of hell on the horizon of the sky, where one explosion can't be distinguished from another and trees with their roots are blown up to the clouds, the land ransacked by gunfire and the harvest churned back into the bosom of the ground, blood-red sunsets, the deep black midnight over the soldiers, who are sucked like leeches into the clay of a dug-out, the eyes of half-mad horses, the deafness from the noise of explosions, the silence and despair of the refugees over their abandoned homes, the grenade-riddled buildings and the field-hospitals full of the living dead, the ghostly moonlight over the carts, full of the fallen, whose still arms do not point a *Heil!* to the Führer, but threaten revenge for the millions of lost lives, the looks in the eyes of old soldiers and the thoughts only of combat and an honourable death on the battlefield; but death, welcome death, which is unique to each one, arrives with a completely different face – so lonely and icy among the decimated ranks, as innocent as the seventeenth autumn of a young boy untouched by bullets and kisses, selflessly dragging from the field of death his heavily wounded friends – with a quality that cannot be analysed, divided into its component parts, it either is or is not under the shadows of the biplanes, which, with their engines switched off, glide in the darkness with their bomb loads, while on the icy roads the "tiger" divisions encounter the iron Josef Stalins, soup in the trenches from thermos flasks, the wives and daughters of the Soldiers' Aid in spirit and flesh, with Christmas songs and pies, sugar-beet beer, the silence before the storm, "Holy Night" with "Christmas trees" – flare rockets which hang in the skies under parachutes, the chaplain struck down by shrapnel from a grenade during a Christmas sermon in Lestene church, the barrage fire and the lice, the grey-blue guts across the trousers of a Red Army soldier, in whose face you can see your brother, a childhood friend or your father, the lightning flash of happiness on a proud march to battle accompanied by an orchestra of Latvian flags, when you know clearly that there cannot be anything more royal under the sun than being in the ranks of this funeral procession in your own land, for your own land, where yesterday's boys are stepping with death's heads on their caps and *Gott mit uns*, God with us, on the buckle of a soldier's belt, singing "Two little pigeons", then an hour later mad processions in the dug-outs, in the white fire of automatic weapons, when the orchestras have fallen silent, and over everything an uncertainty about what it would be right to do at this moment.

Only one thing is still holy, and that is the land that is intertwined with the sky in an indissoluble ring. The land on which one can rely. The black land has been able to raise the cradle-pole, been able to raise even the white rose on the grave. The land of Kurzeme, which taught one to destroy life and love death.

"That isn't possible," says Andrievs. "I can't tell you what I experienced in Kurzeme."

"So what about yourself?" inquires the investigator.

"I became a 'rat at the rear'."

"What's that supposed to mean? You deserted?"

"I received orders to turn up at the headquarters of the 19th Division at Lestene, where they informed me that I'd been transferred to the veterinary company of the division. There, I stayed until the capitulation, carrying out my feeding duties."

"What were your duties?"

"Providing fodder for sick horses."

"How many sick horses were there?"

"About seven hundred."

"That will be enough for now." Having signed off what Andrievs had said and given a juicy yawn, Krop leaves the office. His place is taken by a guard.

The blind darkness in the barred windows is now diluted by a pale dawn. Brīvības Street is gradually coming to life; the early morning tram, rushing past, makes the rails creak shrilly. Andrievs is no longer troubled by sleep, only by an endless internal itch – after so many sleepless days and nights his brain seems plagued by an itching from within. The thought seems strange to him that he is here in Riga, right on the corner of Brīvības and Stabu Streets, where the pavements of his home town are all around him, and familiar people are walking by.

One day the guard knocks on the pane of the cell door, looks through it and says in Russian: "Radvilis, parcel for you!"

Astonished, Andrievs looks at the packet, wrapped in brown greaseproof paper. He opens it to find some sausage rolls. He sniffs them incredulously – white bread, butter and little grey slices of sausage. Marija's kitchen and the view through the window onto the rusty roofs of inner Riga are revived in his memory.

Praise be! A miracle out of nowhere – sausage rolls!

What are hardest to answer are the questions about Andrievs' movements after the capitulation. He carefully relates the version concocted along with Eizens.

"In April, a few weeks before the capitulation, I received an order to go to Ventspils to take necessary medical supplies for the company there. I set off with my two-horse team. Two enemy reconnaissance aircraft were flying at a very great height beyond Matkule. The alarm hadn't been raised, because there was no sense in shooting, owing to their height. It turned out that the pilots had thrown out a few light mortar bombs, on the off-chance. They exploded as soon as they hit the ground, right beside my cart. I was injured, but the force of the explosion killed my mare. In shock, I released the other horse, and then I lost consciousness. I came to my senses in some farmhouse. Some herdsmen had found me, because the one-eyed horse had stood there in the marsh beside the road where I had led him."

"Good – go on."

"Two old farmers lived in that house. The wife dug seven pieces of shrapnel from my arm. They cared for me. I burned my uniform, I wore civilian clothes that they gave me from their dead son's belongings."

"Go on."

"A week later the area was searched by Red Army patrols. '*Ruki vverkh! Otday chasy!* Hands up! Hand over your watches!' After they had ransacked us and relieved us of our watches, the farmer and I were made to go to the meadow at the edge of the forest. We thought we'd be shot dead there, but their command post was there by the forest where they made a record of their captives to send them on to the Kuldīga filtration camp. Nobody knew what filtration was, but this was the so-called pre-filtration. What they called a *troika* turned up. One of them called out: '*Kto umeyet po russki?* Who understands Russian?' Nobody else responded, I went. One by one the men were questioned – who are you, where are you from, why did you leave your home? The old man said I was his son."

"And where did you end up?"

"I went back to their home with the farmer. They let us go."

The interrogation stops, Andrievs is left alone with what he wants most of all to forget.

*

I am Andrievs.

Maška is writhing on the road in front of me.

Probably a broken neck. I can't believe it.

I sit by her head, I hold her head tightly. I can't let her dance in the dust. Birds are calling in the forest, long sweet trills. This morning I couldn't sleep, as if sensing something. What happened after that I don't recall. Maška on the road, a puddle of blood. Her ears bloody, her eyes distended, spread-eagled on the road and wheezing.

There's probably nothing more to be done. The explosion has broken the thill and demolished the yoke. Ješka is still on his feet, rearing, being throttled by the straps.

I had a pistol – where? I rummage in the cart; it isn't there.

I undo the straps that are strangling Ješka. I sit back down by Maška's head on the road. My trusty little girl. That's how I regard her. Delicate, shallow breathing. Breathing quickly, swallowing her blood. I'm thankful to her. I protect her from the sun. Her heart is still beating, her strong, good HEART. I have nothing to shoot with, there's nothing I can do – forgive me. I raise my left hand; my whole side is covered in blood. Gradually I am losing consciousness.

I go into the forest alone. A cool damp dusk. Ješka comes with me. I drive him away. The last contact – the touch of peat across my forehead. Everything goes dark.

Am I still Andrievs?

*

Krop soon returns – he's probably been drinking coffee. That is the smell he has around him. The friendly face of a Cheka major having a snack lunch.

Sucking remnants of food from between his teeth, Krop calmly folds his arms on the pages of notes.

"What's the name of the house where you spent the summer of 1945?"

"Zīžas."

"And the owner?"

"Celms."

Krop writes it down. Then suddenly his kindly expression is replaced by a thunderous bass. "And if I were to tell you now that I've had it up to here with all your tales? If I told you that actually you were living in the forest with the Kabile bandits and you were nursed by the bandits' signalwoman, with the cover-name The Postwoman?"

Andrievs endures the attack calmly. He is still floundering in a mire of memories around the stricken horse. Krop observes him closely – his subject is too immobile, stiff like a mummy. "I don't know any Postwoman," Andrievs waves his hand indifferently.

"All right, we'll start at the other end. What happened after you were released from pre-filtration?"

"I stayed with the farmer until the autumn. I helped with the farm work. After that I set off for Riga. I worked as a loader at the goods station. Later they re-employed me at the racecourse as a jockey."

"Was there a jockey called Antonija Saltupa there?"

"No, she wasn't there any more."

"So where was she, if I may ask?"

"I don't know. She was riding during the war. Since the war I haven't met her again. I heard that she'd drowned in the Daugava."

Andrievs himself is surprised at what he has said. He has never heard any such thing. Krop's face is turning purple.

"Repeat that."

"Antonija has drowned in the Daugava."

The investigator gets up, goes over to Andrievs and hits him on the mouth with his heavy hand.

"Repeat that, you bastard!"

"Antonija has drowned in the Daugava," says Andrievs.

The blood from his lips, like warm salty sea-water, rinses his dry throat.

"Repeat that!"

"Antonija has drowned in the Daugava."

In a sudden fit of unaccountable rage, Krop reacts instinctively, punching Andrievs with his fists like a bag.

"Tone has drowned, you understand?" Andrievs repeats again and again in a shrill voice.

Through the tears that fill his eyes unbidden, Andrievs recalls feeling the same pain in his cheek when his fellow jockey struck him with the whip, and he cries out: "Antonija has drowned in the Daugava, and you won't get the prize, your promotion, you understand, you skunk – don't even hope for it!"

Krop comes to his senses, cracks the bones of his fingers and returns quietly to his place. The guard at the door, a bushy-bearded little Russian, stares intently at the barred windows and pretends not to notice anything.

"If you sleep with dogs, you'll get fleas," yells Krop, as the guard walks past. "All these lies… With all these dogs… While the farmers' houses and the towns were in flames, people like these were sitting in the bandits' lairs. Degenerates! The people were fighting a decisive battle for redemption from the black plague. The nation was going into its last battle for its future – with the red flag of its future, noble and beautiful! You bastard, aren't you a son of your people? Isn't your homeland a sacred concept for you? Hasn't the great Daugava ever called your name? Why didn't you have a machine gun in your hand to drive the Fascist wolf faster into a stinking cave? Answer me! People like you were shooting at me, and even you wouldn't think of shooting me, would you, you piece of shit? There's no point talking to a dog. Beware your people's curse!"

Andrievs feels his teeth with his tongue; thank God, only the insides of his cheeks have been beaten to a pulp.

"You tried to make me stop Grand Hill! You didn't get the money, you skunk! Don't think I've forgotten!"

Krop has now composed himself, and cold-bloodedly replies: "No-one will believe that."

"Why not?"

"His owner and trainer was Giebelhausen."

Say the rest of it, thinks Andrievs; the distinguished trainer Sten Giebelhausen, a Norwegian businessman who was imprisoned in 1941 by the Cheka, and vanished without trace.

"Wasn't he one of the ones who were hurriedly shot and buried in the courtyard of the Central Prison when the Reds retreated? You must know that!"

"I don't have to know anything!" retorts Krop. "I only know that a runner like that can't be better than a Soviet one!"

Andrievs spits out blood and slumps across the table. An absurd ninth wave shakes him like death-throes.

Krop has a guard lead Andrievs away, adding in parting: "I'll be investigating Zīžas and Celms, never you fear!"

His cellmates look on in silence as Andrievs is led in, beaten up. One of them puts a dirty handkerchief on his lips, another gives him his portion of soup, which Prisoner Radvilis is not due to receive today.

They will investigate Zīžas. Let them! And while they're at it, let them gather in the bones of their own!

That is why Andrievs mentioned Zīžas – because he knows well that this large, beautiful Kurzeme farmstead has vanished from the face of the earth.

*

He did go there once, before the Christmas battle, losing his way in the dark, but the impression was so clear, as if he had found an oasis in the middle of a desert. Dark night prevailed all around, but to the south it was uneasy – pale gleams of rocket-fire crackling, fizzing, waves of light ascending, descending, pink auroras flaring up. In the farmstead where about fifty refugees were holed up, all the habitable buildings – the house, the sauna, the byre, the hay-loft, the homemade floating candles glinted in the dark evening. In among the uprooted sugar-beets, the cattle beets or the cabbages, embedded in sheep-fat, was a burning linen wick. Close to such a floating candle one could even read. Although the conflict was going on not far away, the Christmas battles had little effect on everyday life in the houses. Forest plantations and low hillocks separated them from the line of battle. Always the monotonous life was accompanied by constant tension, uncertainty about events. There was no radio, no-one got to see newspapers. They only knew as much as they heard from their neighbours.

When Andrievs knocked on the door to ask the way, at first they took him for a German gendarme. An elderly man came out, but when he understood the situation, he volunteered that he was Celms, the owner of the farm, his son had fallen as a Legionary, and his wife was ill. Everyone else at Zīžas was a refugee. One of the refugees, an adolescent boy, emerged hesitantly from an ancient Danzig-style wardrobe in the front room, having retreated in there in fear of an inspection by gendarmes. How many refugees there were here nobody knew; the living quarters were constantly full to the brim. The residents had acquired a taste for the grain in the granary and the pine-cones in the bunkers that were dug into the ground. Sitting at the big table was a boy, studying by the light of a floating candle an edition of Hauff's tales, published by Jessen, a little collection of the illustrated stories, with faded covers, engrossed in a world of ancient tales.

Mrs. Celms appeared, a shrivelled, bent old woman, white as an apple-tree in blossom.

"What do you want, sonny?"

"I was just… asking the way."

"You'd better come inside. I've got to see to the meal. I have a jug of milk and a big hunk of bread."

The farmer's wife went over to the covered shelf over the oven and put food on the table.

"Take a bite of what God has given. You've probably got a long way to go?"

Andrievs bit into the hunk and told what he knew. Every few moments the farmer's wife clapped her hands together – my goodness! The farmer listened in, weighing it up – abandon their home or wait it out? Some errant volley of fire had already killed a cow. An airborne bomb in the yard had thrown blocks of earth the size of tables from the edge of the garden at the linden tree, and now, in order to dig out cabbages for the soup, they had to climb a tree. Right after the shooting they had wanted to move out, but he had had an unusual dream – an angel of brilliant light had appeared to him and assured him that all would be well. The maddest thing about it was when they were in the lower meadow, removing multi-barrelled mortars, there were cows mooing. When an explosion caused a vacuum, in the rarefied air people were blown to pieces even in their hiding-places. Well, so now they were forbidden to stay here for long; devices had to be removed immediately from the exposed positions. The soldiers would discharge their rounds and move on.

"There's still the threshing ahead of us," interjected the farmer's wife.

It may be Christmas, but the weather continued ridiculously warm. They said they'd managed to talk the German Commandant into letting them get a group together for the threshing. He had said: you can keep all the wheat for yourselves, and if necessary exchange it for rye! You have plenty of hay, but plenty of refugees too.

A one-year-old refugee infant ran into the room. Unable to find his mother, the farmer's wife picked up the crying infant in her arms and sang a happy song to calm him down:

> The girl has white legs,
> Plaited hair, a tied-up ribbon.
> Two are riding on grey horses,
> Who knows where they will turn in.
>
> They were both drunk, the horse was lame,
> They went different ways.
> Do such ones know where Fortune smiles

Where girls like roses bloom?

I yoke up the triple yoke,
Six bay steeds they are,
I leave the dark night to the steeds
For my very own bride.

Bride of mine, bride of mine,
Is there a little warm room?
What use is a warm little room?
What can a little bed do?

Every morning neighbour Jānis
Drags his wooden-clogged feet.
Drag, drag, neighbour Jānis,
You won't get me anyway!

Comforted by the rocking, the little child started to smile. And Andrievs, too, felt so pleasantly comfortable, not having to get up, or struggle back into the dark night.

When he did so, with a friendly goodbye from the farmers, he could hardly find his horse any more. The yard was full of black-clad tank crews. Their armoured vehicles were there too. The whole mood was spoiled.

Later, when Antonija was treating Andrievs in the bunker, she also knew about Zīžas.

Around Midsummer, she said, she had walked past where it stood, although a terrible smell was borne on the wind from there. Nothing was left of the former military railway line, neither rails nor sleepers, no trace of them, only a few burned-out wagons and a locomotive that had plunged into the river. In the forest there were many bunkers, all of them half-full of water. Destruction in the forest, but in the fields even worse – ruins, pits, fragments. She had gone into Zīžas. The bullet-damaged wind turbine was still there, the little pond with its frogs and one half-sunken tank, the cherry orchard. In the courtyard, shot-out mortar-steering devices, pieces of clothing, shards of wood and metal. The grass there had turned brittle and brown. Spent cartridges and shrapnel from the same place were in the dug-outs. Quite close to where the house had stood, as well as further away, the wrecks of Russian tanks were strewn around in all conditions – which ones had arrived in the past hour? No soldiers were buried – each one remained where he fell after the battle. She had looked inside the open hatch in the turret of each tank, and glimpsed the dead down inside. On another vehicle the armour plating was dislocated and ripped out from within by a weapon; another tank remained closed up, burned out, not a living soul could have got out. She had counted about seventeen tanks. She hadn't seen German tanks anywhere. The houses were abandoned, empty. It had been hard to get away – mine-fields all about with trip-wires. Who knew where they were, all gone! By the roadside, munition cases were thrown about, canister-shots and unexploded grenades and men with sagebrush growing through their bodies.

At the neighbours' house they were able to tell her that the farmer's wife at Zīžas had died around Eastertime, while the farmer was incurably ill in Tukums hospital.

*

The next morning a guard leads Andrievs into another, unfamiliar office – to the prosecutor, Major Podpolsky.

"We've been thinking of closing your case, but it won't do you any good. It isn't possible that throughout the whole German occupation you haven't done anything bad! Here is your file, the evidence, the investigator's conclusions…"

Andrievs ruffles through the papers. It turns out that the only charge on which Andrievs has been imprisoned was entered in green ink on several pages of squared paper and submitted by Denisov, the director. "Andrievs Radvilis, a good specialist in horse-breeding, worked conscientiously at the Hippodrome. He comes from a wealthy family and took a responsible post in the Fascist army," runs the wording of the deposition.

"So do I have to admit to what I haven't done?" asks Andrievs.

"No, you don't have to do that."

"So now you'll release me?"

"You're supposed to be sent to work in Siberia, but, look here . . ." Podpolsky indicates the pile of withdrawn case-files. "There's a needle and thread. Mend your clothes. We'll see you again!"

"Goodbye!"

"Don't hurry with the goodbyes!" smirks Podpolsky. "It's my job to see that once a man gets in here, he'll be back."

"I'll look for a strong healer."

"Not only look for one – you'll lead us to her yourself."

The prosecutor gathers up his papers and leaves the office. Only the guard remains, dully observing Andrievs working away at his trouser buttons.

It can't be, thinks Andrievs feverishly, that when someone is thrown out on the street from here, he's simply released? And that riddle – "you'll lead us to her yourself" – what does that mean?

What about his cellmates, with whom he's spent so much blood and sweat? What will be their fate? Even though they're all different, the endless days and nights have annealed them together, fused them like candles from tallow, like the buns they receive. Without this fusing, each would be a different man.

The guard accompanies him to the exit, then vanishes back into the steamy labyrinth of the Corner House. Suitcase in hand, Andrievs soon finds himself on the brightly-lit Brīvības Street. The sun, as it runs past, clutches his heart and bares its teeth like a dog, the March wind blows at his back as at a sail and drives him back along the street. Feeling that his knees are giving way and his suitcase is dragging him to the ground, he supports himself against the rough wall of a building.

Freedom. That word comes like an arrow, bores through him and flies off into the skies. Dear Riga!

He wants to fall to the ground and kiss the street.

Citizens hurrying past the trembling figure's shadow on the street corner look contemptuously at him as he stands there inebriated in the morning! Has he no shame, outdoors in March, in the promise of a new spring under Stalin's sun?

Purviņš and Vītoliņš

We're travelling slowly through Pļaviņas. On one side the town, on the other the Daugava river. Radvilis grumbles: "Pļaviņas, well, what is Pļaviņas? Pļaviņas doesn't exist."

"How come? Look where we are!" I laugh.

"In the beginning there was just the Pļaviņas farmhouse. When that burned down, Count Meden built Pļavkrogs tavern in its place – there, in the middle of town, right opposite the river-crossing. In Ulmanis' times they pulled down the tavern in order to build the House of Unity, renamed the House of Culture in Soviet times – that's how culture gradually grows out of drunkenness. Three places in this area are ancient – Bebruleja, Štokmanshofa and Gostiņi. The old people of Gostiņi, by the way, called Pļaviņas a suburb of Gostiņi. Of course, Štokmanshofa station contributed a lot – especially when they built the Stukmaņi to Valka narrow-gauge line. Now turn right towards the Daugava, please! We'll go along Gostiņi Main Street."

It is evident on Main Street how artificial the merging of Pļaviņas with Gostiņi is. The town lacks a pulse. Trees and bushes slip past. The road crosses a tiny rivulet, which flows into the Daugava right there by the well-tended park.

"Skanstupīte." Craning his neck, Radvilis follows it with his gaze. "Once there were several cascades there, and a deep white dolomite ravine. In the spring, such a racket would rise up over the bird cherry trees that even the nightingales covered their ears. Since the flooding there might still be rapids in the bushes – maybe not. Maybe General Trentelberg's ghost is wandering along the bastion. You can still make out the actual Skanskupīte, the Bastion Stream, by the outflow, not far from Spīgana station.

True, they actually call the river Izmata there. It's typical of this area that the neighbours call this same river by different names. You've never been to Spīgana station?"

"Never in my life!" I laugh.

"So how can you live in this world?"

"And you have?"

"My mother's sister, my godmother, lived at Aizpures, not far from that place. I used to spend a couple of weeks there every summer. By Spīgana station there are fields of white anemones in the water-meadows. The station probably isn't there any more, but the anemone fields are eternal."

The first thing you encounter in Gostiņi is a long white tavern and a sort of low stables built of light grey stone on the opposite side of the street. They are followed by a long row of houses of wood and stone – mostly one-or two-storey structures, each with its own little yard and fence, each with its own face, the eyes of the windows grimacing. The roofs are the colour of horses herded together – grey, piebald, dark bay.

"Gostiņi has many names," explains the old man. "Zarnu miests, Gutville, because of the abattoir that supplied the sausage factories of three whole towns – Riga, Jelgava and Daugavpils – or Žīdu miests, Jewtown, because early in the twentieth century nearly all the inhabitants of the place were Jews. But these are folk-names. The first one you can find on old maps is Evestmunde from about the twelfth century. Just as Glazmanka is known by the Russians after Glazmanka manor. The place is also called Treutelbergi. Because for quite a while a Swedish general of that name lived in the bastion near the Aiviekste. The Jews, meanwhile, know it as Dankere even now – Dankere tavern, on the bank of the Aiviekste, was extremely popular with raft-drivers and river-crossers."

We stop at the narrow end of Main Street.

"We're getting out now!" Radvilis urges. "We can't fool around like this – let's stretch our old bones."

He indicates the church, nestled in a park with a grand portico, which has a low tower and a silver dome.

"How do you like it?"

"Real Treutelbergi." I raise my eyebrows above the shadow of a smile.

"And you're not at all surprised by it? Have you seen any Lutheran churches with a dome? And a chancel right above the altar, an unusual example of late Classicism."

"A dome, yes."

I'm more surprised by the strange peace of Gostiņi. Both of us are shouting in loud voices in the middle of the street, but we are like a reflection in water – a cat crosses the sandy market square without a sound, jackdaws fly soundlessly past the church's dome, settle on bare branches and remain silent. Next to the church, an empty bus stop and a noticeboard. On the other side, in the green, sky-blue and pink wooden houses, a corner of a curtain stirs behind a pane or some shadow shifts in the depths. But maybe it only seems so to me. Maybe it's happening in a dream, in a reflection in water. Here everything seems possible, and at the same time nothing does.

"Let's go to the Daugava," I suggest.

"As far as the Aiviekste, my dear! Here it flows into the Daugava." He chuckles warmly through his nose like a grouse in April.

Along Little Street, past a stone wall we find the white church. The buildings here are small, fitting the name of the street, and by the wire gate a tiny, yapping puppy is guarding the yard. His silvery barking, like shrill bells, finally brings to life the scene at the confluence of the black and white rivers, which seems just like a drawing from Radvilis' portfolio: on wrapping paper, a little in chalk, a little in pencil, a little in charcoal. The objects lack shading, because the light is too dim.

When we turn into Firemen's Street, Radvilis relates: "At the side of the market square there used to be a little wooden booth in which they kept barrels and wheels, a few pairs of firemen's gloves and a ladder. Since fires were a rarity, the stock stood untouched until the end of the thirties, when a huge fire occurred and burned down the river side of Main Street. Until that time anyone could be a fireman, but after that they established a brigade, a proper one, with brass buttons and cockades on their hats."

The street crosses a muddy ford, across which we wade up to the Aiviekste bank. The water swirls black and thick around our legs like curdled blood; the black is a clump of forest on a wedge of earth, beyond which the Aiviekste merges with the Daugava.

"The black marshy waters of the Aiviekste meet the white dolomite waters of the Daugava. From here we can't see it – it's too far. But once I saw it with my own eyes from the bank of the Skanstupīte – how the black swirls with the white. They say it's the eighth wonder of the world – and it is. At the confluence with the Aiviekste, the Daugava immediately strikes out to the left and is quite calm and as deep as a lake right up to the wild rapids of Grūbe. At Aizpures, all the men were raftsmen on the Aiviekste, and they used to tell how, as they entered the waters of the Daugava, they were gradually overcome by a strange feeling. On the Aiviekste the raft seemed huge, but on the Daugava tiny, like a nutshell that the rapids will smash to timbers. In flood-time you had to beware of the Devil's mad whirlpool, but in dry periods you could get by only on the left side. They say they offered bread and biscuits to the rapids, just to get out alive."

"What's that there?" I point to the woods on the opposite bank.

"Grīva graveyard, where the Gostiņi people lie buried. Evestimunde, as it was called on old maps, the first name of Gostiņi. That was where the administrative districts of Latgale, Vidzeme and Kurzeme used to meet. They have a saying: when a cock crows at Glazmanka, it wakes up three districts and nine parishes.* Now, after the floods, sometimes the water laps against the embankment of the graveyard. In the older part, closer to the confluence of the rivers, there was once a simple wooden church, Grīva Church. When it collapsed, Nikolaus von Korf had this church built with a dome."

"I want to ask about something else – why was there a Jewish town here? After all, the Tsar didn't allow Jews to settle in Vidzeme and Kurzeme."

"You think that where we're standing is Vidzeme?"

"That's what they say. Latgale starts beyond the Aiviekste."

"The Aiviekste has never been the border. At the beginning of the nineteenth century there was still a strip of land of the Vitebsk district here. For the Jews this place was really good. The raftsmen were wealthy, and the Jews made a good living from them. Jews were not allowed to own Christian land; they mainly earned a living from crafts and trade, so Ulmanis and his agriculture were not really to their taste. From here, they and their packs or carts went trading in all directions and then returned home. From Aizpures I remember the Jews Moiše and Joselis with their packs; they'd been wandering around ever since the Tsar's time. I was drawn to Moiše's heavy pack; for me as a small child it was fascinating – delicate objects, books on interpreting dreams, pencils and ink at the back. Joselis traded in lightly salted herrings, but he took away rags for the Līgatnes paper-mill, bones, horses' hair and pigs' bristles. Elija Levits drove a tar barrel built into a cart, and Father always used to run up to him with a scoop of axle-grease. I don't know a single rural farm where a Jew was asked to pay for a night's accommodation or not allowed to spend his Sabbath. In the mornings my godmother in Aizpures used to cook ham and eggs for me, but for the Jews she cooked just in butter in a separate pan, respecting their faith. In the stable they always kept a place and an armful of hay for Rubens the glazier's horse. Rubens was a proper craftsman, and Uncle's good friend. The panes he installed are probably still there today. When Rubens got old and couldn't work any more, every time we were in Gostiņi we used to bring him a special treat – a leg of turkey or soft sweet apples. He lived there, not far from the new synagogue. I remember the shops on Main Street at the time – from the same place, storekeepers, tinsmiths, saddlers, cobblers, tailors. From Ginsburgs' I'd buy godmother's medicine, at Lībmanis' they sewed me my first leather boots as a gift when I started school. The owners would stand in the doorway and entice you in. 'Come inside my shop! Come inside my shop! I'll give you a discount – you, sir!'"

"And where did they all end up?"

Radvilis falls silent. The silence becomes oppressive. I stare back at the township, because again I have the feeling that we are being observed. In the end it seems that something's boring into my shoulder-blades. I turn my back to the black waters.

"It was a tragedy," the old man says. "I wasn't there."

"But you do know."

"On the first of August in Krustpils parish by the Kaķīši marsh, on the road between Spuņģeni and Vilkukrogs."

"How many of them were there?"

"A little over two hundred. Overall, a bigger number were shot in the Kaķīši forest, because that's where they also shot the Jews from Krustpils and Pļaviņas, in later years also the Jews from countries in the West."

"Arājs?"

"Arājs was there too, but they say the one who ordered the shooting was the commander of the second company in Arājs' unit, Lieutenant Dībietis, a drunk degenerate. Of course, some local 'patriots' also took part – more than twenty people. Arājs' team had a technique of their own: the front rank, squatting on their knees, shoots at the heart, the second row stands behind them, aiming for the head. The Jews were stripped and laid in a pit – as the dead fell into the pit, so they called up the next ones. The food suppliers brought their killers vodka and sausages. When Arājs' men got tired, they made the locals continue, while they recovered their strength. One of my former schoolmates realized too late what was going on, and acted as if he was drunk – lurching along the road so they wouldn't make him shoot. Many farmers I knew herded their horses into the forest, so as not to have to do the carrying. I remember at Krustpils we met the leader of the Gostiņi self-defence force. He turned up drunk, dragging his gun along the ground. My brother realized something was wrong and asked cautiously 'What's happened to you, Pēteris?' 'A great disaster, Augusts! Today we shot the Jews of Gostiņi.' 'What – all of them?' 'All of them, all of them! Some demon ordered me to get shooting, now I will have nightmares all the way to the grave.' 'A great disaster,' my brother said, a 'great disaster.' That

Pēteris had himself studied in the Jewish school, they say – later he became headmaster of Gostiņi school."

"Headmaster…"

"That's just it, headmaster of Gostiņi school, leader of the Krustpils after-school association – isn't it odd that their pupils signed up for the self-defence unit? The degradation came after they realized that it couldn't be done without a stiff drink, the blood, the robbery and the drinking, for years on end – and they stopped looking like men. Later they tried to appoint Arājs as the commander of the 15th division of the Latvian Legion, but by then the bestiality was obvious. He was dismissed for incompetence."

"What happened to him after that?"

"He was married to Zelma Zeibote, the rich shop-owner. Under that surname he lived in Germany after the war, working in a printing-house in Frankfurt as a typesetter. In the mid-seventies they caught him and sentenced him to life imprisonment. They say he died in Kassel prison in 1988."

Footsteps are rustling along the grassy bank. Like a fuzzy illustration, three figures approach us. The first is a woman, carrying a boy of about one year swaddled in a blanket, with a dummy in his mouth but his eyes closed. He must been wearied by the early morning by the river. The woman is followed by a man with a green folding travelling-chair under his arm, and finally comes a young man, carrying a fishing-rod and the end of a rolled cigarette. The newcomers don't greet us; only the last of them has a smile on his lips.

A pleasant whiff of cherry tobacco wafts back to us.

"I heard that they were wailing loudly as they went along the highway. Then they stood quietly by the pits, as if spellbound. Quietest of all were the children on their parents' arms. Behind them came the carts carrying those who couldn't walk, and at the back came the diggers with their spades. In the big towns the Jews were degraded gradually – they made them sew yellow stars on their clothes, and their property was confiscated – the so-called luxury items; they didn't let them walk on the pavement or shop at Aryan shops. But in places like Gostiņi they simply put notices in their letter-boxes saying that the next day they must gather in the market-place to receive information. When they had gathered, the self-defence unit commander gave a speech saying that the Jews had gone against the Latvian people, sold out the Latvians, because of them Latvian citizens had been delivered into Soviet hands, and now the Jews had to atone for their guilt. For resisting they would be shot, under the laws of wartime. The men were herded into one old synagogue, the women and children into another. The scenario was much the same everywhere – degraded, pushed out, robbed, shot dead and then robbed again. While they were kept for a couple of weeks in a ghetto, they'd be put to work. Farmers in the countryside who needed manpower could get them for a while; they were brought back only to be shot. If anyone was forgotten or hidden, they'd go after him and shoot him on the spot."

Radvilis touches his peaked cap. His bony fingers with their white, curled nails rasp across his brow. For the first time I catch sight of the animal side of a person – it is an old animal standing before me with wisps of grey hair around his face, with paler flecks of skin and dark blotches of pigment like pine-bark. His eyes are pale and dry. The old Jews who were herded into Dankere market-place that day must have looked like this. The same is true of the war-horses, like skeletons draped with skin, who tried to stay upright in all the ravaged and bombed towns of Europe, until they fell and became fodder for those that could still be helped by fodder.

A tenderness stirs in my heart, and I place my fingers in front of his mouth, as if wanting to release him from the obligation to bear witness. I have provoked him with my questions, yet, in spite of the horrors, here and now, I still want to know. But he roughly pushes away my hand and suddenly asks: "Are you cold?"

I shake my head in denial, although the wind brings a cold blast from the water. Dark blue like the famous Prussian blue, which was created from the reaction of yellow prussiate of soda with iron. In this wind you can gradually freeze from within.

I stamp around on the mud, to grow into it, to become a tree. I must stand here and listen to the end. I have to find an answer.

Without it I can't return to the town – to the streets where every window accuses me.

"One more important factor is that no-one really knew anything," continues Radvilis, having reflected for a moment. "For a person used to the modern flood of information it's impossible to imagine how great the ignorance was. I remember how our neighbour Lilija was a witness to the hunting down and shooting of Soviet sympathizers, after the Germans invaded, and she talked about it to anyone who would listen, yet she was put under house arrest for a whole month for disclosing secrets. You could hear the shootings every day, but what did you know about it? Even the propagandist writers who were shooting Jews in the first days of the war, not with bullets but with words – like Corporal 'Lataviensis' Teodors Zeltiņš in his *National Zemgale* – did they have any idea of the consequences, that someone would have to take up a gun and physically destroy? Who knew about the Molotov-Ribbentrop Pact?* The footage spooled forward like a silent film, you had to obey orders. Those same *Aizsargi*,* the Defenders, who had ensured Ulmanis' coup, were made by Ulmanis himself to protect 'USSR forces against provocative acts', so that the occupying army and tanks could enter the military bases unhindered. The *Aizsargi* were ready to fight, but they had to carry out the order to capitulate, with hanging heads. Right after the occupation, at the end of June, the order was given to disarm the *Aizsargi*, and the communists rushed to do it, even before the divisional commissions started receiving the weapons. After that, Ulmanis announced that the order had been issued to liquidate the *Aizsargi* organizations. They had material assets and property! The commissions undertook it diligently until November – until they got them all. In that sense the Reds kept their word: every vestige of the past was crushed and annihilated."

I want to say something, but he raises an admonitory hand.

"Of course there were also people with strong convictions, especially here in Gostiņi… Revolutionary ideas from 1905, from Dvinsk and Riga, quickly spread to Dankere through Kreutzburg,* and especially active here was the Bund, the Jewish Social Democrats. The Stolpers, brother and sister – maybe you've heard of them? They were highly praised revolutionaries. Dankere was more revolutionary than other places around here. That's why the black Cossack *sotnya* unit was more ruthless here – they set fire to the whole of Dankere. Besides – it's hard to explain … the place was small, life was very hard, difficult, but in spite of it all Jewish society was extremely class-bound. People's relationships depended on their material situation. You understand that? It must sound strange to you. In Latvian society there has always been a sort of artificial construct, but for the Jews it was natural. The rich didn't go hungry, the middle classes managed somehow, but most of them were poor, with not even enough money to take the Sabbath off. The only consolation for them was the synagogue – the place to forget themselves in. The poorer a Jew was, the more religious. The richest ones here were the Vestermanis family, leather-workers, famous for their men's trouser-belts and sole-leather, but it wasn't possible for them to mix with the poor – that was beneath their dignity! Zionism was once an activity of the rich – they even called the ordinary people's Yiddish language jargon! That year of the Soviets brought in some changes in the life of the Gostiņi Jews, but no-one was deported to Siberia. That was taken into account, of course. And the demonstrations with red flags too."

"But why didn't they flee?"

"Who knows – maybe they were hoping to redeem themselves. They sensed that the Germans would oppress and persecute them, but they didn't believe they'd be annihilated. Who could imagine that? It's said that they laughed at one old Jew: 'Chuma, how do you look, now that they've sewn yellow stars onto you?' 'Whatever they sewed on, I'll wear,' he replied proudly. Some mother on her way to be shot, in her unshakeable faith told her little girl that now they would both go to sleep together and wake up together in a much, much more beautiful world, and the little one smiled. A mother's love is capable of everything, that's why I don't doubt that it happened as she said… In those places where refugees from Lithuania were coming through, horrific reports were spreading, so they did flee from there. But the Daugava was a trap for most of them – for example, the Jews of Ilūkste had Daugavpils ahead of them, and the Germans were already in charge there. When the Red Army blew up Krustpils bridge as they retreated, many were left behind and remained on the far bank. Or like the Jews of Fridrikštate-Jaunjelgava – they got over the Daugava, wanted to escape through Skrīveri, but the local 'patriots' turned them back."

"Local patriots – you can't believe people would act like that!"

"Yes, but don't underestimate the presence of the Nazi army. Brigadenführer Stahlecker,* who had been given the task of clearing Jews from the Baltic area, was seriously disappointed in this regard. He had hoped for mass slaughter in the streets, so-called pogroms – that word is borrowed from Russia's anti-Semitic past. This is evident from Stahlecker's reports to Berlin. Stahlecker acknowledges that, just by applying the right pressure on Arājs' unit it was possible to start one pogrom in Riga, by burning down synagogues. The pacification of the residents happened quickly, and further reprisals weren't possible. He even acknowledged the fact that in choosing Lithuanian and Latvian shooters, special attention had been paid to choosing those whose relatives or family members had been murdered or deported by the Russians. Then it worked excellently. Germany strove to keep secret the German participation in the annihilation of the Jews in the provinces, passing the blame onto the locals. I remember that one of the murderers, the editor of the newspaper *National Zemgale*, Vagulāns, even lost his position when, in August 1941, he had written public thanks to the German soldiers who had 'carried out the cleansing from the world of the race that gave birth to disasters'. No evidence indicating that the Germans had given orders or encouragement was allowed to be repeated. But the intended pogroms in Latvia didn't take place, and orders had to be given. Maybe Stahlecker was reproached later for bringing dishonour to the German army. In Lithuania at the beginning it had gone dreadfully, but even there with the Germans' knowledge – the Germans disbanded several independent Lithuanian partisan groupings, and in Kaunas, out of three hundred louts they created a single band of degenerates, whose leader, Klimaitis, they instructed that Jews shouldn't be shot but killed with iron bars. That is what the bandits did. There was no shortage of criminals, though, because they found the prisons in the Baltic countries empty – without guards or prisoners. In the biographies of the local 'patriots' you can nearly always find some tendency toward sadism, jealousy, and greed. At least here the majority of the murderers were those who had several times been arrested and sentenced for causing fights, even some who had been murderers in the year of the Bolsheviks, but after that had switched sides to the Germans. In Goebbels' studio they created a weekly survey of events, *Wochenschau,* which was an opportunity to present reality from a Nazi viewpoint – that all East Europeans loathe the Jews and behave as the Germans did on *Kristallnacht.* But in reality the 'natives', as Stahlecker called the locals, were cautious. On the banks of the Daugava the Nazi army did not feel secure, also because of the many remaining Red Army men and partisans, so from the very first days they had to organize protection."

Radvilis circles around me, round and round. The old man is speaking, looking at me and not seeing, far away in thought as he is.

"The most shameful thing about this tragedy, it seems to me, is the greed. Dividing up the spoils after shooting the Jews. Most of it went to the Germans, but the locals, too, were not slow in grabbing and altering a coat right there by the pit. They'd appropriate a horse, or at least a bicycle. The towns established Support Funds – money stolen from the Jews. They paid wages to themselves, to the murderers and the supervisors, they sold off the apartments and orchards by auction. It was not a moral problem to sleep in a murdered Jew's bed or eat from his plate. Field-Marshal Obermeier, the leader of the Glazmanka team in the Wehrmacht, is supposed to have told his superior about one local 'patriot', Winter, the chief of police in Gostiņi and the town's commandant: 'Winter, a former Bolshevik fellow-traveller, shot all the Jews just to rob them'."

"That's enough for now!" I lead Radvilis away. "You'll freeze!"

Having grasped the old man by the arm, I lead him along the path toward the township; he walks tripping beside me, occasionally stumbling on the grass. They're shooting the Jews now, as we run here like two obsessed people, though the empty black meadows of Gostiņi – and what would we do in their place – in the place of everyone that witnessed from behind their windows? Would our faces, behind drawn curtains in an upper room, display horror, mute reproach or sympathy? But how could we help our unfortunate neighbours any more than they did then?

The streets are now crowded; here they all move through me, in crepuscular rooms crying babies are born and old people writhe in their death-throes, wives are drying their washing in the green April mist, boys on the banks of the Aiviekste warm themselves on piles of logs, people beckon me into shops, take me for a ride with a horse. I don't know their names, but I discern their shapes, their fingerprints on the December panes. Are the rabbis not slumbering under the rhubarb bushes with long sideburns on their faces? The old Jews are bearded and stooping, but their grandchildren are as white as marzipan eggs with black chocolate eyes. Their men go to work on Sundays and return on Fridays. Their paupers know how to repair the cuckoos in clocks and to fashion a bicycle out of wood, if you don't have enough money for the real thing. When they really need to, everyone knows how to cut hair and to apply cupping-glasses in the steam-bath. See how the rabbi on the threshold of the *cheder* stares with his yellow hawk's eyes… The boys are as afraid of him as of fire, because he beats his boy pupils with a belt or a birch, raising it behind his ears, piously believing, like his forefathers, that only by main force can the Torah be drummed into the lads' heads. See, a feeble man, moving sideways along the street, fearfully looking at the sky… He was once the carter at Štokmanhofa station, with a little horse whose legs hardly moved. The carter had to feed many children, so he fed his horse only with lashes. When the horse died of hunger, the rabbi threatened that the horse would accuse him before the Almighty for its sufferings. Now the carter has no horse, no job, no bread for his children, and as he goes, all the time he must look to the heavens, to see if the Almighty will strike him down with the lightning bolt of justice. See the bookseller hurrying toward him with a sad, knobbly beak like a raven's… In the bookseller's bundle are cheap novels about sinners who are boiled in great cauldrons by demons. See the private tutor with a scarf around his neck… A cockade in his cap, brass buttons on his kaftan, and he loves to be addressed as Mr. Teacher! Mr. Teacher teaches children to read and write in Yiddish. Latvians and Russians are studying too. I was probably one of his pupils, because I know what the teacher has behind his ears. Behind one ear a pen-holder, behind the other a pencil. He earns a living by composing love letters for whoever needs them – boys and girls. Since he is educated, he likes to read aloud from books, but since he is sentimental by nature, nothing sensible comes out of it – in the most tragic places he starts to cry, and so do his listeners. In the town there is also a medical orderly, an Austrian Jew. What would a town be without an assistant doctor, because there isn't enough money to pay a real doctor, but everyone can afford the assistant. This orderly regards cupping and leeches as barbaric methods; he prefers to treat the sick with enemas and castor oil. He arrives, kisses the *mezuzah* at the door, and if castor oil doesn't help, he goes away, leaving everything in the hands of the Almighty. See the little cottage hidden in a garden, its window open, and a cherry branch in blossom reaches in. An unabating warm wind sweeps clouds of flower petals down the street, and the sound of a gramophone is wafting – it's Abraham Goldfaden's "musical drama", arias from *Shulamith*. Sitting on the window-sill is the village scapegoat – a boy from Daugavpils, an apothecary's assistant. He doesn't go to the synagogue; once he was even seen smoking on a Saturday! He wants to be a theatre director in Gostiņi, to put on Goldfaden's *The Witch*, and the first performance has already taken place on the women's side of the synagogue. Now, under his orders, adolescents are making a stage out of planks in the market square, looking for lamps to light it. It is hoped that soon he'll be moved to another place so he'll stop upsetting this quiet village. But that sad, tall lanky fellow that constantly wheels barrowloads of skin from the abattoir to the factory tannery: that is the gravedigger, recognized by everyone in Gostiņi, because he takes part in all the funerals. "Those people are not only sick, they're dying!" he sometimes exclaims in astonishment. At funerals the gravedigger walks around with a box for donations, and sings a prayer of intercession for the departed soul. If the deceased is rich, it is with a solemn expression on his face; if he is poor, the prayer is said quickly – the fool had himself to blame for coming into the world… As soon as the new carrots have grown in the garden, the gravedigger grates them, mixes them with sugar and orange peel, and boils it on a slow fire in a cast iron pot, until all the liquid is steamed off. Then he mixes in crushed peanuts and powdered ginger, spreads them out in a pan and dries this flat cake on the roof of his hut for two or three days, turning it over now and then. While the *imberlekh* is drying in the sun, the gravedigger bakes the *lekakh* – pounds together honey, buttermilk, sugar, eggs and flour, mixes soda steeped in vinegar, and pours it into a round mould. He shoves the honey cake into a hot oven, and later pours a sour sugar glaze over the mixture and slices it into portions. Last of all he boils the beans. Then he places a little table in front of his house and lines these delicacies up on it, to attract little children like wasps to honey.

A breath like a butterfly touches my forehead – it's Radvilis.

It turns out that I'm sitting on the stone steps of the old Gostiņi post-house. Not far from here is the strange church, here are the bus stop and my car, but I feel that centuries have passed on the step.

A river has passed through me, tearing out a hole around my heart. It is being filled by something new, intangible but very enriching. A noble *Lacrimosa*, more silent than the white snow that falls onto the black Aiviekste.

The old horse-man has heard it.

"There's something else I want to tell you," he says.

"No, that's enough!"

"You have to know this in any case! Two brothers, Motke and Menke Lati, escaped from the Gostiņi ghetto. Motke was hidden for more than a year by the Purviņš – they lived there at the far end of Gostiņi. But the place is small – someone had sniffed something out. It became dangerous to stay any longer with the Purviņš family, so Motke fled through the forest. He was caught in November and brought to Gostiņi for interrogation about where he'd been hiding, and where he had stolen bread. He didn't confess, but Purviņš was still put in prison for three weeks on suspicion. Where Motke got to, nobody knows. They say he was taken back to the forest where he was caught."

"Purviņš," I repeat.

"Yes, Purviņš. They were still just boys, the Lati brothers. The younger one, Menke, got caught too. The local 'patriots', they say, beat him so much that the boy showed no more signs of life. They left him for dead by the roadside, probably too lazy to dig a pit for him. Later a chap called Vītoliņš was passing by. He heard Menke moaning and realized he was still alive. Vītoliņš took him home, treated him and hid him throughout the war years. After that Menke lived in Israel."

"Purviņš and Vītoliņš," I whisper, like a mantra.

Once more I cast my eyes over the empty Gostiņi. We get into the car and slowly drive along Main Street, until the tyres engage the Aiviekste bridge.

Escape

Andrievs knows that it's March, but he hasn't the faintest idea what date. Has he spent a long or a short time in the Corner House? What has happened in the town in the meantime?

By the ugly statue of *The Mother who Sees her Son off to the Partisans* it is empty and quiet. No war invalids. That is so strange. Perhaps this is no longer Riga but a stage-set arranged by the Cheka?

In the apartment, Marija looks fearfully at him, as at a ghost, and for a long time the baron can't really believe it's Andrievs who has arrived. He is grateful for Marija's sandwiches.

"To me it was like worship," confesses Marija. The Englards couple have worries of their own – on the day when Andrievs was imprisoned, the apartment was searched, and together with the tenants' property the Cheka collected the baron's newly begun manuscript and his photograph album.

"Life has vanished as if it was never lived," says Marija. "In it there were pictures from Sofiška's childhood! You're obsessed with writing, and you know they don't like it."

Andrievs is ashamed that these people, already so beaten by the authorities, are roused to further anxiety by his presence.

"I promise, my dear wife, I'll get by without writing, I'll live simply," vows Boriss, stretching out after breakfast on his bunk, straight and stiff as a wooden cane. "What is writing for a pensioner? Too much refinement."

Only now does Andrievs think to ask why Englards isn't at the racecourse.

It turns out that big reforms have happened there. Denisov has made several senior staff members resign, replacing them with younger ones.

Eizens, however, has been taken back.

"They won't trust Eizens to run it, not like me – without an orchestra," declares the baron. "He has a legal education and knows languages!"

"Boris Aleksandrovich, you also know seven languages, but apart from that, Eizens is energetic," Marija says to the reclining man, covering him with a rug. "And yet, believe me, even people like that get to their pension in the end."

"Andrievs!" responds Englards' voice from under the woollen cloth. "On one night, but I don't know which, all the war invalids vanished from the town! Who rounded them up, who took them away? This is a very bad sign."

Having closed the door, Marija confides her worries to Andrievs. "Only work and duty have kept him alive till now. I'm afraid that after losing his job, he'll lose his life too."

Andrievs tries to console Marija, but he has worries of his own – the wallet in his suitcase has no money in it. Everything has been filled in correctly – the wallet is mentioned in the protocol of the house-search, but the money in it is not. Who has so much money that they want to sweep him onto the dung-heap of history?

The greatest pity is Palmer's little book of poetry and Antonija's letters – they too are gone. Andrievs recalls what Krop said, that only imperialist spies read imperialist literature. On the other hand, Irbīte's gift to Andrievs, wrapped in parchment – an autumn scene, two by two inches – was not taken. Andrievs carefully looks it over now, wishing to get back into that cart, where he had conveyed the painter himself – a couple of days before he died.

After the war he found out that Irbīte's life had actually ended there in a cart. At about ten p.m. on the tenth of October, on the corner of Matīsa and Brīvības Streets, during the shooting, he had been sitting in the cabman's dray and taking home some Whatman paper he had bought somewhere. He was killed by some stray shrapnel from a cartridge, which hit him in the head.

In one moment in autumn by a little cottage beside an unknown railway track, the artist entered immortality, but the only one who remembers their conversation is Andrievs. He was unable to convince the vagabond that the concerns about the lack of light in the paintings are completely unjustified. In an Irbe pastel there is plenty of light, enough for several worlds. The bright ripple of the foliage in the trees, the white sky, individual yellowish rays, emerging directly from the black.

Valdemārs Irbe, servant of the light. Andrievs hopes that the artist, freed from his nervous nature, is now looking at the light of the Eternal, splashing in a sea of light, swimming in it, laughing like a child and finally happy.

He sets fire to the prison rags, puts on a new set of clothes, and having stuffed the little board under his arm, sets off for the Central Market, crossing Station Square. Andrievs is intimidated by the labyrinth of old stalls by the station with the railway service offices, the howling chaos that reigns there. By the station the cart-pushers are gathered – the taxis of the proletariat. The station is small; the last wagons of the Moscow trains stretch far away into the suburbs. Trains cross the Latvian border crammed full, so that at Rēzekne, Viļāni, Daugavpils, they hitch another four wagons onto them, bearing the numbers 14, 17 or higher, which are stormed by a huge crowd of would-be travellers. It usually happens that people waiting for a train hang around on the platform for as long as three days.

At Palcmanis' restaurant in the central market one can always meet some buyer of antiques. Andrievs is successful; in the corner by the little table he spots his ever-present old acquaintance Būbinders.

"How's it going?" Andrievs greets him, squeezing onto the next bench.

"Ten spuds a day, a bit of herring and onions, a rare bit of kosher meat, and butter," growls a sickly man with large, flat ears, from which project grey tufts of bristles.

Būbinders is about seventy, said to be still grieving for his wife and daughters, who perished during the German occupation. Ābrahams himself managed to go under cover in a cellar in Lāčplēša Street, thanks to Žanis Lipke, the rescuer of Jews. Recently they say he has started a new family. His wife is half his age, a beautiful Jewess with a medical degree from Russia. They even have a little boy. Būbinders apparently doesn't have much income, so his wife works at her profession and even pays a servant. Būbinders chats away, observant at the same time. His instinct warns him that Andrievs is a customer.

At this moment a waiter runs up to them, seeing that the men are sitting at an empty table. He offers Andrievs frankfurters with cabbage and a glass of vodka, as befits the meal. Andrievs finds this mouth-watering, but he's forced to decline, since he's just got up from a laden table. It wouldn't do to say that he's just out of the Corner House with empty pockets. Even though that is pretty obvious, from the stubble growing on his face. The waiter shakes his head and goes away.

Andrievs stops hiding his light under a bushel. He takes Irbīte's painting from his breast, unwraps the paper and lets Būbinders have a look at it.

"I could've been retired long ago, but I have to work to give me kids a future."

Andrievs agrees that those are fine and serious aims.

With trembling fingers the buyer fumbles and feels the black piece of roof insulation, checking the genuineness of the painting by techniques peculiar to him.

"Good, but not genuine…"

"Received from the hands of the master himself!" interjects Andrievs. "Take a look – don't you recognize Irbīte's background? And the signature…"

Ābrahams excuses himself, studies it further, sighs and exhales, and names his price: "Fifty."

"I'm going away!" Andrievs excuses himself this time. "I'm not parting with it for less than a hundred and fifty."

Būbinders clutches his head.

"Are you mad – a hundred and fifty roubles! Would anyone who looks like me be able to give a hundred and fifty? And for what – for a vagabond! Everyone who isn't lazy is after him! All the swindlers have cellars full of these Irbītes. I could hang him up by the nails in a certain place. Those there –" he angrily points his bony finger at the stalls selling industrial goods – "those old Jews can afford to bargain themselves some capital with roofing nails. My little son, with his pink cheeks – for him I have to risk everything…"

"Am I soft-hearted? If I'm selling it, it's only because I'm forced to."

Andrievs doesn't give up until he has a hundred in his pocket.

Now he could afford even the frankfurters and cabbage, but just like Būbinders, he has to think about the future. He goes out into the harshly sun-drenched market-place where, by the circus stall, a grumpy announcer with a hoarse throat cries out: "Citizens, citizens, come along, come along! The first to come will be first to get a view. Take a look at the world's smallest person on show! Step right up!"

Inside, the announcer kicks at the plywood wall with the heel of his boot. Behind it a feeble orchestra starts rattling out a march. A little group of Lilliputians comes out, bowing in all directions. There are many citizens round about; they stop to look at the parade, but the March wind is still cold and flaps at the dwarves' meagre coats. They soon disappear back into the booth, where their pale bodies are warmed by an electric heater. The citizens disperse again, just as quickly as they stopped. Only a few go inside to look at the display. Meanwhile the compere heads off to Palcmanis' for a nip of vodka and cabbage. Six sessions a day this boy has to endure!

Andrievs goes into a nearby courtyard to the barber's: old Starītis! The expert carefully lathers Andrievs' overgrown cheeks and upper lip, warms them with a towel, then applies eau-de-cologne and cream. A full service and a substantial bill.

The liberated man mixes in among the officers' madames, who prance about town just as fragrantly as himself. It is a windy day of scudding clouds. His legs convey him to a crossroads, to a particular house.

Hard to believe that up there, above the pedestrians' heads, some prisoner is right now being beaten up by a guard! And in the underground caves, men are bathed in sweat, while the guards' matron steals around them, bent over and creeping hungrily, with a bunch of keys and a long knife…

Suddenly Andrievs is seized by a wild desire to overthrow the whole thing.

Just as greedily as a drinker's hands tremble for a binge of drinking, Andrievs is shaking for a gulp of life. Can the scars be cured in a pub? To let your mind go, with some vodka at the Nurses' Club by the City Hospital on Brīvības Street, where the popular Six or the Kremerta dance orchestra have been sweating and swinging on the dance-floor, where chaps with whiskery chins play skat behind closed doors or the suburban gangsters arm-wrestle – Andrievs recalls how Black Mary at the Nurses' Club once overpowered the late Kolya, the *ataman* from Čiekurkalns.* She can knock a man out with her fist. Together with Zilonīte, the Little Elephant, hostess of the Firemen's Club, or Griškene of the Firemen's House, Black Mary was a frequent visitor to the racecourse. She had a talisman hanging round her neck, a little silver elephant, and in that way too the lady is like a brick wall – she rarely strikes twice. Both of them have put money on Andrievs and won. Now, without a word spoken, each of them is buying him a jug of beer…

And if not, there are the clubs of construction workers, of book industry workers, and in the area by the Sarkandaugava …

Or right here, at some *aģitpunkts*, propaganda point, which is in every fifth house. Gradually getting drunk, he would listen to the trade-school pupils, in their uniforms, spinning some records; friends and even enemies would turn up. Like that time when he was summoned into the waiting-room and quickly placed on the wet asphalt – "we'll meet again, count your words of goodbye!" Yet the fight was honest, without knuckledusters and knives. From this place he was helped up, with mouthfuls of mud and dazed, by a somewhat worn lady aged about thirty, and led off to her little apartment in a dilapidated house on Avotu Street. One room in the apartment was closed off, the other contained the lady's furniture – a green leatherette couch, a table and a few chairs. The wardrobe was replaced by hangers in the corridor, covered over with blankets. Surprised by the ghostly, alien environment and roughly pushed onto the couch by the woman, Andrievs watched dully as the lady felt his trouser pockets. Then she explained that she was trying to loosen his braces, later began crying desperately, and confessed that her disease had been only partly treated... Andrievs' presence awakened a romantic strain, she chatted about her work in a zipper factory in a cellar in Lienes Street – on the list there were "dead souls, so you will have to get away from there, before you get a whiff of goosefoot soup". She had already been in prison once – for breaking the passport regulations. A People's Court sentenced her to one year's imprisonment in Corrective Labour Camp Number 6 near Brasa Station. Lucky that the informer didn't know the address of the Corner House, because she wouldn't have got away with less than ten years. It was counted as an invalids' camp, but if more serious work needed to be done, they would buy in those with lighter sentences. There she mixed together paper and glue – papier mâché – and created dolls' heads. All the prisoners were good people, the dolls were beautiful, but a prison was still a prison. Only the thought of your idol – the sniper Monika Meikšāne – helped you. With her grandfather, she had been evacuated at the beginning of the war to Gorokhovets, but like other women, she remained behind the camp gates. She tried with all her might to get to the front, but she was declared to be too young. "They took me to Gorky to work in a factory behind the lines, but in the evenings I'd escape back again." They say she even used purely feminine strategies to get into a division – "it didn't matter which." Then she was ordered to peel potatoes.

"I was so looking forward to becoming a sniper – but unfortunately the war ended." The lively lady didn't hide her disappointment, as she sipped Saperavi from a bottle. "I wrote letters to the command asking them to help me become a sniper, and how to train. I so much wanted to get into the division, get my hands around the bastards' necks, sacrifice myself for our dear homeland. I still can't forgive myself for not living a life like Monika Meikšāne's; she went hunting on her own two feet. She has the Order of the Red Star and a medal 'for valour' – and yet she's a quiet factory worker! Like me!"

On the table an ashtray was stinking – if you collected them all, you could probably get three roubles for the butts in the market. In the folds of the lady's black transparent underwear, insects are active – lice.

"Where are you going to?" she screamed desperately as he ran away.

Andrievs recalls how sorry for himself he felt that night. Did he need to be?

He returns to the apartment, throws a few items of clothing and his sketchpad into the canvas rucksack and takes leave of his elderly benefactors. A sixth sense tells him that he won't be returning here. Free from everything! Palmer's book was probably thrown into the oven at the Corner House, just like Antonija's letters, or filed away in the "case files". Irbe's work was bargained away when he said goodbye to Englards. Now he will have to take somebody's bicycle.

Instinct makes him cross to the other side of the road from the start, in an effort to throw any pursuers off the scent. As if on cue, a procession arrives opposite Riga station with transparent banners: "For Motor Wagon number 100 – a new engine!" The rail-car which plies proudly on the rails is fitted with an electric brake, and a new type of headlight, whose reflectors emit a powerful illumination.

In the open door of the wagon stands a man who calls out in Russian through a loud-hailer: "The workers of the rail-car department have decided to join in a socialist competition! The Lathe Operators' Brigade has resolved to fulfil the daily quota by 200%, the carpentry brigade by 125%, the locksmiths' brigade by 125%, the road-workers' brigade by 120%, the electrical fitters' brigade by 130%, and the armature-winders' brigade undertakes to exceed the daily quota by 190%; the rail-car drivers undertake to travel free of accidents beyond the planned number of kilometres, and compared with the quota, to save 5% of electrical energy, and conductors plan to exceed the quota of tickets sold by 20%."

After almost every word the walkers in the procession cheer loyally and enthusiastically, smashing the bottles they have been emptying right there on the street. These Soviet processions are always reminiscent of gigantic carnivals. Andrievs takes his place in the demonstration, somewhere in the middle among the flags, placards and portraits of the "red heroes" – Stalin, Lenin, Malenkov, Marx, Engels and others – attached to wooden poles.

Immediately behind Andrievs strides a circus elephant, wearing on its forehead a placard: "The elephant supports Soviet power!" On either side of the elephant, the trainers, armed with metal bars, carry little monkeys, dressed in bright costumes, on their shoulders. The elephant is followed by a lorry with opened sides, carrying a tiger and a lion in cages. Last of all run the excited children, who aren't thinking about politics and its stupidity at all, but see only a tiger, a lion and an elephant.

At the corner of Marijas and Merķeļa Streets the elephant places its soft foot on the shards of a bottle. Lifting its leg, it starts trumpeting in pain and charges into a crowd of people, trampling several 'demonstrators' to the ground. Others, including Andrievs, take to their heels and run. With raised trunk, the elephant turns in circles as if bewitched, almost catching the contact-wires of the rail-car on the street, and shakes a lamp-post so that the lamp shatters. The trainers try to control the elephant and drive it back over toward Parka Street, but the animal waves its trunk, jumps around on three legs and continues to rage.

Andrievs, looking back fearfully, gets away along the littered Marijas Street.

Having taken a very circuitous route, he enters the buffet at the Hippodrome. Nona, catching sight of him, bursts into tears.

"Going away, Andryusha?"

"Now that's enough, Nona Nikolayevna." To Andrievs she seems as upset as the elephant with the injured foot. "Maybe we'll meet again."

"How so? Even the invalids have disappeared. They say you have to be heroic, with all your arms and legs, and with medals on your chest. Who rounded them up? God alone knows! Off to some leper colony or laboratory? So are our parasites lacking imagination? This is not a good sign."

At the Hippodrome Andrievs meets Eizens and Vanda.

"Matey, what are you doing here?" Eizens asks incredulously. "Weren't you supposed to be on your way to bright new vistas?"

"I have to ask you something," replies Andrievs.

"Well, the Black Maria hasn't swept me away."

"It swept me away, and it swept me back."

"What are you saying? Really, free of charge?"

Vanda averts her head, and won't look him in the eye. In her opinion Andrievs Radvilis should at this moment be in the Central Prison, together with his cellmates, expecting to serve out the punishment meted out under Article 58 for counter-revolutionary crimes, or in a detainees' wagon heading for Siberia. If that hasn't happened, it should have done.

"Do you really think that I…?"

Andrievs cannot finish the sentence, so troubled is he by suspicions. Meanwhile Eizens' hand rests on his shoulder like an arbitrator.

"Don't go mad, son. There's a complicated situation here. Vanda, tell him!"

"Our class teacher is Valija Ose, the sister of Osis the actor. Yesterday she warned us that there will soon be deportations to Siberia again! She said: Go away, but don't go to your parents! Well, we thought, where should we go now? There's only the Hippodrome."

"I organized a heavy truck for the subsidiary farm; the men are also afraid they'll be taken away," explains Eizens. "Are you coming?"

"I am!" It takes Andrievs a moment to decide. "It's on my way."

"Where has that Knaksis got to?" Eizens frets. "Denisov or Rindiņa will turn up!"

"Let's just keep calm, matey, and have a peaceful smoke."

"You have the makings? Mine got left behind at the office."

With trembling fingers Eizens fidgets with an empty mouth-piece.

Andrievs takes a cloth pouch from his breast.

"This is for you."

Eizens unwraps the package. First class Gercegovina Flor and Java in the little box. A minimalist design – green, black and gold. It also contains Eizens' favourite, sixth-class Boks.

"Well, I'll be!" He exhales emotionally. "Thank you, old chap!"

You could write a treatise about Eizens' passion for "coffin nails". The book-keeper of the Hippodrome belongs to a special class of people: tempered by Soviet *makhorka* before and during the war, he smokes several packets of *papirosy* a day, and even the strongest American filter cigarettes, if he happens sometimes to buy them from some speculator in the Central Market or gets them as a gift from foreign guests; they seem to him more suitable for the ladies.

"Keep it as a keepsake from me," says Andrievs, as they both light up.

"You've still got Nord? They say there'll soon be only Sever. Nord, they say, is only kow-towing to the West."

"They say that Sever is the same as Nord."

"Don't tell me that! At two o'clock in the morning I can tell you which is Nord and which is Sever. They've brought in factory machinery from Germany, and instead of *makhorka* they're mixing in sweepings from cigar tobacco!"

"Are you going too?" asks Andrievs.

"I've got a hundred and fifty heads to feed here; who else would do that instead of me? If something happens to one of them, the arbitration court will take it out on me."

"So then – we'll meet again…"

"Of course we'll meet again – when have we not?" Eizens responds thoughtfully, lighting up a Flor with glee.

One more time Andrievs walks past his trotters – Grand Hill, Vaida, Imaks, Pilots, Kazarka. They don't know how to lie. They recognize their jockeys' footsteps and voices, they prick up their ears and look intently at them. Andrievs feels like a traitor, leaving his companions in strange hands.

There is a place on the hay in the back of the lorry for Andrievs. In the cargo box, gloomy and silent, are huddled the trotters' jockeys with their bundles – one for each of them, piles of rags, suitcases, canvas rucksacks. Whispers are exchanged between Stefānija Medne, Pleša and Mrs. Cīrulis. Vanda is discussing something with her cousin Elizabeta, and with Dzidra and Ērika. There is also little Vilis, Antons' son, the courier for the Hippodrome. Knaksis the driver turns the ignition on the lorry and tries to start the engine. It doesn't start. Knaksis gets angry and jabs his boot on the starter; the green metal interior resounds and convulses.

"What rubbish, all it can do is grumble in the dark!"

"Just take the big crank-handle and give it a turn!" cries Antons, sitting next to the driver.

"The road's slippery, we'll have to take it slowly," says Filips. "If we set off a little earlier or later, what's the difference?"

Finally the reluctant lorry roars into life. Knaksis turns into Miera Street and through the town, heading for the Pļaviņas highway. Andrievs pushes the hay from his face and stares at the sky. Quite close is Vanda's white kerchief; she has been supporting herself with her hand on the floor of the lorry. Close, and yet everyone has glass separating them.

The lorry is now travelling at a fast clip. Riga is left behind with a few sliding lamps. The rows of suburban houses become ever sparser, a sharp wind blows in from the Daugava, and the jockeys sit bent over, covering themselves, wedged against the boards and each other. The night is clear, starry, more reminiscent of spring than autumn, but maybe this coolness comes from the travellers' anxious thoughts, which each keeps to himself. They will slip away, but what will become of their nearest and dearest?

At the beginning of Krustpils Street the vehicle is stopped by two men in uniform.

"Damn – militia!" The passengers in the goods compartment stiffen, neither alive nor dead.

"State Vehicle Inspectorate. Your documents, please!"

Knaksis unbuttons his canvas jacket and pulls out his driver's licence and technical certificate. There is even a voucher – made by Eizens himself.

"Have a good journey!"

The jockeys breathe a sigh of relief, happy that the Soviet vehicle inspectorate is interested only in vehicles, not in passengers and their bags.

And only the driver, cursing his vehicle, jumps out again to crank up the engine.

"Thank God and Eizens! The voucher was approved by Party Organizer Lopatin," observes Filips.

The dark green GAZ starts up with a jump.* At the Hippodrome the lorry is used not only for official needs, but also private ones – it carries belongings in moves from one apartment to another, transports wedding guests, and for funerals the coffin of the deceased, decorated with fir-cones.

The journey goes smoothly only as far as Ikšķile. As early as Kābeļkalns the vehicle starts choking and sneezing, until after a while it conks out completely. Even with the crank the engine can't be restarted.

"What's wrong?" ask the shivering passengers, climbing out of the lorry.

"Seems to be some broken nut. I just fixed it recently! Dammit, what kind of mechanics, what kind of locksmiths are these!" rages Knaksis, ripping open a packet of Belomorkanal. "In peacetime, at Riežnieks' place on Rēveles Street, they would rewind starters, dynamos, magnetos, charge batteries, so that they'd go till they dropped."

"What about Riežnieks, eh? He was also the best of car-saddlers," recalls Sergey Orlovsky, having a smoke with the driver. "We used to take tyres and tubes only to him."

"Will smoking make the engine start?" asks Andrievs, flexing his stiff shoulders. "Where are we?"

"Past the Dance Inn, so beyond Ikšķile."

The road is empty in both directions. The wind is blowing from the southwest into their backs. The moon is covered more and more each moment by a light film of cloud, but there is enough light and the place is high enough to spot a ghostly silhouette on the Daugava horizon – the ruins of the old Meinards church on the bank. On the left side a white sandy road winds away into the foothills and disappears by an old house shrouded in darkness. Knaksis raises the bonnet of the engine and leans over it with a couple of experts. They feel around deep inside the space, fiddle a bit, and confer.

"I can't understand anything, there's a ticking in my ears," declares the driver. "I'm quite hopeless with Soviet technology – to pick up speed, you have to put your shoulder to it; to put on the brakes, you have to dislocate your foot."

From a nearby house, as if going for a walk, a farmer comes striding over in a torn quilted jacket. A dog on a lead barks insistently, its hackles up.

"Refugees?" snaps the farmer briskly, glancing at the jockeys.

"Do we look like tax agents?" retorts Andrievs.

"My wife says – go and look, she thought you'd be genuine, but your caps are different – theirs have a little plug up on top, and a little idiot down below."

The farmer lights up and offers cigarettes to the men as well.

"We're waiting, we can't expect to be towed away." The farmer waves his cigarette in an easterly direction. "At one stage we were over there. Now we've been told that it's starting again and we're on the list. We're supposed to have been brought in illegally from Krasnoyarsk, you see. We'd already been taken off the register."

"I've heard of that," confirms Orlovsky sympathetically. "That decision was published last year – those who'd been released at the end of the war would be put in jail a second time on the same grounds."

"They collected our passports and issued new ones – with Paragraph 38. It was a friendly warning, but – where to run to, where to stay? One night we slept in the forest, my esteemed lady said: that's enough, let's not roam around in the forest at our age. We smashed up our sewing machine, slaughtered the piglet, baked bread, and took it with us. On the way we only had porridge and water. Hell, hell, whoever invented such a hell, I just don't understand. Now we really are in hell! We're living in hell now!"

"They said it would be like that this time – for money you could get to the same place as you were before."

"Nah!" The farmer jabs with his finger. "Travelling for your own money! You have to laugh! Let them go where they want for free!"

From his jacket he pulls a corked glass jar with a transparent liquid.

The men understand without a word.

"That's just what we need!" exclaims Knaksis.

"The other night I mixed lamp spirit with turpentine… A couple of jugs of spirits were left over… Diluted with rain-water it's good."

"Will a lamp burn on spirits with turpentine?" asks little Vilis.

"In a cylinder globe with a round wick, quite well!" responds the farmer. "You just mustn't put a cap on the flame – then it's not so good. And in time, of course, the wick will get silted up, but when you boil out the lye from the ashes, it rinses and dries well, then you can use it again. After the war we started mixing it – my wife was a field nurse at Ogre, she brought spirits home. I got my turpentine from resinous stumps – over beyond the hills there, on the Riga side, there was a huge plantation of trees we had before the war, we found it ploughed up. They say the Germans laid it waste as they were leaving."

The farmer passes the bottle around, and the gin disappears from it as fast as they get it.

"Where are you from?"

"From the Riga Hippodrome," replies Vanda.

"So where are your parents, girl, that you're escaping? Or did they help you?" the farmer enquires.

"We were told we mustn't live with our families! My sister was studying at Saulaine technical college, that used to be Kaucminde; my father works on the windmills at Bauska District Combine, in another district. Mummy lives in Riga district. And we went to Draudziņa secondary school."

"As soon as you live with your family, they start asking who and what," Elizabeta chimes in. "If you're alone, you don't have to look back. They're no longer looking for your family, it's enough for them to transport you."

"At the end of the war we set off from Alūksne, we left everything behind. We went off in two carts, but we had one horse. We went back to yoke him up to the second one. Along the way there were houses – completely abandoned. We didn't have enough flour; at one house the owners were getting ready to leave and said: take what you want," says the farmer.

"That's what it was like then!" confirms Elizabeta. "If you've forgotten something and you need it, then take it."

"How much can you take in two carts then?" says Vanda. "We didn't show up at our own mills. In our parish everyone must think we've gone abroad."

"Where were you at the end of the war?" the farmer wants to know.

"In the Kurzeme Pocket," Vanda replies.

"And what did you do there?"

"We danced all the time at balls in the Pocket."

"Can this be true?"

"What's so strange about that? You know for sure that you'll be deported and you won't exist any more."

"When the Christmas Battle began, on Christmas Eve, we were in Talsi church. It was high up on a hill. Down in the market-place it was probably a slaughterhouse. Vehicles had massed together. You don't go into a church with weapons, but that evening the Legionaries had arrived armed. They listened to the church service, then went out and went away. Major Laumanis was also there, you will have heard that! Laumanis had a sort of elite battalion, it was used as a stop-gap everywhere. He picked the men he wanted personally. He didn't take just anyone. And when they went past, they cleared the place out."

"Do you remember, Elizabeta, that he had one eye?"

"Laumanis? Yes, one of his eyes was bandaged over. What happened to Laumanis in the end I don't know, whether he died, and how, but he was classy. He was a charming man, and he looked as if he couldn't do anything quickly, yet he had lightning reactions."

"The ones that went to Kurzeme remained there, and that's the proper Latvia," declares the farmer. "You can feel it, since that time."

"But the Russians entered Riga without any fighting," Antons interjects. "The Germans went away, and the funniest thing was that the telephone exchange was in the Radio building and nothing got blown up! Pārdaugava belonged to the Germans, but the other side of the river to the Russians. And you could talk on the telephone. My wife was in Pārdaugava with Vilis."

"I rang my father: How are you getting on?" Vanda replies. "We have the Russians here, he says. But we still have the Germans here… Three days passed before the Russians realized they had to cut the telephones off."

"They just can't forgive us for that apartment on Zaube Street," says Antons. "Now that apartment has been a communal one for a long time. Officers with their madams in all the rooms. We ourselves had the smallest room. But no matter – a rich farmer!"

"Quite so," the farmer agrees. "Take away those who have property or those there are complaints about."

Along the dark road blows an icy moon-wind, the jockey's frozen soles flap on the asphalt, turning into a strange dance. Mrs. Cīrulis and Stefānija Medne, skipping down the middle of the highway, begin to sing, mischievously.

> All the little insects in the village are waiting for me to die.
> Don't wait, insects, I won't die in this land!
> I will die in Russia – uuu-baaa!
> In a white bed of nettles – uuu-baaa!
> I'll be borne by dappled bullocks with crossed bridles,
> Russian lords will dig my grave, with red pricks!

"Are you running away just to fuss around, like women!" giggles Sergey, interrupting. "Your singing makes my flesh crawl with ants. Have you got any funnier songs?"

"About a little flower, about the sun – spring, at least!" Knaksis calls out from inside the cab.

"Yes, Friday is Māra's name day…"

After Vanda's words, silence sets in. The name of Māra of the Insects – the day of the Baltic tribes' spring reawakening – now sounds an uneasy reminder of the realm of worms, the grave.

Finally the vehicle's engine springs to life. The jockeys hurriedly scramble into the back and say goodbye to the farmer, who, with a wave of his hand, trudges along with the slowly moving vehicle.

"Travel well!" calls the farmer, with a sigh. "Don't worry about us, we know our way. Just let's not each go his own way. The first time, we were separated, but we got back together in the end. Don't get separated!"

The farmer and his dog remain by the roadside in a lonely little huddle.

A long line of lorries and horse-teams is stopped by Ogre bridge, so the Hippodrome jockeys are not detained long for inspection of documents, and they are allowed through. At the crossroads, soldiers of the Ministry of Security with caps on their heads are smoking. They have to drive through a bitter cloud of *makhorka* smoke.

"You can feel it in the air, now it's going to happen again," whispers Stefānija.

The highway winds alongside the Daugava. In places where the road is closer, in places where they are diverted from it, like a magical belt the river draws the jockeys' gaze. Beyond Lieljumprava church, which serves as a warehouse, with a blown-up tower, Dzidra Baginskis starts to lift her head more often – like a horse that senses the nearness of home.

Andrievs stares at the forests on the far bank of the Daugava. It has always seemed to him that things are better on the other shore, although when he gets there himself, everything is just the same. The little cottages, from which waft thin wisps of smoke, and the forests, full of wild animals and people. When there are people-hunters about everywhere, the forests are even more full of people than the houses.

Flashing by are the supports of the wall of the blown-up bridge. During the war the Germans between Velladobe and the

Dzelmes tavern built a bridge with stone supports and a wooden superstructure. The bridge joined the Taurkalne road and the main Daugavpils road. At Taurkalne were the munition stores intended for the Leningrad front, so the bridge was guarded especially closely. In 1944 the Germans themselves blew it to bits, so that the attacking Red army couldn't get across.

Because of the warm weather at the end of February the ice has started moving in the rapid stretches of the Daugava. Ghostly, shabby grey figures are moving along the bank. The heavy frost at the beginning of March forced up the sludge and has covered the river with new, glossy ice. The ruined ends of the exploded bridge throw long black shadows in the moonlight.

Right here, too, is the avenue to the Viņķelmanis Manor – it's a familiar place from the stories his father told about the Riflemen. The 2nd Vidzeme Division defended the right bank of the Daugava in the November battles. The 4th Valmiera regiment was deployed against Bermont's troops from the Viņķelmanis Manor as far as Salaspils. Lines from Čaks' "Touched by Eternity" come to Andrievs' mind.

> How they shot! A dog can't bite like that.
> Wherever they went – after an hour it was done.
> In their eternally shiny boots
> They seemed not like people, but spirits.

Beyond Viņķelmanis Manor, where the road rapidly winds up the hill toward Velladobe, Knaksis steps on the gas. The GAZ pulls uphill howling. Refuge is so close that they can break into a merry song, so they strike up "Sorrow, my great sorrow".

Before the Skrīveri arboretum the driver steers to the left toward Kalnaveseri. Just near here are Ceļaveseri and Lejasveseri too. At Kalnaveseri since ancient times there has been a limekiln. The houses are walled in together, as well as the long, bright stables. Mrs. Baginskis is waiting on the threshold and embraces her daughter.

"Come inside, dears," she says merrily, observing the new arrivals. "We have to decide what's the best thing to do."

Milda Baginska, graduate of the English Institute, had been working in peacetime at the University of London. After the war she had to prove to the Cheka that she wasn't a British spy.

"They still have the notion that pre-war Riga was one great nest of spies," giggles Milda.

Her first husband, a professor at the University, died of cancer in the Ulmanis era. Kirhenšteins is supposed to have arranged for him to be operated on in Czechoslovakia, but it was too late, nothing more could be done. He is buried in Prague. Mrs. Baginskis was left on her own, but it's hard to manage a rural farmhouse without a husband's help. During the war she got married a second time – to Alberts Veiss from Mazsalaca. Veiss trained trotting horses, and the trotters saved their owners from persecution by Red terrorists.

"By the grace of God, Kalnaveseri is a subsidiary of the Hippodrome; otherwise we'd be long gone!"

The room is warmly heated. On a round table there are mugs of tea and piles of sandwiches, to be shared out between them. The hosts decide that the stables must be emptied. Mares and foals must be moved to the byre, and some horses may stay at the back of the stables.

"There are quite a few of you. You'll have to stay a week or so, until things stop moving."

"We'll clean out the boxes, gather up the straw. We mustn't show ourselves outdoors."

Elizabeta immediately announces that she won't sleep in the stables. A place is found for her in a room. But Vanda is sticking with the older riders. Andrievs thinks crossly that Vanda will sleep in the stables only so that she can eavesdrop, mouth agape, on what the chaps talk about at night.

"Now you're going to get to hear about the horses what you never would have heard anywhere else," Andrievs remarks ironically, meeting the girl apart from the others.

Vanda understands that this is a farewell.

"And you?" she asks. "Will you come back?"

"Who knows – in a little while or a whole lifetime," says Andrievs. "This is for you!"

Surprised, Vanda turns Andrievs' gift over in her hands – a whip made of walrus whiskers.

He puts his bundle on his shoulders and goes across the field towards the arboretum.

Veiss has told him how to get out onto the Silmači road. Six kilometres past open fields – that is where he will be least observed. He has to get to Skrīveri station and wait for a train.

Beyond Jaunzemi he can't find the bridge over the Brasla and fears having to wade. The water from the spring floods is brown and high, it is bubbling and chuckling as it flows. With his shoulder Andrievs topples an overhanging dry tree, and with his last energies holds on to the footbridge he has created.

The clayey Ercu hill opposite Jaunzemi is difficult – the wind over the bare hill is blowing especially severely, cutting through his coat and his knitted vest. Yet Andrievs does not divert his gaze from the proud houses of Ercu – he knows that on the Upland above the Brasla here, the mother and stepfather of the painter Kārlis Padegs had once bought property.

His legs have long since got wet; his woollen socks squelch in his leather boots. To this is added his urgency, his wet back and the strange anxiety in his chest, which is growing with every kilometre. Soon his brow is on fire, and as he draws breath, a stinging pain is wandering around his heart.

At a fast pace, keeping away from inhabited places, Andrievs reaches Skrīveri in a couple of hours.

Skrīveri station, which has suffered badly from the war, has not undergone any reconstruction. The columns by the entrance are ruined and crumbling with coal-dust, the heavy doors half-open, sunken in rubble. In their place a barracks has been rigged up, packed tightly with tired exiles carrying bundles, with nowhere to sit down. When the train will arrive is anyone's guess. Sick and exhausted, Andrievs stretches out on the ground, with his back to the wall so as to be able to see the tracks. Before his eyes is the goods store and ramp, a water-tower with a steam pump, an ash pit and a well.

A passenger train arrives, but Andrievs doesn't get in. In the carriages it's standing room only.

Desperate, he and other disappointed travellers fall back on the floor, which has been trampled as black as tar. His clothes, sweaty from the march, stick to his skin. When his eyelids close and his body starts shaking uncontrollably, a pulsating circle of fire appears in the darkness.

The shrill locomotive whistle, as it brakes, covers everything around it in hissing steam. Reddish cattle wagons are pushed together by both platforms, in endless long rows. Andrievs, who had for a moment lapsed into a kind of unconsciousness, jumps to his feet and sets off urgently along the barred wagons in the direction of Krustpils. Stumbling and falling into pits and mud, and slipping on the heaps of ice covered in coal-dust, he suddenly catches sight of a crack in a half-open carriage door, through which a cat could slip. With desperate force he squeezes through, heaves, pushes and is inside.

The train picks up speed, but Andrievs doesn't sit – he runs and jumps so as not to freeze on the spot. The wagon has small windows, boarded up from the outside, and from the inside covered in barbed wire. Built into the corner is a sheet-metal stove, and in the roof, a little hole, through which a few stars are visible. A moment later, when he sits down panting with fever on the lowest plank, he feels a strange itch on his skin. It seems familiar.

Is he really going to be fodder for lice again?

He has heard tales of how the deportees of 1941 had infestations of lice in the very first hours in barred wagons. These were told by people who were quite credible. Even at the end of the war, the legionaries couldn't escape the lice. Lice are the harbingers of misfortune.

Having lost all his courage, Andrievs sits for part of the way without moving. If these are lice, then it's all over. He remembers Vanda, imagines the warm darkness of the Kalnaveseri stable, at the back of which the bay, the grey, and the piebald are resting, while in the middle people tell their stories. He imagines Vanda's happy face in this darkness, her wide eyes and ears, listening to every word. She absorbs the stories like a sponge, hoping for long life, when she will be able to find a place for these stories – relate them, deposit them…

Andrievs is not looking at the window, but the road itself is whispering its names. This is the road of his childhood, and every turn, every change, is familiar. Aizkraukle, Koknese. The train goes slowly, at times only idling, then suddenly gathers speed, and the rails thunder under the wheels again. Andrievs bends over and looks though the boarded-up pane, trying to catch sight of something, anything. The forests are his friends, he knows the woods even in darkness and misfortune. At the little stations – Paugu sils, Klintene – the train slows its pace. Pļaviņas comes up, whistling and spitting steam at great speed.

What is the destination of this troop train?

Andrievs senses that he is travelling in a carriage of people-hunters, and it would be a good idea to join up with people like himself – young, strong tearaways. But he prefers the aroma of the fears of defenceless herbivores, the slow stares surrounded by the bluish aura of hopelessness.

Beyond the sharp Bears' Bend at Gostiņi the train clatters across the Aiviekste as over an abyss, and it brakes so hard when it stops that Andrievs almost falls off his perch.

He squints through the chink in the door – outside is an open field. Not far from the carriage, among the snow-covered fields, a solitary fire is burning. Unafraid of the danger, Andrievs leaps like a lunatic out of the carriage and goes toward the fire with outstretched hands.

The high place hides from view the distant confluence of the Daugava and Aiviekste.

Now he is at the crossing-point where the black waters of the Aiviekste meet the white waters of the Daugava. Grandfather called it the eighth wonder of the world.

Grandfather?

Grandfather was so long ago that Andrievs has trouble remembering how he looked.

Is he the one who approaches his feverish grandson from the Daugava side like a ghostly little cloud through the frozen crusted snow – a dark phantom, arms stretched toward the flames, just like a mirror image?

Andrievs remembers him as a small, wiry chap, always slightly swept onward like a branch carried in a stream. Around his head he had a wispy wreath of hair, and on his brow a dark blue bargeman's cap with a glossy black peak. His face narrow, his cheeks dry, overgrown with grey tufts of beard, his eyes the colour of faded anemones. He wore a loose rough linen shirt, whose sleeves billowed in the Daugava wind, and creased linen trousers. Over his shirt he had pulled a long padded jacket. He would quietly drop off his wooden shoes and, groaning, arrange himself on last year's grass on the high bank of the Daugava, taking his grandson on his knees. Before him the broad entrance to the river shimmered in the sun like open gates. Grandfather was known as a quiet man, of a thrifty, even niggardly nature, but at those moments his gaze was as passionate and nervous as a March tomcat, and his heart hummed like a honeybee in his breast, when on a sparkling spring day he shifted his gaze from raft to raft, as they slid along near the shore in long caravans. It was on those that Grandfather's young, sprightly descendants worked.

In many ways, the Daugava had soaked right through his body, like a dry root, in his exhaustion binding and entwining his muscle fibres, the blood in his arteries, his sinews and his breath. He had been known to stand on one single log of a raft in the middle of the Daugava's icy current. Re-floating, to stand for hours up to his armpits in the water. With old age his joints were painful and swollen and crooked, and yet his eyes, as if riveted in place, followed the caravans of rafts, the boys bent over the heavy oars, stoking the fire in the middle of the raft on the little turf floors. The spring sun had scorched the lads' skin black; the lifting of the heavy oar had tempered their shoulder muscles. In the sections of the raft between the red pines and dark spruces one could see in the distance, intertwined, some heavy white birches. Tied together in a row, thirty or forty logs passed along the current with their thin ends in front, to lessen resistance. Grandfather had once been a good raft-binder, passing the logs one by one from the stack into the water, and jumping from one to another with a hook, fastening them together in the required row. In his youth, they said, he had single-handedly thrown an anchor weighing almost a *birkavs,* over a hundred and fifty kilograms, into a boat of poles, but now even tapping his pipe caused him pain. "Yes, Andrievs, in those days you couldn't imagine …"

From the sun-burnished shore the first thing you could hear was a song, as a new caravan of ten to twelve rafts at a time arrived. On each raft by the steersman there were twice, three times as many lads. Fires were burning on the rafts, pots of soup were cooking and teapots for grog were being boiled. Bitter as birch-tar and salty as sweat was the smell of the rafts, which lingered on the flat shores long after the caravans had gone.

"However much the lads sing, may it shorten the time till they get to Jēkabmiests – after that there won't even be time to spit, from that township to Maruška. When I was young, by the Zeļķis Bridge, just like the others, I made offerings to the Daugava, so I wouldn't get harmed going over the rapids. There the Daugava is full of money."

It must be said that when Grandfather made the offerings he was quite green, and going on the rafts from Vitebsk right up to the island of Dole, where the rafts were received by the tugboat and taken to the timber terminal. While the water remained high, brown and eddying in the whirlpools, a raft could be transported in five days. As the level dropped, it might take a month or longer. In Riga he jumped off on the shore, bought gifts for his family and, drinking from pub to pub, returned home. For a good while he was followed on the long journey by the accumulated vapour rising from the spring floods. Everywhere the raftsmen were proud of their reputation – raftsmen drank the most, fought most doughtily and loved the girls most passionately.

"If you want to be a raftsman, drink – otherwise the devil will take you!"

The obligatory pose of a raftsman in photographs was with a glass of grog in his hand and a pointed bottle of vodka at his side. The doctors of Jēkabmiests, during the season, had their hands full of work, bandaging the heads of raftsmen injured in fights. When he was young and as hungry as a foal, sometimes

Grandfather single-handedly threw ten opponents out of the pub, and other times he'd beat his chastened opponent senseless and put him in a boat on the current. He had also experienced the sudden disappearance of his best friends under the water as the old raftsmen yelled after them, as if it were torn from their lips, "They're damned!"

"Like that time when Dūnu Ludis was struck by lightning…"

Far ahead, near Koknese, the whole shoreline has been flashing, the lights have faded to black and menacing. On the Daugava shore the birds have quietened, only the silent greenery of the foliage, like a thin slice of meat, has slid ever lower over the river, which was choppy from the first heavy drops of rain. The raftsmen have gone inside in this gloom – and what else could they do?

They can all see clearly how the sky over the end of the raft thickens and darkens into something like a devil's face, like a fist, from which a barb of lightning is released to summon into the sky the first raft-hand, Dūnu Ludis. Criss-crossing over the Daugava are bands of fire; in the middle of the raft the logs are pressed in on both sides by ten *arshins*, over seven metres, but in the air, as after an explosion, shards and spray are intermixed. One section of the raft had burned black and was smouldering, while Ludis was ejected from the world. No-one ever saw him again either dead or alive.

"So little is left over of a man when he dies, but after being struck by lightning even less!" Neither the raftsman's scarf, nor his cap, not even his pocket-knife remained to be wept over. Grandfather, who wasn't in the habit of crying, did shed a few tears on that occasion. Such is a raftsman's life – peaceful – peaceful at night by the swaying fires under the great brilliant stars, mean and dangerous in the daytime, among people.

Grandfather realized early on that, rather than getting beaten up in pubs, he preferred, after being driven into Riga on a raft, to buy a bicycle, ride it home and then give it to the herd-boy. To sleep in the clumps of clover, look at the sky, talk to people he met along the way.

Later, when he had designs on the beautiful Annīte, at first he took her with him on the raft. She was lame because of polio in childhood, but lively, and she sang beautifully. Anna let her voice, clear and supple like the crack of a fine whip, go on ahead of her in the May dawn between the two shores over the swaying, dapple-grey current of the whirlpools, where the nightingale struck its trills in the lilac bushes and the fern-owls called in the snowdrifts of bird-cherry. Anna sang nothing elegiac, it was an ancient song, often sung on rafts. Yet on the river it was sometimes so extraordinarily pretty that a certain languor overcame Grandfather, the heavy oar slid out of his hands and he seemed to melt into the singing, the vibration, the shimmering, the scents and the night fading in the Daugava hazel-bush fields.

> *Pynu, pynu sītu, pynu rašetoju, sapynu venčiku, zam zaļu pļenčiku, vot i horošo!**
> *Pynu, pynu sītu, pynu rašetoju, sapynu venčiku, sapynu venčiku, vot i horošo!*
> *Pynu, pynu sītu, pynu rašetoju, sapynu venčiku, sapynu venčiku, vot i horošo!*

Anna sang, and the lads joined in with their strong voices.

> *Rozpletaju sītu, rozvej rešotanku, rozveju veņčiku, rozveju pļeņčiku, rozvej horošo!*
> *Rozpletaju sītu, rozvej rešotanku, rozveju veņčiku, rozveju pļeņčiku, rozvej horošo!*

Even the deer which raised its dripping mouth from the water on the bank listened to the song as if spellbound and didn't flee, but followed the raft with its eyes of blue silk in which God had put his reflection.

But when Grandfather heard the rush of the rapids approaching, he immediately grasped the oar, cried out to the lads and put Anna to work as well. In one way, this daydreaming had not been good; the raftsmen didn't want women on board, because, as on a ship, they were said to bring bad luck. Because of them, a few bloody disputes arose on the rafts. Better off far from sin, although in terms of salary it was an advantage to take a wife, sister or daughter on board. "Herring and bread on the boat – eat what you want!" people used to snigger about the ways of the Daugava raftsmen.

"I liked going on the rafts with Anna, not for the money but for the pleasure."

When the pleasures of the raft ended and the cares of a family began, Anna stayed at home, and got fat – as broad in the beam as a boat. About that time Grandfather stopped making offerings to the Daugava at Zeļķis, because he had become a real professional. Even in dreams, they say, he was in the habit of disturbing the householders' sleep, blustering loudly: "*Pravo! Levo! Polno! Privalya, Tjagom, Tjagom!* Right! Left! Straight ahead! Together! Together!"

Now, when woken at two o'clock in the morning, Grandfather could name all the rapids and eddies – Pirkaža, Priedulājs, The Mad Whirlpool at Gostiņi, Hell's Organ, Grūbe rapids or Pļaviņas Falls, Brodņa, Zvirbuļi, Ķegums rapids with the Razboiņiks underwater rock. Also the strange counter-current Krūmiņi with the rapids near the Ābeļu Islands. Not only rapids had names, but also every reef, whirlpool, and bend in the riverbank – Kapu – the Reef of Graves, Kumeļu or Foals' Corner, Wolves' Promontory at Vilks, Anna's Current, Lašu or Salmon Spawn, Kraukļa or Frogs' Current. The same goes for the islands – Zvonku, Kofta and Ābeļu Islands, Punga, Kumeļnīca, Daugavsala, Drēģis, Plānu Island. He knew the names of those treacherous places, which were revealed to an ordinary person only in the droughts of summer – the dangerous submerged rock, which every spring swallowed up a few rafts, steered by novices or inexpert hands – Lūsis, Stirniņa, Žests, Udrupis, Lācis, Cūciņa, and especially nasty: that same Razboiņiks, and Vilks at Bebruleja. At its entrance Bebruleja had fierce guard dogs: Dambis and Krustpiniši. Grandfather once saw a raft that rushed at great speed into the rocks and broke up like matchsticks in the rapids the whole length of its seven sections. But now he was an experienced enough waterman not to float rafts from Vitebsk any more. Grandfather became a pilot to be hired at the Bellringers' Inn at Jēkabmiests, and to guide the rafts tied up on the bank onward through the dangerous rapids beyond Jēkabpils.

"What did you think about in those days as you sat on the bank of the Daugava?" Andrievs asks Grandfather. "When you were thinking about it, your heart used to pound loudly."

Grandfather grins slowly and fondly; his face in the firelight is golden pink, like a dandelion.

"About that friend who was struck by lightning. How maybe it wasn't fate at all, nor a curse, but a gift – such a sudden transport to heaven? You see, he didn't experience wetting the bed, or pains in the elbows, or the world war…"

"But Dūnu Ludis didn't get to experience sons and daughters either."

"You're right. A son like my Jēkabs! How could he not experience that? In my memory, he's standing there sturdily in the middle of the yard at Ogles – a little fighter with those blue eyes. He had such supple, powerful legs when he took his first steps…"

As he thinks about it, Grandfather's eyes overflow, like deep lakes.

"If you have a son like Jēkabs, you can wet your pants in old age and put up with pain. Do you think they might have got to Pskov? Will the Germans leave it in peace?"

That, Grandfather, was another time, and I hardly remember you at all, Andrievs wants to reply.

*

At that moment the "tea-kettle" whistles and the clattering carriages are pushed together with a hollow clank.

Andrievs runs back and crawls into the carriage. After squeezing through the door, he looks back.

In the middle of the field, a solitary burning fire.

Dūms and Žīds

The low grey sky is leaking. From the air comes a pale liquid – an intermediate state between snow, ice and water. The splintery roofs of the houses are huddled together as if they're freezing.

"Islands," says the old man, peering observantly through the moisture-streaked glass.

"Houses?"

"That's what they call them now – houses. But I still remember what the old people called them in my childhood – islands."

"So – like villages?"

"Villages!" Radvilis is shocked. "A village is something quite different – a long street with houses on both sides. That's a village!"

I stare at the groups of houses sitting like hats on russet, grassy hillocks.

"They seem to hug the knolls," I say.

"Sorry? Knolls? These are hills! You can't quite see it here, but when my father and I used to walk along Laukezers Lake… Hills they were, from Madona through Kūkas all the way to Trepenhofa right beside the Daugava. Geographers call it the Madona-Trepe embankment. But I call them hills."

All right, hills they are. I'm not going to argue, not about geography. I know that when you walk, and moreover as a child, you see and feel differently.

"In olden times the water level on the Daugava was much higher," he continues. "The dales and marches were lakes then; maybe that's why they built houses around the hills and called them islands. Now there might be about ten lakes left. The most beautiful one in the world, of course, is Laukezers, the clearest lake in Latvia. Water like silk, and white sand. Even the pike are different on Laukezers – bright as silver, with blue-green backs."

He sinks into memories of the bright blue pike, but I am forced to devote my attention to the road. It is wet, with deep ruts in the asphalt like firefly-ploughed furrows. Long-distance drivers approach, forcing the overloaded lorries towards us, pushing forward waves of wind, scattering mud around them.

We alight at an abrupt bend under a disused railway bridge. There the road winds up a knoll, a "hill" as Radvilis would say. On the hill stand a couple of undistinguished walled houses.

"During the war, Stalin's official Soviet spokesman, Yuri Levitan, is supposed to have announced solemnly on the radio: 'After long and bitter fighting the Red Army has finally taken the town of Spungene.' Spuņģēni. This is that big town now."

Yes, this is Spuņģēni, and it is soon behind us. There might have been bitter fighting over some houses, if they're precious. There behind the dim window might be someone for whom all life is Spuņģēni. Maybe he has never been to Riga, Vilnius or Daugavpils. And most likely not Rome or Melbourne either. And yet – who can know that? Just a couple of days ago I didn't know that early on Saturday morning I'd be trundling through Spuņģēni. Life is not good, bad, easy or hard – life is interesting, because you can never know what will happen on Friday. A friend of mine used to say that.

Before Krustpils, where on the left side of the road there begins an endless grey concrete fence with notches bitten out by the teeth of time, and industrial buildings beyond it, Radvilis says: "How beautiful the Krustpils sugar refinery used to be! Even the fence was beautiful…"

I smile. I would even have laughed, if he were not so unbearably sad.

"My father, and people like him, provided loads of gravel here for a long time, before they allowed the factory to be built – to show their support. It wasn't just a sugar refinery, it was politics! Beautiful politics. They were supported by the Farmers' Union and the group of Young Farmers headed by Lūkins, Justice of the Peace in Krustpils. Krustpils got the building contract and celebrated! Look, that's the office building, the only one to be preserved. Windows boarded up, but how beautiful it used to be! We loved our sugar refinery, that's why it was beautiful. Is it possible to love these grey cement molehills, these heaps of wire and plaster, useless sheet metal, created only to cover up the wastage from production? How does it seem to you?"

I am silent.

Sometimes he seems quite mad, but that suits me.

On the traffic roundabout a man waves a horse forward with a nervous hand toward the Daugava. I obey that hand as a choir obeys a conductor's baton. At the roadside a medieval castle glistens white.

"*Krusta pils, castrum Cruxburgh,* the castle next to Koknese, the bishop's grain store," explains Radvilis. "Just who hasn't laid it waste – Kunigaikštis Kęstutis from Lithuania, Ivan the Terrible from Russia, the Germans and the Bolsheviks. Not even they could destroy it."

"Who did it belong to?"

"To the von Korffs, for centuries. The Kreutzburg branch of the Korffs, more correctly, because the Korffs are not only in Latvia, they're all over Europe - it's crazy. Military people they were, these Korffs; for their crusading wars against the Saracens they received rich gifts from the church. Stefan Bathory endowed Kreutzburg to the *voivode** Nikolaus von Korff 'in perpetuity' for his achievements in the Russian-Polish war. So they lived here in perpetuity. The precious wood door, the tiled stoves, the spiral staircase. Where are those furnishings, paintings and plates now? Local people must have carried them off, while the castle lay abandoned after the First World War."

"What about 1905?" I ask.

"I missed that, my dear. The Korffs were progressive, they had good relations with the peasants. The Korffs were like godparents to many peasants, their servants' children. The oldest Korff son was always called Nikolaus, and the Kreutzburgers often christened their sons with that name, but converted it to their own Miklāss."

"The Kreutzburgers?"

"The locals. The Korffs themselves, of course, mixed with their equals, the von Medems, the Rosens. The old baron, *Kammerjunker* Peter Paul Korff of the Tsar's court, took a wife from the Wulffs. The last tsar of Russia, Nikolay II, visited the Korffs here when he was still heir to the throne. In 1905 the von Korffs moved to Dresden, leaving the castle to the younger brother."

"So this is Latgale, or isn't it yet?"

"It is and it isn't. You see, allegiance used to be determined by faith. Nationality was never the question; the question was: which church do you attend, what faith do you have? While all of Polish Vidzeme was Catholic, the Korffs were convinced Lutherans, but they didn't adhere to the 'Tsar's faith', which is what gradually became the fashion, not Catholicism."

The castle observes us with satisfaction through the fog, it brings forth history, and history rises up, revivifies the old emaciated Korff in the eyes of all the young who gaze upon his photograph in the centuries-old vaults of the regional museum – with a bristly beard on his chin and a gold-embroidered uniform.

Radvilis is persistent, so we abandon the main road. We turn to the left behind the castle's park along Barrack Street. The street is narrow and muddy, with water dripping from the branches of the trees. The buildings belonging to the castle are proudly maintained, but here, behind the fence among the bushes, half-collapsed Soviet hovels are lurking, crumbled by time, and in their ugliness powerfully arousing both Homeric laughter and resignation at the transitory, secular nature of it all. A few stone buildings from the time of the estate, some distance from the castle, which have endured socialism, recall the grey elephants huddled under the circus' whips, with the words, written in oil paint, *ne kurit'* or *beregis avto* – no smoking, beware of cars.

Finally we reach the barracks yard. He breathes in that illegitimate mixture of glory and destruction – monumental abandonment. On one side of the broad field there are ancient stone stables, on the left the former barracks. The grand three-storey building with its blinded window-eyes is impressive, its disembodied extremities are lost in a fog of snow.

Radvilis undoes his safety belt himself; I only have to open the car door.

"These barracks were built at the beginning of the thirties, and they were the first monolithic reinforced concrete structure in Latvia. At that time the Latgale artillery regiment was stationed here. How strange that no-one needs it now."

He coughs, leaving a little cloud of breath in the fresh morning air.

The windows and doors on the ground floor are blocked up with reinforced concrete blocks, vandalism and graffiti. On the roof a forest has started to sprout.

"People say a man lives on through what remains in memory. There were more than thirty officers here, in their day. I remember them: Visvaldis Dūms, from Ļūļas at Vietalva, Chevalier of the Order of Lāčplēsis, who, with his battery, helped to defend Riga for the young and impoverished Latvian Army in 1919. I remember him together with his charming wife, Anniņa, daughter of the teacher at Vietalva, Juris Kalniņš-Prātkopis, and their four children, Nora and Rita, Jānis and Andrejs. I remember Jānis Žīds, Dūms' contemporary, from Draudavas in Odziena parish, who was vying with Dūms for the hand and heart of Anna Kalniņa, but unlike his friend was of a slender build, an elegant and graceful man, a social lion. Why did Anna, who had been moving in the circles of the Riga Latvian intelligentsia, give her hand and heart to the stumpy bumpkin Dūms, who only knew how to look after his soldiers in the barracks? Colonel Dūms commanded the Latgale artillery regiment in the mid-thirties, but after him, Colonel Žīds took over the command, and was the commander until the occupation of Latvia."

"What happened to them?"

"Žīds ended up in Litene, the Latvian army officers' graveyard. Those military personnel who openly protested against Latvia's incorporation into the USSR were rounded up right at the beginning of the Year of Terror, but all the others were incorporated into the 24th territorial unit of the Red Army. The

Latgale Artillery Regiment was renamed the 623rd Light Artillery Regiment of the 183rd Division, and Žīds was appointed as Commander. Not long before the fateful 14th June 1941, the 24th Territorial Unit was concentrated on so-called tactical manoeuvres. On 12th June, many Latvian generals and colonels, including Jānis Žīds, were sent on 'courses' in Moscow. Actually they ended up in at the Siberian penal camp at Norilsk."

"And Dūms?"

"Dūms died unexpectedly in the winter before the Soviet occupation, aged 47. He was buried with honours at the Brothers Cemetery in Riga at the feet of Mother Latvia; otherwise he would be lying in permanent frost somewhere, in a shallow dug-out pit. Even if we don't know whether or where they're lying, it does matter. For us who remain it does matter, but for those who have gone – the experts are still arguing about it."

The old man takes out his kerchief to wipe his eyes, as if those two men had invested their breath in him from their invisible presence.

The wide square seems to be built for a historical film-set. Krusts' stone stables by the barracks at the side of Cavalry Street look like frozen icy loaves of rye bread, without a living, warm heart.

"The Brown Lady must be watching over the barracks too," grins Radvilis, with a creaking, rusty chuckle.

"The Brown Lady?"

"In the castle's cellar there is a servant-girl walled in; she fell in love with Korff's son."

We observe the crepuscular barracks house, from which time has removed the flesh, covering over its bare bones. Just there, on the stairs – was that the shadow of a simple brown linen dress flitting past?

"I have to say there's a strong fear of death here," the old man admits, supporting himself with his arm against an empty window frame, with trembling lips. "If this is just a dusty, hopeless, abandoned place? Greying paint, pointlessness, boredom, timelessness, covered in an indefinable – they were so full of life! Dad and Mum, Augusts… Antonija?"

Striding across the barracks ground at this moment is a woman accompanied by a dog, with a cigarette in her hand. She raises her head and looks at us through the empty chinks in the window, but does not see us. We must be standing on another level. The woman continues on her way, with the dog and the evaporating smoke.

"Shall we go?" Radvilis wants the car door opened for him.

"Not yet." I grope for the sketchbook on the back seat and show it to him. "Was this drawn here?"

There are a few fine ink drawings in which the barracks yard is recognizable. Soldiers are giving water to their horses in the twilight by the stables. Some young man with a whip in his hand stands in the foreground. On the next page, a portrait of the same man in a soldier's uniform. Under a peaked cap with a small golden sun on the cockade, a neat open face, from which time has not yet erased the ideals or darkened the attractive glow in the eyes. His face looks familiar.

"Augusts, my older brother," the old man confirms my suspicion. "On Saturday evenings, if he was free, I drew him here when I took the painting courses at Jēkabpils. Augusts introduced the officers, and after that I had to draw for a month right here – on a horse, beside a horse, some of them posed for me. That summer I earned a lot of money, about two hundred lats. – You like it?" Radvilis asks sharply.

"I do."

"He was like you – obsessed! Father kept him on too tight a rein, it's Father's fault," summarizes Radvilis, drawing me away from the pictures. This time he doesn't look too happy about the encounter with the sketchbook.

"Did Augusts serve here?"

"He did serve here, when he graduated from the Faculty of Agronomy. At that time the graduates from the higher educational institutions – the University, the Conservatoire and the Academy of Art – had the opportunity to choose a place to serve. Augusts completed his service as a private first class. The graduates in the platoon wanted to send him, as a successful instructor, to a course for adjutant officers, but he was exempted for the two months extra he had to spend in service, because at the time he thought only about his fiancée. He was lucky! Because in the forces, adjutant officers were mobilized, and ended up first of all in the Soviet and then the German army."

"His bride was Antonija?"

Radvilis turns his head.

"No, it was I who wanted to marry Antonija. I would have, too, if only…"

For a moment he glances at me with raised eyebrows, then breaks into his long laugh.

"Augusts married Margarethe von Greig – the former von Grieg. During the Ulmanis era the only thing that remained to her from the estate was a nose with a bump in it and freckles on the shoulders. She was a dentist."

The old man once again surveys the landscape, as if wanting to fold up the image of the barracks and preserve it in his breast pocket next to his kerchief. Whatever we may think or feel about the past, whatever the paradigms of science, art and philosophy may be, it is quite beyond doubt that all of this has once been touched by these feet standing on the same pavement on which Radvilis now stands.

"Let's go!"

"You were talking about marriages?" I try to draw him out.

"Sorry?"

"About marriages!"

"I'll tell you along the way. I'm frozen to the bone… as if I'd been in a vault."

In the east the edge of the sky has opened a little. This is a great reward, a rug of honour which the sky is unfurling as we drive away along the sandy Cavalry Street – a piece of pale, dishevelled sunlight. The river Lethe is just a stream compared to it.

We're on the road again, slowly winding along the lanes between private houses and the fine-tendrilled garden jungles of the Aiviekste people. Above us the sky is filling dozens of chimneys and smokestacks with fumes. The Kreutzburgers have finally woken up and are cooking pancakes for a late Saturday morning breakfast. The clouds, rushing past, press the smoke, mist and dreams to the ground.

"About those marriages…"

"That was just a joke, my dear. Many men had fallen in love with her, myself included of course. Can you imagine it?"

The old man looks at me roguishly, raising one bushy eyebrow. I shrug.

"Why not? Yes, I can."

"In those days I was shy… You can't imagine how shy I was… Antonija was my first love…Look, Riga Street – we'll go along here to the bridge. In the old days everyone made their way across the river themselves as best they could. The bridge was only built by Ulmanis after his coup and was opened on the national day in November."

"You promised to tell me about the marriages!" I persist, feeling like a tabloid journalist.

"About what?"

"The marriages."

"Oh, that, my dear! Antonija's stepfather was Ludvigs Dimants, a big farmer, trainer of trotters and blacksmith from Jersika. My dad sent me off for a few days that summer to Dimants' forge to learn to be a smith. Dimants had two master smiths working for him – all sorts of smithy work, but mainly shoeing trotters."

Radvilis smiles and fidgets with his fingers: "The story won't be simple – you'll have to solve a riddle!"

"Okay, I'll try." I'm ready for anything.

"One morning, as a game, I yoked Dimants' two-year-old trotter to a cart; no-one had tried to do that before. He had a mad character – it didn't take long to get him to do all sorts of pranks; he trotted like lightning and he was devilishly neat. From the beginning I let him strike out around the circuit; then I calmed him down, lifted all his legs, stroked his head and neck – he was like a drunk, in a trance. I harnessed him, climbed into the cart and rode in triumph through the yard, standing up. Now, when I think about it – terrible thing, passion, isn't it? I was the one who was completely obsessed, not the horse. I wanted Antonija to notice me."

"And she did?"

Radvilis waves his hand.

"She was standing against the gate, leaning on it, chewing on her blond plait. Maruse, her sister, came from behind. In her childhood Maruse had been thrown by the Saltups' trotters and had damaged something in her spine, so she grew up hunchbacked, but by nature Maruse was affectionate, the complete opposite of Antonija, who since her childhood had been as sharp and spiky as a hedgehog. Everything was fine up to the moment when we had to cross a plank bridge over the Siltupīte. Of course I'd harnessed up without a saddle, because actually I had no idea about breaking in a young horse, it's even possible this was the first horse I ever mounted… Just imagine, my dear, the kind of silly things that passion makes you do… When I'd got over the bridge, the cart started to run forward – the collar was sliding toward the poor thing's ears, and the side of the cart was hitting his back legs. The nimble horse seemed to wake up and rushed along the linden avenue. I continued my triumphal ride, but now at great speed. Even now I can close my eyes and see the tree-trunks whizzing past. God knows what would have happened if it had occurred to him to break out through the lindens into the meadow. Anyway, luckily it didn't; he galloped straight down the avenue, until he ran out of steam. Down by Dimants' forest I was able to control him fairly easily. We both walked home side by side, staggering like seamen on shore leave… Anyway, after that ride, every morning I'd find a bunch of flowers by the shed where I spent the night. Freshly picked, warm from the sun, summer morning flowers still wet with dew. As if they'd lain under the head of someone who was crying. I didn't dare to hope that they were from Antonija, but that's what I imagined. I imagined it so much that for a while I even believed it…"

"Of course they were from Maruse."

"You're smart. That's the solution of the riddle. The flowers really were from Maruse. Once I saw her putting them there – after milking the cow she ran through the milky mist. And just at that moment I realized that I loved Antonija… It hit me like lightning, illuminating her as the one who'd inspired me right from the start. It was great happiness and sadness all at once. Because till the end of time she loved Augusts, my brother."

Behind us someone is making energetic signals. We have wandered into history, fallen into daydreams on Riga Street, the main street of Krustpils, and that isn't good, of course. I give a friendly wave to the angry goods carrier, and we roll on.

"Let's turn here, along Celtuves Street," Radvilis says. The shyness he acknowledged has not disappeared.

"Do you see that red brick building there on the opposite bank? It was a fine place: Mrs. Ozoliņa's Belvij'. The finest in the whole township, you could lose your head in a cultured way from her drinks. Until Ulmanis built the bridge, people would make their way in winter across the Daugava by the ice road, in summer everyone in their own boats, or aboard the Gulbis ferry, the Swan, which ran from early morning till late evening. But during the thaw in spring, or the autumn sludge – what then? No movement was possible. Then they'd sit down at Belvija. Some of them sat it out so long waiting for the ice to thaw that a child would be born at the house, if it had decided to get born. Others would squander all their money, their cart, their horse and boots, and have to come home barefoot. The hall upstairs was a theatre and concert stage. That was how Belvija really earned its reputation until the end of the First World War. When they built the Home Guard house, the theatrical performances moved there. Belvija only kept its drinking culture. And I'm not claiming, by any means, that drinking culture is the worst kind of culture."

We roll on slowly along the bank past low cottages which also seem to have entered into history. The Daugava, bloated in its sludge, lies next to us like a star-filled Milky Way, like a brown dark-eyed cow that has just given birth to townships on each shore and now lies with her two brindles Krustpils and Jēkabpils at her udders, spread out between the alluvial meadows and thinking of the distance. She is drunk dry by a thousand little mouths – clumps of bushes, mottled grey roofs, birds flying in the clouds – and never dries up. Under her arms, reeds force their way through, on the brow of the waves the light of the sky always casts its reflection. The Daugava unites the opposite banks and at the same time separates, fructifies and buries.

"Here Antonija and I walked one Easter holiday," Radvilis reflects. "That last spring, when we were all still happy. We happened to meet in Riga in the same railway carriage and we both got off at Krustpils station. I walked beside her as straight as a tin soldier, and I was afraid to breathe; I was carrying a painting under my arm. The snow had just melted. The air was clear and the sun was brilliantly bright, a lark accompanied us all the way, as if attached over our heads. Ādamsona Island, the birches in blossom, encircling the Daugava with a violet glow like in a painting by Purvītis. Regiments of quacking ducks were flitting along the water tinted with bluish light, the herons cried harshly, making their way among the boats on the fishermen's shore. The roofs of the Jēkabmiests houses steamed in the foggy sunlight. She asked what painting I was carrying. I said it was a Varslavāns painting bought by my brother, I was taking it to him. It cost a summer's wages at the mill. How much? She frowned: for a painting? Augusts will probably mature in time; she wouldn't give that sort of money for a painting… As we went past Krustpils Evangelical Lutheran Church, where I was christened, she asked whether I believed in God. The door was open, to let the fresh air onto the walls, the girls were preparing the church for Easter, decorating the altar with evergreen club-moss. I answered that I do, but somehow in a complicated way. I was imagining a mahogany chancel and filigree floral ornamentation, carved in the supports, I was imagining Dūrējs' organ-pipes, and in the tower at dusk a skilfully mounted, masterfully cast bell would ring out. I was imagining the inscription on the altar, in Gothic script: 'Be you perfect, even as your Father in heaven is perfect'. I who see perfection everywhere around me, even in the most humble flower, and yet I am so imperfect myself. How am I to believe in the author of this perfection, if I can't even imagine Him? She laughed at me. I didn't need to complicate things, she said. Her stepfather had educated her at Jaunaglona women's college, next to Lake Rušons; there she had seen a simple faith. Every morning she had run half a kilometre from the boarding-house to the school. Firstly to chapel – the Lord's Prayer. Then breakfast, and after that ordinary school, the humanities. Latin: *Praesens, Perfectum, Futurum, sum, esse, sunt,* all those declensions. The nuns there were Austrian, Dutch, German, very strict. The same as everywhere – girls must be as meek as calves, with velvet eyes and plaited hair. If the sisters at the convent knew that in summer she was a trotting jockey at the racecourse! Merciful God! Antonija had apparently told them at home that she wanted to enter the Red Cross nursing school in Riga, but actually she had applied for the jockeys' courses at the Hippodrome."

"There were such courses? Who ran them?"

"The Army Sports Club. They accepted only horse-owners and stable-hands. I was thinking about those courses myself, because Dad didn't give me any money. When I told him that my shoes were worn out and repairs wouldn't help any more, he hit back: 'At your age I was walking in bast-slippers.' All summer I worked at the Radvilis mills, but he thought I had fed and clothed myself, so I didn't need anything. How long could I go around in his old suits, begging for lats for a cinema ticket or an ice-cream? Then the war came and everything changed its stripes."

Fog and smoke, and chimneys, and finally an expanse before the eyes to lose yourself in – I turn my head and wonder how far I can allow myself to drive.

"This is the Ulmanis bridge?" I ask.

"What, this? This was built in the sixties. A pale imitation of that beautiful bridge, socialist realism, nothing more. That bridge had five lanes! The contract to build the trusses went to England; it had the railway down the middle. The bridge was built by Neiburgs & Co... Ulmanis himself turned up to cut the green ribbon and walked across the Daugava. Afterwards they all had a reception at the officers' club in Krustpils castle – Dad and his brother were there too."

"So what became of that bridge?"

"What became of it? German sappers blew it up. The Red Army wanted to do that in 'forty-one, but it was spoiled for them – one truss collapsed into the water. During the war the

Germans repaired it, but after the war, as they retreated to the left bank, they blew it up afresh. Well, what can you do. War is war, Germans are Germans, and Russians are Russians."

In the middle of the bridge we see the participants in a celebration. I can see that they aren't at a wedding, or a christening, or birthday guests – they're at a funeral. A chap in an evening-suit is scattering ashes from an urn into the Daugava. The current carries away flowers, and a bottle of cognac, no doubt saved for the occasion. Blue-black clouds have scattered to one side, a few rays of sunshine are breaking through, cleaving the river to the bone.

The faces of the mourners don't have the gravity characteristic of funerals. The high bridge, the fast current of the Daugava to the sea, glinting like gold-dust in the sunshine and freely borne away by the stream – this isn't an interment but a liberation.

Radvilis looks on, his head turned back, until the mourners disappear from view.

"Golden onions!" I point to the five domes of the Orthodox church, glistening like mirrors on the opposite bank.

"Without the Byzantines there wouldn't be a Jēkabmiests! That is an Orthodox monastery. And behind the monastery yard a tiny tiny church – twenty by twenty paces – with an icon of the miracle of Jakobstadt. You've heard what happened during the war between Poland, Sweden and Russia? Jēkabs Gudinskis, fighting on the Swedish side, going across the river, saw a little plank floating on the water. He pierced it with his spear, brought it to the shore and discovered blood running down the spear. It turned out that the plank bore the image of the Orthodox Mother of God with the Child in her arms. Seized with fear, he carried it to the *sloboda*, the settlement where there was a little monastery with an Orthodox church. Being a Catholic, Gudinskis adopted Orthodoxy and entered the monastery… At the roundabout we turn right!"

The choir obeys the conductor and turns right.

"The start of the township was the *sloboda* at the Island Tavern." Radvilis points westward with his hand. "In Russia they persecuted the Old Believers, and they were never given asylum.

Foresters, raftsmen, carpenters, builders flowed in from all over Latvia. One or two of the houses they built, over a hundred years old, might still be here. When Duke Jacob of Courland finally established the town of Jakobstadt, it was an important point in the town's rights – only Poles, Lithuanians and Russians could settle here! But later everyone came who wasn't lazy – it was a paradise for raftsmen and innkeepers, and a bear-pit."

"Bears?"

"So what? Around here they earned money from it – there were bears in the forest, so why not? They collected the little bear-cubs, trained them, and sold them to travelling circuses."

We get out of the car and go towards the river along the old Philosophers' Street.

"Now we're going along the same road as that spring with Antonija," says Radvilis.

Feeling the earth of Jēkabpils under my feet, I can imagine their walk through the suburb of manual labourers, where frolicking children laugh in the yards and men enjoy a smoke, leaning against the fences, while women gossip in open windows, filling the window-sills with their ample bosoms like rising dough. I even see Arkliņš the carrier by the lilac bushes, grooming his horse, preparing for the trip over to Krustpils to meet the evening train.

"Antonija wanted to find a few things for sewing a dress – yarns and lace," says the old artist. "Of course I couldn't leave her alone with such an important task! Actually we both always found it interesting to chat. In a circuit along Vadoņa Street as far as the White School, the back along Lielā Street. From the corner of Zaļā Street right up to Smilšu Street past Kacens orchard, where the witch-hazel, the summer rose-bushes and violet forsythias were already flowering in places by the fences. I had to sniff and admire every flower. Finally we'd stop by the Baltmanis house; the best threads were to be found in Mrs. Ramanis' little handicraft shop - made in France, they were. But she didn't go inside, she'd go across the street to Mrs. Urbacāne's weaving-shop with three looms. Still she didn't find what she wanted at Urbacāne's. Next door to the weaving-shop was Birzons' double-sized boarding-house. In the little grocery shop, run by Birzons' sister Mrs. Perls, the customers teemed like in a fish-basket. The farmers, coming in from all around, would buy sugar, salt, kerosene, herrings, while they still could, before going home, because on Good Friday every shop was closed. They also bought delicacies to enjoy after Easter – sausages, pretzels, artificial honey, bon-bons, malt extract. Our mouths were watering."

Radvilis waves at the mud-spattered little building.

"On the way to her shop, Mrs. Sūneklis stopped on her porch – she made artificial flowers, she stretched out her gloved hands and attached to Antonija's coat a little posy of pansies of blue paper. She was so pleased that I dared to take her by the hand and pull her away. We ran as fast as we could. Past Kavišķis' and Rācenis' wine-shop, past Kancāns' and Kiops' bakeries, past Perickis', Elickis', Vestermanis', Suharovskis', Cile's cheap stalls, even past the German Brandmajor Vilde's sausage-stall and Mrs. Ozoliņš' big bakery."

"Where did you run to?"

"If you want to stay on the spot, run for all you're worth!" jokes the horseman, as if checking whether I know the lines from *Through the Looking-Glass.* "Since childhood, water-pretzels had been my favourite delicacy. Threaded with string, sprinkled with poppy or caraway seeds, round and twisted, big, medium and little. But Antonija was stubborn and didn't come with me into the cellar of the Jews' shop, she wanted Krintuss' mother's cakes, the most delicious cakes in the world! Let's be even finer then, I said. On Vadoņa Street, Mrs. Cilinskis sold Ķirze's produce, but we ran to the other side of the square, where there was a Laima chocolate shop. The young girls working there wore chocolate-coloured pinafores with broad white collars and sleeves. In the window they had chocolate eggs made by the factory – in gold, silver and purple wrappers, tied up with ribbons and wrapped in foil, filled with halva, hazel-nuts, walnuts or pecan nuts. Which kind do you want, I asked her, but she just shrugged. Then, on our way, we came across Feldhūns' ready-to-wear clothes shop with five rooms in the basement, from which after an hour's delighted browsing she took away a little bag of lace. After that, Šābels', Jakubovičs' and Špungins' footwear shops. Antonija literally froze at Špungins' window, where there were red lacquered shoes! She went in and tried them on – they fitted like gloves. But she just sighed and we went on our way."

I have to laugh at Radvilis' lively descriptions of women's behaviour and men's torture in shops. In front of us is Old Town Square with its decorated tree at the centre – nothing much has changed: the festivities are being anticipated in the shop-windows just as temptingly, and you stop just as abruptly in front of them.

"There were as many as five fabric shops on the streets of the centre. The first one: Bords' silk shop. Then Mandelštams' and Bebrs'. At Bebrs Antonija spluttered: 'What sort of bumpkin is this! Calico, fustian, sacking material – well, who wants that?' Linen, dungarees and tweed she didn't want at all. It only remained to go on to the haberdashery shops. We went into Putniņš', whose specialities were yarns, wool, worsted – hundreds of colours, kinds, twists. Do you have something ready-made for a Krustpils blouse, asked Antonija. The salesgirl took out of her apron pocket a finely-worked blouse collar and sleeves – still warm, just steam-ironed. A white finely-worked blouse collar and sleeves would cost five lats. They're lovely, said Antonija, I'll buy them! Rejected over the chocolate, I still wanted to buy her something. I was a dumb boy when I got fired up! A swimming costume with Chinese designs? A Japanese kimono? 'Mona' silk stockings, the finest there were? Šermē underwear – natural silk and genuine lace? She didn't want anything, she shook her head. Thanks, I've got everything. We walked along the road – bright lights glistened in a window, picking out the word SINGER."

Radvilis points to the opposite side, by the Orthodox church.

"There's an empty space there now; the war demolished it to the foundations."

"And how did your shopping trip end?"

"As they always have done! I am a fool, I can never cut things short, as with a knife… Wait there, please, I said to her, and headed back to Špungins' shop. I ran out of there with a box of shoes in my hands – I threw away the box immediately for a bigger surprise. I ran like the wind, hurrying back. At the time my brother had a strange, pale horse, Arlekins, an albino of the rare-coloured Estonian Tori breed with light-coloured eyelashes and fish-eyes, as blue as a Daugava wind-flower. That horse was like Augusts' visiting-card. I saw it at once. Augusts had just been at Bauers' picking up Arlekins' new riding saddle of yellow leather; he was standing at the corner chatting with Antonija. But she was no longer the old Antonija – with me she was cool, ironical. Next to Augusts she was smiling from ear to ear, showing her teeth, just like that winter when they both danced at Meņķis' inn… And chewing on a chocolate bar! I hid the red shoes behind my back. 'What are you doing here?' my brother demanded. 'Isn't Dad waiting for you at Ogles?' The question was extremely rude, as if I had disturbed them. Antonija started to laugh, it all seemed amusing to her. Like a foolish woman with drunken eyes, I thought at the time, and for your sake I was prepared to wade across the Daugava? But what I said aloud was: 'I brought the painting', and I gave the painting to my brother."

Radvilis glances at me, confusedly, rubbing his peaked cap.

"Was anyone else there? Oh yes, Šeina Icigsone. Hurrying to her hairdressing salon, she called out: 'You look happy, Mr. Radvilis, like someone who's recently married, congratulations, congratulations!' Antonija suddenly stopped laughing – or else it seemed like that to me. I took advantage of the moment and headed off around the corner to the Daugava. I put the red shoes in the water like boats and pushed them away from the shore, but the Daugava stubbornly brought them back."

Jersika

The silence is so complete that it wakes him up.

Andrievs opens his eyes. The carriage is freezing. High up, in the hatch above his head, a big star is peacefully shining. He must have fallen asleep.

He gets to his feet and approaches the door. Through the chink he can see a dark wall of uniform forest and tussocky field.

Wherever he is, it is no longer Krustpils.

Grabbing his bundle, Andrievs jumps out and heads for the Daugava. The river will tell him how far he has travelled.

Hurriedly diving into a dense new growth of fir trees, he scratches his face.

In the distance the locomotive is whistling, and the barred troop-train carries on its way. After quite a while, Andrievs espies something like a highway. Spattering mud, a column of heavy lorries passes by, each with one headlight on – like a row of wobbling Cyclops. Andrievs lies in a ditch and strives to glimpse what the vehicles' lights are illuminating.

Those are the outlines of Jersika Orthodox Church on the other side of the road. The parts called the 'iron church' – the walls, the external panelling. The roof, the cupola and even the window-frames are cast iron. A hundred years ago a little church was brought from Odessa, where it had been built for the army, initially to Dvinsk, but later, when the people of Daugavpils had built the Cathedral of Boris and Gleb, that superfluous little trifle of cast iron was moved to Jersika at the request of the estate owner Alekseyeva. In Andrievs' childhood the church was served by chief priest Ādams Vītols, invested as Aleksandr by the Bishop of Jersika.

Jersika!

So Andrievs isn't far from his destination. It is still quite a way to Saltupi on the Daugava shore, but it can be done in an hour or less.

On the hillside beside the Old Believers' settlement the horses paw the ground in the darkness, looking for roots and frightening Andrievs. For the Old Believers, who grew their own grain, horses were the main source of income. If one wanted to eat proper Old Believers' bread, then it had to be harvested from a field ploughed by a horse. The racecourse administrators always let the Old Believers keep a state-owned stallion – that meant it would be well kept. They wouldn't let visitors eat with them; they hoarded their delicacies in carts – go home to eat! They would offer drinks from a metal jug in the yard. The hostess would always cry: so where is the *poganaya kruzhka,* the dirty mug? If they invited you for Christmas or any other big festival, they would give you a hearty welcome.

Before midnight Andrievs arrives at Saltupi.

The settlement is small – about six wooden enclosures made of stakes, and grey cottages on the bank of the Daugava. Initially they were communal, as is typical of Latgalian people – side by side with roped-off strips of land – later they were individual enclosures. The grandest house, separated from the others, is Antonija's parents' yard. It was so grand because her mother Rozālija had married the landowner – her stepfather, the smith Ludvigs Dimants, of the neighbouring Dimants clan.

The fact that Toni was hanging around the Dimants stables was said to be the reason why a man like Ludvigs noticed and married the bear-like widow Rozālija. There was no other material in the Saltups gene pool. Rozālija Markunica was a big quiet woman with rough hands, from childhood trained to do hard work. She loved Izidors Saltups, her first husband, she loved her daughters Antonija and Marija, and also loved Ludvigs. She was thankful that he had eased her path, and gave birth to Dimants' son Pāvils. But Ludvigs was as if entranced by his golden-haired stepdaughter Antonija. And Antonija! She was always beside him like a bird of paradise. He sent her to a good school, Jaunaglona

Women's College, although she didn't like it there at all – she ran away to Riga, where Dimants' trotters were running on the racecourse. He wouldn't hear of Antonija being able to ride them. But that is what happened – she became one of the best jockeys in the German era in Riga.

It should be added that, having married Rozālija, Dimants made it a priority to teach his two stepdaughters to run.

Ludvigs had a strange obsession with running. His whole clan were fast runners. It's been said that when the Russian Tsar tried out the Riga-Orla railway line, Dimants' ancestor ran the trains' eleven-kilometre route from Jersika station – from the then Tsargrad to Līvāni, or Livenhof. The tsar took account of it, and had heavy iron running boots forged, which were chained to a rock on the Daugava bank for twenty-five years, like a bear. It may be only a story, but all the Dimants men have been good long-distance runners. True, during Ludvigs Dimants' boyhood it was the era not of runners but of walkers. The world knows the Olympic athletes Jānis Daliņš and Adalberts Bubenko. If Dimants' other passion had not been trotters, then he might have followed in the footsteps of Pheidippides, who ran from Marathon to Athens to announce the victory in the Battle of Marathon.

The cowshed, built of long spruce-logs, glistens white in the darkness against the meadow – the same one that ended the journey of Antonija's father Izidors Saltups. That blond-haired sinewy old man carried logs from the Daugava until he fell on his back, with sky-blue eyes; he was the first of the five Saltups brothers to see the light of the Eternal, leaving for Rozālija as his estate a little room, an unfinished cowshed and four daughters, two who died in infancy, and two who lived. The beautiful but untameable Antonija and poor Maruse.

Antonija was an extremely self-contained child, like her father. When she didn't agree with adults, she would hide under the bed, so you couldn't get hold of her. The only way her mother could catch her was to grab her by her cool, smooth, flaxen hair. But what do you do once you've caught her? There was no point in thrashing her; that was water off a duck's back. Antonija lived just as she wished. The main thing for her was the horses. At the age of four she was already leading a horse to a cart, climbing on its back and falling off the other side. The horses never walked off; they ran as fast as they could!

Compared with Antonija, Maruse was the dark side of the moon. She took after her mother's Polish Markunicz ancestry with her dark skin and black eyes. Her life was darkened when she had a fateful fall under the hooves of Dimants' trotter. On Bare Island, Kailsala, Maruse's spine had cracked against the ice, it twisted, and the girl grew up a hunchback. Stones and ice can touch the flesh, but they were unable to change Maruse's nature – she was and remained affectionate, clever and sympathetic, silently carrying her hump, caring for her younger brother Pāvils, knitting and weaving in every free moment on huge looms, which were put up especially for her in the upper room.

Andrievs peers into the windows, but they are still insulated with oakum from the winter and he can't see anything; only in the kitchen, behind the tangle of geraniums, does a little delicate flame appear to flare up. Andrievs opens the little door to the pantry. He looks cautiously into the kitchen. A black tomcat jumps off the threshold in the darkness.

In its cast-iron holder a taper burns, dimly illuminating the room. On the steps Rozālija is turning a hand-mill. A woollen shawl pulled over her head, her face with its prominent nose sunken into her bosom, her strong shoulders moving in a steady rhythm.

"Good day," says Andrievs.

The grinder, alarmed, drops the quern onto the steps; she peers, but can't make out this latest arrival.

The neighbour women are seated by the window on a long bench. Not young, not elderly, swathed in scarves, with pale faces, rough red hands on their laps. One is holding a handful of tapers, another a hymn-book, a third gets to her feet, looks at the face and finally recognizes it.

"Andrievs – it's you!"

This is Bonaventura Saltupa, a distant relative, he remembers her from the parties during the war.

The other two are Bonaventura's sisters, Anna and Leonija. On the kitchen table, like little strange dwarves, are perched their bags of rye.

"We're having a party here for the neighbours. We're waiting for Ludvigs. He promised to be home soon, but he hasn't shown up yet."

Rozālija doesn't say anything. She observes Andrievs and silently presses herself against the tub in which they ferment birch-juice in spring, sprinkling chaff over it. When the grains have sprouted in summer, the tub is covered with green turf. Under the turf the juice keeps fresh and cool. Rozālija's woollen jacket smells warm, the half-full tub is sourish. Under the stairs that lead to the upper room once hung roasted pigs' shoulders. Now only empty stockings give off a salty, smoky smell. The wet firewood, put on the stove to dry, steams in the dark like an exhausted horse. The odours and the warmth welcome Andrievs more strongly than words.

The look in Antonija's mother's eyes is different to what Andrievs remembers. Like a field overgrown with couch-grass. Someone has locked it up with seven keys and thrown them in the Daugava; sorrow has left its deep impression on her face.

Rozālija shoves some coal into the hearth, and the fire comes alive. She breaks the raspberry-canes and throws them in the pot, where water is bubbling.

"Sit down, I'm making some tea!"

"No more dogs at Saltupi?" Andrievs inquires, because of the strange silence in the village.

"The old ones were carried off by the wolves; those wolves have been multiplying an awful lot. We didn't get any young ones; these days it's better not to have them."

"The bandit-hunters, the *streboki,* shoot them dead straight away," Bonaventura explains.

"These days only the Cheka have dogs," adds Leonija, passing her hand across her mouth in indignation.

"Just like those blabbermouths!" whispers Anna sharply.

"Where from, and where to, if I may ask?" inquires Rozālija, looking sternly at Andrievs.

"I'm covering my tracks."

"So they're after you with dogs?"

"With dogs. Chasing me with dogs."

The women look at each other.

"Then you did right to come here," says Bonaventura. "Nobody's on their lists in Saltupi village. It's been ransacked, nobody left to take away."

"The ice has gone?"

"The Daugava has frozen a second time."

Andrievs grabs hold of the wooden base attached to the millstone. The task is hard, his shoulders soon start to tire. Leonija warns him not to let the grains in the middle of the upper stone run out. Rozālija blows flour onto her broad palm – not ground finely enough. It will all have to be done again.

"Just like on the estate." Andrievs draws breath for a moment, wiping the sweat from his brow. "Do you thresh with flails?"

"With a linen dolly!" responds Rozālija. "Don't laugh – these days everything has to be done on the sly. This rye here, we hide it in the rushes of the roof in autumn in little sheaves, later we thresh it into little heaps in a bag with a linen dolly, and winnow it in the wind. Now give me the mill, you're as weak as a reed's bone, you'll break!"

Andrievs sits down at the table and sips the hot raspberry tea.

"Why don't you go to Līvāni to grind it?"

"We can't," says Bonaventura. "Daddy is avoiding that place ever since his brother was…"

"Ēvalds?"

Bonaventura nods and falls silent. The mill-wheel keeps on grinding.

"They dumped him at the Dubna bridge."

"Our primary school teacher too," adds Leonija.

"Quite a few were dumped there, so beaten up that you couldn't recognize them," says Anna. "Dad had just gone to Līvāni mills to grind some grain. The militia led Dad off to the corpses – they made him confess. His relatives had warned him not to confess to anything, otherwise it would be trouble for him. The Cheka man sneered, 'Well, if your son isn't here, then I can piss on these bandits!' They say they hit his head so hard that his brains were spilling out… It was late autumn…"

"I remember it well, it was the 27th of October," Bonaventura responds. "After that they called me in to the militia. On the way they told me I'd better co-operate. They gave me a red beret, made me climb onto a lorry. We travelled to the Steķi pine forest, up to the place where they shot the Jews when the Germans were here."

"During the war they made us go and clear it up with rakes," explains Anna. "My sisters and I were going along the path – suddenly a fox ran out in front of us with a little child's head in its teeth! We turned around and fled, and never set foot there again!"

"There they made us get out, and the Cheka man says to lead them to the bandits' bunkers," continues Bonīte. "I said I didn't know anything and couldn't lead them anywhere. Then he threatened that I could die right there with the collaborators. I didn't know then that right beside the road, on the left side, they'd burned our murdered forest boys. By 'collaborators' I thought he meant Jews. He made me go forward and then '*Stoy!* Halt!' They counted to three and then shot. At that moment I thought: it's all over now. They shot again, they took a look around – my legs were wet, I'd been pissing myself with fear… Then they pushed me, and I blacked out. I don't remember a thing about how I got to Riga. They took me to the Corner House, to the big boss. He was very kind, it even frightened me, that kindness. Was I sorry for living so long in the forest among bandits? It could all be settled calmly and on the quiet; they promised me all sorts of privileges. I thanked them for the privileges, I didn't need them. Then I said: 'Take me to the collaborators – the Jews you've shot – and shoot me!' He was very angry, made me swear not to disclose our conversation, and said: 'You'll be smarter – you'll come back to me, now you know my office.'"

"When did Ēvalds go into the forest?" asks Andrievs, well recalling Antonija's lively cousin, the violinist of Saltupi.

"Right after the war, when the Reds mobilized everyone into the Soviet army. The Germans would let us stay at home if we had little children or something, but in the Russian army you couldn't do that."

"That was the time of the Courland Pocket*, and they understood that very well – either you shoot your own people or you stay in the forest."

"Even the priest went along with it, with the sacraments and the golden chalices. After the war they tried to make it all legal, but you knew back then what happened to them – they beat them and questioned them, sent them back to the forest, to give people away, and how can you not go, when they're threatening your family? Broņīte Svece got beaten up so badly that her whole body was bruised. She was in her eighth month of pregnancy, the child was born a hunchback. The doctor in the hospital told her: you'll probably want an abortion, with a child like that! Those were the biggest betrayals. There was nothing for it but to give in."

"Are there still some in the forest?"

"There are, one unit. In the beginning they stayed hidden, each one for himself. After that their General arrived from Krustpils, a big strong man, in a German army uniform. He organized them straight away. He had proclamations scattered, saying 'Don't give in!' We're sewing white costumes for them, so they won't be seen in the snow when they're on skis."

"They're listening to the radio too. Waiting for the second front to open. They really believe that help is on the way, to liberate Latvia. They were always promising on the radio: 'See you soon!' but now they say 'Till we hear from each other…'"

"You have to hold out." Leonija stops her grinding.

"And Pāvils?" inquires Andrievs.

Rozālija adjusts her scarf lower over her eyes, takes up the pigs' bucket and goes out.

"Poor little Pāvils was in the forest too, but now he's hidden here!" whispers Leonija. "They shot him, he's very ill."

"Who shot him?"

"The *streboki*, the bandit-hunters. A man called Volkov was stationed here, a very nasty *strebok*. He took Ludvigs in for questioning; after nine days they let him out, unrecognizable. He was badly beaten up. We have a system – if there's something bad, we hang a white sheet out in the yard, the next time we open the attic window, and so on. Then they know, they shouldn't come. But one time, when Rozālija was going to meet Paulītis at an agreed place, Grandmother took her by the hand, saying, you don't need to go there, there's been a funeral procession! Rozālija thinks, what funeral, Granny is having dreams again. But Grandmother meant those *streboki*. Where they'd agreed to meet, Volkov and the rest were waiting for Rozālija, tied her hands behind her back and gagged her. Not far away in the bushes there were a mare and foal tethered. She started whinnying in the dark, and they thought it was partisans. They shot like mad. That poor mare and her foal! But they had warned Pāvils – he only caught a bullet."

Bonaventura's voice slowly dies away, as thin as a hair, then vanishes completely. She sits down at the table and briefly sobs into her hand, so as not to show her weakness but her strength.

"His nerves are really bad. He only comes outside at night. And even then you have to know on which nights the *streboki* are sitting here; they're on the lookout for him. They're combing the whole forest for him, they're always knocking here. When are those English ever going to get here?"

"Because of him they put a 'bandit quota' on us; we can barely get any sawing done. So you're escaping too. Well, yeah, everyone's escaping. The executive committee meets in closed sessions, in blue caps at Līvāni. It's not safe any more."

Rozālija comes back inside, fiercely clutching the empty buckets.

"I need to meet with Toni. Where is she, Mother?"

The neighbours look at each other, the mills stop humming. Rozālija fumbles for some dropped awn. As she straightens her back, her face is calm again.

"Toni's with your brother on the bank over there. If you're escaping from the ones with the hunting dogs, better not to show yourself there. Better take a look yourself."

A horse-drawn cart is squeaking outside. Rozālija pulls back the geranium branches and looks into the yard.

"Ludvigs! Take a lantern, son, go outside, give him some light!"

Andrievs lights the hurricane lamp and goes out into the yard.

Dark shapes are rising in the load under the horse-blanket. The driver himself, in an old greatcoat, bends down past the stable door.

"Hi Ludvigs!"

"Andrievs?"

"Have you got calves with you?"

"Not at all." Dimants pulls back the blanket. "My sons."

Under the blanket lie two foals, their legs tied.

"Remember that Derby runner from before the war – David Duffy? These two are his sons – Dimants and Dufs. The agricultural administrators whispered in my ear: save them from starving to death."

Dimants unyokes the horse and leads it to the stable. The thoroughbred colts, released from their bonds, stand on their feet. Their narrow necks hang like heavy dahlia stems, a white film over their eyes. Andrievs and Leonija support them on both sides, and only then can they manage to get the youngsters into the empty stable, where each of them collapses into his stall onto the hay, breathing heavily.

"Riddled with lice, so you can grab handfuls of them," Dimants whispers, stroking their rumpled manes. "Terrible, those years of starving. You practically have to help the animals to stand. That's because, according to the plan, you have to keep one animal and only that. But they're simply collapsing from hunger! And which of the horses should be fed – the poor little ones that need force-feeding – they don't get it at all. What are they supposed to do with thin hay? Very many have died. Mostly from this campaign."

"What campaign?"

"When the tractors came in from Russia last spring, they slaughtered the horses. A horse was supposed to be a relic of the past. They took them to the slaughterhouse in droves. They were driven along the highway with their tails cut off. It was madness. Everybody wonders why I drink like a fish. I can't take it! When you look back at it – we'd only just begun to live, we got some land, we put up some buildings. A horse was a means of subsistence, we worked the land, we needed to break the stumps, and do a lot of other things, but I always had a good horse for travelling, to go to church with. There had to be a good honest beast for ferrying. But now? What else can you do? Have a drink!"

The neighbour women say goodbye to Ludvigs across the dark courtyard, and go off along the road with their flour-bags like a line of grey geese. At the doorstep the farmer is greeted by the Markuniča grandmother! Rozālija's mother – getting on for a hundred years old, with pale eyes she listens for the visitors' footsteps and breaths, strokes the grey fluff on her chin, then vanishes into the darkness of the room.

"Bonaventura, look, they're getting ready for deportation: dried rusks in bags, torn rags for socks and gloves, and worried all the time that someone will knock on the door."

Over a glass of tea Ludvigs unbuttons his greatcoat and tells them: "The Reds' veterinary service put them to sleep – and officers, you understand? That's what they thought of my mares and stallions! They promised to exhibit them at the Moscow exposition of agricultural achievements. After that Kupris comes in with his papers, my neighbour, a young farmer from the Ulmanis period. At Saltupi everything is going to be nationalized, they say. He described everything, they led the horses away to the Līvāni mechanical tractor station, put them up for hire. They say they're going to help the farmers of ten-hectare plots to work the land. Which of the trotters is a draught-horse, I ask you? Party orders must be fulfilled! After that I was invited there as a horse-breeder. Jesus, Jesus – all my beloved mares and young horses standing there naked in a pasture-ground eaten bare! Soņa, the daughter of old Hill, knew me, came up to me, put her head on my shoulder – ribs like a washboard! I found a bucket, brought her something to drink – the whole lot came running. I gave them about fifty buckets. Then my strength ran out. I ran off to the local veterinarian, but there was the party organizer in front of him. I told them: go off and take a look at the horses, it's a pathetic sight! But they said: everything's all right, you don't have to get upset over trifles!... They say the old farmer woke me up. Soņa was shot by the *streboki*; Pāvils was saved."

"I heard," Andrievs nods. "Did you know that old Hill is alive?"

"They said he was taken off to Gomel. How's he getting on there?"

"Pathetically."

"You'll remember this when I'm no longer around." Ludvigs leans forward and lowers his voice. "The good trotting stallions from all over Latgale are kept at Voronona, beyond the big trees at the track. They're not feed for the pigs! But for every horse that dies, the vets have to hand over the skin. We didn't feed them to the pigs, we didn't skin them. They're all buried in a row with their bridles on, in the proper way. Carol, Petronejs, Signal Hale, Jago, – San Valkers is there too."

At that moment a delicate singing is heard from the little room, as if someone were threading silk in the darkness – singing in Latgalian:

"*Pilna upe boltu zīdu, nadreiksteju puori īti. Bruolits, muosu žālodamsi, laipā lika zūbentiņu. Ei, muosiņa, vīgli puori, nalouz muna zūbentiņa. Duorgs bij munsi zūbentiņis, vairuok zalta, na sudraba. Man ai sovu zūbentiņu tāvu zeme juosorgoj*… A river full of white flowers, I wasn't allowed to go over it. The brother, pitying his sister, laid his sword on the footbridge. Go, little sister, lightly across it; don't break my sword. Precious was my little sword, more of gold than of silver. With my little sword I must guard my fatherland."

Ludvigs wipes the tears from his whiskers and enters the room. You can hear the squeaking of a cupboard door and Rozālija's voice: "You don't have to do that!"

"Have to do what? Make my heart jump out of my mouth, do you have to do that? This is my treat – look, Andrievs! Let's drink to the light of eternity over Jākubs. Jākubs was a great man. Should we call Pāvils?"

"It isn't safe!"

"Tonight it is safe – all the *streboki* are at Leivona, getting ready for withdrawal. I saw it myself. Call him! He's sitting in the well like a weed. Let him come out and join living people!"

Having climbed back into the kitchen, the old man pulls away the tub and opens the hatch.

"Pāvils, my lad, crawl out!"

Sitting down opposite Andrievs and pouring a strong drink, he explains: "He sits in the bunker in the well. In the beginning he was with all the others. With the ones who'd come through the swamps, with a purpose. The Devil's swamp, the Russian's swamp, there were many bunkers, a big group. Juhnevičs, the priest from Vonogi, was also in the forest, calling for them to unite. They were smart: on the army model, they had divisions and regiments, battalions, companies, statutes, 'The Young Eagles' for the younger generation, and goodness knows what else. They had a purpose – to keep the bridge-head in Latvia until the Americans or English came and helped to drive out the Bolsheviks from Latvia as in 1918. But the Cheka sent in its agent, and that one gave away everything. He kept tabs on everyone, and unmasked them everywhere – some at the church, some at the market square, as a warning to others. The *streboki* themselves were observing, not far away – who's going to keep away, who's going to run to them. They'll pick them up right away, understand? For some fathers it was like that – catch sight of your son naked in the snow, tortured and beaten, thrown out for the dogs to gnaw at, but no-one should show any mercy. Pāvils managed to get home before that. He only had God to help him."

Ludvigs pours a measure and shoves it over to Andrievs.

"You'd better tell me: how are things in Riga? Is there still racing at the Hippodrome?"

"I was racing at the Hippodrome, until the Cheka took me for a ride in a Black Maria. I spent time at the Corner House."

"For what?"

"I don't know. They let me out – again I don't know why. I just had a feeling that something was threatening Antonija."

"Antonija?" Dimants' features are knitted together at a stroke, as if rebuffed.

He fills a whole glass of moonshine and tosses it back; from his throat comes something like a scream, at the same time like the cry of a roebuck.

"Oh God, my hands froze, the gloves of reed-bones, oh God, my sides froze, the unmarried bride," he laughs. "Have you heard a song like that?"

"I don't understand – what's it about?"

With his eyes closed, Dimants waits for the hit of the liquor on his insides, then he wipes his mouth.

"Antonija – she's clever! She has good luck, everything turns out right for her. Together with your brother Augusts she established the Good Life agricultural *artel* across the river. She is a small businesswoman, she is an empress. Nobody can control her. She turned up a few years ago, seemed crazy, she urged us to say that she'd been living among us all this time. Where she actually had been, God knows! A rifle on her shoulder, couldn't speak like a human any more. A Soviet activist."

"You let her go yourself," cries Rozālija, entering the kitchen. "Every time, you brought something new from Riga or Jēkabmiests. A silk blouse or a red coat, a tall hat or fine leather boots."

"She burned like a candle, you can't hide someone like her under a veil," Ludvigs remarks.

"And look what that led to!"

"Attagirl! I would do the same if I were young. I'd live life to the full."

"A shameful thing!"

"A shameful thing, a shameful thing – old wives' twaddle! There are new times now…"

At that moment a scarecrow clad in a colourful calfskin coat creeps through the hatch into the kitchen. It's no longer possible to call Pāvils human and recognize him – not at all. The once slim young Dimants has warped into a lump, his shoulders gloomily drooping to his chest like the wings of a water-bird. His feet are shod in bast-shoes, under which are several pairs of woollen socks, which give off a stale, damp smell. In his trembling fingers is a rosary.

"Hello, Pāvils!" Andrievs offers his hand.

"Shake hands, son!" instructs Rozālija, anxiously observing her son. "Andrievs Radvilis, you lived together at the smithy, remember?"

Pāvils is embarrassed and looks around, as if asking for help; then he turns to the wall.

"What kind of Pāvils am I now?" he finally squeaks, like a record. "An anti-state element."

Andrievs tries to cheer up the poor fellow, slapping his contemporary on the shoulder, dislodging a handful of calf-hair.

"Straight back, Guardian of the Fatherland! As long as we can still bear arms…"

Pāvils shrivels up like a grub on a cabbage leaf and starts screaming shrilly: "Don't touch me! Take your hands off me, you…"

Ludvigs calms his agitated son, taking him into the other room. "Calm down, Pāvils! You can't joke like that with him! Come into the room, son, relax, rest…"

Trembling over his whole body, Pāvils creeps over the threshold into the room. Ludvigs closes the door firmly. Rozālija sighs.

"I just boiled up some herbs, but I don't have anything else to give him."

"What's wrong with him?"

"It's bad, his wound won't heal. He's lost himself – turned to a mere nothing… No, you can't say that against God's honour. You know how religious he is. In school he was diligent and studied well. But then he went underground, you could say, he literally went down a well. He doesn't want to save the Germans or the Russians. Many people in the village know where he's hiding, even children and young people – at any moment someone might give him away and get the revenge they promised. But nobody does it… He's regarded as a saint."

Rozālija recites "Our Father, who art in heaven" and "Mary, be blessed". She strokes the tablecloth, her fingers trembling on her bodice.

Ludvigs crosses the threshold.

He has in his hand a violin, which he puts under his chin. "Pāvils really wants him to play when his nerves are on edge," says Rozālija.

Ludvigs starts to play a mazurka by the Lithuanian-born Polish violinist Emil Mlynarski, popular before the war at every Latgalian party, one that Pāvils himself once played with a smile.

The violin sounds monotonous for a while, but with every beat Ludvigs' right hand finishes higher and higher behind his left ear, until the bow flies off over his shoulder and the instrument falls to the floor.

The violinist himself is attacked by strange spasms in the middle of the floor.

"I told you so!" roars Rozālija. "You shouldn't drink! See, isn't that mad?"

But Ludvigs continues his peculiar dance in silence. Some blind force seems to be controlling him, kneading and twisting his body.

"U-baaa!" exclaims Ludvigs, waving his arms like the sails of a windmill. For a moment he squats, then gets up and kicks out his legs as if dancing a Cossack dance. His face contorts chaotically.

"That's enough! You've gone too far! Now it'll be a couple of hours before he runs out of energy and collapses."

The floor-planks are heavy, the ranks of clay bowls containing birch-juice tip over and roll in all directions.

"Ludvigs, calm down!" Andrievs attempts to pacify the dancer.

"The priest said that St. Vitus brought about this kind of uncontrollable dangerous dancing," whispers Rozālija. "The medical orderly too – it's hot blood! A couple of times it's happened now. But I think it's an illness from bad bread. Whole-grain with ergot, that keeps well when it's all you have to eat."

Rozālija puts the bundle into Andrievs' arms and pushes him out over the doorstep into the black night.

"Hunger, misery, disease. What do I know? How are we living now? Hurry! Don't go by the crossing – that's where the Cheka hide. May God be with you and guard your every step!"

She crosses Andrievs and holds him, weeping.

"Bring me Toneite, you hear! There's always a place ready for her with her mother. Say that! Promise?"

Andrievs waves and goes.

The walk – actually, the escape – isn't far. Gradually his eyes get used to the dark, and quietly creeping through the wet turf, Andrievs soon enough feels the strong, fresh breath of the Daugava on his face; his whole body registers the covering of black ice.

Turning his side to the strong buffeting of the wind, he thinks continually of Ludvigs, of Rozālija, of Pāvils. Andrievs seems to have entered another world, where the people he once knew are deprived of their flesh and only their souls remain, bodies of mist, ghosts. Like creatures of the night they haunt the blackness, agitatedly scurrying about in the midnight. What are they doing on earth? How do they endure light? Their pain in daylight must be huge, their suffering as deep as a well.

Has Antonija also become one of these? And Andrievs' life: is that also slowly being extinguished, as time runs through his fingers like sand?

Here on this colossal river he met Antonija for the first time.

Podunai

The road to the eastern Upland, Augšzeme, beyond Jēkabpils, is so lonely.

We enter a realm of flowing perpendiculars, just like Alice, who jumped a couple of squares too far in her chess game beyond the looking glass. Perhaps we are caught in the shafts of huge looms, where the sky is grey linen, the river dark blue linen, the water meadows greenish brown, the road is yellowish pale like tow, but the field beside it, which is being ploughed right at this moment, turned up by the feet, is black and shiny wool?

Two old blue Soviet tractors crawl one after the other across this field, fertile as hemp-butter, the men at the wheels turn the tousled heads of ruddy thistle-pods and look back at us, as we stop at a lonely bus stop to get out on the greyish stone platelets and admire the unimaginably flat expanse.

Radvilis sniffs the damp smell of the Daugava like an intoxicated stag.

I lie down on the newly ploughed earth.

This is a place that can be seen from afar. The cloud cover is like a gentle and porous crust in the sky. I can feel that I have been sitting too long within four walls.

"I remember the dandelions, the dandelions of the Daugava," says Radvilis. "Yellow meadows of them. Looking at the Daugava, I tried to do a picture in pastels, the first landscape in my life. In May I painted dandelions here. On both cardboard and Whatman paper. In colour, those works weren't too bad. The Daugava, yes."

I can only imagine dandelions here in May, and when I think of them my breath jumps into my chest – at a time when there has been no real light here for months.

From the Daugava a large silvery white bird flies over us; I follow it with my gaze for a long time.

"Those peaks you can see from here are the castle mound of Kauprs, on the top of the First Apple-Tree Island." Radvilis points to the clump of pine forest in the distance. "On the bend in the Daugava are two islands – First Apple-Tree Island and, further up river, Second Apple-Tree Island. There was a reserve where the white Daugava anemones and cornflowers bloomed. When I was attending Krustpils primary school, we sometimes went there both with my parents and on school excursions by boat. Next to them were big rapids, really swirling, when we set off for home. In summer the water was so shallow that you could wade from one island to the other."

I want to go to the Daugava too, all the time I'm drawn to it, but the old man holds me back. Every passing landscape makes my heart beat faster and makes me press the brake pedal, but Radvilis only says "not here!" and urges me onward.

"To Dunava! We need to get to Dunava!"

"Why Dunava?"

"Firstly we'll escape from the Korffs to other Kreuzburgers, the Plāters-Zībergs. Like the Korffs, they were sent to the Crusades against the Baltic heathens. Humboldt von Plater was the first known German knight to arrive here from Westphalia. After that his descendants were Polonized, intermarried with the Zībergs and spread out not only throughout Latgale, Vidzeme and Kurzeme, but also Lithuania and Poland. Manors, castles, churches, legends... Did you know that Emīlija Plātere, one of the Poles from Liksna on the opposite bank, is virtually the Polish Joan of Arc? In 1830, when the Polish uprising against Russia began, Emīlija is said to have cut off her hair, sewn herself a uniform and gathered a band of riders, infantry and a couple of hundred peasants with scythes in her regiment. In the spring of the next year she occupied Zarasai, or Novoaleksandrovsk in those days. Emīlija clashed with the Russians near Ukmergė, Šiauliai and Kaunas, and they say she was even made commander of the first Lithuanian infantry regiment and promoted to captain. Unfortunately she died on the way to Poland. Emīlija is buried at Kapčamiests not far from Lazdiai. At the time she was only twenty-five years old."

The old man's face glows as he imagines the scene, his chin buried in his chest, as angular as a cage of thrushes.

"In the Catholic churchyard of Daugavpils lies the Pole, Pan Leon Plater, the organizer of the Polish mutiny from the half-manor of Casanova. A handsome man – have you seen him?"

How could I have seen him? It's not as if I've been wandering the world, taking an interest in Polish revolutionaries.

"A pity; you ought to look at his portrait. It's inspiring! He started the struggle against the empire, but was taken captive and shot outside the prison in Daugavpils, buried in the sand behind the prison beside the roadway. Have you read Rainis' poem 'Sunday and Count Plater' from his youthful epic *Years of the Sun*? It's a great collection of Rainis – juvenilia, from his childhood."

And suddenly Radvilis starts reciting it:

> Young he still was, fair Count Plater,
> When he had to go to the gallows,
> When the innocent had to perish,
> Taking on the guilt of others.
> Involved in revolt was his brother,
> In his castle they find rifles,
> Punishment then is the gallows.
> But he has only just been married!
> But he is only just wedded!
> A fair young daughter of a count –
> Now what will betide his young wife?
> What becomes of the brother's gladness?
> Plater takes pity on the maiden,
> He himself was in love with her,
> Shyly concealed his own devotion,
> Sparing the feelings of his brother,
> Taking the brother's guilt himself!
> Now he is led upon the scaffold,
> At his side the red-clad hangman.
> 'Hangman, what will now befall me?'

'It will not go well for you, sir,
In three minutes you must be dead!'
The sword is placed upon his neck now,
Cleaving thus the young count's honour,
Plater met his death in great shame,
All the people started weeping,
Across the land rang out the death-song
Proclaiming the martyr's piteous fate.

His recitation impressed me. After all, who was the last person to recite a poem just for me, and when? I can't remember. "But how do you –?" My question breaks off in amazement.

It may be that Radvilis has some purely personal issues with this text about brothers. His voice seems to be flowing like the Daugava from distant sources.

But he has caught his breath now, and continues: "On this side of the Daugava, the last of the Plāters-Zībergs was probably Fēlikss Konstantins, the owner of Šlosberga near Ilūkste, as well as the manor-houses of Ilūkste, Ance, Kazimirišķis, Podunaja, Rubene, Kaminča and Subate… He married that fine Polish woman, Ludwika Borewicz, and with this marriage he also acquired a small estate near Warsaw. Where are they all today – Delzabellas and Josefs, Heraldines and Sofijas, Fabians and Henrichs? I have to say, the largest number of them is in the Old Patmaļu cemetery in Līksna parish. Have you been there? You ought to visit them! You simply must see them."

How transitory everything is.

I am still thrilled by the unusual landscape of lines, apparently endless, slowly drawing you into it like a stream. By the roadside there are beautiful stopping places – some excellent spots. The grave-mounds – halts of peace, overgrown with spruces – Nagļu, Meņķa, Dūņenieku, Slīterāņu. Ancient, crumbling, boarded-up inns. The Luģenieki house, around which a dozen elderly horses gather in the muffled half-light of December. Dignāja school – a veritable stone-built castle with a shiny metal roof, decorated for Christmas like a Fabergé egg. Houses at the crossing opposite Līvāni: they seem to be built as a set for some film or simply drawn with brown chalk on a grey cardboard horizon, decorated with red dashes of pelargonium in a fine mesh. Sudrabkalns, Putraskalns, Dignāja church estate, like a mantra recited by the old painter as we drive past the cluster of houses on the sharp bend in the Daugava. "Here lived the raftsmen's wives, they brought their husbands pots of porridge when they moored the rafts on the bank."

"It looks like the centre of a collective farm," I say.

"Later it was one."

The landscape here is noticeably multi-layered. Around the harmonious walled structures sprung up like mushrooms after rain is the asymmetrical sprouting drying kiln, weighing-house and grain silo. Everything here, both beautiful and ugly, has been homogenized by time, covering it all with its brownish-green patina.

Behind the trees, bushes and ragged fields we finally catch side of a noble columned church tower.

"Dunava – look, Dunava as it ever was! The former Podunaja manor-house." Radvilis is quite transfixed. "A pity that there's nothing left of the manor, apparently only the milk-cellars and the apple store. There was also a mill."

I'm turning the wheel towards the church.

"No!" he cries, alarmed. "There's nothing left. A fire – Ruins…"

"I just thought you –"

"To the Daugava," he pleads quietly. Wisps of grey hair lie heavily on his bushy eyebrows.

On the left side I spy a solitary crossing-point, closed for the winter. The platform juts into the meadow, drawn up out of the water.

"Yes, this will be the right place."

Next to us on the bank, a mud-flecked little Opel pulls up. Out of it jump some youths dressed in colourful windcheaters, drawing on cigarettes before going fishing. Their conversation and gestures are lively, they study us curiously. I suspect that is how it is to be local. Instinctively they know every underwater rock.

"Look, they must be heading for the pit over by Kumeļnīca Island. In my younger days, life in summer was spent on the islands. On the Daugava before the flooding there were many more islands. By those big rocks over there the fish swam upstream unhindered. But there were also medium and small-sized minnows too. Big fish require depth. Once I caught a huge one, which bit the horses' rope in two; fish like that live here too."

Meanwhile the visitors have managed to right an overturned boat on a sandbank; the boys are sitting in it, along with a trimming-hook and bait of earthworms. The boat slowly slides into the current, leaving its reflection.

We get out too. The expanse is unfathomable. To the right of the vector of the road, a greenish hillock, sown with winter crops, is shimmering; on the black ploughed earth, a white lacework of snow.

At the crest of the hill is a farmhouse, which across the dimming surroundings seems to roll away the light from centuries of accumulated suns, like yellow amber. In the courtyard, alongside the smoke from a fire, wafts Sunday music, probably a radio switched on. I breathe in deeply, striving not to lose the sense of festivity and communion that was created when Radvilis and I set out on the road, because really, hasn't this trip been a gift to me with every step, even the smallest? To see it with my own eyes and feel the wind on my skin. So then, hasn't someone promised me that, as something self-evident?

As if to confirm it, the northern swans take off over the Daugava – silver threads sewn into the December twilight.

For a long time I follow the swans with my gaze, I hope that in some incomprehensible way my gaze immortalizes them.

Meanwhile, Radvilis has climbed down to the Daugava, feeling with his hand for the familiar blue-black waves like feather-beds. As if he has found a place he will never want to leave.

On the opposite bank you can see a farmyard. A small human figure is slowly walking around the fields. Occasional cars can be seen on the highway. No sound comes here. Our reflections on the water are drawings on a great glass.

"Every water got a song. People got to tell you story to make you happy and safe. Every place got a story," – I recall the words of an Aboriginal artist.

Radvilis is moving like a wind-blown reed-bone that has decided to come back to life.

"You can hear better – isn't there a thundering?"

"Dunava thunders?"

"Dunava must thunder. Don't you think so? They say that the first bell of Dunava church was brought from Aizdaugava and that work was constantly disturbed by the devil, who looked for every way to steal the bell. But the cocks started crowing, and the evil one had to go back to his huts. They say the bell sank in the Daugava, in the place where Zvonku Island now is. It's said you can still hear a bell tolling in the Daugava. Isn't it thundering?"

The silence at this moment is such that I can't hear my breath on my lips or my heart in my chest. Only the water around the reed-beds quietly gurgling, kissing the earth.

Radvilis looks at me, feeling in his jacket pocket. He pulls out a red packet of 7 Seas tobacco and gives a friendly wave.

"Time for a second pipe?" I ask.

Radvilis contentedly inhales the fragrant smoke wafting from the lit pipe. It twines around the old man's warm locks.

"This is where I first caught sight of Antonija."

Antonija

Shrovetide that year came in the second half of February. In Latgale they call it *Aizgavieņs*. A week before Ash Wednesday they had a carnival procession, moving around on sledges, a day before the fast they ate meat and drank milk to the full. At *Aizgavieņs* you have to eat nine, or three times nine, times, and every time there were meat dishes. "On Shrovetide Day you fast even with a sparrow, but at Easter you break your fast even with a sparrow's egg." Anyone who didn't have meat ate blinis or pancakes in the Polish way. A time of excess, which ends precisely at midnight before Ash Wednesday, as if cut by a knife.

Before the great fast everyone wanted to have fun. The chill ended, and it wasn't possible to have snowball fights, so they decided to move around on horses. People from both banks climbed into their sledges and met in the middle of the Daugava.

The bosom of the Daugava, strewn with sparks, burned like a cooled bonfire between the two frosty banks. Strong winds had blown in the middle of the river, but on the side, snow blizzards were blowing, glowing red in the sun like clouds soaked in blood.

That evening Augusts travelled on the Daugava past St. Joseph's church at Podunaja, running his eyes past the Missions' Cross, the statue of Māra, goddess of the land, in the church garden, finally taking a knowing look over the artillery shots in the church wall, which seem to have scarred the place ever since Christ's time, but were in fact tangible mementoes of the First World War. He had hitched a fresh young bay mare to the good sledge, put a frame on it so as to contain the abundant hay from the mill, and, accompanied by a pair of horses from the neighbouring farmer, gone straight between the piles of logs along the bank, onto the windswept ice. On his right hand sat his father Jēkabs, on the frame's poles, the mill-girls, screaming and laughing, lasses with pink cheeks and little white flounced collars over padded coats, but in the witches' place at the back, paupers collected from the poorhouse. Right at the back, standing on a plank, was the adolescent Andrievs. Having scattered on the expanse of the river, laughing and chattering, they proceeded along the river in short hops, toward the sunset. The banks of the Daugava slid past like an open book. Their eyes were dazzled by the richness of colours, the warm mists of snow vapours, which mingled and criss-crossed with the icy breath of the blue shadows. Pure joy struck their ears like a silken flag and warmed their chins, sometimes making them giggle, and sometimes catch hot tears in their throats from the superabundance of emotions.

"Latgalians?" someone called.

They all turned to the right bank, and the laughter subsided. From the east, against the rapidly darkening horizon, a violet spot could be made out ever more clearly, growing like storm clouds, turning into trotting horses and jockeys. Around them moved a cool arc of shadows like a moon-garden, when the speed along the snow-crust took with it the silvery dust lifted off the horseshoes.

"Isn't that the King of Jersika?" someone was trying to make out.

"Right – Dimants!"

The Courlanders halted their horses. The Latgalians jumped off the snow-covered field onto the ice, halted their trotters and made Christian greetings.

"What now then, neighbours? No pigs' ears for Shrovetide?" called Augusts Radvilis.

"No, we have ears up to our necks! We're going for a ride as far as possible from the house, so that the flax will grow as tall as possible."

Andrievs studied his fellow travellers with interest. They had pink faces, heavy beards, tall hats, and goatskin gloves. Suddenly he could see that the newcomers were wealthy farmers. Only those trotters – Andrievs looked with a slight grin over their little horses, like wind-dogs whose withers would only reach the chin of a teenage boy. What a contrast to the upland horses – broad as snowy hills, with necks like bears! Look at their own Maija – withers as smooth as the Daugava, fed at the mill on fine-ground flour, a drop of water wouldn't stay on her back! That is a horse – not those puny Latgalian kittens. Andrievs also overheard Augusts chaffing: "With these bobcats? Do you think you'd even get as far as Līvāni?"

"To Līvāni? Our horses could get as far as Riga! Look – the American, San Valkeris. A record-breaker!"

"Valkers?" interjects old Radvilis forcefully, staring stiffly at Dimants' horse. The Daugava was so quiet that you could hear the thunder of the ice, as it turned around in the river, split in the dusk from bank to bank. The horses had stopped tinkling their belts of bells, only lumps of lather dripped and the vapour rose in the air from their snorting nostrils.

Jēkbs Radvilis got heavily out of the sledge and slapped himself on the knees a couple of times to get moving.

"The very same!" Dimants also got out and proudly offered his hand. He handed the reins to a girl sitting on the ridge-pole in her stepfather's sledge. She had a red coat and a high goatskin hat over a thick blond plait. She was not flushed by the rapid travel, quite the contrary – pale as snow. The girl's ice-blue eyes met Augusts' inquiring look – shamelessly, she didn't even avert her gaze, and laughingly snuggled down.

"Toni from Saltupi!" Andrievs saw before him the girl from the mill as their heads bumped together. Proud! She never greets you – you can tell from that…

Next to Toni in the sledge there was something like a shrunken little bundle of clothes. It was a girl, younger than Tone. She looked timidly from under her scarf at Augusts.

"And the other one?" asked Elza at that moment.

"Maruse!" replied Alīda. "She's the other daughter of Saltupi. Poor girl, she'll never grow big… They say she got trampled as a child by the hooves of her stepfather's horse."

Old Radvilis was meanwhile looking admiringly at Dimants' bay, who was standing in front of him, steamy as the Daugava at midsummer. Under her silky skin he could see every tiny vein. Three legs in white boots, and a star on her brow.

"Bought in Berlin," smiled the Latgalian proudly, wiping icicles from his whiskers. "One mile, two minutes six seconds."

"Palmer the trotter praised her to me in Carolina," noted Radvilis. "He said every foal on his farm dreamed of growing into San Valkers. Is the stallion old?"

"Don't talk rubbish, Jākub!" Ludvigs Dimants shot back. "Old! Compare it to yourself, old-timer! He's been one year with the Latvian state, so he's in the prime of life! At the racecourse he did the thousand metres in one minute twenty seconds."

"The Hippodrome is frozen over; how did you get him into the yard?" murmured Jēkabs, feeling the trotter's legs.

"In winter a stallion can freeze his balls, spending his time in the yard." Dimants surveyed Radvilis' Maija appreciatively. "About fifty mares have already been inseminated. When you have a bag of oats and ten silver lats, then bring your girl to me!"

The Latgalian boys guffawed loudly, gleefully applying what their patriarch said to quite different girls. The maidens of Podunaja blushed as if they'd been slapped.

"A rooster like that won't get on top of my bear-cub!" Old Radvilis clambered back into his sledge.

"We'll add some steps to the cake!" The Latgalian boys burst out laughing again.

"Then it's better to ride with a hare!"

"We'll put them side by side and then see which one wins – your bear or our hare!" The Latgalians are coming over like storm-clouds.

"Well, Jākub, what? To Jersika, eh?"

Maija was dancing on the spot.

"He's afraid!"

"He can't run quickly, but he drives old women, so his calves will grow up fit."

"I'm going to wear my best horse out just for nothing? If you get as far as Līvāni, then I'll pay for your wine at the White Inn."

"You can pour the wine for the Kreutzburg Ladies' Committee! We'll treat you to vodka that'll knock you off your feet!"

Augusts' pride could not stand the test – he clenched his teeth and slapped the reins on Maija's back. The mare set off with broad strides, the other Podunaja people let their horses run behind her. Andrievs could only just hold on to his perch at the back of the sledge, but the cold headwind tore the cap off his head. He looked back, and through the fog of crumbling ice could make out that the hunchbacked Maruse had jumped out of her father's sledge to pick it up.

The Latgalians laughed as they urged on their horses. They needed to – they were playing cat and mouse. Such a big distance had been put between them that they could no longer be seen; Dimants' war-party was pulling on the reins. As is known, trotters are quite the opposite of ordinary horses – the harder you rein them in, the faster they'll carry you.

Dimants' horses, well shod, went flying off. Like a river in spate they caught up with the visitors, caught them from both sides, their fat, well-fed steeds galloping fast with their last strength, and easily overtook them – left them standing.

"You're mad – you thought you could race with Latgalians?" Jēkabs indignantly called to his elder son. "Stop, stop! You'll get black bile."

Maija really was in a lather – more from nerves than from effort. It was, after all, hard to compare Dimants' trained coursers from the Hippodrome with Radvilis' harnessing-horse, which had plenty of feed, but lacked the discipline of work.

The King of Jersika went on beyond Kumeļnīca Island, sure enough, as agreed, to the White Inn at Līvāni. The evening breeze carried toward them the last snatches of laughter and squeezes of the accordion.

There was no sense in rushing any more. Crepuscular silence was falling over the frozen river, finely interwoven with the horses' breathing and the clatter of hooves.

Night was coming on fast behind the travellers, and extinguishing colours. The beauty died away, giving way to a grey lustre. Before the confluence with the Dubna most of the Dunava party took their leave and turned their horses homeward. The Radvilis party hesitated – the millers owed their people some Shrovetide fun.

"Turn toward Meņķis!" called Jēkabs mournfully, as gloomy as a storm-cloud after this defeat. Augusts obediently turned where he was instructed. The White Inn at Līvāni has the best frankfurters and the sweetest sautéed cabbage, but there in front of it stood the Latgalians to taunt him.

When the sledge stopped in the courtyard of the former Meņķis estate, Jēkabs unwrapped himself from his cloak and with his ailing knees stumbled in the night, which was fresh and black like a puppy dozing on a threshold. The lights in the windows of the inn cast long fiery rays over the snow, trampled by the youthful band, who at first could not be made out clearly.

A delicate form could be distinguished in the shadow of the porch, and like a little beetle Maruse pattered up to Andrievs' sledge, amicably passing Andrievs his lost cap.

"Please!" she says, gazing benevolently at Andrievs.

At that moment the arrivals attract other people's attention too.

"Plyease, plyease!" giggle the Latgalian boys loudly. "We've been waiting for quite a while. We've been withering away by the White Inn, as promised. We travelled to Kurzeme to pick you up."

When a familiar bawling voice is heard above the others, Jēkabs sags onto the snow in despair.

"The boyar of Eglona is here at last! What's that there under your feet, Radzivill? Lost your toothbrush?"

Stung by the ridicule, Radvilis noticed something on the snow, and proudly straightening himself up, sighed with relief.

"My sons will have to be sent to help out in the smithy, otherwise Dimants' hooves will be going in all directions."

Something shiny flashed in the air – Radvilis had quickly kicked it, and Dimants just as quickly caught it. It was a trotter's cast-off shoe, thin and light as a shard of moonlight. Ludvigs surveyed it in astonishment.

"In the smithy, Dimants?" Radvilis continued. "Don't be afraid – I promised, I'll pay! You poor man, you've probably eaten your last pig; now you won't see any meat until the autumn. You've hung around too much with those girls – that's why your life is so hard."

Dimants opened his substantial coat. Behind one of their stepfather's shoulders stood Antonija and Maruse, behind the other Dimants' own son Pāvils, dark-haired and narrow-eyed like his father.

"Well, you're talking sense now, Jākub! I have an only son, Pāvils, and he will be an eccentric, a gift from God. Send your sons to me – if they can shoe my horses well, then maybe I'll give away my Tone."

Dimants had been trying to talk big, but the joking fell as flat as the innkeeper Bondars' beard. Everyone was saddened by this poor, tasteless joke.

One story may be endless, while another is brief. So it is with the story of Antonija's marriage. One of the neighbouring farmers had started making eyes at Toni. They said he'd been boasting at the bar about how he was waiting for her to grow bigger and marry him. Dimants merely chuckled and put him off with the words: "You know the old Greek story: you want to be strong – run; you want to be beautiful – run; you want to be smart – run? You want Tone – then run away." The boy took it badly and replied: "I won't run for Tone, but your trotters, I'll outrun them!" Dimants didn't keep him asking for long – he yoked up their sledges, sat down next to the horse by the thill and set off for that boy's village. He gave him back to his relatives exhausted, confused in mind. The relatives just shrugged – if their boy had been that sort of a boaster, then it couldn't have ended well anyway. Outrunning Dimants' trotters – an unheard-of boast!

Old Radvilis angrily wiped his lips on a handkerchief and said: "Don't be silly, Ludvigs! We'd better go and have a drink."

Augusts handed Maija back to his brother's care, and with their father they went into the inn.

On the western side over the Daugava there still lay a yellowish dimness like spilled oil. In the carriage-house there was no more room for the nags. Andrievs unyoked the mare, covered her with a blanket and hitched her to a free place on a wooden peg. He threw some hay in the troughs. He undid the leggings on his tired legs, released the strap and, feeling hungry, dipped into the bag intended for Maija. There was half a loaf and some crumbs of mother's home-made broken bread, a split head of sugar-beet. Since childhood Andrievs had liked the taste of this health food for horses. In one bake, his mother could take care of the whole family; only her husband's fooling around and boasting were not to her taste. Not looking forward to the Shrovetide carnival, she had gone back to Riga.

Standing next to Maija were the Latgalian trotters, covered with heavy blankets, on the grey background of which glistened layer upon layer of white woven half-moons, alternating with a design of the Pleiades. Lamps were smoking at the gate, the horses' white breaths were steaming in the cool carriage-house. San Valkers had a bag of oats around his neck, from which every few moments he snatched with his teeth, and as he chewed he looked at Andrievs with wise eyes, as bright as mirror-shards.

Andrievs stared for quite a while, taking in the composition and the details. It would be so fine if you could convey the full darkness of this life with charcoal on cardboard! Then he turned and went, dived like an eel into the winding, greasy, steam-filled corridors of the inn.

The ground floor of the massive stone structure was since time immemorial devoted to dancing and dining, but the first floor had ten rooms for hire. Being beside the Daugava highway, the inn was sometimes fit to burst with masses of guests.

The whole building was held together by a substantial chimney, in whose oven shelf crackled resinous firewood, while from the cross-beams hung hams and smoked sausages. Right inside it loomed the mouth of the great bread-oven. Behind the dark kitchen was the big bar counter, where the family of Bondars the innkeeper was bustling among the strings of garlic. The gaunt chap poured measures of vodka and fetched beer from the cellar, crying out every time: "Which do you want – a jug or a bottle?" – while his wife Emma stirred sautéed cabbage in a big black pot and offered sausages. "What's for you, sir – Polish or tea, Cracow or London? And you – smoked or hunters'? Jellied, beer or blood?"

But if Sir was a fastidious chap who didn't himself understand what he wanted, Emma also knew how to slice the fine cervelat as thinly as the Germans do, and offer them on a big white plate, an eighth of a pound. As at Shrovetide, the customary pub delicacies – pretzels, buns, lampreys and flatfish – had lost their attraction, everybody wanted to enjoy only meat. Even for the poor of the parish, whom Augusts had transferred from his sledge to the heated rooms, whose pipes wound like grey guts through the inn, there slipped from their laps the gifts of sugared nuts and gingerbread hearts, and their hands rose up for a morsel of liver or garlic-sausage if it lay forgotten somewhere on a table. Making their way through the crowd were the two toiling Bondars girls, themselves as pinkish-white as boiled sausages, but if anyone consumed too much fire-water and picked a quarrel, the Bondars' son would come out of the "buffet room" and throw the drunks outside.

From Martinmas until Shrovetide every Sunday evening there was a dance at the inn. The innkeeper even kept a permanent musical "trio" – bass and fiddle played by two lame soldiers. The accordion was squeezed by a lively girl from a Riga suburb with the nickname Aitu Māle, who, for an appropriate sum, you could take with you to a hired room after the dance until the morning. In the corner by the door which led to the carriage-house, empty beer-barrels were rolled into place, on which table-tops were placed – there the musicians, raised almost to ceiling height, would rip into dance tunes in their shirtsleeves in the heat, to whooping accompaniment from the guests.

The inn was humming like a beehive; there was nowhere to drop a pin, but to two of those sitting at the big oak table sprinkled with white sea-sand, the others made a respectful bow, almost as deep as the semicircle of light that fell from the iron taper-holder by the wall. On entering, Andrievs caught sight of where his father was sitting with Dimants, and moved toward them. He heard how ardently Ludvigs was striving to talk Jēkabs into buying some horse: "If you add a bit of yours to our money, you'd never regret it!" Dimants shouted over the music right into Radvilis' ear. "I saw him in Stockholm – not very big, a long neck, a small head, delicate. Deep bay colour. He's a good trotter, and so pretty! I know my horses. My stallion Petronejs has broken who knows how many Latgalian records, he's the fastest horse in Latgale. And don't even ask about San Valkers – he brought me more money! And fame! Jākub, you won't regret this! Look at me: in 1936 at the Riga Hippodrome the colt I'd raised myself took part for the first time, but now I've got seven running, earning me seven thousand a year. We have great development plans for Rēzekne too. Colonel Kuplais is supporting the Rēzekne Hippodrome this year, the project is already submitted and has got a positive response. We have the support of the Latvian Horse Breeders' Association, the Association of Latvian Farmers' Societies. By autumn it'll all be ready!"

"What's the name of the horse?" asked Radvilis again.

"*Run Hill Dune.* He's an American too, from Carolina."

Some new arrival called out to Jēkabs, and Dimants also went toward the bar.

Some were still taking their seats; Andrievs suddenly recovered his courage, sitting next to Antonija. The beers he had drunk, coupled with the warmth of the inn, had gone to his head, and his heart was split apart in his sudden boldness.

"I saw you last summer at the Hippodrome," Andrievs confided, his lips almost touching her ear.

Tone looked at her companion in amazement.

"Oh, that's nice – are you following me?"

"No, I just happened to… go in with a classmate; his aunt has a stable there. I saw you taking your cap off after a race."

"Yes, I can only ride when Dimants isn't in Riga," says Tone. "He thinks a woman in a cart is a mistake. Sitting with your legs spread out is just like smoking or drinking vodka."

"Those are prejudices from the past. He should have seen how the records in international racing were toppled by Mrs. Kaņepājs or Miss Pūliņa!"

"So go and talk to him."

"They're letting you ride Petronejs?"

"Because he's old... Petronejs is still running on frozen ice but no longer at the Hippodrome. Mitrofanov the jockey is still a good friend to the family; sometimes he lets me ride. Here at the carriage-house is Sirotājs, ridden this evening by Pāvils. He's my favourite! I'm practising his methods."

"What is your method?"

Tone looked closely at Andrievs – was he mocking or serious?

In the small window-pane the moon passed over them with frost-clouded features like a sacrificial head on a silver plate.

"Let's go, I'll show you!" She tugged Andrievs by the arm. "There's absolutely no air in here!"

Squeezing through the crowd, the two pushed toward the Bondars' daughter, who had a plate of sautéed cabbage in one hand and a dish of roast pork in the other. Under her plump chin she had also popped a hunk of bread, and in the white décolletage between her two pink breasts a thin little carving-knife was placed. While this delight billowed and shuffled past Andrievs' eyes, he pressed himself against the bar of the inn, at which, with their backs to him and heads in their calloused palms, sat Jēkabs Radvilis and his neighbour, the old farmer Kāpostiņš. Jēkabs had still not recovered from his recent experience; Dimants' capers chafed at his honour. Kāpostiņš meanwhile, leaning up close, exhaled bad breath along with bitter words in his ear: "Don't look at that Dimants! Only bad can come of that horse-racing, and nothing else... What does a farmer get from a trained horse? What devil is driving him, making his horses run in that inhuman way?"

Radvilis glared angrily at the separate "drinkers'" room in the depths at the back, where grander people could meet. At just that moment Dimants flashed past a chink in the door of that room, talking to the clerk and forester of Dignāja parish, laughing loudly, his whiskers shaking.

"All those changes have to be taken slowly. The farmer will always prefer a good walker, smart at ploughing. Not a scrambler, not a tearaway, he slowly obeys the reins and just strides onwards. Well, sometimes he might let himself go, either at the market, or at a wedding, but it only happens when something gets into their heads, or it's done by people who are known as horse traders, or runners. But the simple farmer, with a clear head – never! Never!"

Radvilis seemed to wake up at these words and struck his fist on the counter, sending a little cloud of flour into the air.

"I'll outrun them!"

Andrievs trembled and made off out of the inn.

Outside it was a stormy moonlit night. The inn was floating in it like a barge filled to the brim with yellow window-eyes. Only for a moment could they stop to observe the stars, full of wonder: at once the cold grabbed those standing in the chilly draught. Frost-fragments whirled about overhead along the huge beams of the ancient inn. Andrievs wrapped Tone's warm body in a coat, amazed at how beautiful it was. With her figure, everything was functional – no superfluous material in it. Andrievs himself put on the dishevelled sheepskin coat with which he walked the streets of Riga like a *bon-vivant,* but in the countryside he was unaccountably ashamed of it.

Usually at night he closed the carriage-house, so that robbers couldn't take away the sleeping journeymen's horses, but at Shrovetide it stood unlocked. Tone stopped Andrievs at the threshold, and then after a moment she came out, leading Sirotājs. The grey was glistening in the moonlight with a blue sheen like March snow. His mane was white, but his tail was as long and silky as that of a bird of paradise. Tone harnessed the horse and invited Andrievs into the sledge. He didn't know how to get in – it was ornamented and narrow, like a nutshell. Finally he settled in somehow on the rearward pole, with his backside pushed out against the side, and now Tone's head came close to his chest. The girl was joyful, laughing, her small hands in leather gloves tightly pulling the reins, and the travellers were, with one bound, on the river.

"Now where to – to Jēkabmiests?" Tone asked playfully.

The moonlight had cut up the surroundings with sharp white lines. Here and there some gaiety broke out; distant laughter was heard from St. Michael's Church on the Līvāni side, or a whinnying horse in Sēlija – some boy must be taking his intended for a ride along the ice.

Worlds collided in the middle of Daugava, but Andrievs and Antonjia slipped lightly through, under the alder arches wreathed in hoar-frost.

The ice of the Daugava, with a light dusting of snow, curved round beyond Līvāni. Sirotājs' shadow in the moonlight fell at the horse's feet like a black moving animal. The horse speeded up without encouragement.

"You see?" Tone pointed. "I train horses by the full moon. The horse sees its shadow and thinks it's his competitor, that's how he thinks. I've never seen a trotter that doesn't want to come first. He can never beat his shadow, but the horse tries. Races are won by the one that runs faster than it is capable of. I was taught that by an old Lithuanian. Every year Dimants goes to watch the horse races on Lake Sartai, usually on the first Sunday of February. This year it was splendid, better than any other time. Have you ridden on an icy lake?"

Andrievs shook his head.

"I haven't ridden at all. Never with a real trotter…"

Sirotājs' hooves thundered like an agitated heartbeat. Towards dawn Drēģu Island appeared, near the Dūņu Inn. Tone turned the grey homeward, and the shadow now fell on the cart, behind his back, like a parachute.

"So take the reins!" she said, her voice trembling with suppressed emotion. "Try it!"

It seemed that it was not Andrievs but Tone who was about to experience the first ride in her life.

The boy cautiously took the reins and felt a tug. He had been flying in dreams, and the power that was in the ends of the reins was the same as the one that pulled him into the air in dreams.

"A horse is a person's wings," said Antonija, clutching her hat. "You stroke a horse – he runs; you hit a horse – he runs. The only answer to everything is to run."

Quickly they flew back to Meņķis. The last bend in the river they took slowly, walking, resting the horse.

"What moonlight!" Tone breathes calmly, grabbing Andrievs' elbow.

Antonija Saltupa! Admired on both banks of the Daugava! An ordinary village lass like that is enchanting, thought Andrievs. A big fellow is steering the horse while she herself can sigh about the moonlight in the sledge – it doesn't quite seem like Tone – strong, beautiful Tone. Maybe she was fooling again?

Andrievs still didn't know how hard it was to be Dimants' stepdaughter.

No-one was near the inn. The walls of the building resounded and rumbled – inside they were dancing the Lithuanian Oira. Tone unhitched Sirotājs, covered him and led him into the carriage-house. When she reappeared out of the darkness, tracing her steps in the snow like a fox in a straight line, Andrievs was unable to do anything else – he gave in to the same instinct that governs a fox, a lynx, a man. He caught her by the shoulders and took her in his arms.

They clung tighter, so that each could feel the other's blood-flow through their clothes. Like a warm bird, Tone's breathing could be felt in the pit of Andrievs' neck. He pressed ever so lightly, his hot cheek against her cool icy brow. Though he was younger, he was taller than her.

The inn was pounding along with the age-old ground it stood on. Those sounds vibrated into them as they stood outside and felt for each other's lips. Those lips were dry and warm, while icy fingers melted in their hair.

As they kissed each other for the first time, Andrievs couldn't dismiss the insistent thought of how to fully appreciate and immortalize the perfection of the moment in his own deep joy.

"I'm going to paint you!" he cried.

"Oh, you dreamer!" Tone burst out laughing, pushed his cap back onto his neck and led him into the inn.

While Andrievs searched for a peg on which to put his outer clothes, their hands unclasped. After that it was too late.

As he entered the room, Andrievs saw Antonija standing in the middle of the hall in the light of the chandelier. Her slim waist in a black velvet bodice with ornaments sewn on. Augusts was holding her firmly by the hand. Tone's face was bright and inviting.

At that moment the music stopped. The girl's breathing raised her breasts high and made her scarves billow; the boys were knocking back jugs of beer. Augusts tossed a silver lats coin up to the ceiling in the sweaty darkness and cried out: "Neigh, neigh, grey horse"!

Tone's narrow waist was grasped as if with pincers by Augusts Radvilis' broad raftsman's palms – not like Andrievs' thin pea-plant paws. In those hands Tone rested, chattering, then flew off across the floor like a silk poppy torn by the wind.

The groups of youths were changing – the exhausted ones were stumbling around the table or going out into the fresh air to cool down, whilst those who had already drawn breath were joining in and leaping and singing, helping the musicians along.

> Neigh, neigh, grey horse,
> Standing in the middle of the stable.
> Weep, weep, young lad,
> As you go off to war.

Augusts and Antonija thrust at each other fiercely.

At first Andrievs tried to escape into the crowd, but the floorboards under his feet seemed to turn in a circle like a log on a raft that has collided with a rock. He was forced to look at the mad dance along with dozens of other fascinated eyes.

> I sent word to Father
> To sell his land,
> To buy me out of the war.
> Father didn't sell the land,
> Didn't buy me from the war.

Yes, but what was Tone to Andrievs? A phenomenon suddenly appearing from the other bank, going for a trot in the moonlight. A dream; it was all just an illusion. Each of them knew only their fathers' competition, the constant war between the two banks. Created, united and separated by the river.

> I sent word to Mother,
> To sell her cow,
> To buy me out of the war.
> Mother didn't sell the cow,
> Didn't buy me from the war.

And who was he, himself? Lanky and awkward with his dark, unevenly cut hair and the first shaved stubble on his chin. A wayward child, crawling onto the punishment stocks of adolescence, looking into himself for the first time and frightened of his own darkness.

> I sent word to my brother,
> To sell his horse,
> To buy me out of the war.
> Brother didn't sell the horse,
> Didn't buy me from the war.

Dimants was also looking at his stepdaughter, and Andrievs saw in her eyes the famous: "You want to be strong – run; you want to be beautiful – run; you want to be smart – run. You want Tone? Run away!" Just now by the Daugava Tone had spoken Dimants' words: "Stroke a horse – he runs; hit a horse – he runs. The only answer to everything is – run."

What great fortune awaits Augusts, even if he manages to outrun Tone?

The Latgalian youths bustled back into the dance-hall, taking up the flow with the next stanza of their story.

> I sent word to my bride,
> To sell her crown,
> To buy me from the war.
> My bride sold the crown,
> Bought me from the war.

Andrievs had clenched his fingers so tightly that he surprised himself.

They will see one day, Antonija and Augusts! Dad and Ludvigs Dimants! All of them.

I'll be myself.

I'll drink with my own money.

I'll run my own colts.

I'll marry who I want.

> Neigh, neigh, grey horse,
> Standing in the middle of the stall.
> Weep, weep, young laddie,
> Coming back from the war.

A peculiar silence came over Andrievs in the middle of the inn under the hot steaming beams, as the floor reverberated under dozens of couples leaping and dancing, but he stood there alone and made himself a promise. Beside him, Maruse, mouth half-open, gaped at Augusts and Tone, in wild contortions, scattering the other dancers aside.

This silence is good, in the eye of the storm. Promises made in such a silence are usually fulfilled.

The musicians stopped playing their instruments and were wiping their wet lips with their shirtsleeves just as the clock on the wall cupboard screwed up its face, the face of an eternally maligned child, and spat out a cuckoo twelve times.

The gospel had rung out. Law entered, and Merriment withdrew. Ash Wednesday was beginning, the great Shrovetide – the stairway to Easter.

Augusts lifted Tone in his arms and twirled her around him a couple more times, as a ship, sinking in a whirlpool, furls its sail.

Dimants waved from the exit. Tone, catching sight of him, melted into the crowd.

Both of Radvilis' sons went to seek out their father. The boyar of Eglona lay drunk on a table, his beard soaked in a pool of beer. Augusts tried to get him to his feet; Barinbaums' suit and Feitelbergs' smart cravat were filthy, drenched with beer. Next to him sat Aitu Māle, giggling at goodness knows what. Dad could only mutter: "I'm running away!"

Andrievs saw that the hair was receding on the back of his father's head, that his ears were drooping, and heat was running over his bones; it was just as well that he took after his mother, not his father! He would never have a bare nape at that age, nor beer splashed down his front. He had indeed just promised himself, like his father, "I'm running away!" – but he had done it differently, without the Radvilis' heavy burden. Let the world not tie him down to the shaft and, wasted away, throw him onto a farm with a heap of slops, laconically explaining: "Too boastful! Wouldn't come to a good end anyway."

Augusts meanwhile, having grasped his dad under one arm, entrusted the other to Andrievs. Like two horses yoked to a cart, the brothers dragged the old man into the darkness of the yard and put him into a sledge, where mill-girls and beggars were already hanging about.

"What kind of a brother are you to me?" complained Andrievs as they dragged their father along.

Augusts looked at him, wide-eyed with astonishment.

"Don't you see that Antonija is just waiting for you to take her by the hand? She's the one who makes you dance! You have Margarēte already, you've just proposed. No, jump up to the ceiling with that tomboy! Till you're unconscious! So is that the co-operative morality of students you're always talking about?"

"What's it to you? You still don't understand anything about these things."

"She'll get you!" continued Andrievs like a gloomy prophet. "Mark my words!"

Someone had mockingly hung a bag of ashes on Jēkabs' back.

"Oh, you … !" Augusts swore quietly, sweeping the ash off into a snowdrift. That's the sort of joke that Dimants might play, thought Andrievs.

The brothers harnessed Maija and travelled back to the house, the reins relaxed, relying on the mare's memory. At the mill they hauled their father into Maruse's clean made-up bed.

Without his boots, of course.

Jēkabs Radvilis did overtake Ludvigs Dimants; in the middle of that year he bought the American trotter Run Hill Dune, outbidding him for the former world record holder in Stockholm.

On 30 July 1939 Run Hill Dune was entered for the Group One race at Riga Hippodrome for the first time. The horse was starting to run after only half a season, but by the end of the year he was the highest earning trotter. He was an excellent runner, born in America in 1930, who at the age of three years had set the US record, running one kilometre at a speed of 1m.16.1. As years passed he lost none of his strength. Even on 18 June in Sweden he had set a course record of 1m. 20.7, and a month later he was running in Riga.

The experienced jockey Mitrofanov, selected by the owner for his first start, had injured his knee the previous evening. Andrievs arranged that Antonija would ride instead, wearing Mitrofanov's colours.

Many people knew this, but the fathers of the two youngsters didn't.

The race took place, and Antonija won it. The horse took first place and won its owner 750 lats.

Only in the stable-yard did she dare take off her cap. She released a sea of blond hair over her slim back that July afternoon.

Their hands were hurting from the congratulations and handshakes. After the races, though, as is known, their fathers thrashed the two conspirators.

Augusts

Hands stretching out in the dark sink softly into last year's grass on the bank.

Before Jersika the Daugava is not wide, but before the spring floods it still runs high and swiftly. Sunk in thought, Andrievs strides robustly along the black, rain-washed ice, avoiding the ice-holes, and doesn't notice that he has crossed the river. His legs have carried him to the edge of the opposite shore quite a way downstream from Dunava. Andrievs makes his way along the embankment, keeping to the bare, ice-nibbled roots of black alders.

In finding his way he's helped by moonlight – the wind blows away the cloud cover, and through the torn curtain a somewhat faded chalk-pale toad looks curiously down to Earth. The moon, like the people, is not getting any sleep on these nights. Andrievs looks with gratitude at the face of this strange creature, which reviews the life of man, visible to all – he is born, grows, fades away and vanishes, to appear once again.

Having got up onto the road, he hears a horse and cart approaching. There are two riders, their cargo covered with spruce branches, the horse limping along at a slow trot.

"Where are you heading?" Andrievs calls out when the team catches up with him.

"Not far now," replies the man sitting at the reins. "To the Radvilis mills."

"Then that's on my way. I have relatives at the mills."

"Come, take a seat! You don't have to bust your tongue for our sakes – I can see already that you're running away."

The other man frees up a place on the frame of the cart; Andrievs nimbly jumps up with his hip against the back of the cart. The horse takes the opportunity to slow to walking pace. The man at the reins no longer urges him on.

"Exhausted – been on the road all night."

"Don't you have your own mills then?"

"There you have to first of all show your certificate from the parish or village council, and hand over a tenth of your grain." The holder of the reins spits angrily over the side of the cart. "They want to force you to pay your dues. Round our way, more than thirty farmers have been thrown into prison. There are few threshing machines, few steam engines – how are we supposed to pay those taxes? But here you can grind it with no worries – they don't ask for any certificates."

"You're not afraid of travelling at night?" asks Andrievs, looking at the undergrowth.

"Afraid?" The man sitting next to him surveys him suspiciously. "Of what? Of partisans? They all have support at home. What would they rob travelling men for? The Cheka, they're robbers."

"Restless times – let's sleep here for a couple of nights." The man at the reins lifts his gun. "Your folks at the mills are sort of half-Red – as they say, when Satan rules, then creep under Satan's skirts!"

"If you're not at home, someone else will take your place," says the other one gloomily. "They have to fulfil the export plan, anyway. The list of names comes from the District."

The conversation peters out. Andrievs observes the Daugava, which is etched in the darkness by his left shoulder – a line, a vein, an invisible boundary. Like death, which always stretches its arms far and wide.

The cart turns rapidly off the main road onto the path to the mill, and travelling becomes difficult, because the marshy ground is a real bog, pitted by the easterly wind. The horse pulls, dragging on its collar. The men jump off, to make it easier going for the cart.

Andrievs gradually falls behind, striding along the greyish water-meadows to the side that is darkened by the wall of spruce-trees. Andrievs recalls school holidays, when he travelled from Riga to help his father and brother with the haymaking and walked this same road, swinging the sagebrush – free, care-free.

*

Mummy – as Andrievs called his mother – Emma Radvile was no match for her energetic partner, worn down as she was by social obligations and work. Therefore, when Dad built his first rental house in Riga, she moved into one of the apartments, choosing a separate life and solitude in the big city. About that time Andrievs started high school, and moved in with Mummy. From his mother he had inherited not only her grey-green eyes, slender figure and curly hair, but also her way of thinking. Andrievs' elder brother Augusts, whose property the Radvilis mills became, was like his father – stiff and self-righteous as a fencepost, with wiry white hair and broad raftsman's hands, blue eyes full of a consciousness of superiority.

It was good to grow up with his mother close by, in the calm, cool half-darkness of the rental house, which for years afterward smelled of fresh plaster and parquet varnish. The lace of the curtains and the thick green satin cast mysterious shadows in the bare light. Right from childhood Andrievs liked to imagine and sketch this and that with a pencil on paper. The house in Riga gave the dreamer peace and shade. "Don't dream a life – live a dream," his mother instructed him, and there he could afford that.

The Radvilis water-mill was something quite opposite – a hothouse filled with dazzling light, kindled with a masculine fire. Windows without curtains, chopped trees, so as not to block the light – Dad didn't like shade and shadow. On summer days the only refuge was the cool bosom of the mill-pond, or the thick walls of the mill. But there was never any peace even there. Shards of radiance pricked the sweltering, half-naked bodies; father had endless tasks. Hardest of all was haymaking time, which was often passed in a lather of sweat under oppressive black storm clouds.

As the haymaking time began, the mill was in operation only three times a week, because the mill-owners worked shoulder to shoulder with their staff. They converted the sharp grass of the water-meadows of the Eglūne River into hay, reaping it, drying it, taking it to the barn. Around sunrise they reaped, after breakfast they turned it over, in the afternoon they stacked what was dry.

Your head would be spinning from the constant wakefulness; instead of blood, grass-juice flowed; sleep came like water, in streams, even painfully. If you happened to lean sideways or rest your back against the mill wall, quite often you would suddenly wake up from falling asleep standing, like a horse. The soles of your feet would be covered with thick skin, blisters would break out on your palms, and keep breaking out, and your skin, browned by the sun, moistened with sweat, pricked with bent-grass, stopped feeling. Haymaking time was a special period each summer, which covered Latvia like heavy green velvet. Life was a feast; every usually forgotten muscle would throb and smart. Even your lungs seemed to be covered from within by a fine coating of hay.

The horses allowed Andrievs to settle into the men's sweltering world and even love it. Perhaps these two realms fed each other. The silence of the horses and their silky smooth skin, though which came the iron strength of their muscles, the fall of their manes, their elegant gait and their intoxicating scent – who could be left indifferent by it? From the beginning Dad was breeding heavy Oldenburg draught-horses for the Army's needs, but later, urged on by Dimants the Latgalian, he started to keep trotters.

Emma, a Krustpils woman, never grew to love the Radvilis mills. Nor, for that matter, her hot-blooded husband, and yet maybe – was he the love of her life? Like a waterlogged English rose she always found something over which to bend her fair head in sorrow. Sorrow over her little daughter, who perished in Pskov during the escape from the First World War. Over some real or imagined dalliance of her husband's, and their estrangement. Until suddenly she surprised the whole family by starting to play the racecourse totalizator. Possibly to spite her husband, who had enough enterprise to take a world-famous trotter to the course, but lacked the time and the will to climb the twenty or so steps to his wife's apartment.

Unable to fit into her husband's life, Emma, fumbling blindly, sought out her own. "Everyone enjoys life – am I the only one who shouldn't?" she asserted, when Andrievs made some objection to her too close friendship with the Ābens family living in the farmhouse. Ābens was a young swindler with gold teeth, a dealer in the literal and figurative sense of the word. He worked on the stock exchange, played chess for money in Riga cafes or draughts in the harbour, bought and sold everything possible – even horses. Ābens knew Riga businessmen of all nationalities and groupings. His wife had a summer-house at Melluži, a splendid situation in doubtful company, and many and various invitations to house-parties near and far. Everything he earned Ābens put on playing the totalizator at the racecourse, even drawing Emma Radvile into secret dealings. He never borrowed money – Ābens didn't do that – but it turned out that Emma herself liked to risk, lose and borrow. They enjoyed most sitting with a cup of coffee in Emma's living room, the so-called "green salon". They were never short of conversation topics, but Ābens took care to provide certain intoxicating substances. Spending her days like that – was it any wonder that Mummy grew nervous and couldn't sleep?

The other members of the family scolded Emma, making her feel guilty. A foolish old woman who'd got mixed up with a young chancer! Squandering her property! Andrievs thought his mother was doing nothing wrong: it was accepted in the Radvilis family that everyone lived for themselves, everyone loved themselves, not caring much about their next of kin. So why should Emma be an exception?

Mother had more than her fair share of imagined guilt in front of a married friend during the time of the Red Terror. In 1941, warned about the Stalinist deportations, Emma immediately went off to her husband's place at Ogles in Krustpils, and the two were deported together to Stalin's camps. In the cattle wagons the soldiers separated her from her husband again. Andrievs had no further information about his parents' fate. They must have been laid to rest in the permafrost, but not side by side – just as in life.

The millers' cart rattled hollowly in the dark across the little bridge over the Eglūne River.

The water-mill is part of the ensemble of buildings on the Podunaja estate – the servants' quarters, the granary, the smithy, the stables. Around them rustles the ancient parkland. The so-called castle, which had once been a typical central building of a Polish landowner, had sadly not survived. It was built on substantial foundations with walls about a metre and a half thick, which is clearly visible here and there from what is preserved of the ruins. With fifteen rooms, intended for the landowner's family and servants. The great cellars in the wall were still being used as a prison during the war. The New House on the estate has survived, and after he acquired the mill it was Augusts Radvilis' family home.

The nephew of the Eglona estate-owner, Baron Boriss Englards, having returned from Russia in 1927, regained his lands in Latgale, and among other properties, an ownerless shack in the Upland Augšzeme. After ten years, having got to know Jēkabs Radvilis, the baron offered Radvilis the neglected, abandoned water-mill, which Jēkabs, with characteristic impetuousness, bought immediately, digging up the molehills and putting the place in order. The Radvilis family felt at home in this setting, among these people, who spoke the same *augšzemnieku* Upland dialect as Krustpils people.

When, shortly before the war, Augusts married Margarēte, a descendant of the bankrupt Izabelina estate and a dentist by profession, he installed a modern dental surgery in the New House, and a comfortable waiting room for the patients. A society of her medical peers came into being – doctors and pharmacists and their families. Augusts named the restored mill the Radvilis mill, in honour of his father. In order to prove that he had not studied agronomy in vain and knew something about farm management, he introduced crop rotation in the fields, put the farm buildings in order, bought pedigree stock, and bred and dealt in horses for the army's renovation commission. He got up and went to bed at the same time as his mill-hands, whom he had inherited from his father. He only needed to modernize the equipment. The good reputation of the Radvilis mill was enhanced, and there was plenty of work. Augusts spent his Sundays hunting; his hunting bag was rarely empty.

The events of 1940 drew a line under everything. A year before, when Margarēte, as a Baltic German, declined to be repatriated to Germany, maintaining her faith in her newly-married husband and the land of her forefathers, she had her nights' sleep troubled by bad presentiments. Officers from Poland, which had capitulated, arrived from Riga, asking for shelter and work. Then the news followed that little Finland had ventured to attack the great Soviet land and started a war. It was forbidden to write bad things in the Latvian newspapers about the Soviets' new-found allies, so everyone was forced to appear more stupid than they really were. After the tough winter followed the spring, when Latvia's orchards stood black and lifeless, while the German forces attacked Denmark and Norway.

There was not long to wait for the tragic continuation of this gigantic chess game. On 17 June 1940 the Red Army entered Latvia, while Latvia's defence lines were commanded to defend the railway lines, as long as trains with troops and tanks were moving along them. Some army units were billeted at Krustpils castle. The lats was pegged to the chervonets, and Soviet officers' wives in Jēkabpils went on a buying spree. They were hoarding dresses, coats, silk stockings and leather gloves, they were sewing dresses from curtain tulle. Officers were buying up all the box-calf boots and shoes, women's nightdresses, and chocolates, filling their back-packs, thinking that this strange abundance, specially laid on for them, would soon come to an end.

When they found out that Ulmanis' government had been replaced by Kirhenšteins' cabinet, the Radvilis were not very concerned, because the newspapers were reporting that there would be parliamentary elections, in which, apart from the communists, a non-party bloc would take part, led by the writer and teacher Atis Ķeniņš. Only when a few days had passed and Atis Ķeniņš was arrested, did the naïve people realize that there were already troops in Jēkabils, and they themselves were under a hostile and harsh occupying power.

The Radvilis family experienced several nationalizations. First of all the Riga house passed to the state, then the Radvilis mill, after that their family home at Ogles in Krustpils, their car and the horses. The general meeting of the local Agricultural Association was attended by Otomārs Oškalns, Second Secretary of the Jēkabpils committee of the Communist Party. The Association's previous board was dismissed from office; Oškalns read out the composition of the new board. It was a great surprise that Augusts Radvilis was included in it. He, like the others, was elected unanimously.

So he now became the district agronomist, travelling around the parishes, instructing old and new farmers, giving lectures, directing the young farmers' winter school, and strenuously preparing for the sowing of taraxacum rubber dandelions.*

At the beginning of June the next year everyone started to sense that preparations were going on for some extraordinary event. In great secrecy the Cheka drew up the first deportation lists on 14 June 1941.

Someone had warned Augusts that he and his close associates should hide that week in the meadows by Biržu forest. They slept in huts of branches by the haystacks. Every day they went to Jēkabpils on the lookout, until it emerged that some people had been imprisoned. Andrievs and Augusts' wife Margarēte, who was in the last months of pregnancy, had gone to some acquaintances at Dignāja. Nothing happened to them, but Andrievs was tortured by foreboding. He immediately cycled to his father at Krustpils. With his eternal spitefulness Dad believed that the repressions wouldn't touch him, an old man – "they'll only carry me away from Ogles with my boots first!" How mistaken he was! Jēkabs was shown a long list of "crimes" in the eyes of the new Soviet authorities. Mummy, having arrived at Ogles from Riga, was indisposed – the doctor had diagnosed inflammation of the gall-bladder and blood poisoning. In their lifetimes they didn't often meet, but now that the deporters had made them gather their things and climb into a truck, Dad had apparently cried and begged forgiveness if he had been bad to Mother, but Mother answered that he should forgive her for being no angel either. This was related later to Andrievs by their long-serving maid Vincentīne, when he found her in tears. What was most tragic was that there in the cold room, on the table, had been placed the coffin of Grandma Pīcka, Mummy's mother, who lived in Ogles. She was over eighty years old, and apparently she had fallen down in the cowshed a couple of days before with a heart attack. The deporters, Russian soldiers, had left the funeral arrangements to Vincentīne.

This was the sight that Andrievs beheld in his beloved birthplace, Ogles – his faithful sheepdog Čarle shot dead in the doorway, his dear Grandma, in whose care he had spent his whole childhood, in a coffin in one room, and the maid weeping and dishevelled in the kitchen. Grandma Pīcka lay in her coffin, grey and shrunken like a little towel wrapped around an ironing roller. Andrievs touched her cold hand and recalled what she had always said when she wasn't well: "Žaniņ, hold my hand."

With an acute pain in the heart he ran outside; it was already dusk, Vincentīne had let everything go, the cows in the shed were lowing in pain, making a terrific noise, from not being milked. For a few days that June an icy, stormy wind had returned there.

It wasn't clear to anyone on what principles the list of the deportees had been compiled. Marked for deportation were both public servants and oily-handed mechanics, the biggest farmers in the neighbourhood, people who worked in *artel* associations and co-operatives, even railway conductors. There was talk that Stalin's plan was to transfer all of Latvia to Russia and bring in the Siberians.

When the deportations were over, Augusts' and Margarēte's little girl was born, Grandma was buried, and the remaining Radvilis carried on living. A couple of weeks later the war reached them. German Luftwaffe bombing destroyed the narrow-gauge railway lines, and Krustpils railway station was bombed. One night in a powerful explosion the Krustpils-Jēkabpils bridge was blown to bits. In the morning the last Red Army units crossed the Daugava in boats in great haste, while the Radvilis mill was full of German soldiers deeply asleep on the floor. To grab his bag, Andrievs had to climb over these slumberers.

The mill was untouched, the horses were in the stables, animals reserved for other farmers returned to their sheds. Even the mill-hands remained as before; only a few Soviet activists, who didn't feel safe, went off in an easterly direction. Nazi propaganda created and stirred up a spirit of retribution. People were accused according to their Communist activity in the year of Soviet occupation. Arrests of Soviet sympathizers began, and Jews were rounded up and shot. This was repellent to the Radvilis. Augusts didn't hesitate to speak out against the slaughter and he earned a nickname as a Communist. Yet he was powerless to do anything.

Sometimes he had to meet with the leaders of the German district enlistment office in Jelgava – Freiherr von Medem and the men on his staff. Augusts took Margarēte with him. Her Baltic German origins, her excellent knowledge of German and her diplomatic skills helped to settle relations successfully. The district's *Kreislandwirt* – the army's financial service – did once accuse Augusts of sabotage. A commission of men in black SS uniforms arrived, and the non-fulfilment of purchases of agricultural produce was investigated. Augusts pleaded a shortage of threshing-machines, which he had been forced to lease to Lithuania, where the grain harvest was going even worse.

Andrievs returned to Riga, living with a friend from his father's time at the racecourse, Jānis Eizens, and started working as a stable-hand, in the summer also as an apprentice jockey. He didn't meet with Augusts often – he only knew that Augusts' family had grown quite a bit: in the spring of 1943 Margarēte and Augusts had a second daughter, Johanna, and after a while Augusts brought home two Latvian boys from Russia, orphans from the "People's Aid" supply-train.

*

The mill is lustrous, giving off bright electric sparks. The waters of the Eglūne are working a dynamo too. In the yard, beyond the river, stand a row of yoked horses with raised shafts. Andrievs' drivers are lifting a beer barrel and a honey-pot, shoulders of ham, a pile of blocks of butter, carefully wrapped in parchment, off the cart.

Andrievs pushes back the heavy door of the mill and slowly enters the great room. A fire is burning, someone is sitting, someone is sleeping by the wall, with a suitcase as a pillow. On the broad square table are the sacks of grain, and some of the grinders are there chatting with the millers, whose blue overalls have a dusting of white flour. Two young girls are bringing in beer and pancakes, which, like yellow oily suns, are bubbling on the huge cast-iron pots above the stove.

Andrievs sits down at the end of a bench. Among the clay salt-dishes, two little children with short-cropped hair and gaunt faces have laid their heavy heads on the table. It isn't possible to tell their sex; their eyelids are heavy with sleep. Some chap, with a dry rasp, is telling a story:

"A farmer wanted to buy himself a dragon. He went off to Riga, made some inquiries, went into a big house. Once he got in there, he took a look: all the rich men from his district were sitting along a table, carousing: they were using horse-skulls as dishes, bones as spoons, claws as drinking bowls, and the devil himself was serving them. He was busily bringing them all their food and drink. The farmer looked around for a moment: a shudder ran through his bones – he just wanted to get away. Finally he thought again: 'Why should I escape – they're having a fine time!' He stayed, and then soon enough he got to meet the one who was selling dragons. He started to negotiate – and the seller gave him a little box, saying 'When you bring the box into your house, say to your wife: The devil in your heart!' But he loved his wife very much, so he turned the words around: 'Wife: the devil in your backside!'"

The children seem to have fallen asleep, but the teenagers sitting opposite chuckle at him.

"As soon as he'd said that, the box fell out of his hands and shattered – there was no dragon. The next year, when he was in Riga, he demanded his money back from the dragon-seller. But he just laughed: 'How could a dragon live with you, when you talk so shamelessly?'"

Andrievs takes the girl's hand as she puts on the table a yellow bowl of melted fat, with pieces of white bread floating in it.

"Where's the boss?" asks Andrievs.

"In the little room," replies the girl, and then goes to fetch some still-warm flour for the next bake.

Andrievs crosses the hall, with its wooden floor, and heads off out the back, where a corridor begins beyond the bars and the tank. At the bottom of the stairs he opens the door to his father's former office – and is shocked at how much it reminds him of those times when he came here as a boy. But who is that sitting at Dad's dark desk with its turned legs? Dad himself.

Augusts has put on even more weight. But that isn't the right word. He has acquired bulk – like a table, a cupboard or a bed. His features have sunk into his face, his shoulders, his body, Augusts has expanded and hardened within himself like an ornament on a clay oil-dish.

He looks blearily at Andrievs, as at a ghost over the dishes and the spattered surface of the table, on which there are two vodka glasses, bowls full of food and a bottle of a dark brown drink. His blond hair hangs tousled over his glossy cheek. Is this really Augusts, Andrievs' brother?

Andrievs well remembers their last meeting at the Christmas battle of Džūkste.

A command had arrived from the company commander to leave their digging and proceed through the forest to the railway line. There they had to take up a new defence position. The enemy was observed in the forest beyond them. Andrievs was repairing a damaged yoke and was therefore delayed in arriving. He was entering the group's empty bunker to collect his things when the Stalinists attacked the trenches from the front. Two men appeared in the bunker – the first to enter was a thick-set bearded man, and behind him a slighter, gaunt, blond-haired one. The big man made to stab Andrievs with a bayonet, but the thin one tapped the side of the large man's weapon.

"Don't shoot, Lin – that's my hostage!"

The big man turned around on his heels and ran outside.

The two Radvilis looked at each other.

"Sit down, brother," said Andrievs. "Heavy fire from our artillery is about to start, and our men will come on the counter-attack. Meanwhile, you can stay out of it."

The ground and the sky were soon thundering with peals of artillery fire.

There was no sense in saying anything, and for that brief moment nothing could be heard or said.

When the counter-attack began after about half an hour, Augusts crawled back along the ground ploughed up by the firing.

On the third day of the attack the Reds withdrew their Latvian division from the 19th division's front and transferred them to Saldus district in exchange for German units. The hearts of these Red Army fighters were with the men of Kurzeme. The armed Red soldiers answered their pursuers' cries of "*Ruki vverkh!* Hands up!" with "Calm down, chaps! We won't shoot you – don't shoot us!" The enemy that was observed in the background proved to be the Latvians who were enlisted in the 43rd division. For quite a while they had been observing from the bushes how cannons and cartloads of munitions were passing a few metres from their noses. At first they were ready to shoot, but then they heard the riders talking in Latvian. They decided: "no shooting, those are Latvian boys."

The big bearded one, and a few others, were caught. Andrievs led them to the company headquarters, asking about his brother on the way. The bearded one was apparently Lin Peņko, a young Communist from Viesīte.

"The fascists had caught me, but Augusts bought me off with a pig," Lin told him. "They slaughtered an old pig, divided it in half and went off to Jēkabpils. At home he'd said that they had to kill that pig for the Germans, she's old. They'd never been so hungry. The Germans didn't say anything, they ate the bacon, the crackling, and finally they let me go."

When it was announced in the summer of 1944 that even those who had a certificate in their pocket that they worked in an essential occupation would be mobilized, Augusts tried to avoid serving in the German army, hiding with Lin in the bunker that was installed at the base of the wash-room of the mill. On the eighth of August, German forces withdrew from Jēkabpils, the Zeļķis railway bridge over the Daugava was blown up, and Krustpils was occupied by Captain Kristaps Kaugurs' battalion of the 308th Latvian Riflemen's division of the Red Army. Augusts and Lin came out of the bunker. Peņko would not leave Augusts' side for anything, hanging onto him for dear life. His reputation as a Communist helped Augusts this time – the two underground men were not sent to the Gulag, but mobilized into the 130th Latvian Riflemen.

Peņko begged and pleaded to be kept in the ranks of the Legionaries, but not in the trenches, because he didn't want to fight on any account. He was assigned to cart duties in the cavalry regiment. Someone said that after the capitulation Peņko had gone on living a long time in the forest and he used to shoot back at the hunters with a heavy Russian Maxim gun from his shoulder.

"Well beyond midnight, but the mill is going at full pelt," says Andrievs. "You must have bought yourself a dragon!"

"Yes indeed," smirks Augusts. "They're milling all day long. Endless feasting."

"Feasting in a time of plague."

"Why are you gadding about at night?" Augusts slurs the words crudely. Only then does Andrievs realize that his brother is pissed out of his brain.

At that moment a gaunt, swarthy man in spectacles comes in. His gaze is distracted; he's buttoning up his fly. On seeing Andrievs, the newcomer is startled.

"Brother, Kazis," slurs Augusts. "My man."

Kazimirs finds a third glass and shoves the free chair towards Andrievs.

"Sit yourself down!"

Andrievs sits down hurriedly. His exhausted energies allow him to think of only one thing – the goodies on the tables, the like of which have been appearing to him in dreams. A mountain of pancakes glistens in the middle of the table. A fish swimming in butter; bacon. Jellied meat and porridge in brown clay dishes.

"Go ahead!" Kazimirs invites him, seeing Andrievs' burning look. "You're welcome."

"Are you hiding?" Andrievs asks straightforwardly, chewing rapidly.

Kazimirs fills the glasses and just as straightforwardly replies: "I'm escaping."

A refugee doesn't look like that – unlike Andrievs, he is wearing a good autumn coat, a hat, a pressed shirt and even a tie.

"*Smersh?*"*

Kazimirs waves his hand.

"And – the scar?" Andrievs points to the pink lesion that cuts into the newcomer's face. Andrievs has one himself, on one cheek.

"The scar – their colleagues on the other side. The Gestapo. They told me straight out that there would be no way back – they'd make sure that the Communists themselves would shoot me. They sent out a provocative wireless message saying that I worked for the Gestapo. *Smersh* let me lay down my arms after the fight against the Hitlerites, and only then did they capture me. They couldn't prove my guilt, handed me over to the security forces, and now what will happen, will happen. What is there to wonder about?"

"A haze of grim suspicions!" intones Augusts with heavy emphasis. "Based on the unity of all partisans! And their supporters!"

Kazimirs clinks glasses with the brothers.

"The people's support is the partisans' air supply."

"Kazimirs, comrade in war, party organiser with a capital P!" Augusts points at his guest: "Commander of the 'Men of the Daugava' partisan unit. A radio operator betrayed him, the Gestapo locked him up. He agreed to collaborate. But what other option was there, tell me, please? He got away to the Latvian partisans in Byelorussia and reported to Moscow. How many future Gestapo victims did he save by doing that? But now they're holding 'witch hunts'! The machinery of accusation, so to speak, has got into gear. The official tone has been set, the course laid out. Traitor to the fatherland, you know…"

"Where were you, party organiser?" asks Andrievs, biting into some sautéed beef, so as to continue the conversation as long as possible over a full plate.

"In the border guards."

"And how did the Latvian border guards get mixed up with the Bolsheviks?"

Kazimirs views Andrievs with disdain for a moment, then dismisses him with his hand, his anger dissipated.

"It wasn't hard, believe me! In the war years when you travelled to Riga by train, everyone could see that not far from Rumbula station people were being shot. Men, women, children, half-naked, waiting in line. So do you think that many supported 'the new order'?"

"Where did I keep that bit of paper?" Augusts opens the door of the desk and, after ruffling for a moment through the drawer, pulls out a torn page. "The German SS newspaper *Der Schwarze Korps*. An article by Rosenberg, the German minister of state. Plans for the Baltic lands – annihilation of the disobedient, Germanisation of the remainder in Latvia… Read it, Andy!"

"In our family there were five people – father, mother and we three brothers." Kazimirs throws back his head and stares at the ceiling. "All three dreamed of an education. In the Daugavpils district fourteen hectares of land belonged to us, of which eight were arable. What kind of arable? Trenches dug in the First World War and bunkers, tangles of barbed wire and stones. We tilled that land for ten years, and what do you think it meant to crowbar the rocks, pull them out of the ground, split them, carry them to the station? We earned a living from the rocks, but that hot smell of forging still sticks in my throat. And when I finished second grade at Aglona high school, the moment arrived when Father said with tears in his eyes – forgive me, I can't send you to school any more! I cried when I said goodbye to my school, yes indeed, I sat in the swamp and poured out my tears. What sort of future would we have? My older brother would go off to the country and be a parish clerk. The younger one and I would have to divide the land in half, or else one of us would have to go off and be a farmhand with some big farmer in Zemgale or Kurzeme province. Latgale was a source of cheap labour. They looked on us as second-class people. That was to be the future for the average Latvian farmer in Ulmanis' time. But what about the people who really were poor? Grim!"

"Then you accepted Soviet power enthusiastically!" Andrievs continues to eat the hunk of black rye with butter.

"I can say without exaggeration – for me and people like me, the changes back in '40 gave a prospect of a new life! With our level of knowledge at the time, we were the ideal Leninists! We were actively learning the basic ideas of socialism, humanism and democracy. We didn't know anything about those Gulags!"

"You didn't know anything about the deportations?" asks Andrievs incredulously.

"We didn't even ask! It didn't affect our family."

"And when the Soviet tanks crossed the border uninvited?"

"What was that to us? I was serving in the border guards, in Number 1 Dagda Battalion. An alarm was declared at the borders, but we were commanded to show no resistance to the Red Army, if necessary to show them the way. Why do you ask?"

"What do you think of these actions?"

"I tell you once again – it was a neighbouring state with which Latvia has a treaty of friendship and non-aggression, a socialist state, 'the first beacon in the world'. The simple working people, who were dissatisfied with Ulmanis' regime, greeted the tanks with flowers, they even sang. Because all the leaders of the resistance were sitting in prison at the time."

"Doesn't it seem like a hostile act by a big nation against a little state? There isn't even a word for all this – people call it 'the June events'. Why was the first government – Kirhenšteins' government – put together in a foreign embassy? That doesn't worry you? You, as a Communist – what would you call that?"

Kazimirs digs in his ear and examines what he finds.

"It happened so unexpectedly. The army threw the whole thing at us."

"But if you yourselves, in the underground, had been able to organise it, how would it be?"

ıe first government, I tell you, was very cleverly put ..ogether. We were almost intoxicated, thinking it was an expression of fraternity, nothing more."

"Proletarians of all lands, unite!" cries Andrievs.

"Exactly." Kazimirs appears not to notice the sarcasm. "That this was some sort of reckoning by the great powers didn't even occur to me. Vilis Lācis was so proud to be recognized in the embassy of the great socialist power. For me that embassy was a pure temple at the time. The embassy of a brother nation – it has a ring to it, doesn't it?"

"Deeply naïve and honourable." For Andrievs too the vodka has quickly gone to his head in the warmth. "Moscow gave you a part to play in a big theatre – how proud you were! First they reconciled you to your own kind – Rainis' party, the Social Democrats, traitors to the working class."

"Rainis, you don't criticize him!" Augusts blurts out.

"So that's why you're sitting here at the mill. You're so naïve!" Andrievs replies. "Because you've been acting according to the commands of the old republic, you didn't know what was going on, and you don't want to know. The so-called socialism in Russia is a fiction, terribly bloody and unstable. You can't pretend you haven't seen it, you just don't want to open your eyes and admit it."

"The further socialism is strengthened, the more it proves itself, the deeper is the rift between the classes and the opposition of hostile forces grows."

"That's well known from the 'short course'." Andrievs dismisses it with a wave of his hand. "So what was there to wonder at, when in July '41, apart from Shustin's institution,* you were also active – you, the Latvian Communists, and the responsible Young Communists! You took up the arms that were given to you, you were under orders as 'security men', you knocked on the doors of apartments at night and you put to death little innocent children, you took out old people in their blankets and threw them onto trucks! It probably didn't even occur to you that the little group that opposed you could be rounded up. Shame on you!"

It seems to Andrievs that this is why he had pined away for years like a dumb man, so that he could now shout these words loudly to those sitting opposite.

"If we're talking frankly, in '40, '41, I didn't notice any heated hostility in this district," Augusts admits. "There was a strange quiet expectancy… like before a thunderstorm… But then, after 14th June, an explosion!"

"What are you telling him?" Andrievs waves his hand and reaches for a pancake. "First he said he hadn't heard anything about deportations. They hadn't affected his family. But every one of them mentions how horribly they treated the Soviet activists when the Germans came in. Is that why they behaved horribly? Because of those little children, that June, those old people that they kicked with their heavy boots."

"You weren't anywhere near!" screams Kazimirs. "What about those who had to carry out orders? And they didn't know what they had to do until they entered their victims' apartments!" Time is mildewing their temples, driving the naked life through their veins, they know how to speak, but they can't communicate. "Only those at the top knew about it – the town and regional committee secretaries. The rest, who had to go along with Shustin, only found out on that day, at that hour…"

Augusts shrugs his shoulders.

"Many people from our parish weren't rich, and didn't belong to any organisations, Kazimirs. So what would they have done, who would they take revenge on? And did they have to be treated that way? For nothing."

Kazimirs pulls out a packet of cigarettes and offers them to the others.

"I don't know about them. Like other Latvian Communists, I was thinking about the liberation of Latvia. That I would be building and shaping everything differently! That's why I say thanks to you, Augusts, I was able to find shelter at your place at a difficult time."

"Whenever you like," nods Augusts.

"Augusts is an admirable man," opines Kazimirs, blowing thick clouds of smoke into the air. "He helps people and doesn't ask for anything in return. I'm not talking about people like Kalnbērziņš, who never risked his life, always sitting in the background like a rat with a 'special ration-voucher' supply. For all the authorities, Augusts was a partisan! In the forest battles too, when everything was changing by the minute, you had to think on your feet, you had to foresee what was possible, what was impossible."

"You can't predict everything," sighs Augusts. "Like our good friend Oškalns."

"The old devil," Kazimirs concurs. "I met him with my people in the winter of '42 – '43, when they came over the front line from Staraya Rusa. About a hundred men. He said it had been a senseless war, Oškalns did – they were fighting and blowing things to bits, but they hadn't seen Fritz with their own eyes. Their commanders were Samsons, then Moravsky the Russian from Riga, and Oškalns himself. Soon after, Oškalns formed his own brigade."

"Wasn't he in Kurzeme for a while?" Augusts enquires.

"No, Macpāns was in Kurzeme in the summer of '43; he wouldn't give the fascists any peace at Abava and Usma, with his partisan fighting unit, the Red bullet. At Piltene, Kārlis Salmiņš and the Red Army officer Vasily Red'ko were co-operating; in Pape and Ance parishes it was the two mobile partisan units of Āboliņš and Valtsons, the Arrow, and the Hawk. Near Spāre station – the Stende area, to the north, Sēme's section. In the forest of Kabile there was Nikolay Kapustin's front-line reconnaissance group, the Seaman."

"What about Oškalns?" Andrievs repeats. "They must have buried him a couple of years later?"

"That's just the thing. He drank himself to death."

"I have a clutch of poems by him, hand-written poems." Augusts searches through the drawers again, but he can't find them. "He left them on a tree-stump when he had to escape. We met. I wanted to give them back – he wouldn't take them. He said that words are not real life."

"He was bitter, in the end it was terrible," Kazimirs agrees. "Oškalns and Laiviņš paid dearly for the fact that the parish executive committees had appointed the good old specialists from the 'bourgeois colleges'. That was unacceptable to Lebedev and Titov. And they were dismissed for that. After all, it was Vilis Lācis, in Moscow in the last summer of the war, who approved the list of local people who had attended courses, leading officials of commissariats and Soviet executive committees who had higher education. Nowadays you can't find a single one of those cadres! They weren't allowed to work. Is it any wonder that Oškalns drank himself to death after such disloyalty?"

"We'll drink ourselves to death too, Kazi," Augusts observes laconically, pouring out the vodka.

"You won't drink yourself to death," objects Kazimirs, clinking glasses with him and tossing it back in one gulp. "Maybe I will – I'm drinking all the time, I'm drinking to forget. But as for him – only tonight! Eh! Your brother's a genius of a man. They've all paid bitterly – the leaders, the scientists, and the farmers. But Augusts Jakovļevičs goes and sets up the 'Good Life' co-operative!"

"Not on my own! Ten or twelve farmers came together, we talked through the night about what we'd do and what we wouldn't. We didn't take on the lazybones and the drinkers."

"Simpletons with rifles!" Again Andrievs can't suppress a wry grin. "No wonder they say the Soviet revolution was made by *yevreyskie golovi, latishskie shtiki i russkie duraki* – Jewish heads, Latvian bayonets and Russian fools."

"Why are you talking like this now, comrades?" Kazimirs looks through the crate of bottles by the leg of the table. "It all happened on a voluntary basis."

"I'm no comrade of yours. Tonight or tomorrow, people will be carted off to Siberia – will that be 'on a voluntary basis'?"

"That's because of the agricultural tax, brother," Augusts explains. "It can hardly be otherwise – the city's situation is hard. They didn't grumble either, those farmers. They were deprived of their grain, and gave up as much as was asked. But there are always informers, you see! And the pressure from Moscow: why are you spending so much time with those *kulaks,* those bourgeois farmers? Speed up collectivization!"

"So what happened to the voluntary principle?"

"The idea of the *kolkhoz* is a necessity!" interjects Kazimirs. "A necessity, not a luxury!"

"Why do the farmers have to have both their cows and their only working horse taken away to the *kolkhoz*," says Andrievs, recalling Ludvigs. "Must animals be compelled to be in the same shed, where they forget to feed and water them? And these Communists who come from the factories to be bosses – do they understand anything at all about the land?"

"Those are just details!" Kazimirs dismisses him. "The forest is what is making the farmers protest. The forest!"*

Augusts disagrees: "I don't know why Moscow exaggerates about the forest. We don't have much need for the services of the Cheka's internal military forces. In Lithuania the forest is still holding out, and only because of their uncrowned king, Žemaitis. In Latvia the forest was finished long ago. I mean the political forest. The mass one."

"We're getting by with the forest on our own," Kazimirs is forced to acknowledge. "The Communists have been negotiating with the forest folks. If they come out of the forest voluntarily and lay down their arms, there'll be a promise not to retaliate. Live and let live, for everyone."

"When they did hand in their arms, they were shot like dogs," interrupts Andrievs. "Loaded up like firewood at the roadside."

"Yes, and people like you – I'm sorry – from the sidelines, are to blame again!" cries Kazimirs. "The Communists have cheated again! They shot soldiers from the Cheka! It wasn't the fault of the Latvian Communists, but just another order from Moscow."

"But you – clever-clogs!" Augusts suddenly leans over the table and bores into his brother's face with his hostile gaze. "Now you've got out of the shit, then don't witter on! Don't forget you're under my roof."

The heat and the dazzle of the electric lights in the narrow room remind Andrievs of the room in the Corner House; his insides are burning with nausea.

"It's not worth us arguing; let's just keep to our own views. It's right when they say: a dog's eyes will be opened on the ninth day, but a Latvian's, never. See you in the morning!"

Andrievs goes out to the hall, where, putting a little sack on the headrest, he stretches out on a free bench.

Even his sleep is accompanied by the roaring of the mill-wheel and the quietly intoned song of the young girls.

> For a Lithuanian I'm singing, for a Lithuanian I'm rejoicing.
> Aila-raila-railaa, ra-laa-laa-raa.
> For a Lithuanian I'm wearing my garland of acorns.
> Six black colts will come to me from the Lithuanian.
> Six black colts, four little forged wheels.
> The Lithuanian's black colts are running, turning their heads.
> They run turning their heads, kicking up the white sand.
> That's where I'll go, that's where I'll stay, that's where I'll live out my life,
> Aila-raila-railaa, ra-laa-laa-raa.

Andrievs wakes up in bright daylight, having slept all night on just one side. There are different millers in the kitchen, other girls are cooking the pancakes for breakfast, only the wheel turned by the current is still shaking the thick walls of the mill as before.

For a moment he stares at the floor, which is covered by a grey layer of dust from chaff and awns, of bran and stalks of straw. In the corner are sacks of shelled nuts, peas, beans. Then he stretches out like a frog which is slowly regaining its frozen limbs from the ice in spring, and goes out to the wash-house of the mill to bathe.

Abandoned on the toll-shed is a child's cart made out of wicker, open and tall like a racecourse trotter's.

The scene around him encourages him to believe in the durability of life and the fact that he is still the same Andrievs who fell asleep on the bench at the mill the previous evening. Across the land scud sudden squalls, which immediately make the sun's rays sharp, falling like swords onto the fermenting dough of the road and remaining there, reflected in the puddles. The thin and refreshing icicles of sunlight pierce his aching temples.

Andrievs takes off his thick jacket, then his shirt, and bends down over the rainwater-butt. In the night it has frozen over – the water a greenish bright jewel encrusted with a brittle network of ice.

The reflection is so peaceful. Scooping up handfuls of water, pouring it over his neck and shoulders, Andrievs recalls a poem by Rainis.

> …The sun with reviving eyes
> Looks down on the dead land,
> Until gradually the stiffness loosens,
> The throttle of ice melts and falls away…

It is "Early Spring" from *Distant Moods on a Blue Evening*. It is still early spring. But not the kind that Rainis was dreaming of.

Along this road past the mill, Rainis' father would have travelled more than once. And little Jānis Pliekšāns himself would have jogged along too in his little perambulator. No, not a pram – in a sprung drosky at least, if his father was an innkeeper who could afford to build the Tadengofa villa, from which, after the Polish uprising of 1863, seven families were driven out of their homes. A place to which Rainis never returned in his lifetime.

Is something else happening here today, Andrievs asks himself, and can't find an answer. Some will be taken away, but in the foundations of a burned-out house a child will be born again who will say to himself: I am scooped from the sun, there will be enough for my whole life… And with the power of beauty he will try to put in order this ugly, absurd world of chaos, and make it habitable.

"Good morning!" a cheery voice rings out. Standing before Andrievs is Maruse, Antonija's sister, with a linen towel in her outstretched hands. How lovely she would be without those hunched shoulders – it's as if she's shackled to a cross, and cast aside.

"Is the morning good?" Andrievs takes the towel. "Everything still in place?"

Maruse's face darkens.

"I've been running around where the drivers of heavy lorries are, leaving notes even for the timber carriers behind the line of horses – 'Don't stay at home tonight!'" she says quietly. "So they don't make the mistake of being deported."

"Thank you." Having dried himself, Andrievs gives the towel back to Maruse with a smile. Not for a moment would he want to make her feel guilty of anything. Maruse has grown older and seems to have shrunk. The thinness is not marked, but it is wearing out the poor girl's hump.

"Augusts is calling you to breakfast at his place."

Two swarthy boys hover there with faces scarred with the pimples of adolescence. They stare at Andrievs with interest.

"Kims? Eduards? Do you still remember me? I'm Andrievs; we went swimming in the Daugava together."

The boys shyly offer their clenched hands in greeting. They are Augusts' stepsons, orphans sent from the Latvian border area in the second summer of the war on the 'People's Aid' train. The first ones were taken on by farmers and were raised up into strong youths and women, who were helpful in the work. Nobody wanted the little brothers. Augusts had taken the two boys into his home and admonished Margarēte to love them as her own children.

They're going to the new house at the mill, where the table is laid in the dining-room. Augusts isn't there yet; Maruse is heating the water for coffee.

Andrievs stands by the mirror, and pulls his wet, curly hair back into a knot. He sees his reflection and doesn't believe what he sees. Is he still Andrievs?

"Where have you come from?" asks Maruse.

"From the riverbank."

"How are Mother and my little brother doing?"

"They're all alive and healthy. Pāvils sits in a well, saying his prayers, Rozālija is milling flour. Actually Ludvigs is sick ..."

"Sick – with what?"

"He dances."

"Yes, indeed, he dances," sighs Maruse. "When this deportation ends, I'll go visiting."

"Are you sure about them?"

"I heard it with my own ears! In February, when they started making lists, Mum had visited Augusts – wasn't I in danger? Augusts rang up somebody in Līvāni, then he said: you can go home safely, you're in no danger."

"So where's Antonija?"

"Please don't mention that name! You mustn't say it so aggressively, just like Grēte! It's a sin! But she can't be persuaded… She looks down from her high horse, to the manor born, even though it burned down long ago, that manor, and all the people in it are gone…"

"What has Tone done to her?"

"She's done nothing. But Augusts…"

"What?"

"It was so good when the two of them started up that 'Good Life' together," sighs Maruse.

"Good for whom?"

"Everyone. It was good for everyone."

Maruse looks apprehensively at the outer door, but there is only sunshine and the shadows of clouds, and a milk-can on the threshold.

"It was very hard for Tone right from the start. Very hard. She was the vet here. She couldn't stand all that drinking. She had to take blood from the cows, and the chaps said, Doctor, if you won't drink, we won't keep those cows! What were they offering? Moonshine, of course! She took a swig, and after that she couldn't hit a vein in the cow. The same thing over and over again. In the end she said: Put plenty of clover in my cart… That was at the secret farm…"

"What do you mean – secret farm?"

"There's an illegal one in the forest," whispers Maruse. "You can't milk enough from our cows to meet the quota, so there are these forest farms, secret ones. I was helping; I said: I'll do the carrying in a drosky. So I took her, lying among the clover. Then later she said: Comrades, I don't drink moonshine! Okay, then try something else! Since that she hasn't been able even to look at other people drinking. She's cured of drinking for life. But it's terrible! Just look at the nasty things that are going on here! If you don't cheat and you keep animals in the numbers that are prescribed, they go hungry, it's a frightful thing. The piglets die, they all have diseased livers. I gave her books about what kind of contagious disease it is, when so many piglets die. She read it aloud and laughed like mad: '*v Sovetskom Soyuze nye vstrechayetsya!* It doesn't exist in the Soviet Union!' But the papers need to be filled in! God forbid that anyone would reveal that no diagnosis was made. But you have to do it sensibly, so that people don't suffer…"

The two boys stride into the vestibule with armfuls of firewood, put them down in the kitchen by the stove and go out. Andrievs recalls how everyone laughed when Eduards told them that his brother was called Kims* in honour of the Communist Youth International.

"She doesn't love the boys," says Maruse. "Her own daughters, she does. But she drives them like servants. So does she need to command those boys to be milk-carriers? They can't even lift heavy milk churns onto the cart. At the dairy they roll them sideways on round hoops."

At that moment, Augusts comes in with Margarēte and their daughters. Maruse falls silent immediately and ties up her scarf, pulling the corners of the material tight under her chin. But Margarēte doesn't notice anyone; she walks with big strides back and forth across the room, her clothes around her gaunt frame rustling like treetops in the wind as she turns. Her nose has become prominent, as on a corpse or a bird; her face is pale.

"Maruse," she appeals quietly. "Aspirin."

The hunchback hurries off to the kitchen, where after a moment the door of the commode is heard creaking.

Augusts has slept off the drink. The mollusc from yesterday has crawled back into its carapace, hiding in its shell. The dark blue miller's overalls are dusted with flour. Having taken them off, he immediately takes a glass of tea and starts vigorously stirring it.

"I'm coming," Augusts indicates to Andrievs and disappears into the next room.

"How are you doing, girls?" Andrievs pulls the noses of Augusts' girls. "I'm your Uncle Andrievs, do you remember me?"

"No," grimaces the elder one, Ilze, pulling away. She's already a big girl, blonde and blue-eyed like her parents; she doesn't like this kind of treatment. Both girls are dressed in new, recently made brown dresses with pleated skirts and white buttoned collars, with black satin pinafores. They wear *burkas* on their feet – specially sewn boots of double wool padding, stitched with soft fox-fur on the inside, covered by galoshes.

"How old are you?"

"Eight."

"Then oughtn't you to be in school?"

"Daddy took us out to be safe," the younger one, Johanna, explains gravely, as delicate and agile as a little stoat. "There are thicker walls at home and it's more secure."

"How do you like school?"

They both look at their mother, who stands indifferently, her back pressed against the lukewarm tiled stove.

"It's cold," says Ilze. "The classroom can't be heated, the stove's always smoking, and the cold creeps in from the corners and stops the warmth."

"Mrs. Verningena irons the mattress with an iron in the evenings, but in the morning our plaits are frozen to the sheet anyway," complains the younger one. "Ink freezes in the pots. We sit all bundled up, we can't learn anything."

"Who sewed those pretty little *burkas* for you?" asks Andrievs, looking at the girls' feet.

"Maruse!" they both cry at once.

"But the fox was caught by Daddy!" says the little one.

Andrievs laughs.

"Now go and wash your hands and stop complaining! It's even harder for other people. Many people don't go to school because they don't have clothes."

"That's why Daddy donates to them, and Mummy makes wishing wells," calls Johanna over her shoulder as she rushes into the kitchen.

"Maruse, for God's sake!" scolds Margarēte. "Where have you been?"

"The eggs will boil over, ma'am."

"My God! Let a hundred eggs boil over – bring me an aspirin!"

"I've made you some barley coffee, ma'am."

"Give me three!"

Maruse hands the tablets and a jug of coffee to Margarēte. Something about this scene reminds Andrievs of the scene by the canal at the Central Market in Riga, where a black jackdaw cautiously approached a herring gull, pecked at its wing and made off.

Margarēte takes the tablets and blushes as if slapped in the face.

"Mummy has a migraine," sighs Ilze.

Augusts arrives, takes his place, and the two brothers sit down as well, having washed their hands and combed their hair properly. Maruse rushes around, buzzing like a dragonfly. The girls look curiously at Andrievs. He feels their approval.

At this moment there is something there of the ancient harmony – the sense of home and family as in bygone times, when there was still no rift between Emma and Jēkabs Radvilis, the foundation stone of the rental house in Riga had not yet been laid, when Andrievs had his puppy Charley, there at Ogles in Krustpils, in his sunny nest on the bank. Only at the beginning of life can things be like this, when the seed is sown but hasn't begun to grow. Growing up inevitably brings its pains, like the pain of light in an eye accustomed to the dark.

The tablets finally take effect, Margarēte gradually returns to life. She folds her arms and prays. The others also try to feel gratitude, with bowed heads.

Then they get to work on the fried eggs.

"Do the bells still ring on Sundays in the church?" asks Andrievs.

"No, they don't," replies Margarēte. "Nowadays we're a weekday people, we don't hear the bells any more."

"The table is still round." Andrievs examines the strength of the wooden masterpiece with both hands. "From Zabelīna's time?"

"You know, I had half an hour to get moving." Margarēte looks at Andrievs as if noticing him for the first time today, and explains: "Straight after my family moved, I was sent away from the house to a barracks on the outskirts of Jēkabpils. Izraelsons, the old merchant, gave me a horse. Only thanks to his kindness was I able to take with me what I needed: a bed, a redwood wardrobe and this table here."

"It was like a bolt from the blue," agrees Augusts. "I was in Riga that day."

"My dear, what a bolt from the blue – you know what Latvians are like," says Margarēte sharply. "If Ulmanis has said 'Let them go! But for good, then!' then they throw stones and cry out: the rats are leaving the sinking ship! But that's nothing, of course, compared to what happened to Izraelsons in the Soviet year. They were rich people, timber merchants. I had actually brought them some honey. After that some female party organiser came from Moscow, sniffing around every drawer and watching little Ārons eating white bread and honey! That caused a fuss – that's how they were bringing up children here, while theirs were eating grated beets with viburnum, frozen potato blinis, and sucking on beer mash! They only got to taste white bread for the first time in Moscow. It was shame for a proletarian state, bringing up children like that. And so they loaded the Izraelsons into those barred wagons."

"A pity that we always end up meeting at times when someone wants to establish order here again," declares Andrievs.

Margarēte raises her eyebrows quizzically. The freckles are still warmly present in their old places on her cheeks.

"I seem to remember… when there were German women from two countries here? They'd probably arrived here from Munich to visit their party functionaries, the back-room heroes?"

Andrievs nods.

"I remember them saying something about uninhabited land, a sad, melancholy, abandoned land… That's how it appears at first to everyone who comes from a world full of barracks, department stores and shiny boulevards."

"And how you need to take this wild land in hand and lay out the roads. How is your family doing – is there any news?"

"Wretchedly," sighs Margarēte. "They really don't know what it means that Hitler is calling on the Balts to maintain the lands claimed from Poland. The Balts – who have first-hand experience of the injustice of confiscated estates. It was terrible that in those new places, the talk was always the same. All of us here had gone over to the Catholic faith, and that's why my relatives had such a bad experience of the injustice done to the Catholics in Poland. My cousin Konrāds, who was married to a Pole, spent several years in a horrible hovel, refusing to accept someone else's estate as his own property, which he officially had the right to claim. In the end the Gestapo shoved him into the deepest and most dangerous mineshafts of Upper Silesia, where they say he died."

"Is there any news of Eižens Englards?" Andrievs is inquisitive about Baron Englards' nephew.

"He was fighting against the partisans in Byelorussia. He was trying to be humane at a time when one savage beast – mankind – was fighting with another savage beast – mankind. He wrote me long letters. I clearly remember one sentence – 'they'll have to shove it under the moss, send it to the Moon – that's how they describe something as noble as death here'... Over and over again he expressed his sympathy for the innocent, those penned in between two fronts. Such destruction, when the fiercest enemies are neighbour against neighbour, brother against brother, separated from the front! Justice or injustice, treachery or heroism, it isn't possible to tell them apart in those circumstances. With all his heart he believed that the German Baltic lands would emerge again from the carnage, but –"

"He's dead?"

"Yes. Last autumn, from lung trouble – he's buried somewhere in Bavaria."

Silence sets in around the table, each one in their own thoughts. In this silence the children's shy conversations at the table can be clearly heard.

"And who's your best friend?" Kims asks Johanna.

"Moon," the little girl replies. "When he's round, I can't get away from him. It's a shame to go to bed and sleep, I want to be with him all the time."

"Johanna!" her mother calls. "Eat, don't talk – your egg is about to spill onto your dress!"

"Children become adults so fast," says Andrievs, looking at Kims and Eduards.

Margarēte nods.

The blood-vessels affected by the migraine are still thundering and throbbing in her brain; suddenly she very clearly remembers a dream she had the night before Augusts brought his two stepsons home.

In the dream it was wartime, with strange absurd regulations. There were many people around her, strangers and ones she knew. One little refugee child had been left without his parents – a year and a half or two years old. And that infant was very swarthy, like a child of Gypsies, of Jews, of Communists. Yes, maybe Communists – all the Communists she had met in her life were slightly built, with dark faces, ragged. It must quite certainly have been a child of Communists who was left without his parents, like a dark little innocent flower of the forest. And in this dream the rules of war decreed that children like that must be buried. All children without parents were buried alive. Margarēte and Augusts had just lost their dog Sultans – so it was funny that Margarēte would think that in a dream, because Sultans was her dog as a child at Zabelīna, he couldn't have been contemporary with Augusts. And since Margarēte's dog is dead, then it happens that Margarēte does for once have to bury a child – she is entrusted with that task. In the coffin – an ornate coffin of light turned wood, there was still room for a child next to the dog. She wanted to place the child in that coffin, but the dog's large paws with their familiar tawny fur were already as stiff as posts; they could be broken, but not bent as they should be. Somewhere between the dog's legs Margarēte tried to insert the child. He lay there, looking back at her trustingly, but then Margarēte thought – when the coffin is buried, the child will cry out shrilly at first, alone in the dark and airless vault. The child's sobbing will be heard from the ground long afterward. Margarēte knew that she wouldn't be able to go through with it. Her heart would break. She went up to the others and begged to have the child at least put to sleep before burial. In wartime you can find some doctor who'll give a child an injection! But they turned her away. It wasn't an accepted practice to do that. Finally Margarēte understood that no-one would assist her. They would close the heavy lid with white silk tassels. Immediately the child would be laid in the ground. And then the thought occurred to her – she and Augusts could keep the child! That would be an opportunity to get out of this place and time, away from the dream with its absurd regulations. Where one child could survive, so could another, she told Augusts; never mind that he's small and a dark child of a Communist. That's nothing. It's a trifle compared to the wailing of a child buried alive. Augusts agreed at once. Joy and peace emanated from this decision. Those around them, even though they were astonished and surprised, were also delighted. It seemed to Margarēte that also present in this dream were her parents Georg Johann and Friderika, and her sister Gertrude. Of course Augusts and their two daughters Ilze and Johanna were also in it. Even Maruse, Andrievs and Ludvigs Dimants with Rozālija, like a giant gnome, and Antonija were there.

But what was Platacis the millhand doing in this dream?

The last thing Margarēte dreamed was the Communists' child trying to start a conversation with their Ilze. The two silently held onto the table, twirling the curls on their temples in confusion.

"Just like now," thinks Margarēte, looking across the table at the two of them. In the place of Ilze is Johanna, who was born shortly before the boys arrived in the family.

After that she woke up and went about her daily affairs in the mighty shadow of the prophetic dream. When the presentiments were as taut as strings, when her head hurt so much that it seemed it would split, her husband's official car entered the yard.

Margarēte pushed a disobedient strand of hair from her brow and came out onto the threshold.

"Mummy – Daddy, Daddy!" called Ilze in the park, crying from Maruse's arms, but this news was no surprise to Margarēte. She looked on silently as Augusts stepped out of the car with two little darkish boys, older than Ilze. He pushed them encouragingly ahead of him toward Margarēte.

"You're going to have two sons, and Ilze and Johanna will have two little brothers," said Augusts. "Be nice to them, because I love them just like you."

Augusts glanced at Margarēte, then at his stepsons. He well remembered how practised his speech was, with a heightened boldness.

It wasn't certain that Margarēte would accede, he thought as he brought the orphans home. She has a right not to agree to it. Two little Communists, from the same bloodline that destroyed Margarēte's family… Yet Margarēte was strangely calm, stroking the boys' heads and making Vabole the maid set the table.

At lunch the boys learned to hold a knife and fork. Ilze and the boys looked at each other shyly and curiously.

"They don't speak Latvian yet," explained Augusts.

"They'll learn," responded Margarēte.

"Do you remember anything about the old days?" Andrievs asks Kims at that moment. He shakes his head.

"I do," nods Eduards. His voice has already lost its childish timbre, and turned deep.

"Liar, you were too little!" Kims objects.

"I'm not lying," Eduards hits back. "I even remember the name of the house: Velikoye selo. They were shooting over our heads all the time – Germans here, partisans there. The Fascists set fire to our village; we lived in the ground like moles."

"Like moles?" laughs Johanna.

"The Germans took us away in trucks to the station and shoved us into cattle wagons. It was very cold. The whole time I was sitting up by a little window, afraid. Once I fell down, because the partisans had laid a mine on the rails and the train braked! In Jēkabpils we lived in a barracks for a long time; there were bugs there. After that they gave an order for the farmers to take us off to their homes. The whole time I kept hold of Kims' hand; I didn't want us to be separated. Nobody wanted to take us, because we were too little. And then Daddy rode up on his white horse!"

The two boys' faces are turned toward Augusts like sunflowers. He blushes and coughs, taking out a packet of cigarettes.

Complex, contradictory feelings are registered in Margarēte's gaze, turned for a moment toward her husband.

"Thank you, Maruse!" she says, turning her head aside. "Without you there wouldn't be this meal, or properly raised children. And now get changed, girls, we're going to the Daugava!"

The girls are blown away as if by the wind. As Margarēte says goodbye, Maruse starts clattering the dishes in the kitchen.

Augusts offers Andrievs a smoke.

"Thanks for sheltering me," says Andrievs, taking a cigarette.

In his mind, though, he is repeating the words he heard from Leonija: "It was the Kurzeme Pocket then, and they understood that very well – should they go and shoot at their own people, or flee into the woods?"

"Why are you looking so preoccupied?"

"I can't forget those trenches in Kurzeme."

"I have actually forgotten, on the other hand!" says Augusts testily. "They say that in times of confusion the man with too good a memory is not happy."

"They also say that justice and success flee from the victors' houses, and disappointment comes in their place."

The brothers light up, each from his own match.

"What are you after?"

"I wanted to meet Antonija. Where is she?"

"At the *artel* co-operative."

Augusts seems to have been expecting this question a long time, but his eyelids start to twitch treacherously and his jaw muscles clench, as if on an invisible brick. He starts speaking quickly, as if wanting to dismiss his own fears and presentiments: "I've got away from there. Why are you all getting at me? Who do I have to tell how few of our people will be deported? I've been feeling for a long time that there's plenty more to come. According to those documents that came from the centre I understood that the system will be the same as in Russia, that there could be deportations. I was the first one to start talking about what we could do so that the taxes aren't so great, because for those farmers they were huge. Last year I – we – started talking to them. There was an order to send lists of the ones to be deported. The list is short – they had all fled to the city – we had warned them. We had a very good understanding with them, only now – it's women's thinking, it's unfathomable."

"What did you do to her?"

"What could I have done to her? Isn't she a great person, who doesn't know what she's doing? What does she think? You saw with your own eyes – the girls, the brothers, Margarēte, that's what it comes to! For my sake Grēte didn't go away with her own people, she stayed, and now…"

Augusts' hand, which he had contracted into a fist to beat on the table, remains still. It lies powerless on the crocheted white tablecloth.

"Where is that *artel*?"

"Up along the Daugava. The former vicarage."

Andrievs gets up, not knowing what to say in farewell.

"That's how it is, brother. It can't go well for everyone. Especially now, this time of confusion …" Finally he turns and heads out into the sun, without looking at Augusts.

Augusts, tired, stubs his cigarette out. He ought to go, but his body won't obey. As if made of clay, it pulls him back into the depths, the dust. At this moment the sun shines joyfully in through the window as if it knows nothing of the troubles of mortals.

It used to be such a positive time! How he and Antonija loved to be together in the office of the *artel*! Spending the evenings. Planning. Projecting. He would write something or read aloud, pacing up and down across the room, she would tidy the room or, gently puffing away, heat the stove.

One hazy evening he noticed that the stove was cold, Tone was no longer smoking, and her waist was not slender. Had the mist from the Daugava crept into the room, so that his eyes couldn't see clearly?

Tone sensed a gaze full of suspicion resting on her body. The first snowflakes were falling outside, a peal of them, resounding. The bend near the vicarage – the lorries were passing by, with howling tyres, the horses were panting as they pulled their loads by the shafts. Suddenly such a noise, it was incomprehensible.

Augusts got up, with furrowed brow. Tone placed herself by the door, with light, anxious fingers undoing the buttons that he had done up with firm movements.

"Where are you going? You didn't say you had to go… You love me very much?" She was only able to say what was unnecessary.

All the time it had been so good without words. And now they were intervening. Her gaze, like a lighted taper, slid across the features of the man's face.

"What can I say to you now? You know how things are with us," said Augusts.

"What – what can you say? How things are with us? They're good, aren't they? Aren't they?" Tone pleaded desperately, feeling that the room was pursing its lips as Augusts was pursing his – as if preparing to spit.

"I don't know what to say to you." His hand roamed across Tone's waist and recoiled as if scorched.

How that snow was pouring down! How it fell onto the frozen ground – such a hollow sound! Tone pressed his hands against her body; Augusts tore them away. He felt as if he'd been hit.

Thundering, droning, booming. Tone's heart was thundering too, as well as the little heart inside her. All the blood seemed to run to her temples, her cheeks, the veins in her neck. Her pupils were large, black, her nails crooked and twitching against Augusts' chest, like the claws of the wolf that he said he had strangled in the forest in the crook of his arm. And she, a fool, had got ready, had hoped that the thunder had passed, that she would never have to hear that cursed thing ever in her life!

"But I'm going to have your child!" said Tone, releasing her fingers.

In his power! "Whatever you want, whatever you do, it's all up to you," – and before her eyes danced the image of Ludvigs, rising up and then squatting.

"I already have children, I don't need any more."

"What about me?"

"You? You do what you want, as you always have done. And is it my child? I don't believe it is."

For a moment it felt like an eclipse of the sun setting in. Everything went cold for Tone, and a shiver ran through her bones. The snow was falling in lumps, and running down the glass like thick blood.

"I haven't been with anyone else!" she breathed, clenching her teeth.

"People are saying a lot of things."

"This is your child, Augusts! I know that for sure!"

"With or without a child – I just want to be free!"

Augusts pushed Tone away and walked to the door.

"You know, it seems to me now that I'm at war and my comrade has betrayed me!" she cried after him. "My beloved, the one from whose hand I've drunk blood alone!"

And suddenly inside her a tiny seed of sunlight started to unfold. Then it fell silent. Augusts looked at Tone. It moved again. She cried out and grasped herself around the waist, as if wanting to strangle it. Then she started crying uncontrollably, leaning against the cold stove.

Tone, Tone. The beautiful red fox, finally in a snare.

Thundering, booming. Out on the road, Augusts' horse whinnies, then all is silent.

The Stadium and *Sakura*

Having covered quite an arc across Augšzeme, past Tadenava, Rainis' birthplace, then having turned back over the Eglona River along the raised forest road, with its steep black wall of firs on both sides looking out with the eyes of elks, and the countless hunting towers reminding us of the concentration camps – through places apparently untouched by time or mankind along the Biržu road in the late morning, we return to Jēkabpils. Our car is like a molehill, spattered with mud to its very roof.

At a roundabout my telephone rings.

My husband is ringing, asking how it's going. He tells me about our child.

Having forgotten the entire world, I listen to his voice as I circle around the roundabout. Like a paper decoration, a blue road sign "Dunava 40" rolls past me, and then the white Catholic church of Jēkabpils.

"How are you doing?" asks the distant and yet very close voice.

We're doing well.

As I end the conversation, I glance at Radvilis. He looks like the Man of Straw from last year's Shrovetide carnival who has got into a tumble-dryer and is going wide-eyed round and round. The long journey has exhausted his strength.

"What are we doing here?" he asks, as we park in the courtyard of a café.

"You need a bite to eat!"

My companion pulls a face.

"My dear, I'm fasting at the moment. You go in alone, I'll wait!"

"How come?"

"I fast four times a year for ten days, if you don't count the weekly fasts. My head works better that way," he explains.

"And the fast is right now?" I am desperate. "Just before the festival?"

"It's due to the lunar calendar," he says unapologetically. "What can I do about it?"

"No, nothing! I'll get back on the road again. We'll fast together."

"We need to find a hotel, my dear," he ventures shyly.

"Why?"

"It's getting on for two o'clock, I usually have my nap at this time. But I can't get to sleep in the car – I've been trying."

Oh, I see!

"Maybe you know one?" I ask.

He doesn't. I drive on the off-chance, until I see a sign, "Stadium", picked out in lights at the edge of the forest, almost at the end of Jēkabpils.

"Here!" He jabs his finger. "This'll be the right place!"

Beside the hotel is a new modern stadium with stands slightly reminiscent of the racecourse.

Huge garage gates on the ground floor, and a sign saying "Car Servicing". Having grabbed our things, we climb up the grey cement stairs to the first floor. Behind a window in a little booth nailed together from plywood sits a young receptionist with glossy black hair, and explains to us that this is a hotel for the sporting association; at the moment it's full of builders and foresters. Only one twin room is free, for 7 euros. The price is incredible.

In the foyer of the hotel, between high windows, a fir-tree decorated with strings of lights spreads its flickering, brightly-coloured reflections all around – so strange against the background of a snowless black winter.

Radvilis tries to hear the girl, his good ear cocked by the little window. She hands over the keys.

The room exceeds all expectations.

It has a window like a screen facing the stadium and the Daugava. In one corner of the room a square lacquered table, in another a wardrobe, and two beds. The bedspreads on the beds seem to be relics from Soviet times – heavy, with real woollen padding. The pillows, too, are big and hard, stuffed with feathers. These I remember from my childhood.

Radvilis stands looking out the window, while I unpack his pillow and blanket and put them on the clean bed. I have only one thought in mind – eating!

As soon as he's lying on his back on the bed, he clasps his hands over his prominent chest and in a moment falls asleep, breathing evenly through his nose; I reach for my bag of food and pull out a triangular packet of sandwiches. A bottle of juice comes in handy too. Life is a feast.

Later I'm sitting on my own bed, leaning against the wall, and I see that the afternoon light has woken up the old artist. Radvilis suddenly opens his eyes and is present. Marvellous!

"You looked worn out," he smiles at me. "You need a run!"

"What do I need?" I can't believe my ears.

"Once I almost died – after I returned from Siberia. Only running saved me. I had such asthma from those wormwood fields on the steppes that I couldn't walk even a few metres. I took up lodgings in a fisherman's hut by the seaside for the summer and started running. At the beginning I'd run fifty metres, then a hundred. By the autumn I was doing one kilometre."

He goes over to the window and takes a sip of water, looking outside. The stadium fascinates him. And me too, of course. The pink, deserted track, the stands covered in darkness, and the little emerald-green room in the middle, glistening in the electric light.

"Are you going to run?"

Radvilis stands in front of me with his bushy eyebrows, the curly grey nest of hair on his head, then turns sadly aside.

"I've always been running, but now…"

"I know," I say, staring at the stadium. "I saw the hospital papers on the desk in your room."

"Well, yes."

He sits back down on the bed.

"Perhaps you didn't need to run away from there? Nowadays medicine works wonders."

"Not at my age. It's old age, my dear."

Radvilis takes an apple from his pocket and starts cutting it with a knife. The soft peeled flesh he gives to me, but he himself eats the peel. It lies on the table, thin and transparent as curls of birch-bark.

"Doesn't an apple count as a little bit of a sin during a fast?" He gives a long, rich laugh.

"I'm inviting you for a cup of green tea in the centre of Jēkabpils," I say. "We've earned it."

"Yes indeed," Radvilis immediately sees through me. "In other words, my dear, you're hungry."

"It's snowing!" I exclaim.

Outside the window immense amounts of big white feathers are flurrying, as if some madman had overturned the hotel's old pillows and shaken them out.

"At least it won't be a Christmas without snow."

On the way here I had noticed a coral-pink sign, Sakura, by the Old Town Square, above the staircase down to the cellar of a house. If my senses don't deceive me, there might be sushi, plum wine and wok food on offer. I wouldn't say that I crave the plum wine, but I could do with some sushi, and the green tea is already promised for Radvilis.

Through the park we go out to Brīvības Street. The unprecedented blizzard drives us the length of the town over the asphalt. The facades of ancient houses look out like so many people's faces. Peals of fireworks suddenly resound from some dark garden. Whistling and howling like dragons in the air, the colourful rockets twist, a jubilant cry of 'Hurrah' goes up from many voices – as if heralding an attack.

At the Sakura café the first thing to greet us is a doll dressed as a geisha under a plastic cherry tree. A computer is churning out French music. Just let the sushi be good! Two young women put their heads together at a table in the little room. A grubby couple is sitting in the depths of the room on a sofa. It's evident that the man wants to sweep the woman off her feet and she is trying to appear in the first bloom of youth, but the traces of tears under her eyes have long ago etched grey paths on the dolomite rocks of her face.

In the bigger room, where there is a place for us, a funeral dinner is nearing its conclusion. The long table is on a small stage in the celebration room, as if on a pedestal. The glass door is shut. We are seated at a little round table in front of the stove, facing each other closely.

Only about a dozen mourners are left at the meal. I notice the old man in a dinner-jacket who was pouring ashes into the Daugava from a bridge. A woman wearing a black dress and blood-red socks and with long dark hair is at present offering a dish of meat to her neighbours. The mourners are enveloped in their intimacy and strong feelings. To watch it is like observing love-making by strangers, making us avert our gaze and pay attention to the sushi and tea. The sushi is good, the tea is green and strong. Across the wall from the cellar, car headlights cast an arc of brightness; outside, the French language mingles with the swish of asphalt. I remember what my father said – somewhere and sometime, the creature that will eat at your funeral is being silently born.

An elegantly dressed old couple bursts into the café – a lady and her husband, covered in snow and drunk.

They laugh unsteadily, and as they pass, toss cut-off pieces of home-made cake onto our plates.

"We're pretty pissed already!" they laugh. "We're celebrating our sixtieth wedding anniversary by going around handing out the cake!"

Radvilis is fasting, so I will eat for the two of us. The cake is really delicious.

"Congratulations!" I say, and call for plum wine for the "newlyweds".

Reflections are strolling behind the windows, reality is dissipated in the music.

"Shall we go and look at the snowfall?" I ask Radvilis.

He follows me.

The Good Life

The vicarage, laid out in a semicircle on the slope of the Daugava, seems like a crumbled ship, majestically furrowing the river of time – that is how it must have looked in the time of the Tsar, of Ulmanis, of the Nazis, of the Soviets. Evidence of a new order is the weigh-station set up in a muddy pool, and the board nailed to the end of it, inscribed *Zhenshchini v kolkhozakh – bolshaya sila. I. Stalin:* Women in collective farms – a powerful force. J. Stalin.

The brick-walled stable in the depths of the garden has a new roof of chipboard. At the end of the stable, like a swallows' nest, is an annex put together from plywood, inscribed "Agrozoovetpunkts", Vetinary Station, packed with besoms.

The first thing Andrievs encounters at the vicarage is the smell of smoke. Behind the office building a field kitchen is in operation. A stocky woman wrapped in a scarf and a lanky youth are peeling potatoes into a bucket. Past the fish-smoking grid set up in a barrel strides a thin man, wearing a woman's apron.

"Hello! Where can I find Antonija Saltupa?" Andrievs calls to them.

The man fixes his full lips into a smile, showing long hare's teeth, then raises his eyebrows high, like a roof on his forehead.

"At the meeting of the gods!"

"Meeting of the gods? What meeting of the gods?"

"Oh!" The thin man brushes an invisible speck off his sleeve, furrows his brow gloomily and suddenly gives a sunny smile. "*Bednyak, srednyak, kulak, i na posil!* Paupers, beggars, prosperous peasants – to be deported! Meeting of the gods, yes! Deciding whose guts to rip out!"

"Hold your tongue, Gubashlyop," a woman suddenly calls in Russian as she peels potatoes, wiping under her nose with her red frozen palm. "Why are you talking to him? Don't you see he's a bit of an idiot?"

She disappears behind the corner of the house, shoves the window-pane open and shouts inside: "Antonyina Izidorovna, they've come for you!"

When Andrievs enters the cold, unheated room, with "Hall" written on the door-post, Antonija is sitting on a bench at a long table. Behind her the surface of the table is littered with piles of papers. Lying among the documents is a Russian PPSh automatic rifle with a drum magazine. In the corner of the hall a layer of bed-covering made out of straw, in the middle of which has been flung a Maksim machine gun. Tone's long canvas coat is half-open; under the coat she has pulled on a red woollen dress, gathered at the bosom. In the grey light the room seems strewn with ash, yet it is easy to see that the woman is pregnant.

"How drawn you look!" he says, the first thing that comes into his head.

"War changes everything."

That really is Antonija's voice now! For so many long years he has got by without that voice, he has forgotten it. A voice is something so intimate, much more delicate than anything else in the human body.

And then she laughs at Andrievs' foolish remark – a flash of the old Antonija. The uncontrollable brightness of laughter breaks unexpectedly through the excessive weariness and irritation of the day, like blood from a cut artery.

"But what will the child be like? Won't he carry his history with him, and his homeland too?"

"What part of you is in my child?" Antonija rocks her leg angrily like a cat swishing its tail. "Language, homeland, all those things – I'm not interested in anything you could say about it. Now it's easier for everyone to be born without a gender and without a homeland. Don't say anything!"

The chap who has been dozing at the other end of the table lifts his head.

"Are they here already?" the snoozing man asks in Russian, rubbing under his chin and scratching his spade-shaped beard vigorously. "What are you arguing about, youngsters?"

He introduces himself, energetically buttoning up his bright jacket over a crumpled blue shirt. "Spiridon Feoktistovich Yegorov, authorised operations officer."

"Andrievs," replies his confused interlocutor. "Jockey."

Tone starts to laugh again, then bites her lip.

"Jockey, that's good!" nods the officer in charge of deportations, looking questioningly at Tone. "We'll need jockeys!"

The chap takes a carafe off the table, fills a glass to the brim with vodka and empties it at a gulp.

"My head aches so much that even my hair is leaving it."

Having regained his breath and revived a little, he looks out of the window.

"So the major isn't here yet? Where the hell's he got to? No need to argue. Really marvellous place, this, Antonyina Izidorovna! Next time I'll definitely bring a fishing rod."

Yegorov knocks forcefully on the door of the office.

"Bogdanich! Get up!"

A moment later a red tuft of hair appears at the chink in the door.

"Dunya! Tonya, call Dunya!"

The window-pane springs open, and the woman who had earlier been peeling potatoes outside looks into the hall. The scarf around her head is tied up in the Russian style. She has the resolute face of a simple country woman – round eyes, wide cheekbones, lips made pink with beet and puckered in an offended expression.

"I'm making food, Yuzik, what are you roaring about?"

"Bring me a shirt!"

"It isn't dry yet."

"Doesn't matter, bring it, it'll dry on me!"

The red-headed man comes into the room, shaking his fiery curls, which are a contrast to his black whiskers and his black woolly chest. His extends his only hand to Andrievs.

"Jāzeps Bogdaničs Blaha, instructor."

"Andrievs, jockey."

"Augusts' new number ten," Tone explains.

"Tear up a newspaper, roll me a little ciggie, mate!" Blaha smiles at Andrievs. "Everyone says: good that they ripped off your left arm, but I tell them: I was left-handed all my life, what's so good about that, eh?"

Andrievs picks up a copy of the newspaper *Socialist Countryside*, dropped by the stove, tears off a strip, sprinkles into it some brown grains of shag, and rolls it. The red-head nips the coffin-nail in his mouth with satisfaction, goes over to the table, and pours a glass of what's left of the vodka.

"Nicely rolled. I can see at once that you've been at the front. Where were you fighting?"

"Nowhere," Andrievs lies. "A white card – they wouldn't take me because of my lungs."

"Tuberculosis, then." The red-head wags his index finger. "Well, look! You still rolled the fag well… Just like Tonya – eh, Tonya? At the *artel* I'm organizing courses in shooting, but then she turns up and gets a bull's eye on all the targets! Like a bandit – ha-ha! Tuberculosis patient – for your sake I took Berlin, I lost my arm – now for my sake you can strike a match!"

Andrievs pulls out a match and helps Yuzik to light up.

"Sorry, but you're an idiot about striking matches – you do it towards yourself, Grandma-style," he instructs. "You need to strike away from yourself. Anyway, why can only two people light up from one match? You know?"

Andrievs shrugs his shoulders, although he knows very well. And he'd struck the match Grandma-style deliberately. He mustn't fall in with him, the way he did with the cigarette.

"While the first one is lighting up in the trenches, an enemy sniper notices the light; while the second one is lighting up, the sniper raises his weapon and takes aim; if there's a third one lighting up, he'll have time to take aim and fire, you understand?"

"But why can't you take a light in your hands from the cigarette when someone else gives it to you to light?" the gaunt old man butts in. "Explain that to me, instructor!"

"Because you mustn't, Comrade Colonel – and that's all!"

The red-head laughs, coughing and farting. The one he called Colonel takes a packet of foreign cigarettes out of his pocket.

"In our work it's important to notice details! You may crumple a Soviet cigarette, but an imported cigarette, you mustn't. Soon as it's carelessly handled, it'll crumble. If a spy starts crumpling a foreign cigarette – it's over, that's the end! He's given himself away with his Soviet habit."

He lights up and smirks.

"Ah, those were the days! There was no money, you'd get through the day on two packets of fags, two glasses of *kvass* and a box of matches…"

"Romantic!" the red-head responds dreamily.

"You're smoking the place out even in the early morning, Spiridon Feoktistovich!" Antonija angrily throws open the window and, wafts out clouds of smoke, wrinkling her nose. "I've got a headache."

"Don't take on so, Tonyechka," begs the colonel, trying to grab Antonija's hand. "You mustn't get angry. You're in the full bloom of maternity, so to speak."

"We'll blow it out the window; maybe you really do have a headache," calls Yuzik. "That's why we painted posters at school: 'Smoking pupils learn worse than non-smokers.'"

"Under Communism, you might not be a smoker, but at the moment tobacco is as necessary as air!" the Cheka man reprimands the party organizer.

Meanwhile Yevdokiya comes in from outside with a long Russian shirt in her hands and puts it on Yuzik. She also puts on his jacket, and tries to stuff the empty sleeve into the belt.

"It's fine, calm down. Comrade Colonel – we're still waiting!"

"We're waiting, Comrade Party Organizer!" replies Spiridon. "We're waiting!"

"I think we could start now…"

"Then let's start!"

Andrievs helps Antonija to clear the table.

He notices a round seal in the middle of the table.

"That's the round seal of the Krustpils Temperance Society!" Andrievs shows it to Antonija.

"Quiet!" she whispers. "There was a request for a round seal! Where do you get one? I took this one, none of them understand what's written on it…"

Heaping the documents into a pile, Andrievs comes across a map on the top. "Map regarding Operation Coastal Surf in the Latvian SSR, 1949. Top Secret" is the title written in Russian; it depicts Latvia and its railway stations and the number of massed cattle wagons specially prepared for the deportation of people. Big red arrows on the map indicate "loading points", stations, as well as indicating from which districts of Latvia people must be conveyed to these stations and "loaded". The map is approved by the Chief of Internal Forces of the MVD, the Ministry of Internal Affairs of the USSR, Major-General P. Burmak.

At this moment the outer door opens, and in come Yevdokiya and Gubashlyop with steaming dishes. In one, scrambled eggs, in the second, pickled gherkins, in the third, bacon. From Antonija's side a large glass bottle of home-distilled liquor appears.

"Extremely grateful, extremely!" murmurs the colonel with glistening eyes. "A family atmosphere."

Gubashlyop sits down next to Yegorov. He has taken off his apron, and now he looks attentively at the Cheka colonel and fulfils his every wish. He piles a steaming heap of potatoes onto the plate, adorned with meat-balls and gherkins. Just in case, he sprinkles pepper and salt on it.

Yevdokiya and the boy sit by the non-existent right hand of Yuzik. The place on the other side remains empty. The party organizer's whiskers smile, he bares his teeth like a wolf, surveying the goodies. The colonel gets up with a glass in his hand.

"While we're waiting, I want to say the biggest thank-you to the Soviet activist Antonija Izidorovna Saltupa, who has invited us and is our host. The sauna was excellent! You've renewed my faith in Soviet man. Tonight we'll be doing a bit of cleaning, tomorrow we'll be loading up, but after that I want to donate to your *artel* a permanent cinema!"

Gubashlyop applauds.

Blaha listens, squeezing the glass in his red-haired fingers. His face has an awkward, sensitive expression, his whiskers are drooping, and moisture gathers on the ends of his eyelashes. He shrieks: "Irma! Where the hell are you?"

Out of a room comes a slender woman in a tight-fitting dress who sits down without a word to Blaha's left. Bored, she cups her chin in her hands and studies her nails. Both sides of Irma's face are enveloped by abundant shoulder-length hair.

"Dunya! The jacket!" cries Blaha.

Yevdokiya hurriedly pulls the jacket off the party organizer and tucks in the sleeve of the remaining arm.

As he spoons steamed fish onto Andrievs' plate, Gubashlyop whispers in his ear: "Poor man, Blaha! Stalin punished him with two wives – one Russian, one German."

Yuzik raises his glass ceremonially.

"Thank you for your kind words, Comrade Colonel! A year ago… As a Soviet activist, I saw it all! Antonyina Izidorovna, tractor and trailer driver, veterinary nurse, cultural organizer and postwoman rolled into one, and Augusts Jakovļevičs, the miller of Radvilis, front-line soldier, hero of the Great Fatherland War… Where is Augusts Jakovļevičs?"

The party organizer glances at Antonija.

"He won't be here."

For a moment the silence of the grave reigns, in which you can hear the buzzing of awakening flies on the panes.

"These people sought new methods for the increase of agricultural production. My advice fell on fertile ground. I invited them to seek guidance from the press, I helped them… And so the *artel* co-operative came about in this forested environment, bad for traffic, the rich farmers' abandoned nests – in a word, a den of *kulaks*. Tonya was elected chairwoman by majority vote. That was how it should be… This person, she… is a real Soviet person! Brilliant! Let's drink to her! Tonya, may I pour for you?"

"She's pregnant," cries Yevdokiya.

"Tonya is pregnant, everyone can see that. But soon she'll be giving birth, a mother! There will be one more Soviet person on earth. So many have fallen, been brutally tortured, tormented, – oh! Such things! Many more are still missing. The bosses gave the *artel* a radio. Because of the premises and the bad roads the locals can't develop culturally at present. And we can't form a basic Young Communist organization. We're still hampered by malice, infections and illnesses – but this will change! The main thing is for the comrades in the *artel* to lose their doubts about the new economic order! If Comrade Yegorov has decided to donate a permanent cinema to the *artel*, then for my part I'll be offering next winter, as director, to build up the drama troupe and the orchestra – accordion, violin, guitar and cello!"

Gubashlyop applauds again.

"I'll volunteer!"

"I'll lend you my dress, Gubashlyop, I've got a new dress and shoes," giggles Yevdokiya.

She bangs on the table and gets up.

"You do what you want, and I'll tell you how it is," declares Dunya, her gaze fixed on Yuzik. "I was an orphan, nobody needed me, nobody's child. I trained as a nurse. I liked to travel the world, I liked speeding. Roads, trains, cities. Everywhere I've defended my own Soviet order. Then I met him, ten years younger than me, he was beating up bandits before the war outside the village. I really liked the way he spoke simple understandable words that everybody needs. I put doctoring aside, and started following him, I loved him. Now, since the war, you see for yourselves how his sleeve hangs down. You know, he has kept the habit of taking off his jacket and tucking in his sleeve, and only then does he start speaking. Passionately, with conviction. Without me there'd be no-one to hold his jacket, there'd be no-one to ask to tuck the sleeve in. And so I hang around behind him on dusty roads, on icy tree-clearings, on dirty stations. Where has that led me? Ha-ha, you see for yourselves! To you, Jāzeps Bogdanovičs!"

During this speech, Yuzik is slumped on the bench.

"Not again, Yevdokiya Matveyevna – too long-winded!" He looks anxiously at Irma, who is twirling a glass in her fingers. "Needs to be more concise…"

The colonel is also shifting uneasily in his seat. Long speeches parch his body and soul.

"Let's drink, comrades – too many words," he says. "Where are our colleagues from Riga? It's time we got down to business!"

"Indeed," agrees the party organizer. "Many difficulties still ahead!"

"The struggle with bandits is a dangerous struggle, but that doesn't mean it's the hardest. During the war I toiled for *Smersh*, I know what I'm talking about. The hour is not far off when Latvia's forests will be completely free."

Sitting at a distance from the others, Andrievs is thoughtfully sketching what is going on, on sheets of brown wrapping paper. There is the round stove, behind it Stalin's portrait, the little corner ends at the window-sill. There's the PPSh on the table, the Maxim on the floor. The bottle, glasses and faces under the crooked beams – Yevdokiya, Irma and Antonija. Possessed by a sudden longing, he also draws Run Hill next to Antonija.

Meanwhile Gubashlyop is walking around the table with the big bottle. For a brief moment he stops by Andrievs' drawing, his lips pursed appreciatively.

"Tonya, ah Tonya! She has no mercy," Gubashlyop whispers in Andrievs' ear. "If she calls you to the veterinary station, don't go! No-one has come back alive from there."

Antonija, sitting right there at the other end of the bench, has heard this.

"Let me introduce – my admirer," laughs Tone. "Viktor Belogub, known generally as Gubashlyop, shot his grandmother dead in 1919, and in 1941 – God."

"How did you shoot God?" Andrievs asks, wide-eyed.

"Symbolically," replies Belogub. "I shot an icon, and I accepted Stalin into my heart."

"Just like that?" asks Yegorov.

"Of course. I don't go anywhere without a weapon."

At this moment some soldiers stumble cheerily into the room – two from the Cheka forces and three militiamen, five in all.

"My little eagles," Yegorov says quietly, hoarse from the strong moonshine.

Then he suddenly cries: "Where the devil have you been, you blockheads, while I've been sitting here all night without protection? Where's Mark Akimich!"

One of the fighters replies: "Comrade Colonel, allow me to report, Comrade Major and his men are delayed in Jēkabpils! Car in a ditch – can only be towed out with a tractor."

"Sit down!"

Overhearing the Cheka men's conversation, Andrievs can no longer control his pencil. He carefully folds his drawing and puts it into his sketchbook, leaving it at the corner of the table.

How to tell Tone about the dangers to come?

The armed men are knocking the muddy snow off their boots by the stove, unbuttoning their greatcoats, laying their weapons by the wall. Yevdokiya and Belogub rush off to get some more dishes of food. Through the open door you can see that two more soldiers have remained on guard on the slope by the white cedars.

"Where were you flying, eagles?" the operations officer asks more mildly.

"*Gosproverka!* State inspection! We were tracking down the dens of bandit supporters, Comrade Colonel! Where we arrested the two telephone operators on the 15th of March."

"And how?"

"*Chudaki pokoynyiki* – strange little corpses. They'd gone into the forest."

"In one house we found the grandmother," explains another. "Well, our dander was up – we said, if you won't tell us where they slipped away to, we'll set fire to the houses. We brought some straw, we were going to set it on fire, but that was enough to frighten her. We did set fire to one of them further on, because they'd been hiding animals."

"Couldn't do it more 'culturally', Comrade Platacis?" inquires Yuzik menacingly. "Go off and question them, but shoot the pigs?"

"Aren't they delicious, those pigs?" asks the one called Platacis sarcastically, nodding toward the table, where blood-pancakes are piled up, made of flour mixed in blood.

"But why did you piss in the cabbage barrels?"

Laughter rings out.

"For you – it's a laughing matter," sighs Blaha. "But this is an *artel*! How is Antonina Izidorovna supposed to live and work here, after you've been past?"

"More 'culturally', you said?" Platacis challenges him. "In February they took over the village council; the whole day they were heating the stove with Soviet documents! More 'culturally'?"

"Did you get Siliņš?" Yegorov interjects.

"No, we didn't!" Platacis grimaces. "Siliņš' wife is a friend of mine from childhood. She was still at school when I was already running a farm. I used to ride past her on my horse, wanted to take her home, but she always turned me down…"

"Is that why you drive a sledge, winter and summer?" chuckles another fighter. "Big farmer you are! You don't even have a cart!"

"Shut your mouth, Platacis, don't you malign the working class!" The first Platacis pulls his cap down over his eyes. "Yesterday evening I had a look – she was at home. We went in. I said: Go to the shed, you whore – you've got a bandit there hiding in the straw! I'm going to shoot him! So I drove her out to the barn – oh, you'll get it now! She goes and she's crying. Oh, you're crying, I say, are you sorry for him? Ah, when you got married, what place were you thinking of? Stir up the straw, whore! She answers back: stop that 'whore' business, have you no shame at all! Shut your mouth, whore, I say…"

Irma suddenly starts to cough, louder and louder; she moves away. Then she runs outside to escape. Yevdokiya follows her with an ironic gaze.

"Apparently Siliņš has gone to Ilūkste," says the third. "So they say! He's in the forest, all the boys are in the forest. He's not at home, that's what they all say: he's in Ilūkste. We did catch one relative, we had a talk with him – he shat his pants, but we didn't manage to get anything out of him…"

Yegorov pushes over the pile of papers.

"Let Siliņš go, we'll deal with Siliņš later. The Major's thinking of an action; if it's carried out, then we'll get further with this…"

"Siliņš is being protected by Radvilis," the second Platacis lets slip incautiously. "We know that from Rubene… My fingers are itching to grab that bloody miller by the arse, just once!"

"I don't believe it!" exclaims Yuzik. "What has Radvilis done to you? Father of many children, four times wounded, awarded the Fatherland War Order! For shame!"

"If you're a believer, go to church!" spits the second Platacis, leering at Antonija. "Father of many children – for shame himself, the boaster!"

"You're a fine one to talk, Platacis!" The party organizer won't be left out. "You're always staring at Tonya like an elk over a bog…"

The colonel rubs his hands together.

"No need to argue, chaps. First of all Operation Priboi, then we get stuck into combing the forests! There'll be no shortage of work, I promise you. Who's going to be the guide for the operational group tomorrow morning?"

"We will – the Platacis boys from the village of Platacis!" The three stumpy brothers get up; from their faces you'd think they were triplets. "The three Platacis brothers, we're all militiamen."

"Why only one rider?" Belogub asks Antonija, looking at Andrievs. "Are you taking a truck?"

"No, a horse and cart."

"How many can go on that?"

"There won't be much to carry," says Antonija.

"Damn it! I must've got lice here!" Yegorov is nervously rubbing at his beard again with all ten fingers. "What witchcraft are you doing today, why are you laughing all the time, Antonina Izidorovna?"

"If you want to send someone, send me!"

Yegorov exchanges glances with Blaha.

"See, women!" The colonel is displeased. "Women's logic! So what then? On the very eve… Antonina Izidorovna! A list of people to be transported was sent from the region. Where is that document?"

Antonija turns on her heels and goes out.

"I'll look for it…" Blaha starts digging in the pile of papers. "Whims of a pregnant woman."

"Go outside and smoke, you buggers!" The colonel drives away the fighters, who, after the substantial meal, are getting out their packets of shag. "You're making my head ache!"

Yegorov goes into the smallest room – the *artel* office, hearing someone pick up the telephone receiver and call the switchboard: "Priboi! Priboi! Can you hear me? Please reply at once: Priboi!"

After a moment he comes out of the room and rubs his chin, confused.

"I don't understand..."

He goes over to the window, opens the pane a little and calls in a soft voice: "Tonya! Antonina! Antonina Izidorovna!"

His voice is frail and suffocated by the gusts of wind raging in the bare trees.

The first Platacis pokes his tousled head through the window.

"What's happened, Comrade Colonel?"

"Telephone connection cut off! Might the wires have been cut?"

"Ugh, nonsense! Some tree by the Daugava has fallen again," says the fighter, waving his hand. "Come to the fireside! Everyone, come! We're going to sing with our colleagues."

Yegorov studies the shrubbery suspiciously for quite a while. Then he puts on his leather coat and goes into the yard, letting Blaha and Andrievs go ahead of him.

"Please come on, comrades, I can't stand it if someone gets left out."

A cool dusk has thickened over the river. The sunset sky of jagged clouds is torpidly reflected in the Daugava.

A fire is lit by the spruce hedge on the south side of the house; around it, sitting on the cut-down boles of apple-trees, are the fighters and the blue-caps. Under the spruces, through the old grass, snowdrops are curling like lambskin. Yegorov sits down by the fire, Gubashlyop immediately pours him a glass, and the colonel drains it dry without flinching.

The Platacis boys start to sing the song of the Red partisans:

Darkness covers over the traces,
In a birch-grove the partisan sits
And with his comrades surveys the highway.
As darkness gathers all around
We must await the enemy
To trample him just like a beast.

In the window as the day is melting,
Sister is not waiting for us,
Mother no longer lays the table crying,
We have no family any more,
Our homes are already destroyed,
Only the winds wail over the ruins.

Over our homeland, sudden
And far sweeps this wind,
Counts the tears, torments and scars.
As darkness touches the land
May the partisan be able
To avenge the pain and sacred blood.

Andrievs glances beyond the coach-house of the vicarage in the hope of seeing Antonija.

There, among the apple-trees overgrown with green moss, with their covering of snow, wanders Irma, with someone else's coat on her shoulders. Standing on guard under the white cedar is the owner of the coat, one of the blue-caps – a Cossack. Irma pulls out a cigarette, the Cossack lights it. For a moment their heads are together – pale grey silky hair and a heap of wiry black curls, light blue and black eyes, skin brightly pale and copper-brown as if singed by fire. The message is the same, but every letter is written differently.

The twilight wind shakes the bare branches, jumps over the crooked apple-trees. On the dry grass stands a fluttering shadow: Blaha is watching Irma.

From the direction of the Daugava comes a sound:

It was dark that night,
The moon was buried in the clouds,
Suddenly vehicles careered into the ditch.
It was the enemy's curse,
Brought down on the fascists,
There on a mine they met their death.

The swath of clouds vanished,
The moon emerged pale,
Men came out to hurry on their way.
The woods are silent again
Only the leaves rustle
Slowly covering the executed fascists.

"Help me light up," Yuzik forces through his teeth. "I never thought I'd be such a cripple."

"You've managed so far," responds Andrievs cautiously. "In the towns there are war invalids wandering around without any arms or legs at all. You manage as best you can."

"They're not wandering any more," declares Blaha. "I saw them in Ilūkste – all collected together in a full monastery. They sleep on the floor, where it's draughty and damp, unbearable living conditions. I wanted to organise help – the guard said it's not worth it. Soon, they say, they're going to transfer them to some island. Just as well summer's coming, they said; if it was winter, that'd finish them off. They'll take them out of sight, to the quiet taiga."

"Why are they treated like that?"

"It's supposed to be Stalin's decree – that's why they were arrested. It doesn't look good to have them in places where foreigners might turn up."

"It seems to me – it's because they were too free. I know one of them… half a man…"

Andrievs doesn't finish the sentence. Nor does he say that Blaha seems like the same sort to him.

Darkness covers over the traces,
In a birch-grove the partisan sits
And with his comrades surveys the highway.
As darkness gathers all around
We must await the enemy
To trample him just like a beast.

But maybe Yuzik has understood that himself. With squinting eyes he looks at Andrievs, then sighs heavily, looking at the slope where Irma is walking through the apple orchard.

"You have to watch those Prussians!" complains the party organiser. "Sluttish woman."

"Beautiful."

"Other people think she's a nun. She's never the first to start a conversation. Everyone laughs that I've got two wives. They told you that too, didn't they?"

Andrievs can see that what Blaha said about a nun was just his imagination. Irma is talking quite animatedly to the Cossack – she even throws her head back and laughs.

"I met her in Dramburg in 'forty-five, in the last days of March. I remember that Ilya Ehrenburg wrote in the *Army Pravda:* 'All Germans are the same: villains, bourgeois or proletarians.' Did you read that? He was a great inspiration! Imagine it: famine in Berlin. Drawno, Spandau, Neustettin – everywhere the same. Robbery and violence. And the women from all over – Jews, Russians, Yugoslavs, Poles, Estonians, Latvians too, as my major said – all the whores of Europe. They'd all gone mad with joy that the war was about to end; people had to find some comfort at any price. In Poland they started those pornographic pictures and venereal diseases. Animals got foot and mouth disease. Mud on the roads, fallen horses, rotting in their skins. Soldiers took the German women who were working on the estates, took them off to rape them without the slightest fear of punishment. The authorities complained that they were being kept away from their work. And they were robbed as well. Gold rings disappeared into thin air, there was blood and many, many tears. Fittings were ripped from apartments, and trophy cigars. They'd rape them by the score, in the presence of children. Mothers would willingly hand over their youngest daughters to be raped, to save the frailer ones, but even the ones who were hidden got hunted down. German women in Berlin were fighting over scraps of food, and drunken soldiers were right there with their offers. The authorities had them driven away from the kitchens… That May, how the apples blossomed! They bloomed under the roaring of the aeroplanes."

Yuzik nods at Yevdokiya, who has crouched down with her son by the wood-shed, glancing at her husband every few moments.

"She's checking on me! Dunya's pretty too, but in a different way. Their beauty is not the same kind. Irma is an animal, a wild egotist, raped many times. She was ill with scabies. They wanted to shoot her. I tried to understand her thinking, I couldn't. I don't understand the German psyche at all – if you knew how they carried out the orders of the Red Army! Soon as an order came to headquarters, they all went to read it, and simply carried it out. Complete submission and loyalty. German dogs – they would bark and bite. We didn't waste bullets on dogs – we'd spear them with pitchforks."

From the brick-lined opening of the cellar, Antonija emerges. She places full buckets on the stone step and wipes her hands on her sides, straightening her back. In the bare, sap-filled birches over her head, thrushes are twittering woozily.

"Irma – now she's exhausted, delicate, tormented by her cough, but in those days she was seventeen years old – a very strong, wild German girl, often raped. I don't know why she attached herself to me like that. I fell in love with her, you understand? That was the biggest mistake. Falling in love in the midst of Sodom is a great sin. But she lies so snugly beside me – *liebe Josef!* I wanted to protect her. My major screamed: Let those German women get raped a thousand times, what has it to do with me? I don't understand! She wouldn't go home, terrified of what was waiting for her there. That was in Dramburg. Her mother wanted Irma to go with me. She herself had her doubts. Why did I agree to it?"

Flushed with anger, the one-armed man looks piercingly at Andrievs.

Antonija, having rested her back, lifts the buckets onto the yoke. Andrievs wants to go and help her, but Blaha won't let him, grabbing Andrievs' sleeve in his fingers.

"Flatow. We travelled in torment as far as Schwiebus. We were drowning, sinking. We had a captured bus, a red one, without documents. I couldn't stay beside her the whole time. There she was raped many times – my major and the major's aide. They made her wash the rooms at the Red Corner, and they raped her. While I was taking Number 1 Company to headquarters, Number 2 Company broke in. It was organized rape. She was so tired after that. She got pregnant. Possibly from the rapes. She wanted to hang herself. Asked to be shot. She'd told other people that she loved me! She wouldn't abort the kid. She wasn't going to get married. She would go back to Dramburg… The forests were burning, there was a fog of smoke all around. The desperation and the unspeakable shame! The child perished inside her – from the hardships of the journey. She aborted the foetus. She was in extreme pain, she asked for a cigarette. Then I proposed to her. Among these predators she put her trust in me, abandoned her home town and left with the enemy. But I already had a wife of my own here – Dunyasha. And a little son…"

Andrievs sees Antonija approaching with the yoke on her shoulders.

Yevdokiya seizes her chance and calls out in a shrill voice: "Look, what times these are! A pregnant woman walking on ice, while the big fellas are gossiping. Antonina Izidorovna, you're not going to the shed tonight; Pasha and I are going to sweep it out!"

"Why do you think I've done so much harm to this unfortunate woman, bringing her with me?" Blaha asks, upset, looking Andrievs in the eye. "I did it to save her and help her, but there was little I could do."

"Don't fantasise so much!" says Andrievs angrily. "You fantasise too much! You've made it all up yourself. In our lives we meet dozens of people – what do we know about them? You have to walk around all the time with a mourning band on your hat…"

Blaha looks thoughtfully at Irma. Andrievs breaks off and hurries over to Tone. He takes up the buckets which she lets him carry into the hall and put on the table.

"So much beer!" exclaims Andrievs.

"I've got plenty of beer – work out for yourself how much is in fifteen buckets. The men from Riga will arrive and they'll drink them dry, don't you worry."

"I'm not worried, but you should be! We need to have a talk, Tone. It's very important!"

Breathing heavily after her exertions, Antonija scrutinises Andrievs, and then lights the hurricane lamp.

"Help me see to the horses."

Andrievs throws his bundle onto his back, and they head for the stables, at the end of which is the "Agrozoovetpunkts" annex.

From the Daugava a black cloud is driving a storm forward. It gets dark quickly, before their eyes. Rain patters on the chipboard roof overhead. Tone's canvas coat is spattered with dark patches; her wooden clogs sink into the manure by the threshold. She slips on the ice, but Andrievs has time to grab her by the waist, amazed that what was once such a supple body has suddenly become as heavy as lead.

In the stable Antonija leans against the neck of a grey mare. The mare, with her soft lips, feels around Tone's shoulder and neighs softly; she wants oats. Another bay horse reaches over the high railings. The further part of the stalls is sunk in complete darkness; the cows there are lowing, long and hard.

"Put out some hay, give them water," says Antonija. "There are no oats."

She raises the lid of a flour-box, then sits down on it and watches Andrievs carrying hay.

"That one on her own is Geja. But the grey one is Puķe. She's so sharp! Very smart mare. She doesn't want to be tethered. She unties everything very delicately with her lips, and then stands still. Now I don't tie her up any more – wherever I go, I leave her there, and she waits for me."

"They're your horses?"

"Mine, but they're counted as the *artel*'s. I take one horse riding in the morning, another in the evening, there's quite a lot of moving around to do. In winter the wolves run behind us. I have two places, and I have to have time for everything. If it's terrible weather, I just ride and ride. You can't do anything here without horses; the *artel* people that I have to ride to haven't always got a horse. They simply ring up: Doctor, doctor, can't you help? I say: well, ride behind me! No, we've got nothing to ride. Winter, frost, rain, mud – they don't matter. I have a sledge and – look over there, on the wall, a sheepskin coat with a collar – when you put it up, you can't see anything. The horse comes home by itself… When I started working, there was a Machine and Tractor Station here. From the start I lived at the mill for about half a year, while they were putting this place in order. They put the windows in."

"How long have you been a veterinary doctor? You used to be a human doctor."

"I'm not a vet. I'm a so-called orderly. One time the paramedic was drunk, and I got to do an autopsy on a horse that had fallen on the road. It had been hit so that it fell. On a muddy road. You couldn't say that it was malnourished, but it had too big a load. These newcomers don't understand that it's a horse, not a machine. But when you're doing an autopsy, you have to be careful if you're writing down that the horse was shot – you know what you're threatened with? The laws are very strict; for every one that falls you have to write an autopsy. In fact they're dying from malnutrition, from not eating. But if you write something like that, it can get unpleasant for everyone. That time, I found something to blame, and I wrote it down, but after that I was really cursing those guys. Later they said they'd never heard words like that coming from a woman… The paramedics dismissed me, sent me off on courses."

Scrawny cats are slinking among the animals' troughs, afraid of Andrievs. A pregnant striped tabby seeks solace and, with eyes screwed up, rubs herself on Antonija's legs.

"Once they brought me a puppy, supposed to have choked on a bone, and I looked for the bone…" says Antonija. "I couldn't grasp that it wasn't a bone at all. Foam wasn't coming out of his mouth – that happened a little later. I put him in quarantine, and after two days it was clear that it was rabies… Those injections in the stomach were terribly painful."

The horses are well fed. Antonija gets up ponderously from the flour-box and takes the lantern. Through a little doorway along the stable wall she goes into the veterinary station. The tabby cat bumps against her legs, and Andrievs follows at a distance.

The lantern illuminates an empty room with two narrow, sheer little windows at the south end and a huge table in the very centre. Under the table is a drain for blood and a curled spiral of hose.

Andrievs looks at the iron table and smiles.

"That man warned me not to come here with you. They say no-one's come out of here alive."

"Gubashlyop." Antonija dismisses him with her hand. "What a buffoon! A primary-school Pioneer leader in the first year of the Soviets. Throughout the war he hid with farmers and dressed in women's clothes. Now the war has ended, but he just can't give up those clothes – he takes my outfit, shoes, make-up, shaves himself and goes to dances."

Antonija presses a button, and the table, squeaking, slides into a vertical position.

"The bosses from Leningrad donated it, showed me how to use it… You see, here you can tether a cow or a horse, and then the table rises up again hydraulically, because you can't lift it, the animal, to dissect it. But they all need to be dissected. Even now I can't grasp much of it, but it's not up to the one who's working. In the beginning I was ringing up Ludvigs every evening, for he's a sort of animal doctor after all, and I was asking who, what, and how. I said – I don't understand it! He said: nothing to get upset about; write what you want, no-one will understand it anyway. The main thing is the actual autopsy. Where I go, they're already piled up, swollen and stinking corpses. I say: I'm going to be sick! He says: Tone, buy some *mahorka* tobacco, the strongest kind, light up, then do it. So I did what he said. And then that Gubashlyop tells everyone: this terrible doctor cuts them up quite calmly with a fag in her mouth. That's how things are for me here. The maddest year of my life."

"I could imagine all that – but, you sitting here, guarded by the Cheka, and cutting up animals… Antonija!" Andrievs bursts out.

She presses the button again, and the table rises with a hum.

"I dissect animals, but if some traitor needs a bullet in the ribs, I can do that too." Her voice has suddenly become different. "You probably still haven't understood that Gubashlyop is telling the truth."

His memories of Antonija were bright, but this real Antonija standing before him is a darkened one. Her always limpid face is emaciated, browned with dark flecks from last summer's sun, with some new wrinkles around the eyes and mouth.

"A traitor?"

"What do you think? On the second morning there were two carloads of Russians there. One old farmer had a chance to warn me. There were three of us – two patients and I. I managed to get away, but they had the works thrown at them in the bunker…"

"I didn't give anyone away, Tone, word of honour!"

"What happened then? Tell that to the dead! If anyone had told me beforehand that you'd betray us, I'd have scratched his eyes out. I treated you for four months, getting you on your feet. But that's what men are like. That's what they're like."

Antonija presses herself against the operating table. Andrievs is next to her. Now, instead of the past, the eternal present is taking over – the warmth of bodies side by side, and her strong aroma, flowing from her hair in streams. Andrievs feels his veins quivering and glowing – his mind recalls one thing, his body another.

"You remember, you once asked me if I believe in God?" says Andrievs quietly and simply. "At the time I didn't know how to answer. Now I'd say I'm full of gratitude for what's happened according to His will, while my will would've only spoiled it all. At the time, I had to go. Because I loved you."

She moves rapidly, as if wanting to escape. But she only takes off her scarf and tucks it under her arms. Antonija's hair is the same as it used to be – like the thick, light grass by the Daugava.

In the bunkers of Kurzeme it grew down to her hips, and it seems not to have seen any scissors since then.

"I told you that. You laughed – passion, nothing more! All the time you talked about going away: you said I was cured, it was time to part. But I loved you very much. You couldn't imagine how much. I had to be the first to go. Otherwise I couldn't."

As if shielding herself, Antonija folds her arms on her stomach.

"You know when I was a military rider, one Legionary died in my cart. Many died, but he had in his pocket a poem he'd written in the trenches… I don't know whether he was identified or was buried in a common grave as an unknown soldier. And I don't believe it can be that the man for whom he wrote this poem never found out about it. But maybe. May I read it to you?

> If it were so that eyes were dazzled in brilliant light,
> But not by flame-throwers – by festive fires,
> I would carry you, pressed to my bosom,
> As my comrade in arms through the artillery shells.
>
> If it were so that we two were fated to live
> And see our children's childr en through the blizzards,
> I would carry you off to the graves of the fallen
> And beg for your hand from the departed."

Antonija sits as still as the frozen Daugava. For a few moments there vibrates in her memory that morning when she wanted to be the first to leave.

I am Antonija.

My heavy sleep is broken towards morning like a little vein on my brow. Andrievs has overheated the stove again; he's always freezing.

Lying with eyes open in the hot darkness, my pulse beating rapidly and loudly in my temples, it's worse than death.

A hawk begins to call at the boundary of the daybreak between night and dawn.

I get up and put my coat on. I feel my way on the stairs and step outside like a corpse rising from a grave. As I push the slats of the outer doorway, sand and dew are blown into my face. Outside the daybreak is blazing; white handfuls of August fog are gathering over the brook. Somewhere the hawks cry, persistently, as if imposing their will.

Before me slumbers a huge, dense spruce-tree, like a grey she-wolf that has opened her flanks full of countless heavy branches. Urged on by a sudden desire, I open my mouth and bite into one of its cones. I am an elk, picking at the shoots, feasting on the goodness of the forest. If my conviction is really only the product of a sick brain, if I am an abscess that just needs to be cut out of healthy, happy Soviet flesh – if everything human inside me has turned out wrong, then at least there remains my animal side. They too have their place under the sun – the lichen, the hawks, the elks.

Maybe there is a substance in spruce sap that will cure the bleeding cracks in the corners of my mouth, my fingertips and the festering, hard-dried thick soles of my feet. These cracks are definitely from lack of sunlight, which no longer shines down into the well of my body, which is inhabited only by dark, animal craving.

I get down on all fours and gobble the wood-sorrel, and I want sorrel, watercress and the tiny crab-apples by the stream. The sun is climbing ever higher above the horizon, the forest is starting to steam. The cold dew leaves the branches and curls upwards in a supple body of vapour. The opaque, wild, peaty dampness – the forest of my mortal life.

I don't want to think about what causes my fear and anxiety. All day long Andrievs is working a generator, operating a radio that he listens to like a famished man – just stay there, in your forests, until someone comes and saves you… I sense that no-one will save us.

Why am I gnawing on pinecones and green apples? God in heaven, make it so it's not too late! I'll go away, right away, I promise!

And I, Antonija, really do fall on my knees and beg you, God, ardently, with all my heart, as I strive to discern some sign in the indifferent face of nature.

From the meadow beyond the stream the one-eyed horse limps towards me with hobbled legs, quietly neighing in response. I have been heard.

I stroke the animal's neck; the dew on its veins is hot. The black horse's scars are now healed, the scabs stick to my fingers and flake away from the bony body, as light as birch-bark. The horse's gentle, shy muzzle seeks me out. Pressing our nostrils together, for a moment we breathe the same air.

"Ješka," I whisper, amazed that a one-eyed creature can enter another's heart so deeply.

In my coat pocket are a cigarette and matches. Relieved, I light up.

The sun is rising, the flies are buzzing, the hawks are crying. The soft moss encloses our bare, broken nails and hooves.

I perceive it suddenly; it reaches me like a military command – I have to go away!

No-one may do such a thing to another. We're young, but we're not living our own time. We have to command love: do not come! We are your children, we are the evil spirits of the underworld – love doesn't belong to us.

I lead the horse back to the meadow beyond the stream, where he remains, pursued by midges, and solitary.

I lift the wooden lid of the bunker with the spruce-tree placed across it and let myself back into my coffin.

Andrievs has woken up, feeling around in the dark, searching for me. His youthful body is burning as he leans over me and calls forth from me a rushing, uncontrollable passion, breaks into me desperately and deeply, as if wanting to stay there for eternity, beyond breath, beyond skin and arteries, beyond our lives, which will certainly part, because love is not meant for people such as us. The human side of me, which flared up so brightly at daybreak, is extinguished again. We are animals living underground, and this is our only youth. Youth, which is a force in itself. It isn't love, which is why I bury Andrievs inside me, and the darkness folds its wings over him. Again and again. Tomorrow it may not be like this.

Tomorrow there may not be anything.

Am I still Antonija?

"It isn't love," says Antonija, as if waking from a deep sleep.

Andrievs turns his head quickly.

"I was told thatJeška had been found after the war," he forces himself to continue the conversation, as if wanting to show that this doesn't hurt.

"Yes? I thought he was shot by the Cheka back then."

"The passport commission got in touch. His real name is supposed to be Nordpol, from Hanover, bought in Brandenburg."

"That may be," nods Antonija. "He was a thoroughbred. The best thoroughbred I've known."

"Where did you go to that time?" he asks after a moment's silence. "To the Lithuanians, as you wanted to, and after that to the great Polish forests?"

"All over the place." She shakes her hair, as if wanting to throw off the cobwebs of the past. "From Kabile I went off to the Ugāle people near Misiņš. Among the Ugāle people there were many left over from Rubenis' battalion. Actually they had joined with the Piltene people. There was always someone for me to treat. Unrest all the time. Many of them were old people who couldn't do anything. Nearly all of them were sick, those old rich farmers who came into the forest so that they wouldn't be deported. And the paramilitaries – they were quite old too. Those people who had someone in the forest would call me to their homes. I went myself to Ugāle, to the chemist, and bought medicines."

"And after that – you got legally registered?"

"It didn't cross my mind! I slipped away from there before it all started. I had a bad dream, let's say that. I had a strong wish to get away. I met a man who was on the run on his own. So he and I went into hiding until late October, helping out the farmers who supported us, with farm work. One day he didn't show up any more – after that I found out he'd been shot dead in his hiding-place. I applied to join a tractor-drivers' course at Lielplatone."

A convoy of lorries is passing the vicarage on its way towards Jēkabpils. Individual lamps in a snaking patterned line can be made out through the rain-streaked pane. Andrievs is seized with alarm, but the vehicles drive on.

"What did you want to say? Speak quickly, before Dunya comes to milk the cows."

"The Cheka picked me up. They questioned me about you. The Postwoman, who's the Postwoman, where's the Postwoman?"

"And what did you say?" Antonija narrows her eyes, like those of the pregnant tabby cat lying on her lap.

"Nothing, of course," declares Andrievs. "They let me go…"

"Then they tailed you?"

"No! That I can swear. The elephant started to go mad."

"The elephant!" laughs Antonija. "What are you gabbling about? What elephant?"

Churns are clattering in the shed. Yevdokiya can be heard ordering the boy about.

"Why did you come?" whispers Antonija. "You came for your own death. It's too late! I can't do anything any more. It doesn't matter whether you love me or not, you hear? Because you're the only one who came out of that forest alive. You're the only one who knows who the Postwoman is."

"But I –"

"Whether you betrayed us or not that time, whether the Cheka says something now or not – doesn't matter! We pulled you out of the swamp, treated you, took pity on you. You went away, but we didn't leave our bunkers, we stayed faithful… And what came of it? They were all shot. You have to die, Andrievs."

Antonija's face suddenly becomes as malevolent as an old fox's; she raises a bony finger to the window.

"And he will see Siberia too! With this hand here, I wrote down his name!"

This same Antonija Saltupa, who fled from the nuns of Jaunaglona and was mobilised into the Nazi army, who fled from her own Latvian, German, Russian and Jewish admirers, even escaped from her stepfather in the end, who knew how to avoid the Gestapo, the Cheka and Andrievs… But she won't be able to escape from this child forever.

"Pretend not to recognize them! Go over to the other side of the road when you meet them!"

Tone vigorously blows her nose in a corner of her scarf and is once again the chairwoman of the Good Life *artel* collective.

"This is how it will be! They won't deport from the Chilly Marshes, or from Caurkubuļi, or from Akmeņāres, from Sieriņi and Pupiņas, from Ašņēvere and Griķupeles – no! But the song of the mill has been sung."

The cat, who has heard the jingling of the milk-churns in the shed, hangs around the door, mewing like the devil.

"Don't do that!" Andrievs implores her. "Don't you understand that they won't take him alone? They'll take Margarēte and the children too!"

There is a diabolical gleam of revenge in Antonija's eyes.

"With everyone it's the same, when they're stroked the right way they slide under your hands like dogs, but then bite you in the bum! I think it would be no great loss to the world if people like that vanished from the face of the earth."

These cynical words shock Andrievs like a bucket of icy water, but he controls himself.

"Now you listen to me, Red Queen! That Major Mark Akimovich who's waiting here is Mark Krop, who wanted to know everything about you."

The great black pupils of her eyes bore into Andrievs' eyes in the semi-darkness, as if wanting to read the future; her face looks ugly from the excessive tension. The two stand close together, breathing each other's hot breath, enough to last a lifetime.

"You don't have much time yourself, Postwoman. Go across the Daugava, you hear? The rain has cleared the ice, your footprints won't be seen."

"Where to?" She starts to cry like a child waking in darkness.

"To your mother."

"Who shouted 'Tramp!' after me as I was leaving!"

"She told me to bring you home. You'll always find a place with her, she told me."

"And all those old women and gossips! I won't be able to…"

"Times have changed, haven't you noticed? For the communists a fatherless child is no shame."

"If not shame, then fear, all the same… Creeping back into the cave bunker with mad Pāvils? I'd be better off with the Lithuanians, the forest is still strong for them… or to Riga…"

"What? Riga! You have to think of the child now."

The door opens, and the brilliant light dazzles them as they stand there. Yevdokiya is standing on the threshold with a steaming pail of milk.

"I thought there were rats scuttling around –"

"We were just going," says Antonija.

"Let's take the churn, the two of us, Pasha. Tonya, you take the bucket. But you –" Dunya commands Andrievs, "leave the door ajar when you go, so that in the morning people won't faint as they stand in line shitting themselves. Prop it open with a plank…"

They go off, chatting. Andrievs sees Antonija's form one more time in her canvas coat, then the lantern disappears and the path goes dark.

"Puķe, Puķe," – he goes over to the grey foal. Good that he's noticed where the bridle is hanging.

The trotter's nostrils flare anxiously against the darkness and rain. Andrievs jumps on her back and turns the horse toward the Radvilis mill.

"Go on!" he whispers, crouching against the mare's neck. "You'll get home by yourself."

The Postwoman

"What happened next?" I ask, looking out of the window at the bluish snow.

"I warned Augusts. He decided to go into the forest with his family for a while. But he left his sons at the mill. When the deportation crew arrived toward morning, they took Maruse and me, and the boys. They needed to have a certain number."

"What about Augusts?"

"They were shot in the bunker at Rubene."

Only under snow can silence be so stupefyingly quiet.

The sketchbook is lying on the table, damnably alive. At any moment it is possible to open it and touch the occasion when Antonija looked at the drawings in the cave bunker, running a finger over them.

"It's interesting that Ludvigs died a couple of years later at Strenči on the very day when Run Hill fell at Gomel. Explain that if you can."

The bedsprings squeak. Radvilis turns toward the window and pulls up the blanket. He wants me to leave him alone.

Outside the window, it continues to snow.

And I don't remind him that I no longer believe explanations. Telling the story is enough.

The Daugava. Still thundering in the dark trees of the park.

I see them all *simultaneously*.

In a provincial neuropsychology clinic for old men, someone dies, dancing a Cossack dance. The distinguished trotter, an ex-world-record-holder, who is collapsing at this moment on the Gomel racetrack. And the little girl sits under a blanket of rags in the middle of Rozālija's big bed listening intently to the silence of the unheated room, waiting for the thunder of the footfalls of the postwoman's horse beyond the corner of the house.

The old man's name is Ludvigs. The man's body is aged, but in his hair there is only the odd silver thread. His drooping whiskers are a deep black, yellowed and twisted at the ends from too much smoking. The clinic is located in the border area of the Latvian Soviet Socialist Republic, at its very northern edge; beyond it are only forests of red pines, with the marshes of Estonia in the blue distance. But this he doesn't know, as he examines his knotty fingers, splaying and retracting them into fists like a cat's claws. Through the windows of the ward flecks of light fall onto the stone floor, lying on the ground like long bony-white mourning widows with shadows in the hollows of their eyes. St. Vitus is hiding in a corner, invisible, moment by moment jerking the man by the arm, the leg or the ears. Shivering like this day and night, Ludvigs wails piteously, but no-one responds to his whining. Today he gathers all his strength and finally tears himself away, he escapes from everyone, with his mournful and slightly cunning face like a big child's – smooth, oblong, with narrow, dark eyes. He gets into the corridor, where a trolley like an old sledge with dull metal wheels has broken away, and aluminium chamber-pots are stacked up, with damp red stone tiles under his feet and a low greenish vaulted ceiling, which suddenly reminds him of the osier bower that grew thickly over the shingly path by his home. For some reason these in turn remind him of a woman's honey-brown arms around his neck. Rozālija's firm lips, the sudden rush of memories pulling him back here, make Ludvigs stiffen like a ram that has been clubbed between the horns, in the middle of the day. The illness exploits the brief moment of stiffness and enters his body, plays it like a harp, he cackles and convulses. St. Vitus will not let go, it grasps him and starts tickling ever more strongly. The old man, weeping, stoops, straightens and skips, straightens and skips, his whiskers shaking with the effort. With his fists Ludvigs beats himself on the chest, then hits out at an imaginary enemy, at one point even driving away a couple of orderlies who cross his path. Roaring every time he squats down, he approaches a distant window there, at the end of the corridor, from which waves of calming spring light are flowing in.

The Cossack dance!

The Ukrainian dance!

His heart is beating along with him, faster and faster, until something in his chest bursts and Ludvigs rolls to the ground at the end of the corridor like a bag of flour fallen off a hook in the mill. The ends of the bones in his joints are protruding through his parchment-thin skin, the breath enters into him for the last time and, faithful as a dog, remains seated in his chest. He lies in the light, which has won him over, and with deep gratitude at last he can feel the beginning of a stillness which fills him like the Daugava enfolding him in its bosom.

At that moment, at the horse stud near Gomel on the fringes of Byelorussia, an old trotter collapses behind the finishing line on the track. The spectators cry out and whistle, the drunken jockey jumps out of his cart and tries to raise the jade with the whip. Just for once this is too much. The best horses always go to younger ones – how can they stand idly by! Being a devoted smoker, he has recently lost a leg, but is that any reason to dismiss him from the job? He had saddled up this old nag, known as Pet'ka Burzhuy, and driven out of the Baltic district who knows when. For a long time he couldn't even get him into pasture, Burzhuy wouldn't let anyone near him, he avoided them, you had to call for help from the little children who had got bored playing with leeches in the reeking ditches. It would rain all day, the children needed a diversion, they want something to laugh at! So, the children, whistling shrilly, energetically chased this gaunt steed, ready for the knacker's table, with wide, wheezing nostrils, but a emphysema-tightened thorax like drum-skins stretched between the ribs, from inside of which every few moments there resounded creaking, tearing noises. Clouds scud across the mirror of the earth with their deep shadows; the rain always starts suddenly, as if someone has turned on a tap. The water stops pouring, and just as suddenly as it began, it is driven back into the sky as soon as the hot sun shines. The children chivvy the old horse among the pillars of white vapour. They call this horse

Pet'ka, that's what they say, adding – Pet'ka Burzhuy, supposed to be from the Baltic district, *prizovoy risak*, prize hare – a racer, but born in some place way beyond the Baltic, and Pal-Palich the smith was informed that this horse had seen the light of day in the imperialist States, and his name had been Run Hill Dune. During his Burzhuy period and later, too – in the fascist Baltic in the Great Patriotic War it was a great pastime – he had run at the Riga and Tallinn racetracks, bringing not inconsiderable sums into the pockets of punters. This horse is old, worn down to the skin, not looked after by anyone, roaming around under the bird-furrowed skies. Clusters of horse-fly maggots on his neck, the flesh on the bone around his loins is broken, and the deeply cut tissue from the narrow fissure seeps out with every movement like birch sap from a hollow in spring. It was difficult to get near this carcass, his eyes sharp and wary, although old age has drawn a bluish film over them. When the jockey slowly approached with outstretched hand, hiding the other hand with the halter behind his back, the wreck turned his back on him. The children are smart; they start chasing him, throwing stones, to catch him. But the old warhorse of the racetracks was not losing his powers so quickly. Only when the mob of whistling children drove Burzhuy into a narrow place between two enclosures did they manage to catch him. The jockey put the bridle on him, and led him to the cart. In their anxiety the children put their dirt-stained fingers in their mouths. All around such a silence reigned that the twittering of sparrows in the sand sounded like screams, while the foals in the distant paddocks wheezed like steam engines. Burzhuy's broken hooves, stamping nervously, left rounded impressions in the sand.

Proudly Tikhon mounted the cart and seized the reins. This was his star moment, the 2nd of May 1952, a Friday. Usually the races took place on a Saturday, but the 1st of May was switched to a Saturday, so that the working people would have two days to celebrate. On the track were his competitors, fellow jockeys and their fast horses – Gromootvoda, Lovlya, Lyubopitnuya, Gips, Kursant, Rodnyik, Vecherinka. And he was on Burzhuy. Quietly he turned the old horse in a loop. He could feel that Burzhuy was a real trotter – as soon as he was on the track, he was scrambling to be first. Tikhon forgot about his wooden leg. He whacked the horse between the ears with the whip and placed the shaft back under his legs – it seemed that he wouldn't need more!

The old crack racecourse sprinter was running marvellously, his ears pinned back. As mournful and malevolent as a snake, adhering to the track, he beat out time, his thin nostrils gulping great quantities of the damp, steamy air. A faint memory was revived in the horse of what he was created for. Of different laws to those that prevail elsewhere, where the body is engulfed in speed, when one manages to escape from one's ego, from desires and wishes, from blows, thirst and hunger, from boredom, pressure, cold, heat, evil and fate itself – when one manages to divest even one's own skin for speed. Run Hill Dune is running one more time, as only he knows how. Like a powerful cannonball Pet'ka Burzhuy shoots in front, his hind feet chopping widely, flattened against the ground, boring into time and space.

The jockey whooped, turned to the stands and waved as he crossed the finishing line first. A few steps later, the dark red horse fell over his own shadow like grass under a scythe and remained collapsed under the carriage. The jockey flew forward several metres and somersaulted, rolling into the grass beside the track.

At that moment, rain starts to pour. Droplets thunder down onto the trotter's steaming skin. The curtain of rain covers him and also the jockey, who cracks his whip to make him get up; it covers the village of Gomel and the sagging roofs of the horse-stud.

Beyond the moment of the trembling, moving curtain of rain, something like a little red thread, a kind of frenzy, a humming, is set in motion. As if a broken heart were a butterfly which, trembling with all its might, were striving to send out into space one more wing-beat. One heartbeat.

For whom is it meant, this thundering through time and space?

For the little girl in an unheated room in the middle of a drenched garden?

She is called Madelaine, she is three years old, with crooked legs stricken by rickets, dressed in a white linen blouse and a blanket kicked off from Rozālija's bed after her daily nap.

Whatever has woken her up is approaching the window-panes. It is a horse's snout, and then an eye... large, black, all-encompassing, observant... The eye is black, as the sun goes down in it, like a mother-of-pearl in a pearl-oyster. Then there is a heavy clatter of hooves, and the horse disappears, turned around on the spot. Smoking dust shuts off the movement and slowly settles back onto the stones from which it was disturbed. There remains only the thundering, the distant thundering against the horizon, but on this side of the dewy pane, the rhythm of a worried heart and a tiny hot breath.

Soon Rozālija will come, having attended to the calves on the *kolkhoz*, and will look for her Madaliņa, her pet name for the girl. She will find dew from the garden in her lap and will scold her, not yet knowing that this afternoon in a distant psycho-neurological clinic Ludvigs died while leaping in the Ukrainian Cossack dance. The soft-hearted man with the droopy moustache who used to carry Madaliņa in his arms, cajoling the exhausted and angry Rozālija: "Let the child stay in the yard!" Even when she was an infant, he didn't hand her over to the children's home – this orphan of living parents from the other bank of the Daugava, the stain of shame from the Good Life agricultural *artel*, the fruit of the frivolous Tonija's free love.

Madelaine's heart is often pounding when she wakes up from sleep. Rumbling even breaks into her dreams, and wakes her up. Sometimes it is the thunder of a galloping horse at the window. The *kolkhoz* named after Molotov has a new postwoman, who delivers the post riding a black stallion. The *kolkhoz* has allocated it to her. Madaliņa wants to glimpse the postwoman, but the black horse and its rider are always far off on the horizon galloping along a dark fine line along the white roads. Or else she dives into the billowing wisps of the mist which threads its way in the mornings from just about every little swamp, pool and lake in Jersika.

"Will the postwoman be here today?" asks Madaliņa, importuning Rozālija.

"You've fallen in love with that postwoman, have you?"

Once Rozālija declared, in Madelaine's hearing, that the new postwoman was like Antonija, Madaliņa's mother. Since that moment the girl has been longing to see the postwoman. But sleep is so sweet, and Mada's little body is so feeble that she can't resist slumber. Like a deep well it swallows her up whole and spits her out on the sandbanks of waking only when the clock on the yellow pinewood cupboard by the opposite wall vibrates and calls out hoarsely: Finished! The postwoman has already gone.

I see how she wakes up – she leaps to the threshold and tries to open her parched eyelids – she is constantly plagued by those itches, probably from cows' milk – but when she gets her red eyelids open, before her eyes is only a white, empty road.

She bends over the mound overgrown with green grass which Rozālija for some reason calls Pāvils' grave, which on high days she usually decorates with flowers. Without any pangs of conscience she falls once again into the well of sleep. Rozālīte comes along and scolds her, grasps the sleeping child by the shoulders and shakes her by the arms, but the lass is dead to the world.

And then she complains that her heart is knocking. It's thundering.

Thundering, thinks Rozālija, seated on a tree-stump, bent over her chapped hands, looking at her sleeping grandchild, here on the road, as the postwoman gradually vanishes.

Where does this thundering come from?

She thinks about that morning, about a bright May morning three years ago, when she didn't hear her daughter's footsteps.

True, that wasn't thundering either, it was the quiet squeaking of shoes. Rozālija can imagine how Antonija, having climbed out of the well, came to the window in her town clothes – a blonde, lithe she-cat, the most beautiful of Rozālija's daughters.

How she stuck her hand through the open ventilation window and undid the hook, holding some kind of bundle in the crook of her other arm, a roll of clothes. Carefully she opened the window and stooped over her mother, who was sleeping profoundly, exhausted like a dry twig on an oak tree.

How she put her bundle in the crook of Rozālija's elbow, crossed herself and cautiously closed the window. She looked at the horizon before she left, and her features were lit up by a solitary, confused smile. Smiling foolishly like that, she had a while before entered Madaliņa's church with her two-week-old infant, as if seeking refuge, but the bare walls were smeared with mineral fertiliser, and the bells had been stilled.

She went outside again. At her feet flowed the Daugava, rushing to the sea.

No-one told her, so she didn't yet know, the boldest of Rozālija's daughters, that she couldn't flee from her child even as far as the horizon. Not even hide in death, the great shuffler of cards.

The most frivolous of Rozālija's daughters, she still had no idea that the meaning of life, with Madelaine's birth, had passed from Rozālija through Antonija into Mada and would continue thus – Mada's fortune would be Antonija's fortune would be Rozālija's fortune, till death did them part…

It would continue thus – Mada's life would be Antonija's life would be Rozālija's life, till death did them part…

Mada's death would be Antonija's death would be Rozālija's death… no! There would be no death!

Rozālija looks attentively at Madelaine's little face, to see what it portends. It's doesn't portend anything bad, it is simply the face of a frightened child, tired too early.

I did what I could. The big woman crumples her scarf in confusion, lifts up her granddaughter, feeling the child's fragile, knobbly ribs, and carries her to her bed.

And when I say *simultaneously,* I mean *simultaneously*, on the same day, in the same white, tired hour.

The metronome on the piano, the racecourse in a cloud of hot dust, echoes of the war, footsteps through a blooming garden, approaching her mother's bed, stealthy steps, retreating from her child, the Cossack dance in the barracks, the front-line combines, the trains of beef-cattle wagons and *kumiss* mares,* the troop-trains full of people, the clanking of wheels over the points, soldiers marching, the crackle of sparks in a fire, the firing of shots at a stone bridge, St. Vitus' dance in a provincial clinic, the ice thundering away, the Daugava, the din of it, the thundering.

Thundering

I come to my senses in a darkness of dancing snowflakes. The light from the snow has filled the room with a vibrating alarm. Was I asleep? Where is Radvilis?

He isn't there, the bed is empty. The blanket is neatly folded on the big pillow. Outside the window, the snow-white stadium and stands.

Feverishly I search for my things. He's taken the sketchbook with him. I have no-one who can show me the direction to go.

Radvilis must be thinking that the map has been drawn. And I haven't told him that my mother is Antonija's daughter.

Quickly dressing, I take my bag and run out into the corridor. It's four in the morning. I wake the receptionist. Rubbing her eyes, she emerges from her veneered pig-sty – surprisingly good-looking though she's disturbed in the middle of the night.

"Did you let the old man out?"

"An hour or so ago." Yawning, the girl glances at the round clock above the Christmas tree.

"Did he say where he was going?"

"Yes." She smiles lazily. "To the Daugava! He says he always goes to the Daugava at three in the morning. He was glad that my name is Dina. And he was sorry that he can't listen to beautiful girls any more… Funny guy, amusing!"

"The bill!" I cry out, and in a moment the girl catches my urgency. She sits in a chair behind a pane, turns on the lamp and writes out an invoice.

"You're not staying any longer?" she asks, leaning forward.

Snowflakes are falling on the hazy windows of the hotel, dark heaps lie on the turnings of the concrete staircase, the Christmas tree, decorated with a string of lights, is flickering and changing behind her – now red, now yellow or blue. The receptionist's round breasts in her skimpy black jumper are still pinkish at the cleavage, while the clock is moving its black hands at a threatening pace across its pale face.

Are we not staying any longer?

"We're not staying any longer," I confirm, having understood that she's asking about our stay at the hotel.

The receptionist takes the money I hand her and goes down to unlock the door.

"Fine." She can't contain her pleasure, and pulls out a cigarette, looking at the snow. "Everything will be white tomorrow."

Great flakes of snow are ceaselessly peeling off the black infinity and hitting me in the face.

Quicker!

I drive toward the centre, carefully studying the empty blizzard-lashed street, although I sense that he won't be here. There is only one bridge in Jēkabpils.

And someone is indeed standing right in the middle of the Daugava. Pressed against the railings, looking as if hypnotized into the depths below.

I stop the car at the beginning of the bridge and switch on the yellow hazard lights.

Slowly I approach Radvilis.

The snow thunders down onto the Daugava and does not melt.

Notes

p. 20 Imants Ziedonis: a Latvian poet (1933-2013).
p. 22 Kārlis Padegs: a Latvian artist (1911-1940).
p. 39 Mežaparks: a forest park in Riga.
p. 44 Augusts Kirhenšteins: a Latvian microbiologist, politician and educator (1872-1963). He was Prime Minister of Latvia from 20 June 1940 to 25 August 1940 and Acting President of Latvia from 21 July 1940 to 25 August 1940.
p. 51 *artel* co-operatives: a semi-private Russian venture.
p. 59 Irbīte: an affectionate diminutive form of the name of Voldemārs Irbe, Latvian painter (1893-1944).
p. 59 Romans Suta: Latvian painter (1896-1944).
p. 61 "Pūt, vējiņi": "Blow, winds", a well-known Latvian song.
p. 61 Andrejs Upīts: a famous Latvian author, 1877-1970.
p. 61 a nest of Ulmanites: followers of Kārlis Ulmanis (1877-1942), prime minister and later authoritarian president (1936-1940) of Latvia.
p. 69 blackheads: an ironic reference to the medieval guild of the Blackheads in Riga.
p. 73 the Cheka men: the earlier name for the Soviet secret police or internal security organization, established by the Soviet Bolsheviks as the 'Extraordinary Commission' (abbreviated to Ch.K. in Russian) for combating counter-revolution and sabotage. Later transformed into the NKVD, later still the KGB; its modern Russian equivalent is the FSB.
p. 74 Kārlis Zāle: a Latvian sculptor (1888-1942).
p. 76 *jukurrpa*: i.e. 'Dreamtime', a Warlpiri word from Central Australia meaning the laws and protocols set by the ancestral beings who created the world.
p. 82 Michurin, Lysenko and Pavlov: Ivan Vladimirovich Michurin (1855-1935) a Russian practitioner of selection to produce new types of crop plants. Trofim Denisovich Lysenko (1898-

1976), a Russian-Ukrainian agronomist, leader of a campaign under Stalin against genetics, natural selection and science-based agriculture; he blamed genetic science for the earlier Soviet famines. From 1948 Lysenkoism was taught as the only correct theory. Ivan Petrovich Pavlov (1849-1936), a Russian physiologist, known as a pioneer of the study of conditioning, Nobel Prize winner 1904.

p. 82 Marshal Budyonny: Marshal Semyon Mikhailovich Budyonny (1883-1973), founder of the Red Cavalry, who developed the Budyonny horse breed.

p.84 Latvian Riflemen's processions: a military formation created under the Tsar during World War 1, and which, though it later sided with socialist forces in the Revolution, came predominantly to represent Latvian nationalism.

p. 108 Andrejs Jurjāns: a Latvian composer and musicologist (1856-1922).

p. 110 Čaks: the poet Aleksandrs Čaks (1902-1950).

p. 110 Rainis: the pseudonym of Jānis Pliekšāns (1865-1929), Latvian poet, playwright, translator, and politician.

p. 152 Saxo Grammaticus' *Gesta Danorum*: a medieval Danish history by the 12th-century author Saxo Grammaticus. It is an essential source for the nation's early history, and also one of the oldest known written documents about the history of Estonia and Latvia.

p. 152 a Curonian: the Curonians were a Baltic tribe living in what are now western parts of Latvia and Lithuania from the fifth to the sixteenth centuries.

p. 153 in many languages *Duna* means 'dune': *Duna* is the original Latvian title of this novel.

p. 153 Jaunsudrabiņš: Jānis Jaunsudrabiņš, a Latvian writer and painter (1877-1962).

p. 161 The horse: from Walter Butler Palmer's book *Heart Throbs and Hoof Beats*, San Jose, California, Hillis-Murgotten Co., 1922. Palmer (1868-1932) was a US poet and horse-breeder.

p. 165 Palmer's little book of poetry: the quoted passage is from the English original.

p. 171 UK Schein: Unkömmliche Schein = a certificate of exemption from military duty on essential work.

p. 171 *Schutzmann* units: a special police unit during the German occupation.

p. 173 ROA group: Rossiyskaya Osvoboditelnaya Armiya, a Russian military unit in the German army.
p. 184 Chapayev: Vasily Ivanovich Chapayev, a celebrated Russian soldier and Red Army commander (1887-1919).
p. 197 M.T.D.I.L.T.P.D.N.K.L.D.F.T.H.I.W.M.D.ch.D.L.Z.L.U.ch. xAmen: this is a riddle for which the author can provide no solution. They seem to be initial letters from Scripture, maybe the initials of guardian angels which mothers wrote down as an incantation to protect their sons.
p. 200 Ūdris: the surname of an artillery 'spotter', whose job was to spot the source of enemy fire and call out the co-ordinates, so that the artillery could aim precisely at enemy gun emplacements.
p. 206 Arājs: Viktors Arājs (1913-1988), SS collaborator and leader of a commando unit which belonged to the Latvian Auxiliary Police, subordinated to the Nazi German *Sicherheitsdienst.*
p. 206 Simons Šustins: in Russian Semyon Shustin (1908-1978), head of the NKVD (State Security organ, predecessor of the KGB) in 1940 and largely responsible for the mass deportations of Latvians to Siberia.
p. 206 the Bund: the General Jewish Labour Bund of Latvia was a Jewish socialist party in Latvia from 1900 to 1940, abolished under the Soviet occupation.
p. 207 the Poale Cion (Zion): a Marxist-Zionist labour movement in Poland and other European countries founded after the Bund rejected Zionism in 1901.
p. 207 Jēkabs Peterss: a Latvian Communist revolutionary(1886-1938), one of the founders of the Soviet Union, and of the Cheka, the secret police.
p. 207 Lācis-Sudrabs: Mārtiņš Lācis(-Sudrabs) (1888-1938), a Latvian Soviet Communist revolutionary and a high officer in the State Security organization.
p. 216 Voldemārs Irbe: see note to p. 59.
p. 219 'Christmas trees': German signal flares, used to guide the bombers to their targets.
p. 219 *Tēvija*: 'Fatherland', a newspaper.
p. 219 *Vlasovites:* supporters of General Andrey Vlasov.
p. 224 the Bermontians: the West Russian Volunteer Army was an army in the Baltic provinces of the former Russian Empire during the Russian Civil War in 1918-20. Named after its commander Pavel Bermont-Avalov.

p. 230 the bone-saws: the nickname of the German machine gun MG-42, or Universal-Maschinengewehr Modell 42, famed for its devastating precision.

p. 239 the Christmas battle near Bitšķēpi: the Christmas battle, or third great battle of Kurzeme, lasted from 21 to 31 December 1944. It started near Saldus, with 20 Red Army divisions on the offensive on an almost 35-km. front. The focus of the battle, between Dobele and Džūkste, engaged the 19th division of the Latvian Legion and the 21st German division. The Red Army gained only a little territory and suffered huge losses.

p. 256 Glazmanka: the Russian name for Gostiņi.

p. 261 the Molotov-Ribbentrop Pact: a non-aggression pact between Nazi Germany and the Soviet Union, signed 23 August 1939. The secret protocol defined the borders of Soviet and German spheres of influence across Poland, Lithuania, Latvia, Estonia and Finland.

p. 261 *Aizsargi*: a paramilitary organization ("Guards Organization"), or a militia, in Latvia (1918–1939).

p. 261 Dvinsk, Dankere, Kreutzburg: the Jewish names for Daugavpils, Gostiņi, and Krustpils.

p. 263 Brigadenführer Stahlecker: Franz Walter Stahlecker (1900-1942) was commander of the SS security forces for the Reichskommissariat Ostland in 1941–42.

p. 274 *ataman*: a commander of Cossack cavalry in Imperial Russia. Čiekurkalns is a suburb of Riga.

p. 281 GAZ: a Soviet make of lorry for military and civilian use, from the initials of Gorkovsky Avtomobilny Zavod (Gorky Automobile Plant).

p. 295 *Pynu, pynu sītu*: a traditional women's song in a mixture of Latgalian and Russian. The rhythm is more important than the meaning.

p. 300 *voivode*: a military commander in Central and Eastern Europe.

p. 323 the Courland pocket: the name given to German forces who were surrounded by the Red Army in fierce fighting in Kurzeme province, western Latvia, in 1944-45.

p. 366 taraxacum rubber dandelions: Taraxacum was a plant of the dandelion family introduced into Soviet agriculture as a source of urgently needed artificial rubber.

p. 373 "*Smersh?*": abbreviation of *Smert' shpionam* (Death to spies), the Soviet wartime counter-intelligence organization.

p. 376 Shustin's institution: see note to p. 206.

p. 380 The forest!: the Soviet hunt for members of the 'Forest Brothers' partisan groupings was causing disruption to Latvian agriculture.

p. 385 Kims: the Russian initials of the Communist Youth International are K.I.M.

p. 438 *kumiss*: fermented mare's milk, used as a liquor.

Translator's Afterword

The north-east corner of Europe, skirting the Baltic Sea, has for centuries been a crossroads of ambitious conquerors, whether political, commercial or religious. In the twentieth century, the fates of Latvia and its two neighbours, Lithuania and Estonia, were sometimes neglected by people of the English-speaking countries in favour of the larger theatres of war and conquest. This novel, by Inga Ābele, attempts to set the record straight. History is usually written by the victors; and the Latvians are victors only in the sense that they have managed to preserve their nation against tremendous odds.

The events outlined in this novel had a dramatic effect on the life of every Latvian. There can hardly be a single Latvian family who did not lose a member or a loved one during the tragic happenings between 1940, when the Soviet Union forcibly annexed Latvia and its neighbours, and 1949, the deportations that were culmination of the events depicted here. I need not go into detail here, as the author has done that more eloquently in her introduction. Latvians were cast out into the world far and wide. Growing up in distant Australia, I heard often enough the references to recent immigrants from the Displaced Persons camps as "Balts", indiscriminately alternating with "Reffos" (refugees) as pejorative terms.

From 1940 to 1991, Latvia was a constituent republic of the USSR. Inga Ābele, born in Riga in 1972, was just coming out of her teens when Latvia regained its independence. She has written other novels, detailed and well-researched, that explore the lesser known byways of Latvian history; in a just world, they too would be translated into English. But this novel, in my opinion, is a gem.

To reflect a whole swathe of history through the person of one protagonist requires real talent, real human empathy, real insight. The colourful and unexpected imagery that peppers the novel was a challenge to translate; the historical detail required some diligent research on my part as well. My frequent consultations with the author about little details of the story have turned this translation into a true collaboration.

Andrievs, the hero of the story, is seen both in the present day, in reflective old age, and in the very thick of the traumas of the nineteen-forties. He is a victim of the treachery of the Communist regime in the directest sense. But whenever human beings let him down, there are always horses, those ever reliable, unquestioning, noble and beautiful servants of man.

Running through the whole novel like a silver thread is the river Daugava. Starting from Riga, the novel follows its course upstream, intertwining past and present, eastwards into the province of Latgale. (The river rises in Russia and flows westward through Belarus, through Latvia, and empties into the Baltic at Riga.) Andrievs' modern-day journey, accompanied by the nameless female narrator and driver, never deviates far from the banks of the river, though it evokes memories of theatres of battle elsewhere.

The novel came about in 2017 as one of a series by different leading Latvian authors, to celebrate the centenary of Latvia's first independence (1918-1940). Each novel in the series focused on a different decade of that century: Inga Ābele concentrates here on the nineteen-forties. The series was collectively called "We. Latvia. The 20th century" *(Mēs. Latvija. XX gadsimts).*

You will gather from the author's introduction that the novel is based on extensive research. The author has based her characters mostly on real people, particularly those associated with the Riga trotting track in the years after the communist takeover. What you read of historical events in the novel really did happen. This was brought home to me vividly when, after I'd completed this translation, the author sent me a copy of a "Top Secret" report from the head of the Latvian KGB to his masters in Moscow, summarizing the progress of the "operation" to deport Latvians who were members of socially undesirable classes on and around 25 March 1949. It is a chilling document.

This is not the first of Ābele's novels to appear in English. In 2013 Kaija Straumanis' translation of *High Tide* (*Paisums*) appeared from Open Letter Books. Her work has been translated into several other European languages. She has also written poetry, drama and short stories.

One of the knottiest problems for me as translator was to render the passages in the Latgalian language, which is close to, but different from, Latvian. It would have been merely comic to put it into some kind of English dialect, so the differences are shown in other, subtler ways. The extensive gallery of characters in the novel, who are often called by different names or titles in different passages, can make it hard for the foreign reader to follow who is being referred to. Names have therefore been clarified in the translation.

A word about the title. The original, *Duna*, was the hardest word in the whole book to render into English. In Latvian it conveys the "thundering" sound of horses' hooves on a track, but somehow "Thundering" didn't seem quite right. ("Duna" is distantly related to the English word "din".) There are numerous references to "thunder" and "thundering" in the novel, but eventually we decided to rename it after a unique feature of that fateful year of 1949, "The Year the River Froze Twice".

Finally, my thanks as translator go to all those who have helped this volume toward production: to Janet Garton of Norvik Press for having faith in this novel and for her wise editorial advice; to Deborah Bragan-Turner for her meticulous proof-reading and editing; to Sarah Death, Elettra Carbone, Claire Thomson and Essi Viitanen for all their advice and encouragement; to the Latvian Literature organization for their financial support; and finally of course to my author, Inga Ābele, who has shown patient faith in me and given unstintingly of her time in answering hundreds of niggling questions that arose in the course of this challenging, but always enjoyable and awe-inspiring task.

Reading, August 2020
Christopher Moseley

ILMAR TASKA

Pobeda 1946: A Car Called Victory

(translated by Christopher Moseley)

In Tallinn in 1946 a young boy is transfixed by the beauty of a luxurious cream-coloured car gliding down the street. It is a Russian Pobeda, a car called Victory. The sympathetic driver invites the boy for a ride and enquires about his family. Soon the boy's father disappears. Ilmar Taska's debut novel captures the distrust and fear among Estonians living under Soviet occupation after World War II. The reader is transported to a world seen through the eyes of a young boy, where it is difficult to know who is right and who is wrong, be they occupiers or occupied. Resistance fighters, exiles, informants and torturers all find themselves living in Stalin's long shadow.

Ilmar Taska is best known in his native Estonia as a film director and producer. *Pobeda 1946: A Car Called Victory* is his first full novel, and is based on a prize-winning short story from 2014.

ISBN 9781909408425
UK £11.95
(Paperback, 246 pages)

VIIVI LUIK

The Beauty of History

(translated by Hildi Hawkins)

1968. Riga. News of the Prague Spring washes across Europe, causing ripples on either side of the Iron Curtain. A young Estonian woman has agreed to pose as a model for a famous sculptor, who is trying to evade military service and escape to the West. Although the model has only a vague awareness of politics - her interest in life is primarily poetic - the consequences of the politics of both past and present repeatedly make themselves felt. Chance remarks overheard prompt memories of people and places, language itself becomes fluid, by turns deceptive and reassuring.

The Beauty of History is a novel of poetic intensity, of fleeting moods and captured moments. It is powerfully evocative of life within the Baltic States during the Soviet occupation, and of the challenge to artists to express their individuality whilst maintaining at least an outward show of loyalty to the dominant ideology. Written on the cusp of independence, as Estonia and Latvia sought to regain their sovereignty in 1991, this is a novel that can be seen as an historic document - wistful, unsettling, and beautiful.

ISBN 9781909408272
UK £11.95
(Paperback, 152 pages)

ANTON TAMMSAARE

The Misadventures of the New Satan

(translated by Olga Shartze and Christopher Moseley)

Satan has a problem: God has come to the conclusion that it is unfair to send souls to hell if they are fundamentally incapable of living a decent life on earth. If this is the case, then hell will be shut down, and the human race written off as an unfortunate mistake. Satan is given the chance to prove that human beings are capable of salvation - thus ensuring the survival of hell - if he agrees to live as a human being and demonstrate that it is possible to live a righteous life. St Peter suggests that life as a farmer might offer Satan the best chance of success, because of the catalogue of privations he will be forced to endure. And so Satan ends up back on earth, living as Jürka, a great bear of a man, the put-upon tenant of a run-down Estonian farm. His patience and good nature are sorely tested by the machinations of his scheming, unscrupulous landlord and the social and religious hypocrisy he encounters.

The Misadventures of the New Satan is the last novel by Estonia's greatest twentieth-century writer, Anton Tammsaare (1876-1940), and it constitutes a fitting summation of the themes that occupied him throughout his writing: the search for truth and social justice, and the struggle against corruption and greed.

ISBN 9781909408432
UK £11.95
(Paperback, 258 pages)